Fundamentals of Being a *Good Girl*

It all started with a series of tropes: just one bed, forced proximity, and a dash of enemies-to-lovers, and now, ten years later, Julie Murphy and Sierra Simone are best friends and coauthors of the *USA Today* bestselling *A Merry Little Meet Cute* and *A Holly Jolly Ever After*. Separately, Julie writes for all ages, with titles including *Dumplin'*, *If the Shoe Fits*, and *Dear Sweet Pea*. Sierra is the author of several titles, such as *Priest*, *American Queen*, and *Salt Kiss*. When they're not writing, Julie and Sierra enjoy forcing their families to go on vacation together and eating an array of pies while watching delightfully bad movies.

Also by Julie Murphy and Sierra Simone

A Merry Little Meet Cute
A Holly Jolly Ever After
A Jingle Bell Mingle

JULIE MURPHY
& SIERRA SIMONE

Fundamentals of Being a

Good Girl

HarperCollins*Publishers*

HarperCollins*Publishers* Ltd
1 London Bridge Street,
London SE1 9GF

www.harpercollins.co.uk

HarperCollins*Publishers*
Macken House, 39/40 Mayor Street Upper
Dublin 1, D01 C9W8, Ireland

Published by HarperCollins*Publishers* 2026

1

Copyright © Bittersweet Media LLC and Sierra Simone 2026

Julie Murphy and Sierra Simone assert the
moral right to be identified as the authors of this work

A catalogue record for this book is available from the British Library

ISBN: 978-0-00-871855-8 (PB)

This novel is entirely a work of fiction. The names, characters and incidents
portrayed in it are the work of the author's imagination. Any resemblance to
actual persons, living or dead, events or localities is entirely coincidental.

Interior text design by Diahann Sturge-Campbell
Map by The INKfluence LLC

Illustrations and art throughout @ channarongsds; Oleksandra; michaelray back;
Raman Maisei; Veronika; Kate; amorroz; Oleksandr Babich; Kamenuka; SQB Creation;
Morphart; Natasha-Chu; Good Studio; Sad; vectortatu; guliy-art; croisy; Adndrii_Oliinyk;
Turaev; Pagina; francovolpato/Stock.Adobe.com and bioraven; Canicula; Arthur Balitskii;
Natalia Samdiuk; Intellegent Design; Anastazja91/Shutterstock.com

Printed and bound in the UK using 100% Renewable
Electricity at CPI Group (UK) Ltd

All rights reserved. No part of this publication may be reproduced,
stored in a retrieval system, or transmitted, in any form or by any means,
electronic, mechanical, photocopying, recording or otherwise,
without the prior written permission of the publishers.

Without limiting the author's and publisher's exclusive rights, any unauthorised
use of this publication to train generative artificial intelligence (AI) technologies
is expressly prohibited. HarperCollins also exercise their rights under Article 4(3)
of the Digital Single Market Directive 2019/790 and expressly reserve
this publication from the text and data mining exception.

For more information visit: www.harpercollins.co.uk/green

For Flavia, the very best good girl

Put on some lipstick and pull yourself together.
　—ELIZABETH TAYLOR

Fundamentals of Being a Good Girl

PROLOGUE

The Dry Bean
8:49 P.M.

"He's not bad-looking, if you don't mind people who look like they play Minor League Baseball," Sloane says after a minute.

"He looks like a ferret." An amendment: "A ferret who's gone to rehab." This comes from Leo Saint James, Sloane's cousin.

Leo isn't wrong. The man in question walks by, *rodently*, and the table collectively shakes its head.

"Okay, so not Jeremy Allen White's embarrassing uncle for your first postdivorce smash," Joey says, "but I'm not giving up hope! You deserve an epic love affair! You're beautiful and smart and nice . . ."

Joey is starting to tear up now; he always gets a little maudlin when he drinks. But really! Sloane Saint James was married to a controlling douchebag for ten years; tonight is her first night of official, legal freedom, and Joey just wants her to be happy. Have a good time like they did in the old days, when they'd crowd into this same bar for cheap shots and loud music and end up on the floor of Sloane's apartment in a tangle of blankets and friendship.

That's the real problem with being in your mid-thirties. At some point, you stopped making new memories and settled for hanging on to the ones you already have. You stopped doing stupid shit like drinking shots called the Wisconsin Lunchbox and started upgrading from liability-only car insurance instead.

And that's mostly a good change—Joey does like the other stuff that comes with being in his thirties, like having a funny wife and three little girls who cover him in glittery eyeshadow before they have tea parties—but why can't they all make new memories once in a while too? Why *can't* Sloane make a bad decision with a rat-faced man tonight? What's stopping Joey from ordering a Duck Fart followed by a Chuck Norris followed by a French Pension Protest?

Why can't they have one of the Andromeda Club's patented Best Nights Ever, even though they now have a few gray hairs and some mortgage payments between them?[*]

"I want to have a Best Night Ever," Joey says abruptly to Bram, who's just come to the table with a round of drinks clutched easily in his large hands.

Bram calmly—Bram does everything calmly—sets a beer in front of Joey, a glass of neat scotch in front of Leo, and the usual extra-*extra*-dry martini in front of Sloane. For himself, Bram has a reddish ale that looks like something a hobbit would drink,

---

[*] Formally, the Andromeda Club began in the eleventh grade, after Leo noted that they always seemed to hang out at Joey's house on Andromeda Avenue. Joey was so excited to have a group name that he drew up an Andromeda Club charter then and there.

which is on track for the only professor at the table tonight. The man lives a life of rumpled button-downs, dusty books, and boring the pants off people about moss.

Finally, Bram says, "I'd settle for a Medium Night Ever at this point," and then sits down and runs a hand over his face.

The table stares at him. From Bram Loe, the goodest guy—the guy for whom the term *unruffled* was invented—this small act of stress is basically the same as flipping over a table and making snow angels in the broken glass.

"You okay, champ?" Joey asks.

Bram takes a drink, his hand nearly dwarfing the glass. (He might *live* like a hobbit, but Bram himself is well over six feet of muscle, stubble, and hard-earned suntan.) "You know," says Bram after a minute, "it was a rather frustrating day, now that you ask."

Joey looks up to see the Saint James cousins exchanging gray-eyed glances. The cousins—aside from being obscenely wealthy—also share the same pale skin, platinum hair, and silver eyes. (The main difference between the two of them is that Sloane is nice and Leo is a Berluti briefcase full of scalpels.)

Sloane's impeccably manicured fingernails tap against her martini glass. "Do you want to talk about it?"

Joey expects Bram to refuse—not because Bram doesn't trust them, but because there's never been anything in the history of ever that Bram hasn't been able to handle. Knocking up his high school sweetheart at eighteen? Marrying said sweetheart and refurbishing a crumbling Queen Anne house? Surprise twins? Tenure? Divorce? Bram has always taken everything in stride, like those broad, sweater-covered shoulders of his can carry any conceivable load.

But Bram surprises him again by taking a long gulp of his drink. "The twins fed Sara's dog chocolate ice cream," he says after he swallows. And then, as if upon reflection, he polishes off another quarter glass of ale.

"And why is Sara's dog at your house?" Leo asks in a drawl. "Surely the most salient benefit of a divorce is never having to lay eyes on that beast again."

"Right, why is the dog at my house," repeats Bram with a teacherly nod, as if a student has asked exactly the correct question. "Sara's glacier research grant went through at the last minute, but we had almost no notice and no time to make plans for . . . well, for literally anything. And there weren't any dog boarders or pet sitters that could take Hester Prynne for as long as Sara needed."

Joey loves Sara—she's a part of the group too, and she and Bram parted ways as friends—but Leo has a point. For anyone else, an ex's post-split giant dog goes squarely in the *not your problem* category the minute you light the Freshly Signed Divorce Papers candle.

But not for Bram Loe, their goodest guy.

"Anyway, I have to get this research proposal in by the end of the week, and I thought I could take the twins out for ice cream, bribe my oldest to keep an eye on them, and sneakily work on my laptop while everyone was distracted with treats." Bram stares at the bubbles racing to the surface of his drink. "But Fern was on her phone and then the twins thought Hester Prynne looked hungry and then suddenly I was dealing with a puking dog and a four-hundred-dollar vet visit."

"So is the fiend dead or not?" asks Leo.

Bram gives him a mild look. He never rises to any of Leo's bait, something not even Sloane can manage. "Hester is fine. No thanks to the brat who stole the last parking space on Tombaugh. I had to park on Andromeda and carry the dog all the way to Dr. Sackrider's office."

The table shares a moment of sympathy for Bram. Andromeda to Tombaugh Avenue is a bitch of a walk, even without a puking, hundred-pound dog.

"Anyway, it's all okay, except the dog has to stay overnight at the vet, the twins are traumatized, Fern is giving me the silent treatment because she has to babysit tonight, none of my work is done, and I still don't know how I'm going to manage being a single dad for the next eight weeks." Bram scrubs his hands through his dark hair and sighs.

"You need an au pair," Sloane advises in the tone of someone who grew up thinking au pairs were standard issue. Leo is nodding lazily next to her.

"I've already put in an emergency request at a local agency," Bram says tiredly. "At least for help in the afternoons. Otherwise, it'll all be down to Fern, and she's already got enough going on after that shithead boy dumped her."

Bram says *shithead boy* with the same neutral composure that he uses for everything, but Joey doesn't miss the subtle twitch of Bram's hand around his glass when he brings up his daughter's ex-boyfriend. (None of them have forgotten that an undergrad Bram once explained in great and drunken detail how he would hide a body without getting caught. It involved carnivorous plants and a trip to the fine arts department's pottery kiln.)

"I know what you need," declares Joey, "and it's not an au pair. You need to get laid, my brother. Just like Sloane."

"But not like me?" Leo inquires.

"Leo, you were in flagrante delicto when I called you this morning to ask about Aunt Cassandra's birthday dinner," Sloane remarks dryly. "I don't think you need any encouragement in the sex department."

"Trust me on this, guys." Joey spreads his hands wide, ready for his TED Talk moment. Maybe he's not a professor like Bram or a fancy, galas-for-good-causes person like Sloane, but he *is* an expert in the long-term health benefits of great sex. "Riley and I have sex all the time—"

"Yes, we know," Sloane says.

"—and my blood pressure is great, my cholesterol is great, my bench press is better than it's ever been—"

"I don't know if that can be ascribed to biblically knowing your wife," observes Leo.

"—and I just really think you need to get *out* there with those gonads, and leave nothing on the gonad field!"

"Thank you, Coach," says Sloane.

Bram hasn't been listening at all. "I can't believe she stole that parking spot from me," he mutters.

"Who?" Leo asks.

"The *brat*." It's the most irritated Joey's ever heard Bram. "I was there with my blinker on, waiting to turn in while Hester Prynne was throwing up all over my car, and then she just shamelessly *took my spot*. And when I rolled down the window and told her I'd been waiting for it before she got there, she flipped me off!"

For someone who deals with undergrads, a teenage daughter, and twin first-graders on a daily basis, Bram sounds uniquely peeved by this act of finger-based rudeness.

Joey shakes his head and finishes his beer. Bram really needs to cut loose—they all do. And Joey knows just the answer.

Leaving the others to deal with Bram's bad mood, Joey goes up to the counter and flags down the bartender on duty, who is also the owner (and also the reluctant short-order cook). Robbie has owned The Dry Bean since long before Joey and the others discovered its hallowed halls as fake-ID-bearing college students, and Joey genuinely doesn't know if the man is in his fifties or in his eighties—the only evidence of the accumulated years is in Robbie's long, wispy eyebrows, which make him look like a great horned owl with rosacea.

"You got any shots that will make a table of thirtysomethings act like they're twenty-one?" Joey asks.

Robbie thinks for a moment, then taps the chalkboard sign hanging behind him.

SHOT OF THE WEEK: ACADEMIC AFFAIRS

A shot of Copperhead pride! A splash of gin, rum, tequila, vodka, triple sec, and Midori, topped with edible copper glitter.

Joey grins, delighted. "That looks awful. I'll take four."

9:17 P.M.

Joey returns with the shots as the lights dim and the familiar strains of Lesley Gore's "It's My Party" start playing.

"Someone's about to get birthday spankings!" Joey calls out fondly as he passes out the shots. (He bought an extra shot for himself, something called a Big Guy Touchdown, and as a big guy who is a high school football coach, it was clearly calling his name.) "Okay, on the count of three, everyone!"

"What's *in* this?" Leo asks as he holds the green and copper drink up to the barely there light.

Joey doesn't have the time to fight with Leo about this and also, he doesn't remember what's in it. "It's your medicine. *Our* medicine. We are going to drink these and then we are going to have a Best Night Ever. You hear me?"

Leo looks doubtful, but Sloane is nodding and Bram looks too ready to wash away the memory of dog vomit to say no. They hold up their shots, clink them together, and chant, "*Optimus noctem!*"[*] Then they all give a good, old-fashioned Astra University Copperheads hiss before they toss the shots back and slam the glasses on the table.

"You brought us glasses of poison," sputters Leo when he can speak again.

"Glasses of *magic*."

"I wish Alessandro were here," Leo says, and Sloane nods. Alessandro Ottaviano is a professor of neurosurgery at the Astra University Medical Center in Kansas City and is too busy digging inside people's brains to come hang out. He's the only one of the group aside from Sara who isn't here tonight.[†]

The DJ comes on the microphone and shouts over the music, "Please give a big old Mount Astra welcome to tonight's birthday girl, Maddie Kowa-kowaltch . . ." A pause. "Maddie from California!"

The bar hoots and cheers as a fair young woman with golden hair takes the stage. She's fat, with smaller curves up top and hips and thighs for days, all of it showcased in a tight sweater set and pencil skirt. Her mouth is a little too wide and sinfully full, and her large eyes are as green as a pit viper's.

"That's her," Bram says.

---

[*] "Best night ever," translation courtesy of Leo's prep school Latin.

[†] Except for Cole McKenney, whom Leo has never met and doesn't believe is real because he coincidentally transferred to Mount Astra High School the year that Cole moved away.

Fundamentals of Being a Good Girl

His voice is strange . . . low and breathless. Like he's just won a race but he's pissed about it.

"Who?" Joey asks, plucking his Big Guy Touchdown off the table.

"The *brat*."

The DJ now has Maddie from California facing the side wall with her hands splayed inside the Sharpie'd outlines that have contained the hands of scores of birthday spank-ees throughout the years. The green and copper paddle comes out.

Next to Joey, Bram stiffens.

"How old are you today?" the DJ asks.

"Twenty-six!" chirps Maddie.

"Your safe word is *cash tips only*!" the DJ says, and starts swinging. The swats start out as mere taps, but the bar shouts along with the DJ as if each tap is a catastrophic wallop, and Maddie looks to the side at the crowd, a smile on her plush mouth.

And then she and Bram lock eyes.

Bram's hand is a fist on the table. His jaw clenches.

His eyes have hooded a little, and when the DJ gives Maddie a final, no-shit swat with the paddle—hard enough to make her whimper—Bram sucks in a breath.

"Maybe you should go discuss parking etiquette with her," Leo suggests. "After you can stand up without committing a crime of public obscenity, of course."

"Fuck off," says Bram, distractedly. His eyes are still on Maddie as the DJ helps her off the stage.

A slow smile pulls across Leo's face, making him look briefly like one of God's favorite angels, all sculpted features and gorgeous symmetry. "Did Bram Loe just tell me to *fuck off*?"

Joey claps his hands together. The shots are working already!

"More shots!" Joey yells, and Leo holds out his credit card, the black metal one that looks like a prop from a movie about Wall Street stockbrokers.

"I'll get this round," says the rich asshole. "I want to see how far we can push Professor Nice Guy tonight."

10:02 P.M.

Joey skips up to the bar for another Big Guy Touchdown and watches Robbie come down the narrow stairs before slipping behind the counter and reaching for a fresh shot glass.

"You still living upstairs, Robbie?" Joey asks.

Robbie shakes his head. "Moved out years ago. Been slowly renovating the space up there to make it easier to sell the place."

"You can't sell it!" Joey exclaims, panicked. "This bar is a staple of the community! The Dry Bean *is* Mount Astra, Kansas!"

Robbie pulls a battered wallet out of his jeans and thumbs around for a picture. For a minute, Joey thinks he's going to see a picture of Robbie's spouse or kids or grandkids, but when Robbie unfolds the picture and sets it on the bar in front of Joey, it becomes clear that it's a picture of a pontoon boat. A very old, very ugly pontoon boat.

"She's waiting for me," says Robbie wistfully. "At the Lake of the Ozarks. All I need is to get my name off this shithole's deed."

10:57 P.M.

Joey bumps into someone tall and evil, and Leo spins around to glare at him. "I'm in the middle of eavesdropping," Leo says tightly, his voice like jagged ice. "And I will kill you if I miss my cue."

"Your cue? For what?"

Leo looks down his perfect nose at Joey, a slight sneer on his face. "For announcing my engagement."

"You're not engaged," Joey says with mostly complete certainty.

"And I'll never be if you don't shut up." And then Leo shoves him away.

11:32 P.M.

Bram is looming over Maddie the Birthday Girl. She has her back against the wall and he has his forearm braced next to her head, his face dropped to hers as he speaks sternly to her, presumably about parking etiquette.

He lifts his finger, to scold her or to make a point, and Maddie from California dips her head and bites the tip of it with pearly white teeth.

12:01 A.M.

Sloane is sitting at the bar talking to Robbie, the picture of his pontoon boat clutched to her chest as he gestures at the water spots on the ceiling. Behind him, mounted to the wall next to the Jägermeister sign, is a framed poster of the *Lonesome Dove* miniseries, signed by Danny Glover and Steve Buscemi.[*]

Sloane pulls out her phone and starts tapping away, still cuddling the picture of the pontoon.

---

[*] The saloon in *Lonesome Dove* is called The Dry Bean. *Lonesome Dove* is Robbie's favorite book, TV show, and topic of conversation. He has never ridden a horse nor been near a cow.

12:28 A.M.

Joey finishes singing "Barracuda" to the approving roars of the crowd. Someone is calling for an encore. He asks the DJ for "Tequila" by The Champs because he knows all the words.

12:56 A.M.

Joey is at a table arm-wrestling one of his former football players while people shout and drop dollar bills onto the table. Someone shoves another Big Guy Touchdown in his free hand and he finishes the shot as he shoves his opponent's hand to the table.

Look at all the money he won! Twenty-seven dollars!

His chest swells. Riley is going to be so proud of him. He's provided for the family. He is a hunter and a warrior. Maybe she'll still be awake when he gets home . . .

1:07 A.M.

Joey's vision is blurry, but he is pretty sure he sees a pair of muscled thighs clad in brown corduroys disappear up the stairs to the empty apartments above the bar. Looks an awful lot like Bram's brown oxfords too.

Is that also the pale blue of a sweater set?

1:20 A.M.

It's official.

Bram is gone. The Saint James cousins are gone.

Time to Uber home.

Fundamentals of Being a Good Girl

Joey Fucking Kemp's House
2:21 A.M.

"Do you have a condom?" Riley whispers. They always have to whisper. The curse of having three girls who sleep like little princesses atop heaps of peas.

"What can one time hurt?" Joey whispers back. Also the condoms are *so far away*, like all the way in the bathroom.

Riley seems to think about it. "Okay," she says, yawning a little. "I guess I'm still breastfeeding. I don't think I can get pregnant again yet."

Best night ever.

CHAPTER ONE

Bram

"He's awake," a little voice whispers. "You ask him."

"No, you ask him."

"Let's get Fern to ask him."

Two pairs of tiny feet pound away, and I roll onto my back—into a wall of cardboard. A sheet falls onto my face, and I don't even bother pulling it off because at least it's stopping the sun from stabbing into my brain.

It is . . . so bright.

I breathe in through my nose and try to absorb as much information as possible without opening my eyes. I'm on a creaky wooden floor—*my* creaky wooden floor. I'm still wearing my belt and shoes. My head hurts, my mouth is dry, and my dick is sore. Sore like it hasn't been since I was eighteen.

A flash of last night comes to me—stripping off a condom and having to use a spare tucked inside the brat's purse. And then having to use another.

Three times. Jesus. I haven't gone three times in one night in . . . years.

"Dad," comes the unhappy voice of a teenager. The sheet is ripped off my face and I force myself to blink my eyes open. My eyelids scrape over my corneas like fine-grain sandpaper.

"Yes?" I croak, and then try to sit up (a mistake). I knock over another wall of the cardboard fort that the twins have been building around me, pain lances through both the frontal and occipital bones of my skull, and then I have to confront the quiet judgment of my oldest daughter.

It occurs to me that I am too young to have a seventeen-year-old evaluating my fully legal bad decisions. (Thank you, Kansas sex education in the 2000s.)

"What time is it?" I rasp.

Fern stares down at me with her mother's dark, dark eyes. Her expression doesn't change, but it's very clear that she has thoughts about her dad having slept fully clothed on the floor. "Nine in the morning. The twins have been up for *hours*."

"And have *you* been awake for hours?" I ask as I glance around the living room and attached parlor. Old textbooks and battered dictionaries pin sheets to tables—sheets that are definitely supposed to be on beds upstairs—and the crushed exoskeletons of juice boxes litter random counters and chairs. The tinny noises of a YouTuber's video game commentary emit from a place in the fort both mysterious and abandoned, and when I look over at the antique aquarium where the pet frog lives, I see the glass lid hinged open. No frog inside.

"Well, I just got up," Fern concedes. "But they woke *me* up to wake *you* up to tell you that they want pancakes."

I catch movement just beyond the parlor, where the staircase is. Two heads of dark curls, bent together in either espionage or suspended conference.

"Is that true?" I ask the twins. "You two want pancakes?"

The twins step out of the shadows. They're wearing a motley sampling of the makeup that Sara's mother bought them for Christmas paired with superhero costumes, and they clunk over to me in some high heels they stole from Fern's room. Letty—the spokeswoman of the pair—clears her throat as Berry, my shy one, crawls into my lap. She smells like apple juice and sunshine.

I kiss her soft glossy hair as Letty itemizes, in order of priority, the toppings they would like, starting with whipped cream, all the way down to sliced bananas.

AN HOUR LATER, and I'm Advil'ed, showered, and gathering syrupy plates from the kitchen island as the twins dash out to the backyard to enjoy their last day of non-school sunshine. I put the plates in the dishwasher, look around the ground floor of the rambling old house that Sara and I bought as a foreclosure, and allow myself a tired sigh. We picked the Queen Anne because 1) we had no money and it was cheap and 2) it looked like the kind of house that would forgive a mess or two. Sara and I have always been the kind of people to favor homey clutter over sterile minimalism, and the Queen Anne, with its fussy fireplaces and stained-glass windows and ornate metal doorknobs, practically came pre-cluttered.

But it's too cluttered even for this old place, and I resign myself to spending the afternoon cleaning (and gently herding the twins into cleaning with me). We can leave part of the fort up in the parlor, maybe, because I do like to encourage their imagination and ability to problem-solve structural engineering dilemmas, but we'll never find the frog if the *whole* floor is covered in sheets and couch cushions, and we need to find the frog before I collect Hester Prynne from the vet—

"DAD!" Fern rushes into the kitchen. Her bronze cheeks are flushed with panic and the August sun. "My car won't start!"

"Okay," I say, setting the dishwasher and closing the door. "I'll come take a look."

"I'm supposed to meet Sophia at the library to make back-to-school posters," adds Fern. "It's really important, because Olivia has already flaked and Emily can't help because she broke her pinkie finger playing lacrosse."

"Well, when are you supposed to meet Sophia? I can get the twins gathered up and then drop you off—"

"I was supposed to meet her fifteen minutes ago," Fern mourns, already going to the back door. "I'll just walk."

"Fern," I call calmly, "it's no problem for me to drive you. I just need to round up the twins—"

"No time!"

The back door slams just as I shout, "I love you!" There's, of course, no *I love you* back, or *goodbye*. Teens.

In the silence that follows Fern's exit, I reorder the day's tasks in my mind. I need to clean, find the frog, and look at Fern's old Honda . . . and get Hester Prynne . . . and finish my proposal.

First, though, I go upstairs to start a load of laundry, finding my button-down shirt from last night and getting ready to sort it into the cold-wash pile. There's a smear of pink lipstick on the collar.

The brat's mouth on my throat, nipping at my earlobe.

Her jaw in my hand and those green eyes on mine. Her mouth was wet and open, shining in the shadows of the empty apartment above the bar.

"Someone needs to teach you some manners." I barely recognized my own voice. Low and heavy and stern.

She shivered and shivered, a brat in a blizzard of her own making. "If you say so," she whispered, and then opened her mouth like she wanted my fingers in it.

I press the heel of my palm to the fresh hard-on swelling behind my zipper, irritated. I'm thirty-five—inconvenient boners are supposed to be a thing of the past! Especially since I need to map sea tides and chart lunar cycles just to find a few minutes of time alone as a single parent.

But god, *her*. Her too-full mouth, her too-large eyes. Her cunt like liquid silk when I'd finally gotten inside; so hot that I thought my skin might catch on fire as I moved between her legs.

My phone rings in my pocket, and I wince as I dig it free and the fabric pulls against the raw but endearingly hopeful erection I'm sporting.

"Loe," I answer as pleasantly as I can while 90 percent of my brain is still fucking a parking-space thief above The Dry Bean.

"Bram, it's Ali," says Dr. Ali Darwish, my department chair—and then, not waiting for a response—"the butterfly perverts from Oregon are saying they still don't have the website copy you sent over for the pollinator seminar series, and I told them I *knew* that you'd sent it over because you'd cc'ed me, but they're probably too busy drinking microbrews to check their spam or whatever, so do you mind sending that again, because you know they'll want to Track Changes the entire thing before we can put it on the website, and I want to go live before we meet with the dean next week."

I take in a belated breath and mentally revise today's to-do list to include dealing with the visiting lecturers from Oregon.

"Of course," I say. "That's no problem at all."

"Great! Then I'm going to archive that email and forget it exists. Hey, congrats on Sara's grant, by the way, that's amazing."

A side effect of being married to a fellow academic and having worked at the same institution for more than a decade is that people still think of us as a unit, even though we've been divorced for five years and Sara's been engaged to someone else for two of them. Our accomplishments are still funneled into the joint bucket of *Sara and Bram*, and I'm not generally bothered by it, except when people offer me praise that rightfully belongs to her.

"Ali, I had nothing to do with it, it was all her. But I'll pass on your kind words."

"Behind every great glacier scientist is an ex-husband with an air fryer and crumb-covered booster seats," Ali says distractedly. "Okay, the rest of the inbox awaits. Talk soon, Bram."

I hang up, but before I put my phone away, I see a text from Sara.

> Arrived safely in Fairbanks! Do you think I can FaceTime the kids later?

I arrange a time that I think will work—with as much as Sara's research takes her away from Mount Astra, we try to prioritize her connecting with the kids at least every other day—and then I put my phone away and take a deep breath.

On the bright side, my erection has settled down.

I put a load in the washer, change into a worn Astra University Copperheads T-shirt in anticipation of getting under the hood of Fern's car, and then take the lovingly restored stairs two at a time.

Clean, frog, car, dog, Oregon, phone call. Proposal.

I can do all of that, right? And make sure the twins and Fern eat something resembling real food? And not think about the fact that I fucked a stranger in a bar last night and wish I could do it again?

Clean, *frog*, car, *dog*, Oregon, *phone call*—

The doorbell rings.

I pause at the foot of the stairs, consider the warren of cardboard and fabric between me and the door, and admit defeat. I drop to all fours and crawl through a cardboard tunnel, my shoulders knocking against everything. The doorbell is ringing again by the time I reach the door and swing it open.

And then I feel like I've been lit on fire.

The brat from last night stands on my front porch, wearing a floral sundress and pearls like she just came from Sunday brunch at the Congressional Country Club, her sinful mouth painted in a demure shade of pink.

"I'm Madelyn Kowalczk," she says. "The agency said you needed a—"

She finally realizes who she's talking to, and she stops. We stare at each other.

Which is the moment the missing frog chooses to emerge from the fort. The frog gives us both a salutatory *ribbit* and then flings herself out the front door and toward the road.

"Well, fuck," the brat says.

CHAPTER TWO

Maddie

There is now what appears to be frog goo on the toes of my thrifted camel-brown Coach loafers, the ones I was very proud to debut last year at Gentry's grandmother's birthday party (proud until his mother complimented me on my Burberry dupes, at least). Which was really just one of the many moments of foreshadowing that brought me here—to the doorstep of my hot, nameless hookup who also just so happens to be my new boss. Great.

"Okay." I press my fists into my eyeballs as though I could literally shove the memory of last night into the furthest recesses of my mind. Except . . . nope. It's all still there. Fresh as a daisy. Giant, burly, bossy daddy pulling and yanking on my ponytail as he filled the first of three condoms. Him eating me out from behind—a terrifying but thrilling first for me. Me coming so hard my scream might have actually been loud enough to compete with the bar noise below. Walking back to my car, sore and absolutely content. (Content until now.)

"Okay," I say again, pulling my fists down as my vision slowly blurs back into focus. "This cannot be—"

"Porcupine!" screeches a little girl with unruly dark brown curls, wearing oversized high heels and a superhero cape. A silent but equally adorable and nearly identical girl tromps down the steps of the porch after her.

"Not the street!" Bossy Daddy bellows as he barrels past me after them and into said street.

I spin around to see the frog bounce back onto the sidewalk and in the direct path of an oily teenage boy on a scooter slurping a Mountain Dew Baja Blast.

"Fucking frog," I mutter, and sprint down the steps to the sidewalk, where I jump out in front of the boy, sending him flying into the grass just before he flattened the stray amphibian.

"Hey!" he snipes at me.

"Maybe you should watch where you're going next time," I say as I retrieve the frog (*blech*) and give him the same withering glare I'd used on opposing counsel during various moot courts and mock trials. The boy practically melts into the grass before silently retrieving his scooter and walking it past me. I wish—not for the first time—that I'd mastered that glare in high school.

"Porcupine!" the girls sing as they crowd around my knees like little cult followers who have chosen me as their idol.

I gladly hand the frog off to one of them before wiping my hands down the front of my floral dress. And then think about how I'll manage having a wardrobe that's mostly and ill-advisedly dry-clean-only in my current circumstances.

"Dad! She saved Porcupine," says the first girl who ran out into the street. She looks up to me. "You're our hero. Thank you!"

"And you're so pretty," the other girl says softly as she takes possession of the frog, who I can only assume is named Porcupine.

Bossy Daddy swallows as he nods, and the way his Adam's apple bobs reminds me of my tongue on his neck last night.

I look down to the girls. "You're welcome and thank you." My style is more on the bland side than it once was, but I would be lying if I said I didn't live to impress little girls. I glance over at their father (who I have to stop mentally referring to as Bossy Daddy before it slips out). "This isn't going to work."

He roughs his fingers through his still-damp hair before smiling down at his girls. "Letty, Berry, can you girls head inside and put Porcupine back in her aquarium?"

The pair skip off to the front door, leaving us alone. Just the two of us and a wall of sexual tension.

I take a step back. Not that I would pounce on him in broad daylight in his front yard. No, my life is messy enough without this further complication. "So, yeah," I tell him. "Your kids seem really sweet, but this can't happen. Good luck."

I turn to walk back to my car, parked across the street. I need this job, but my horny, heartbroken ass had to go ruin it all because I was feeling bad for myself on my birthday. Now, what felt like a harmless and truly memorable hookup is setting me back even further. I immediately regret even letting myself go out last night and spend money on frivolous things like shots and cheese fries and a cupcake from that food truck between the shots and cheese fries. It had been my first birthday alone, and I was convinced that it was no big deal and that it hardly mattered . . . until I had no one to share my cupcake with and it suddenly felt like it mattered a lot.

"Wait," he calls, and that same commanding tone sends tingling sensations down my spine. I hate myself for stopping and turning around the moment the word leaves his mouth.

"Just come inside for a minute while I call the agency, okay? Maybe we can get this sorted out." There's a hint of desperation in his expression that there was definitely no trace of last night.

"Fine," I concede. Maybe a client call would at least be faster than contacting the agency completely on my own and waiting to be reassigned.

He steps aside and waits for me to walk up the stairs ahead of him. "There must be some sort of mix-up. The agency had said that the childcare provider they were sending over was a lecturer here at Astra."

I turn back. "Do I not look like academic material?"

One single brow arches in a no-nonsense way. "That's not at all what I said." He redirects his gaze to the California plates on my car. "I'd just made the incorrect assumption that they'd already be settled here."

Ugh, fine.

"My name is Maddie, by the way," I tell him. "I don't think either of us thought to get each other's names."

"Well," he says, and then . . . he blushes. It's cute on such a large man. "They did announce yours before your birthday . . . spanking, but I guess I had other things on my mind than giving you mine. I'm Bram Loe. I'm a professor of ecology at the university."

"I'm adjuncting in the political science department. I suppose fucking my coworker is better than fucking my boss."

The edges of his ears are glowing now too, but he is otherwise unruffled, which feels like a challenge, honestly. The last three years of my life have been dedicated to being as palatable as possible. But something about Bram makes me want to get a rise out of him.

Bram's home is lived-in. Not in a hoarder sort of way, but in a way that unspools the tension in my shoulders. Gentry Cooper Wade *the Third* and I had lived in a townhouse that was tidier than the model home we toured before he bought the place. Other than the tasteful portrait of us from our first Christmas together, there was no evidence of life. Our toothbrushes were put away every morning and night. There were no stray glasses of water and he squeegeed the shower door every day after his morning rub and tug. (Sex was strictly reserved for the hour of nine thirty to ten thirty in the evening. Morning sex was not conducive to focus.)

As Bram scrolls through his phone before pulling it to his ear, I realize he's in a threadbare Astra University shirt instead of a repeat of the button-down he wore last night with the rolled-up sleeves. The vein coiling up his forearm and past his elbow disappears into the sleeve of his T-shirt as he waits for an answer on the other end of the line. And all I can think of is the way that same vein twitched when he pulled me to him with my back flat against his chest and reached around, flipped up my skirt, and molded his hand to my pulsing center. As I begged him to pull my panties aside and slide a finger through my wet folds.

Woo. Okay, I need some air. And maybe a splash of cold water to the face. Even when Bram is no longer officially my boss, hooking up with him again would be a bad idea. I need this job, and while I'm sure the university has some highly specific human resources song and dance for romantically involved faculty to adhere to that will make it permissible and aboveboard, a one-night stand—was it still a one-night stand if he went three times?—anyway, a horny little hookup was not really how I wanted to kick off my on-campus reputation.

Bram paces the kitchen, rolling a pen between his fingers, as he explains the situation to the staffing agency in broad terms.

He pauses, his eyes roving over me for a moment before he nods to himself. "Yes, we discovered that we have a . . . conflict of interest."

"Nice one," I whisper.

The only recognition I receive is one very annoyed arched brow.

"Right," he says. "Well, I suppose that's good for business." He pauses. "Um . . . no. We will discuss first and I'll call back if necessary." He nods, his gaze finding mine as he ends the call. "Yes, thank you. You too."

I lean forward on his kitchen island with my hands steepling over my lips. "That didn't sound very promising."

He shakes his head slowly. "Turns out there was an IVF baby boom in eastern Kansas three years ago and the plains are now overrun with twins. The agency says the soonest they can reassign someone would be in a month, which does me no good, because their mother is gone *now*, and it's just me."

"Yeah." I move to stand up and smooth my skirt. "That's bad news . . . for you."

Now he's the one leaning on his kitchen island, scrubbing his hands over his face. He takes a few deep breaths before standing up straight, and his face is the picture of calm. "I'll give you a twenty percent raise."

"I didn't realize we were negotiating." My voice comes out more like a purr. Am I sexually aroused right now?

"We're not," he says flatly.

My face falls into a pout with my lower lip sticking out and my chin dropping. First, he and his great dick are costing me my job before it's even started, and now he's ruining my fun by not even letting me negotiate. Not that I'm entertaining his offer, because if there's one thing I've learned from my brother, Nolan, it's that you don't fuck at work. (The fact he married *his* work hookup is irrelevant; Nolan's sexual omnivorism meant that the odds of him marrying someone he *hadn't* worked with in some capacity were unfavorable at best. So I still rest my case.)

Bram's expression softens, and it stops me in my tracks.

"I'm desperate here," he says. "I promise to make this the safest, most ideal work environment you could ever ask for. Besides, the whole purpose of your job is that you're here when I'm not. We'd be ships in the night, Maddie. That's all. I wouldn't be asking you if I wasn't completely out of options."

He is right in that we would likely never see each other outside of passing along information about the kids. Berry and Letty *are* adorable. And the agency did say that the third child was a seventeen-year-old girl who could drive. God, is he even old enough to have a teenage daughter?

I shouldn't do this. In fact, I hadn't even decided on if I would, but I couldn't help but wonder if I could push him just a tad more. He might have said his offer was nonnegotiable, but I'd be kicking myself all day if I left without testing the waters. Just for fun, of course.

I inhale through my nose and pull the strap of my purse over my shoulder.

He reads my body language loud and clear. "Twenty-five," he says. "Twenty-five percent."

I rock back on my heels for a moment, ready to push, but he holds at twenty-five. A rush of adrenaline chases up my spine when he shakes his head. It's rare that someone can keep pace with me when I'm bargaining, and it's kind of sexy how quietly and mildly he can do it.

But I'm not quite done. "I have rules," I say. My mouth is on autopilot at this point. I'm like a cat who has to know that the glass full of water will indeed spill and shatter the moment I knock it over.

"Anything you want," he says, walking around the island and closing some of the distance between us.

Now it's my turn to arch an eyebrow.

"Within reason," he clarifies.

"No more sex."

His jaw clenches. "Of course."

"We will, under no circumstances, be alone together in this house."

"That's not a problem."

"The job description says that I cook five days a week. I propose homemade meals three nights a week and takeout for the other two."

"I have a binder full of local menus."

He's too goddamn agreeable. I've pushed him this far and he hasn't blinked. Now I have no choice but to say yes. Why couldn't I have just left?

I cross my arms over my chest and try one last time to push him over the edge. "I want a credit card in my name for all incidentals and gas for while I'm working."

He eyes me thoughtfully for a moment. "I'll have one rush delivered. You can start tomorrow."

My jaw begins to drop, but I stop myself before I look like an absolute buffoon.

Sometimes the problem with negotiating is winning when you least expect it.

He walks me to the door, and I can feel his hand hovering above my lower back like he's guiding me. Protecting me.

I'm fucked.

I get in my car and wait for him to close his front door before I turn around and make the cursory inventory I do every time I return to my car. My pillows are there. My blankets. My sleeping pallet—a twin bed mattress topper. It's all there right alongside the toiletries I keep tucked under the passenger's seat.

Tomorrow I'll be chauffeuring around two little girls, which means I'll have to reorganize the trunk, where I keep most of my belongings—including my wardrobe. I don't want my personal things out in the open where the girls can see.

I'd hate for Daddy Bram to come home after my first day with Letty and Berry to learn that their new nanny is sort of—okay, definitely—living in her car.

CHAPTER THREE

Bram

The next afternoon, I walk into my office and find Leo Saint James on my love seat, feet propped on a stack of books, tossing an apple up into the air and catching it with efficient flicks of his wrist.

I skirt around Leo's long legs to get to my desk. "Busy day at the Saint James* office?" I ask mildly as I set down my leather satchel and start pulling out my things.

"I pay people to be busy for me," says Leo, not bothering to sit up from his long-limbed slouch.

I sit down and crack open my laptop. "And you didn't want to be un-busy in your own city?"

---

* Saint James Chocolate Co., founded in 1923, started as a tiny confectionary store in downtown Kansas City, Missouri, and is now a vaguely evil chocolate conglomerate.

"I had to visit the Mount Astra factory, and the idea of driving back was too exhausting. I had to come here and rest."

"It's a half-hour drive back to your office," I reply. "It probably took you twenty minutes just to park and walk here."

Leo leans his head back against the edge of the love seat and closes his eyes. The apple dangles from his hand. "Exactly. Now I'm doubly exhausted. How is Dr. Loe today?"

"Good. Had my first Bio 1 lecture of the year." Bio 1 is a massive course; even chopped into three lecture sections, each section has over four hundred students. Four hundred students with new backpacks and flushed cheeks from having rushed over from some wrong building or another. Half took unnecessarily detailed notes, while the other half looked like they'd already found a source of cheap beer on campus. All of them reminded me of unsteady kittens about to fall face-first into a bowl of milk.

"Ah. Science babies," says Leo. "When do you get to teach the big kids?"

"This afternoon."

In the interest of fairness, our department divides the 100- and 200-level courses among the teachers evenly, and while I know some professors prefer the smaller, upper-division assignments, I never mind teaching the early stuff. It's mostly first-years, and yes, they are exhausting, but they're kind of adorable too. And nothing beats watching a student discover that they *like* science, that they can be *good* at it, that this is only the beginning and there will be more and more and more, as much science as they want.

"By the way," Leo says, in a voice that is too casual to be truly offhand, "that cute little hookup of yours was scurrying to Salih while I was walking in."

Salih Hall houses the psychology and gender studies departments . . . and the political science department.

And I knew Maddie was teaching here, I *knew* she'd be in the building next to me, and yet—

I guess I thought it wouldn't affect me. That I wouldn't immediately think of Saturday night, of the plush curve of her ass while I had her bent over a kitchen table in an abandoned apartment above a dive bar.

Of how wet my cock had been every time I slid free of her body.

I look over at Leo and find him regarding me with a shrewd silver stare. His lidded eyes and bored expression might fool the poor souls who are ensorcelled by his angelic features and enviable hair, but not me. Leo and I have enough history that I can recognize when his interest has moved past curious to *here be dragons*.

"Yes," I say finally, having found my *this is neutral information* voice. "She's adjuncting here."

"Mm." Leo gives his apple an indolent toss. And then another. "And this is information she disclosed to you while you were upstairs explaining local parking regulations to her?"

The tips of my ears burn—one of the few things from my awkward childhood that's followed me into my thirties—and I look back at my laptop. "She's going to help out with the twins. Actually."

The apple stops.

"The twins," he says.

"And Fern. Sometimes. Maybe."

"Bram, *you slept with the nanny*?"

"She's a childcare provider," I say, a little sternly. "And we didn't have an employee-employer relationship when it happened."

"Sure, sure," reassures Leo. "I mean, it *would* be the most interesting thing you've done since you and Sara went all *FernGully* on construction equipment in your twenties, but I know our rebellious Bram is all mature and well-behaved now."

I'm not really listening at this point. I have the semester course listings pulled up on my laptop, and I've already found the classroom Maddie is teaching in today. If I go now, I can still catch her.

I stand up before I have a chance to talk myself out of it, and Leo blinks up at me. Then he grins. "Are you going to go *find* her? Your childcare provider?"

"I should make sure she has everything she needs for this afternoon, since it'll be her first time alone with the kids," I say. I think it's plausible. It's plausible enough that I believe it myself.

I just don't know if it's the entire truth.

Leo surges up from the love seat. "Excellent, I'm coming with you."

"*Absolutely* not—"

But he's already up and walking toward the door, his expensive shoes gleaming along with the apple in his hand. It only takes me a few strides to catch up with him—despite being much shorter than him for the first part of high school, I'm every bit as tall as he is now—and then we're pushing out of Gerhart (molecular biosciences, ecology, and undergraduate bio) and into the late August sun.

Leo tosses his apple as he walks, silver watch flashing on his wrist, the lines of his Italian cotton shirt pulling at his shoulders and arms. His trousers have somehow kept their perfect crease even after he's sprawled all over my office, and the sun catches the sharp perfection of his jaw and cheekbones. Undergrads of every gender stare open-mouthed at him as we pass, something we both ignore. When it comes to Leo Saint James, admiration is to be expected. Particularly when the admirers have no idea how cutting, cunning, and cruel Leo can be when he's in the mood.

Leo suddenly stops just before we reach the steps up to Salih's glass doors. "Bram," he says in a whisper, yanking at my arm. "*What the fuck is that thing?*"

I follow his eyes to the bench by the stairs, where a gray and brown beast is watching us with unimpressed gold eyes. Its ears barely emerge from its fluff, its face is framed by drooping whiskers and what looks like a beard, and it's so round that the shadow it casts on the sidewalk is a perfect circle. It gives a low growl of warning.

"Oh. That's Dr. Monty Python."

"*Dr.* Monty Python?"

"The humanities department gave him an honorary doctorate in *litter-ature* last year," I clarify.

"I— This makes no sense."

Oh my god, finally! A kindred spirit! "I've been trying to say this! It makes no sense to name the Astra University campus cat after a *python* when our mascot is a copperhead snake, which is a type of viper! Pythons are nothing like vipers! Pythons strangle their prey! Vipers strike! Vipers are venomous! I don't even know who came up with this stupid name; probably somebody in Fine Arts—"[*]

"No," Leo interrupts. "No, this creature makes no sense. That is not a cat."

"We're certain it's a cat," I say. And then amend, "Well, maybe like seventy-thirty that it's a cat. Actually, the oSTEM club is trying to get an internal grant[†] to run a feline DNA test on him."

---

[*] It was.

[†] The Out in Science, Technology, Engineering, and Mathematics club did first try to start a GoFundMe for their cause, but they were in violation of some university rule written by someone who hates cats. Probably.

"You should do that," Leo says, fear and disgust edging every syllable. "Because I'm pretty sure that thing came from hell. We're very close to Stull, you know."[*]

Leo follows me cautiously up the stairs, careful to keep me between him and Dr. Monty at all times, and then we go through the doors and find the large tiled staircase up to the second floor. I haven't been in this building since I was an undergrad myself, so it takes me a minute to find Maddie's class. The door is closed; she's still teaching. I can hear the appealing alto of her voice, and when I come up to the window set into the door, I can see—

"Oh, she's poli-sci, all right," Leo says. "Look at her. She looks like she's running for mayor of a mid-sized town in the upper Midwest."

Leo isn't wrong. If yesterday Maddie looked like she'd just come from Sunday brunch, then today she looks like she just came from a casual sit-down with the morning news. Wide-legged trousers and a white silk blouse, both of which look understatedly expensive. She's wearing a tidy strand of pearls that nestle at the base of her neck, and her long, blond hair falls in loose curls over her shoulders. She looks focus-grouped.

She looks beautiful too.

"What is this section?" Leo asks.

"Intro to US Politics."

"She doesn't have the room," observes Leo, taking a bite of his apple. Juice shines on his lower lip and he licks it away, and a student walking toward us accidentally drops a stack of handouts onto the floor.

---

[*] Stull, Kansas, is rumored to be a hellmouth. (It was Mount Astra students themselves who started the rumor in the 1970s.)

I turn away from Leo's latest convert and see that he's right about my brat—ah, childcare provider. Maddie doesn't have the room, and while I don't know her well, it feels completely out of character based on everything I do know about her.

She's in the front, futzing with an uncooperative laptop (something we've all lived through but that can be extra brutal on the first day), and I can see at least seven sleeping students from where I'm standing. A clump of football player–shaped boys are talking openly in the back, and several students are looking at their phones under their desks.

This close to the door, I can hear Maddie clearly as she starts speaking again, the words coming out lilting and a little uncertain, almost like she's waiting for someone else to tell her the right answer. Nothing like the fearless brat who unflinchingly negotiated herself to a 25 percent raise yesterday.

"So . . . that will be the judiciary section. We'll have one final section on the media and politics, and . . . did you have a question? Just stretching? Sorry. Um, media will be the last section, and then we'll have the final. And—that's it. That's all. Does anyone have any questions?"

One of the muscled young men in the back raises his hand, going from slouched backward to sitting completely upright, like he's trying to touch the ceiling with his fingertips. "Professor Ko—Kowow—uh, Professor K, can we go now?"

"Yes," Maddie replies faintly and there's a backpack-jostling scramble as the students race down the steps of the small indoor auditorium and rush for the door. Leo and I step back just in time—the door crashes open and students flood out, already texting, shoving, wedging earbuds into their ears.

We walk into the classroom after the students leave, and Maddie's head swivels at the movement, sending her curls bouncing. She glares at me.

"What are you doing here?" she hisses.

Leo glances between us, his eyes sparkling with amusement. "Great question, sweet," he commends, and then turns to me. "Dr. Loe?"

"I just wanted to make sure you had everything you needed to pick up the twins," I say.

"You," she accuses, pointing her finger at me, "were watching me from the door."

I slowly drag my eyes from her finger to her face, the blood suddenly kicking so hard in my veins that I'm almost dizzy with it. I want to wrap my hand around that finger and pull her close and tell her exactly what's coming to her for that little show.

And then I suck in a deep, quick breath through my nose. What *on earth* am I thinking? She's my employee. She's almost ten years younger than me. And even before I gave up on dating, I still wasn't the . . . the *you've been a bad girl* guy.

Maddie spins away, back to the podium where her laptop is still sitting open, obviously upset about something. Possibly me. Even more possibly what just happened during her first class here at Astra University.

I look at Leo. "You should leave."

Leo bites his apple smirkingly in response. Only Leo Saint James can bite into an apple smirkingly.

I sigh. "Please?"

"But where would I go?" he asks when he swallows, looking suddenly like a lost angel, bewildered and innocent.

"I don't know, Leo. Your home? Your office? Your local library?"

A flicker of something unnameable moves through his eyes.

Then he smiles, one of the amused, vicious smiles that used to signal torment for me when we were boys. Now I think it might signal torment for someone else.

"You're right," he announces, tossing his half-eaten apple in the trash without looking at either the apple or the trash can. It lands perfectly in the middle with a *thunk*. "I should visit the library. Pick up a book. Get to know a librarian. It'll do me good." And without another word, he leaves, sauntering off with his hands in his trouser pockets.

"Sorry about that," I say to Maddie as I turn back to her, but she's already shaking her head.

"Don't be sorry for him, I don't even know him! Be sorry for you, lurking out there and making me nervous!"

I lift my hands, palms out, the posture of an innocent man. "I wasn't trying to make you nervous. I only wanted to touch base with you before you left to get the twins. That's all."

Her mouth, immaculately painted in Focus Group Mauve, curves into a luscious scowl. "Look, *Dr. Loe*," she says, her gaze narrowed into black-lashed slits of irritation, "I might work for you at your house, but you're not allowed to give me a performance review *here*."

Oh, I want to give her a performance review, all right. Over my lap. With those pointy kitten heels up in the air.

"Understood," I say with a mildness I do *not* feel. "I promise I'm not planning on doing anything of the sort. I'll be home around five thirty; you have my number if you need anything. See you tonight, Ms. Kowalczk."

I HEAR SCREAMING.

I'm halfway out of my weathered hybrid crossover, one hand

wrestling with the door and the other with the satchel I'm trying to drag out of the passenger seat, and I finally give up on the satchel and the door and bolt around to the backyard, leaving the car door hanging wide open.

There was a time in my life where I did a lot of adrenaline-fueled bolting, where I had a knack for ruthless, reflexive action, and when I clear the corner of my house, my mind is already sorting through the possibilities—that there will be blood, broken bones, a strange dog that Hester Prynne, despite being a massive German shepherd, is too cowardly to chase away—and then I wrench myself to a halt, the split second between my photoreceptors turning light into electricity and my brain turning that electricity into information stretching into years.

Letty and Berry are jumping through the sprinkler, shrieking at the cold water, shrieking at Hester Prynne, who is trying to bite the water, and then shrieking at Maddie until Maddie chases them back through the spray again. Fern is tucked away on the patio, chatting to a friend on her phone while she works on one of her many embroideries in progress (a hobby that sounds wholesome until you see the things she embroiders).

No one is bleeding. No one is broken.

The screams are happy ones.

I let out a full exhale for the first time since I opened my car door, and Maddie walks through the sprinkler to me, a challenging look on her face, like she's ready to revisit our earlier disagreement. Satisfaction—strange, uninvited—blooms inside my chest as she comes closer.

I want the challenge. I want her to try me. I want her to step closer and let me see those flawlessly lipsticked lips and those wicked green eyes.

And then I make the mistake of dropping my gaze.

Something much, much stronger than satisfaction rips through me.

"Thank you for playing with the girls, they love the sprinkler," I manage to say when she's close enough.

She tosses wet hair over her shoulder, and *oh god oh god*—it's not just that her blouse is wet, but the thin bra underneath too, and I can make out the pink of her nipples. I can see the hard shape of them.

She might as well be wearing nothing at all.

"I was happy to," she says briskly. "Now, about you showing up randomly to my class—"

"It won't happen again. And can we speak inside the house for a moment?" I sound gruff and a little stern, but that's better than lewd and panting, I guess.

She regards me with enough miffed suspicion to make Dr. Monty proud, and then lifts her chin and marches to the kitchen door and goes inside.

"Fern, will you keep an eye on the littles?" I ask my oldest. I get a nod from the teen, and then I follow Maddie inside, no idea how to say what I'm going to say next, but also knowing with certainty that I'm going to say it.

Maddie has drifted from the kitchen to the dining room, which in my house is lined with bookcases, and is perusing the spines of some vintage gardening books with a dilatory finger.

"Ms. Kowalczk," I say, and she huffs.

"You can call me Maddie, you know."

"Ms. Kowalczk," I repeat, "do you want a dry T-shirt to change into?"

Maddie turns to face me. And with the warm glow of sunlight pouring in from the west, I can see through her wet shirt in here just as clearly as I could out there. I drag my eyes up immediately, my entire body tight and breathless and eager to fuck, but she sees, of course she sees where I was looking.

"A dry T-shirt," she says. "Hmm. Is something bothering you, Dr. Loe?"

I step closer to her and she draws closer to me, and I see that challenge again in her face, like a dare—like a question too, maybe—and I study her eyes, her flushed cheeks, the teeth digging into her bottom lip.

"You," I tell her softly, "have a smart mouth."

"You going to fix it for me?"

We are so close now. Close enough that she has to tilt her head almost all the way back to look at me. Her neck is flushed. Her pupils are massive pools of black.

I say in my sternest voice, "I think someone should teach you how to behave."

Her lips part on an inhale . . . and she shivers.

I nearly do it. I nearly break our rules and reach up to touch her. Rub my thumb along a furled, pink bud until her knees buckle and I can push her back onto the table. I'd peel the wet silk from her skin and taste her nipples and kiss my way down her stomach. I'd slide her trousers off her hips and toss them to the floor, and then I'd get to my knees and lick her until she shuddered out a climax with her thighs by my ears. I'd unzip my trousers and push all the way inside. I'd show her everything I'd been thinking about since Saturday night—relay every depraved, quivering, sweat-misted detail.

I take an abrupt step back and scrub my hand through my hair. Without looking at her, I say, "I know you must be cold. I have T-shirts or I have some button-down shirts, if you'd rather."

Maddie doesn't answer at first, but when she does, her voice is largely devoid of emotion. "It's fine, Dr. Loe. I have a change of clothes in my car."

"You can call me Bram," I offer, looking up right as she starts walking to the front door.

"When you call me Maddie," she counters, a bit petulantly, and I can't help but smile a little as she goes outside to her car. I watch as she pops open the trunk and starts rummaging through what look like plastic containers, the big ones meant for storage. She must not have unloaded her car after getting here from California.

She pulls out a shirt, slams the trunk closed, and when she looks up to see me watching her through the window, she visibly flinches.

My small smile slips into a frown as I watch her bypass the front door and go around back with the girls instead.

The frown stays on my face as I go outside myself to finally shut my car door.

CHAPTER FOUR

Maddie

There is an art to sleeping in your car, and I am proud to say that I have had my first decent night's rest since moving to Mount Astra two weeks ago. Thankfully, I clock in at five two, so that's one less thing to worry about in my 2000 Volvo S40.

For the first few nights, I camped out in the Mount Astra Methodist Medical Center parking lot and I found that sleeping in the back seat was more comfortable.* But then I had a little bit of a scare when a man pounded his fists on my car and shouted about loose women being damned. I could barely scramble into the front seat before he was yanking on my (thankfully, locked) door

---

* It is rumored that Leo Saint James lost his virginity in that same parking lot to a nurse on her break while Leo's homecoming date was being treated for an allergic reaction to asparagus.

handles. After that, I tore down my window covers and spent the rest of the night sipping coffee at Waffle House.*

But last night, I discovered the glory of rest stops. You'd think being surrounded by eighteen-wheelers would be intimidating, but there seemed to be some mutual understanding that everyone had the common goal of an uneventful night's sleep.

I wake up with a slightly stiff neck, but it's worth sleeping in the reclined driver's seat after the incident in the hospital parking lot. I barely even miss my mattress—and I definitely don't miss the man I shared it with, who slept with a Tempur-Pedic body pillow between us because he was a fussier sleeper than a person who was nine months' pregnant with twins.

As someone who's been in school for the last seven years, it took little to no time to source everything I might need to fill in the gaps left by living in my car. The campus gym opens at six and the showers are pretty decent when you get to them first thing in the morning before they become a pit of loose hair. And there's not really anything suspicious about an adjunct putting in a quick morning workout before running to the library to take advantage of the free coffee bar courtesy of an absolutely angelic librarian.

Speaking of, I hold the door open for Junie as she scurries into the library today with her arms full of flavored creamers. "Thank you," she says as she blows a loose curl out of her face. "I got a new creamer for us to try."

Junie is the curvy, adult form of the *before* version of Mia Thermopolis in *The Princess Diaries*. Poofy, untamed hair. Plaid

---

* The parking lot where Joey Fucking Kemp lost his virginity, followed by a drunk lecture from Bram about how virginity is a construct. The lecture was followed by celebratory waffles.

skirts that are a few inches too long. Sweaters that swallow her and loafers that she definitely purchased after reading hundreds of reviews written by swaths of elderly shoppers. In one word, her look is *tragic*.

I didn't want to like her, and trust me, I tried not to. The moment we met, I could tell that she was the type of person who lived to accommodate. But she wormed her way into my good graces with her array of creamers and insider tips about Astra University. (Example Number One: The campus bookstore sells expired fruit parfaits and no one is willing to stand up to the dictator of a store manager to have it addressed. Example Number Two: A Phi Gam named Dustin was running an underground cologne ring from the back of a local dry cleaner. I took the liberty of visiting the dry cleaner while the owner was working, tipped him off about the bottles of smuggled Acqua Di Giò and Tom Ford, and he was so grateful that, after firing Dustin, he gave me free dry cleaning for the semester.)

The truth is Junie is sweet. Genuinely sweet. No ulterior motives or passive aggression. Just sweet. And maybe I picked up on her people-pleasing vibes and found them annoying because . . . blah, blah, self-reflection.

I follow Junie to the coffee bar, where I help her organize the new creamer additions.

"I know it's early, but they already had the fall creamers out, so I just went for it. Seasons be damned."

"Daredevil," I tell her with a playful nudge.

She rolls her eyes.

"It's really nice of the university to provide complimentary coffee."

"Well . . ." She clears her throat and adjusts her headband. "It's not provided by the university in the traditional sense. It's more that the university provides me with a salary and I earmark a portion of the salary to stock the coffee bar."

I pause mid-whiff of fresh coffee. "Junie, these punk-ass kids must be bleeding you dry. You walked in with fifty dollars' worth of creamer this morning, at least."

She shrugs. "I want this place to feel cozy. Last semester, the library was a ghost town until finals. If I don't have enough traffic, I risk a budget cut. So complimentary coffee it is. I'm thinking of doing doughnuts on Fridays, though—"

I smack her hand before it can drift to her chin in thoughtful contemplation. "No," I tell her. "Bad librarian."

She lets me loiter at the reference desk for the next thirty minutes while she tells me all about my favorite kind of gossip: drama between people who I will never have to deal with myself but am vaguely aware of. The latest is about an old high school friend of hers and a recent run-in with her former bully. The first guy sounds like a tool and the second sounds like a dick.

Before I leave, I berate her once more about blowing her own money and plant the seed that she should include the coffee in her future budget, especially if it drives traffic into the library.

She lets out a long *hmmmm* as we both watch a first-year boy fill two cups full of nothing but mocha creamer before pocketing a handful of wooden stirrers.

"Were we all that feral during undergrad?" she asks.

I laugh, but fail to mention that I am currently as much of a mooch as that kid.

"Don't forget to grab the campus paper on your way out," she says. "There's a coupon in the back for a free appetizer at Cinzetti's." She winks. "No purchase required."

"Has anyone ever told you that you're too pure for this world?"

"No, but I do have to wear medicated sunscreen."

I'm not sure if the nearly translucent hue of her skin is constitutional or earned by spending every waking moment in this cavernous, neo-Gothic library, but either way, I believe her. I say goodbye, scoop up the coupon, and drop it into my leather tote bag before heading over to Salih for my first section of the day.

When I applied for the job at Astra, I was hot-spotting off my phone in a Costco parking lot eighteen hours after Gentry Cooper Wade *the Third* broke up with me. Well, technically his family's longtime political adviser initiated the conversation. I had graduated a month and a half prior and was still studying for the California state bar exam when Penelope Pike sent me a calendar invite. She wanted to meet at our townhouse, which I assumed would involve talking strategy for Gentry's first run at the California State Assembly that we were all gearing up for this year.

Back in January, Penelope had sat me down for a conversation with an action plan after some polling she had run (unbeknownst to me). Apparently, I was lacking in image and likability. Men felt like I appeared to be unhealthy, which very clearly translated to *fat* and *unfuckable*. Both women and men found me to be stiff, overly rehearsed, and lacking warmth. Which translated to *a bitch*. No one mentioned the endless hours I'd spent doing philanthropic work in the midst of full-time law school and occasional work-study programs. And they definitely didn't mention how I'd untangled the financial mess that was the domestic violence arm of the Wade Foundation and salvaged the programs planned for that year after Gentry's seedy great-uncle had gone on a cocaine bender with cash he had pulled from the foundation accounts.

After graduation, my polling results plummeted even more. It could have been any number of things. There was the charity auction I was required to attend with Gentry's mom during the week of finals where I was asked by a reporter if I felt that the National Association of Pet Sitters was a worthy cause and I gave a clipped response about the importance of subsidized childcare. Or the time I wore a two-piece swimsuit to a family weekend at the lake and posted a picture online. Gentry's fitness-podcaster cousin reposted the group photo only for his loyal listeners to fill my comments with concern-trolling about my weight and claims that Gentry was only dating me because I had dirt on him. I love being a woman on the internet. Truly.

So I wasn't surprised that Gentry was breaking up with me, but I was surprised to find Penelope was doing it for him. As a parting gift, she even provided me with a copy of the fully executed NDA I had unwisely signed the summer after undergrad.

I sat gobsmacked, and after Penelope was through, Gentry gave me a one-armed pat-on-the-back hug like I'd just lost a Little League game. One year of secretly fucking, followed by three years of dating, and it all ended with a pat on the back.

Three years spent drowning in law school courses that I wasn't even sure I wanted to take and curating a palatable image of someone who was anyone but me. All because I thought Gentry and I could change the world together. I was bit by the political bug back in high school and it only took volunteering for a few underdog (and often female-led) campaigns to wonder if I could do more good in the passenger seat of someone like Gentry's life than I ever could on my own.

So after living the last four years in service of someone else's ambitions, the adjunct job was a desperate attempt to return home

Fundamentals of Being a Good Girl 49

to Kansas, where I was born and raised. It was a place where I didn't feel like I was existing under a microscope.

My brother and mom had moved to LA a few years ago, just after I graduated high school, so there was always the option of going to stay with them, but I couldn't stomach the thought of being in the same state as Gentry. Not when he had just won the primary and his name was beginning to be a regular in the news cycle. Sure, a state assembly campaign wasn't normally a big deal, but it was when the only heir to the Wade political dynasty was making his debut. It also didn't help that despite their attempts to be supportive, it was painfully obvious that my family didn't like Gentry or the person I had become. I'm good at a lot of things, but admitting that I'm wrong isn't really one of them.

So I fled the state and took the first job I could get . . . and then also signed up with a childcare agency to supplement my meager adjunct income, because I'd worked at a church nursery on Sundays in high school and had liked it fine enough.

What I did not do was a good job of planning where I would live and how I would survive before I got my first few paychecks, hence the car camping. Anything I had saved from my work-study programs before graduation was spent on the trip out here.

I walk into the classroom with just a minute to spare. I made the mistake of showing up to one of my lectures too early last week and was met with the empty stares of the first-years who had waited too long to register and therefore ended up with my 7:30 a.m. class. Not to mention that I was cornered by one of my later-in-life students (who looked like the Unabomber and smelled like beef jerky) so he could get my thoughts on filing a

FOIA request related to some unhinged theory involving legislators in the basement of a pizza parlor covering up proof of aliens.

As I stride to the lectern, I call out, "Good morning, class."

I'm met with a chorus of *good morning*s and groans. In the last two weeks, my class size has visibly shrunk. After I got my first list of student drops, I hid in the shared adjunct office upstairs and spiraled. Could I get fired for this? What if they just kept dropping and eventually there was no class at all? Was I really that bad? I had TA'ed for a legal-writing class during my second year of law school and I felt like I'd done a decent job. But there were just so many students, and it was an intro class mostly full of people who *had to* rather than *wanted to* be there.

The political science department chair, Dr. Miranda Salazar, found me about thirty seconds away from huffing into a paper bag when she explained that this was totally normal for an early morning class full of younger students. It helped that her voice was soothing to me (if you found the *Real Housewives* franchise to be a source of calming energy) and she looked like Marissa Tomei in *My Cousin Vinny*, but twenty-five years later. I'd read online that she was a retired New Jersey state senator who'd moved to Kansas after falling in love with her husband, who was a higher-up with Hope Inc.,[*] which was headquartered in the Kansas City area.

I have found, however, that I like the smaller class now, actually. It feels more manageable, like I'm dipping my toes into the

---

[*] The holiday powerhouse parent company of the Hope Channel, Hope After Dark, and Hope Greeting Cards and Gifts. The headquarters are rumored to require their front desk staff to dress as elves for the entire month of December.

Fundamentals of Being a Good Girl

warm pool of academia rather than taking a cold plunge. My second section, however, is another story.

"Let's move down to the first five rows," I say to the very sporadically filled auditorium.

The students at the back huff and loudly gather their things before moving down. One girl with fading blue hair that looks like it's been soaked in chlorine crawls over four rows of seats because she can't be bothered to walk to the end of the aisle. She's really matching the energy of her fleece Winnie the Pooh pajamas, which I can appreciate. Another girl refuses to move while she taps away on her phone and the guy behind her is so dead asleep that I wonder if he just spent the night after a class yesterday evening.

While I plug in my laptop and dongle (what kind of Silicon Valley perv came up with that name?), I go over a few reminders. "Don't forget that next week I'll need your topics for our constitutional amendment project. You are free to work in groups of two to three or by yourself. Choose wisely, because groups will be uniformly graded."

A quick glance at my class tells me which students are eager to pair up while some of the quiet ones sink down into their seats to avoid getting cornered.

"Professor," says a guy in the second row, "is that really fair? If you do the project alone, you're doing the work of three people and then if you're in a group of slackers, everyone else is getting credit for your hard work."

A few nod along with him.

"I hated group projects during undergrad," I tell him as I walk out from behind the lectern and hop up onto the desk, which looked more graceful in my head than it actually is despite the help of my sensible two-inch heels. "But I wouldn't have known that if I didn't try it. I'm not saying that you need to work with a group of classmates to know if that's your speed, but I am saying that you should consider the structure of this class as important as the material itself."

He crosses his arms, and his eyebrows lift up to his hairline. "Think of this as natural selection."

"Wait, we're getting dropped?" someone asks.

Sweet, sweet babies.

"No, no. Imagine you as a person, with all your traits and quirks, are being stirred in a pot. The longer you're in the pot, you'll find that the ingredients will either dissolve or remain if they're hearty enough, right? You've been simmering in a pot since birth. College turns up the heat. So think of this decision as a chance to figure out if you're A, a group project person, B, a lone wolf, or C, a lone wolf with no backbone who can't say no when approached by a group and will learn the valuable life lesson that is the power of no."

The guy huffs out a sigh, but I notice a few other students leaning forward, their interest piqued.

"Does that answer your question, Mr. . . ."

"Jordan Mallory." He peers around at his classmates. "And before any of you assholes ask, I'm working alone. I'm not about to sit around and wait for someone else to do the work I'll get stuck doing anyway."

A girl in the front row rolls her eyes and then swivels around. "Don't worry. None of you are missing out on anything. The classroom isn't the only place Jordan doesn't wait for other people to finish."

A low chorus of *ooooohs* rolls through the auditorium and I am immediately nostalgic for a time when I was showing up to class in yesterday's clothes. Back when Gentry was just the irritating upperclassman who I found to be both suspiciously charismatic and deeply attractive.

We move on to talk about federalism, and in the last fifteen minutes of class, the collective sleepiness finally wears off and the students are in a heated debate over whether or not marijuana should be federally legalized.

The class is so involved that no one even notices when we go three minutes over. That is, until a man in a tweed vest and dusty-looking corduroy pants walks in and says, "Class dismissed. Everybody out."

My jaw drops, hackles rising, and my temper goes straight to my quickly reddening cheeks. "Excuse me," I say, but my class has already heard those magic words and they're disappearing like it's the Rapture.

The girl in the fleece Winnie the Pooh pajamas stops by before I can storm over to the man who I now recognize as Dr. Wallace, the resident expert on Eastern European politics.

"Hey," she says without making eye contact. I take a deep breath and force my blood pressure to ease up. "That was pretty cool. My brother got picked up on the wrong side of the state line for having weed in his car. He didn't even realize he wasn't in Missouri anymore. He had a warrant for an outstanding speeding ticket, so they arrested him over a holiday weekend and he couldn't see a judge for three days. He ended up losing his job at Tanner's Bar and Grill after no-showing on his shifts. He has two kids and a pregnant wife." She shakes her head.

I grimace. "Ugh, I'm sorry. It's Whitley, right?"

She looks up then and nods, giving me an almost smile and a half-hearted wave before slipping out the door.

When I turn around, Dr. Wallace has already closed my laptop and set my materials on the desk in a haphazard pile. Fucking prick. The man is the definition of entitlement. He's every reason why I think tenure isn't always a good thing and why I am very much doubting my decision to dive headfirst into academia.

"Dr. Wallace, I don't think your class starts for another nine minutes," I say.

He glances at the heavy gold watch on his wrist and snorts. "And your class ended six minutes ago. I have patiently waited outside of this room for the first two weeks of the semester, but enough is enough, Mrs.—"

"*Professor* Kowalczk," I say as I stuff my papers and laptop into my tote bag.

"It wouldn't hurt for you to learn some respect for your fellow faculty. Especially those of us who are teaching more advanced courses that might require the full fifteen minutes between classes to properly prepare."

"Right." I've got this bag of dicks' number, and now that I do, I look forward to spending the rest of the semester getting under his skin with a smile on my face. "I am so incredibly sorry, sir." My voice is high and fluttery. "How careless of me to run over my allotted time. And especially when you must prepare for a class with such complex concepts. I bet you use all the ten-dollar words during your lecture."

His brow furrows. "I do have quite the extensive vocabulary."

"If you'll excuse me," I say with a warm smile. "I have to grade my online quizzes from this week and make sure that my students all spelled their names correctly."

I leave him in a confused state of limbo, unsure what to make of me. Either way, he definitely underestimates me, which I've found is the most advantageous of positions.

In the hallway, Dr. Salazar is hovering near the door. "Professor Kowalczk, just the person I was hoping to see."

"Hi, Dr. Salazar—"

"Please call me Miranda," she says.

"Only if you'll call me Maddie."

"Quid pro quo," she says, her thick black brows raised. The streaks of white through her dark hair feel purposeful and the black pencil slacks and cobalt-blue heels she's wearing stand out among the cozy, warm tones of Mount Astra. "I just wanted to let you know that I might be popping in to observe at some point in the next few weeks. No pressure. Just standard practice."

"Great," I tell her. "I love surprises, and by that I mean, please put me out of my misery and say you'll sit in on a class sooner rather than later."

She laughs and the sound of it is loud and almost crass. I immediately want to pick her brain and figure out how she outsmarted the focus groups and got elected.

"I'll do my best," she promises, and then steps in a little closer as the hallway begins to quiet and classroom doors begin to close. "And Maddie, you can't let that old man talk to you like that. Especially in front of your students."

My mouth opens and closes, looking for an excuse or a reason that I would let Dr. Wallace bully me.

"This is the kind of thing I could fix for you," Miranda continues, "but I don't think that will do you any good in the long run. Especially given how male dominated the program is this semester."

She's right. The political science department is currently a sea of ungroomed nose hair and rumpled tweed. I was hired so quickly because the three women and nonbinary professors were poached by a private think tank while two other faculty members are doing their research intensive semesters this fall.

"You're right," I say. "I'll figure out how to handle it."

She claps me on the shoulder before speed-walking past me. "I'm here to talk you through anything you need, Maddie. Pop by my office anytime. Even if it's just to escape the boys' club."

I don't want to make a name for myself in the department as being difficult to work with, but I also know exactly what Miranda means. This is the kind of situation where I have to assert dominance or else it will turn out like the first time I met Penelope Pike and I let her talk me into removing my nose ring and getting highlights in less than fifteen minutes of knowing her.

Before I head upstairs to the shared adjunct office, I step outside for some fresh air and to peel the orange I tossed in my bag this morning.

While I savor each slice and occasionally lick the juice as it drips down my wrist like a mannerless animal, I open the campus newspaper, *The Astra Star-Herald*.

The front page is all football and student government elections—which I am honestly triggered by after managing Gentry's campaign for student body president when I was a second-year and he was a third-year.

The second page delves into the upcoming production of *Thoroughly Modern Millie* followed by Greek life and the initiative to expand the campus sexual health resource center next summer. I take a bite of my last orange slice as I land on the final page. The header on the bottom half reads *Throwing It Back*. There are photos of faculty and students from the last few years and even this summer.

Right there in the bottom corner is a photo of Bram and a statuesque woman. The photo might be grainy, but she is clearly stunning with her long black curls piled atop her head. He has a stack of papers wedged under his arm and a rucksack on his back. The woman is wearing hiking shorts, her lean thighs muscled and burnished in a deep, deep tan. Her elbow is propped up on Bram's shoulder as she rests her chin on her wrist in a familiar pose. She's grinning at the camera and Bram is smiling at her in an all-consuming way.

Let the record show that Bram has never smiled at me.

The caption below reads: *Dr. Sara Loe is pictured with colleague and husband Dr. Bram Loe after leading graduate students on a hike in the Rocky Mountains to study a colony of snow-loving moss.*

Oh.

Oh.

The paper crinkles as I involuntarily clench my hand into a fist.

Not only does he not smile at me, but he's *married*. As in legally wed.

Their mother is gone for the next eight weeks. Why did I just assume . . . I mean, there hadn't been a wedding ring, but that doesn't mean shit. Fucking hell. I've never slept with a married man. What does that make me? And what right did he have to involve me in his infidelity? The poor woman is probably off on sabbatical, or hell, I don't know, helping out with a sick relative while her husband, the green fucking giant, is just boning his way through a college town with his stern voice and rolled-up shirtsleeves and slimy-ass pet frog.

Everything in me wants to storm into his building right now and quit. Leave his cheating ass high and dry.

The money. Come on, Maddie. You need the money.

And okay, the twins are adorable and funny and make me forget for a few hours every day that my life is in shambles. Fern is pretty great too, even though she's barely spoken to me.

But I have to find another job. Then I have to move out of my car. And then I can quit working for Bram Loe.

My phone buzzes in my bag, and I dig it out to see Nolan's contact photo. My brother, who's several years older than me. I swipe to ignore the call. I'll talk to him soon. Mom too. But first I need to get on my feet and I need to do it on my own.

Nolan was in a boy band ages ago, and after a few rough years (which were perfectly timed with most of my adolescence), he's back in the public eye.[*] He would help me if I asked. I know he would. But I was the one who dealt with the bills when Nolan was busy or gone, and with Mom's medications, and leaky sinks and broken-down cars. After doing all that, I know I can handle my shit myself—plus, if my teenage years and splitting up with Gentry have taught me anything, it's that relying on anyone other than yourself is a fast track to disappointment.

Anddddd, okay, *fine*. Admitting the truth about my abrupt move and vehicular lodging to Nolan would require admitting he was right about Gentry and Gentry's overall suckery and that I had indeed been turning into someone Nolan didn't know anymore. Someone *I* didn't even know.

And that is a conversation best had with a roof over my head. One I paid for myself.

---

[*] See the Hope Channel's viral hit *Duke the Halls* and its many, many sequels and spin-offs.

CHAPTER FIVE

Bram

"Daddy!" Letty yells. I look up from my potting bench to the glassed-in breezeway that connects the house to the greenhouse I built the year I got divorced.

(Sometimes a thing can be the right choice—like a divorce—*and also* leave you feeling weird and bored after it's done. Building a greenhouse seemed like a better alternative than a more destructive hobby, like online dating or getting into *Warhammer*.)

"What is it, sprout?"

Letty runs through the breezeway, my phone in her hand. "Berry was trying to show Mommy the new things we've put in Porcupine's tank, and Porcupine got out, and now Hester Prynne won't come out from under the bed."

"Really sorry about that, Bram!" Sara's voice comes from the phone. "I didn't expect my hundred-pound German shepherd to be terrified of a frog."

Letty sets the phone down on the potting bench and then tears off, probably back to monitor the dog situation with Berry. I pull off my gloves and pick up the phone to follow in Letty's wake. "In fairness, I didn't see it coming either. Hey, Asher. How're you doing?"

Sara and Asher got engaged two years ago, and the minute I met the environmental researcher and activist, it was like solving for x after years of scratched-out answers. Sara and I had made the marriage thing work for so many years because we'd been bound together by the girls, because we'd been horny enough, because we'd been even hornier for science and science was a thing we did together anyway. But over time, our connection started to fray, cardboard puzzle tabs repeatedly forced to fit in the wrong cardboard sockets.

And from the first words Asher spoke—bitingly intelligent, charged with meaning—I immediately understood why Asher was the right puzzle piece for her, and I hadn't been. I'll never be a mix of tattooed mystery and charisma; I'm not in demand as a guest on podcasts or television segments; I don't get any joy sparring with congresspeople about climate change. I *like* that people don't notice me, that they underestimate me. I like not arguing, I like staying put, I like anonymity.

I like rules and gentle routines and the soft quiet of my greenhouse in the mornings. I like being the invisible person behind someone visible, taking care of them, supporting them, making sure they get enough to eat and that they get enough sleep. Sara needs something different. A co-activist. A co-performer.

"Hey yourself," Asher says, giving me that enigmatic curl of a smile that I know must have killed before they settled down with Sara.* "Seems like a busy Sunday over there."

"About the normal amount of chaos," I say as I go into the house and make for the stairs. "I did ask Maddie to come over today so I could have some time to work on the book."

I'm tenured now, so it isn't quite publish or perish these days, but the book is a project meant for a general audience, not an academic text, and finding time to write among parenting, teaching, and all the behind-the-scenes curriculum and committee work of academia has been next to impossible. So in a moment of desperation—and despite having done my best to avoid extended time spent with Maddie over the last couple of weeks—I asked for a weekend shift at double her normal rate.

"You should take some time off," Sara says seriously. "See if Joey wants to grab a drink or something. Have a Best Night Ever."

Just the idea of *a drink* makes my stomach turn. "We actually hit it hard a couple of weeks ago to celebrate Sloane's divorce, and I don't think I have another Best Night Ever in me for a while."

"I'm bummed I missed that." Sara sighs. "I've been waiting for Sloane to leave that knoblord since the day she married him."

Sloane is the only one of us who didn't go to high school in Mount Astra—she went to a prestigious day school in Kansas City

---

* Verifiably true. There was once a Tumblr account called Ashes to Asher filled with anonymous submissions recounting unrequited love for the atmospheric scientist. There is also an (unverifiable) rumor that Asher was featured on an underground *Hotties of NOAA* wall calendar one year; finding this calendar is a holy grail for many science horndogs.

instead—but she and Sara have a certain bond as the only women in the group.

"*And* you were her divorce coach too," I say. I can hear Hester Prynne whining as I reach the top of the stairs.

"In fairness, we quickly reached the limits of my expertise. Lucien made leaving as hard as he could on her, whereas divorcing Dr. Bram Loe was more about keeping track of filing deadlines. I think the only thing we fought over were the bonsai scissors."

"They're Sasuke."* I push open the bedroom door to find Porcupine looking out onto the room from the top floor of a Barbie Dreamhouse and Hester Prynne partially wedged under one of the twin beds, quaking.

Porcupine gives a magisterial *ribbit*.

"They're *mine*," Sara says smugly. And then, more seriously, "I meant what I said about taking a break, Bram. I know you never let anything bother you, but it's okay to be a *little* bothered and need a night off once in a while."

It's true that I don't let much get to me—save for one very curvy, very feisty exception.

I have no idea why Maddie makes my jaw clench when twins, a teenager, two animals, and daily emails from the athletic liaison trying to get their athletes excused from my already very easy labs don't faze me.

Is it the lipstick? The emerald eyes? The bratty attitude?

"You'll be back in Mount Astra in six weeks," I say, scooping up

---

* A wedding gift from Leo's parents, who forgot that a $35,000 present might be considered extravagant by anyone who didn't own an international chocolate conglomerate.

Porcupine. Her bright green throat quivers in silent fury. "Then life will get back to normal."

"Yeah, but *normal* for you, Bram, still begs for some fun," Asher says, adding a lifted eyebrow for emphasis. (Asher is one of the few people to keep their brow piercings from the aughts and have it look good on them.) "You know, if the dating pool at Astra is tapped, I'm happy to introduce you to some friends of mine at NOAA. There are a lot more fish in the sea in Kansas City than in Mount Astra. And the commute isn't so bad! I get through a lot of podcasts."

The twins crowd around me to check on Porcupine, who is, as a tree frog, currently trying to climb my hand like a tree.

"I haven't tapped the dating pool," I explain. "I'm just . . . not good at it."

"You barely tried!" protests Sara. "I had a robust postdivorce ho phase. And you went on two dates that didn't even get to second base and called it quits."

"Three dates," I correct without heat. I'd wanted a ho phase too; I'd started dating Sara so young that there hadn't been a chance to explore my nascent bisexuality, and so after the divorce, I'd planned on spreading my bi wings and making up for lost time. But something about dating felt . . . perfunctory, I guess. *Commercial*, even, like I was shopping, and my dates were shopping too, and the actual date was just the part of the shopping trip where you took something off the shelf and glanced at the price tag.

I didn't want to shop. I didn't know what I wanted instead, but I knew that much. So I gave up, and now here I am, with an engaged ex-wife and a childcare provider whom I think about in the shower.

"Okay, say goodbye to Mommy and Asher," I say to the twins as I start walking toward the stairs with a squirming frog in my hand.

"Bye, Mommy! Bye, Asher!" the twins sing, and then fling themselves back onto the floor to give Hester Prynne post-frog therapy.

I hear the sound of the front door swinging open, a sound my body now pornographically responds to.

Maddie is here.

CHAPTER SIX

Bram

"Bye, love you!" Sara calls to the girls as I'm walking down the stairs. I see Maddie standing in front of the door looking like a ripe peach in a yellow sundress with her Focus Group Pink lipstick.

"Sara, I've got to go. Call tomorrow?"

"Wouldn't miss it for the world," she says, giving me a quick wave before hanging up. I finish descending the stairs and carefully place Porcupine back into her tank. She climbs onto a moss-covered rock and then blinks giant black eyes at me as I swing the lid shut, as if to demonstrate her amphibian innocence.

"Good morning, Ms. Kowalczk," I say in my best *nothing to see here over at the frog tank* voice.

Maddie doesn't return the greeting, swinging her golden hair over her shoulder and looking up the stairs. "Are the girls up in their room?"

"For now," I say, frowning a little. Maddie and I are currently in what could charitably be called an armistice—we avoid each other on campus and keep our communication about childcare as brief as possible—but she's never been outright *uncivil* to me. "If you come with me, I'll show you where we keep the swimming stuff in case you take them to the pool. It's the last weekend it's open, so it might be a good idea to go."

"Fine," she sniffs.

Okay, then.

We go out to the garage, where I point out the plastic tote full of pool noodles and goggles and inflatable water wings that the girls don't technically need anymore but still want to bring. Then I lead her to my office so I can give her the key to my crossover—I figure that'll be easier than her trying to wedge pool noodles into her sedan—and fish it out of my satchel right as she says, with some layer of meaning I can't decode, "Was that Sara on the phone?"

"It was." I hold out the key, and she snatches it away, like she can't bear to have contact with me for a second longer than possible. But she doesn't flee the room. She doesn't turn on her heel and stalk off with that comportment-lesson-straight back. She instead lifts her chin and crosses her arms, her green eyes flashing in the late morning sunlight. She's looking at me like I owe her money.[*]

I step back, so that I'm half sitting, half leaning against the edge of my desk, and cross my arms too.

My office is on the ground floor, in the large octagonal turret that sold me on the house the moment I saw it. It was the hardest space to restore—if I never have to strip hardwoods in an eight-sided room again, I'll die a happy man—but now it's my favorite

---

[*] Bram has never owed anyone money.

place in the whole house. Built-in bookshelves line half the walls, while the other half consists of tall windows trimmed in stained glass. My desk, given to me by Leo and Sloane when I was officially awarded my PhD, faces those windows and my big cottonwood tree outside, which my dendrology friends tell me is older than the house itself.

Botanical prints hang wherever there's room, books and papers crowd two of the deep window seats, and the other window seat has a basket of Fern's latest knitting project tucked into the corner. The twins have left a carnage of construction paper scraps and broken crayons near the door to the office closet, which is supposed to be where I keep paper files and old research, but has long since been turned into Letty and Berry's "apartment."

If there's any room in the house that sums up my life, it's this one. The room where my teen curls up in the window and crafts while I work, the room where the twins scoot around on their knees and crawl into my lap and have me watch their YouTube "videos" that they perform live for me. The room where I grade, where I write, where I quietly sketch plants and mycelium and where I think about how *nice* life can be sometimes, how we have beautiful mosses and wafting ferns and clever mushrooms, too many books and funny children and ridiculous friends.

And now, for the first time, Maddie is standing in the middle of it.

I like the way she looks in my room, surrounded by my things, framed by my books and prints, lit by the sunlight coming in from the tall windows. She looks like she belongs here.

That is a very dangerous thought. I push it away.

"Is there anything else, Ms. Kowalczk?"

Her lips press together, roll in, purse into a plush, pink bloom. A thousand words considered, almost spoken, discarded.

I wait patiently, still leaning against my desk, watching her decide whether or not she wants to pick a fight with me. Outside, a hot breeze washes over the front yard, and the cottonwood sings back to it with a rustle and clatter of dry leaves.

"No," Maddie finally says, and turns to leave the office. Then stops and adds, "Look, it's not really any of my business what you get up to when Sara is away. But I don't want anything to do with it again."

"What I get up to when Sara is away." I repeat her words slowly, sure I'm missing something. My mind flips through memories of frozen chicken nuggets and extra screen time requests and a handful of other venial single-parent sins.

"That's right," Maddie says, warming to her cause as she fully turns to me and unloads. "You know, my ex did this same shit to me, and it was only the one time, but that one time was enough to fuck me up for months. I'm still a little fucked up over it and the laundry list of other awful things he did to me, if I'm honest. And I think cheating is the mark of a coward. And a narcissist. And a . . . a dickhead."

My body stills as I begin to piece together what she's implying. "And to be clear, you're saying that I'm a coward and a narcissist and a dickhead?"

She gives me a look of such unfiltered scorn that a lesser man might have withered right on the vine, but I meet her stare with a level one of my own, my eyebrow lifted ever so slightly.

"Obviously, that's what I'm saying," she bites out.

"It sounds like you're building conclusions without gathering any data first," I say, and then straighten up. "Do they forget to teach the *science* part over in Political Science? Or is it all about disingenuous op-eds over there?"

"You're thinking of Journalism," she says, glaring up at me as I step closer to her.

"No, because the journalism students bother to interview their subjects."

She takes a step back as I get close enough for my shadow to brush hers, and then another step back until her heel hits the bookshelf behind her.

"I don't need to interview anyone." Her eyes are pure dragonfire, green and mesmerizing, and an angry flush spreads across her throat and chest and rouges the tops of her cheeks. "It seems to be common knowledge."

"Hmm." I stop mere inches from her. "*Common knowledge.* That's quite an assertion."

She narrows her eyes as she looks up at me. Her chest is heaving. "It's not an assertion. It's a fact."

I'm breathing harder now too. I can smell her, and she smells floral, delicate—jasmine, I think. I have some in the greenhouse. I want to touch my nose to her neck and trace it up to just behind her ear. I want to bury my face in her hair.

I lean forward until my lips are at her cheek, and breathe, "If you have a question, Ms. Kowalczk, then ask it."

She pulls in a shivering breath, and I give in to temptation and brace my forearm against the shelf next to her head. Our bodies are nearly pressed together now, separated by nothing, by mere atoms of nitrogen and oxygen and argon.

"Fine, *Professor*," she says, and I think she means for it to be cutting, but it comes out soft and tattered, like it's a word she's whispered to herself in the dark. "Are you cheating on your wife?"

"I'm not," I murmur. From this angle, I can see the dark roots of her hair growing in, I can see down her bodice to the enchanting gap between her tits. I imagine myself running my fingertips along that gap. I imagine myself taking her waist in my hands and turning her around to face the books, guiding her hands up to grip the edge of a shelf as I kick her feet apart . . .

Maddie pulls back to meet my eyes. "You're not?" she asks suspiciously.

"I don't have a wife. Sara and I divorced five years ago, and she's engaged to a much smarter person than me now. I'm not dating anyone, I'm not hooking up with anyone, I am as single as anyone can be. Now, may I ask why you came into my house like a little storm cloud, so certain that I've made you an accomplice to adultery?"

Her mouth twists adorably to the side—abashed, defensive, pouty. "The campus newspaper had a throwback picture of you and Sara on some trip. I guess I might have . . . jumped to a conclusion or two."

"If your ex cheated on you, then I understand," I say. Anger at this anonymous ex scratches at the soles of my feet and the middles of my palms, itchy, restless, but I keep my breathing even and carefully set the anger aside for another time. Anger is a mint plant—best to keep it in its own pot, far away from everything else. "I'm sorry that happened to you."

"Thanks," whispers Maddie. Her eyes are wider now, her mouth softer, but she's still breathing like she's running for her life.

"I don't cheat. And if you must know, you were my first since the divorce."

"Oh," she says, breathlessly. "Okay."

Fundamentals of Being a Good Girl

"Do you like that?" I murmur, and oh god, what am I murmuring? What am I saying? We have *rules*. But I have to know. I have to. "Were you jealous when you thought I was still married?"

Her eyelids are hooded now, her long, dark lashes nearly brushing her cheeks. "*Yes*," she releases on a low note. "I was jealous."

"You want me all to yourself?"

She swallows and closes her eyes all the way. Nods.

I do what I definitely should not do, and I brush my lips gently over the shell of her ear as I speak. "I'm not scared of your jealousy, Madelyn. I've got nothing to hide. But if you're going to come flaunt your bad manners at me, I'm going to assume that you're looking for attention. And you should know that I'm happy to give it to you."

A barely audible gasp.

"You like that? Does it get you wet to think about me fixing that bratty little attitude of yours?"

We're still not touching, save for the graze of my lips over her ear, but my words have her trembling and trembling. She finds my hand, and keeping her eyes closed, she pushes it up her skirt. We both inhale when my fingertips encounter hot, wet silk.

She's soaked.

"Madelyn," I say as I find the top of her panties and slide my fingers down, down, right into heaven. "You're *such* a bad girl—"

A broken moan.

"But you know what I think? I think you're a good girl, deep, deep down. In fact, I think you want to be my good girl." I don't even know what I'm saying—it's a fog, it's a fire—all I am is this fucking *fever* for her. Burning in my blood. Swelling my cock with need. Hollowing out my belly with hunger.

It doesn't matter, though, because the moment I say those words—*good girl*—it's like everything in Maddie changes. A low, whining whimper quivers through her as her cunt grows hotter and wetter and softer. Her lips part and her eyes open and she has this expression of shock, but *good* shock, and she's nodding then, quick, desperate.

"Yes," she says, and now she's trying to fuck my fingers, her hands grabbing at my forearm. "Yes, please. I'll be your good girl—"

The front door opens and slams shut with a glass-rattling *bang* and the sound of teenage sobbing fills the ground floor.

Maddie and I both freeze, eyes meeting, my fingers still buried in all that soft heat.

I blow out a silent breath, my fatherly concern briefly warring with the very selfish urge not to move. And then my better angels take over, and I carefully free my hand and adjust Maddie's dress so it hangs straight again. (And then adjust myself.)

"Wait," Maddie says quickly as I'm about to leave the office to find Fern. She grabs my hand for the second time today, but this time, she lifts my fingers to her mouth. And licks them clean.

Fuck. Me.

I watch as her tongue curls around each knuckle and pad, and when she whispers a quiet *that's better*, I nearly die.

"Good girl," I tell her, and I relish seeing that delicious shock ripple through her again. Has she never been called a good girl before? Has she never *been* someone's good girl before? Then again, maybe not. Maddie is argumentative and bold and confident, everything you'd expect a law school grad with an interest in political science to be, but not always what the world expects a woman to be. And maybe a person can only go so long being told that they're the wrong kind of girl before they say *fine, fuck it, if I can't be a good girl the way I am, then I'll be a bad girl the way I want to be.* Like Milton's Satan with a thwarted praise kink.[*]

But I don't have time to consider what it means that my brat secretly wants to be a good girl. Reluctantly, and with some bodily pain, I leave Maddie in the office and go upstairs to knock on Fern's (shut and locked) door.

"Fern, honey, is everything okay?" I call.

"Go away!" she cries.

"I'll give you space if you need it, but can you at least tell me if you're safe?"

A loud sniffle. "I am."

"And the other kids at school? Everyone is safe as far as you know?"

"Yes. Now, go away!"

I hate leaving her like this, but it feels ham-fisted and futile to force her to open up when she clearly doesn't want to. I have no idea what's worse—leaving her alone to face something clearly upsetting or unhelpfully crowding her when she needs to process something on her own.

Teens need to know they're supported! But also teens need to learn resilience and independence! Like, why the hell is parenting a teenager so complicated and contradictory? How can this be nature's plan for us??? Get it wrong, and you risk all sorts of horrors: self-harm, addiction, start-up culture. Get it right, and they hate you anyway for chewing too loudly at the dinner table.

---

[*] "Better to reign in hell than serve in heaven" and such.

"I'll be in my office if you need to talk," I offer. Probably pointlessly. "And we can always talk tonight after you've had some time to think. Or we can call your mom. I love you."

No reply, save for more sniffles.

With a sigh, I go back downstairs, and find my office empty of panting adjuncts.

The jasmine smell, however, lingers for the rest of the day.

CHAPTER SEVEN

Maddie

I roll down my window and poke my head out to see what the holdup is. School let out five minutes ago and the pickup line for the twins is at a standstill.

Ahhh, the culprit is indeed a dad who didn't realize he needed to have the laminated paper in the window with the name of his child and now he's stomping his feet about having to pull over so they can get him sorted.

The woman in the minivan next to me catches me looking and rolls her eyes at the petulant father like we are fellow comrades in arms. The rows of her back seat are stuffed with booster seats. "This is why I don't let my husband pick up the kids. I'd be getting death threats from the room mom."

I have to stop myself from blurting out that I'm not actually picking up *my* kids and that Letty and Berry's father has their every move and routine memorized, but she's already rolled her windows up and turned her audiobook up to max volume.

Bram gave me very specific directions on how to pick up the girls on their first day or else I'd probably have looked just as foolish as the dad holding up the line today.

As my wait continues, my mind wanders to this morning, when I'd managed to score one of the private shower rooms at the student center. The steam from the shower clung to the air while I slid my hand between my legs and let myself delight in the thought of Bram in his office. The memory of his eucalyptus and cedar scent. My back pressed against his shelves and his words tickling my ear. My fingers this morning were a pitiful replacement for his, however, and it only left me feeling more frustrated.

I don't know how I'm going to see him again today. But I also don't know what I'll do if I don't.

The line is frozen again, and I twist to see what the holdup is this time. It's wild to me that something as innocuous-sounding as a school pickup can be thirty minutes of idling purgatory, and honestly, I've been thinking for the last two weeks that this horrible fucking line is designed with a cloddish attachment to the *appearance* of efficiency, not actually the spirit of it, and if they'd just—

I don't know how it happens, honestly, because I've spent the last three years—four, if you count the year Gentry and I were hooking up and I was whittling away pieces of myself to keep him coming back—biting my tongue until it bled when stupid shit happened in front of me. (It's not the job of a political spouse to have any opinion whatsoever on stupid shit. We are supposed to be stupid shit agnostic.)

But I'm not engaged anymore and biting my tongue has gotten me nowhere but a rest stop parking lot and also, just—this could be better, there's no reason for it not to be better!

Fundamentals of Being a Good Girl

And that is how I find myself with the car pulled to the side and parked. That is how I find myself walking toward the woman in charge of car purgatory.

"Hey!" I say, my face already transformed into the smile that won me second runner-up in Olathe, Kansas's annual Sweet Six contest, my voice both *hey girl* and also a little conspiratorial. "Oh my god, is that a *Wicked* lanyard? I love *Wicked*, I've actually loved Jonathan Bailey since *Chewing Gum*, and have you ever thought about splitting the pickup traffic into two lines? I know it seems like it wouldn't help, but I think if you had an extra staff member just there to radio the numbers back to the person at the door . . ."

Fifteen sun-soaked minutes waving cars around later, and the now-split line is rolling forward like a precision-engineered watch. Berry and Letty race toward my car and then both pile into the back seat. They sling their backpacks onto the floorboard and the moment their seat belts click, they are a tornado of conversation.

"Silas Reynolds ate a dead worm today," Letty says.

"Only because you dared him to," Berry adds.

I glance up to the rearview mirror. "Berry, how was music class today? Any easier?"

She nods once and then twice, her chin dipping into her chest.

"Mrs. Barrett said Berry didn't have to play the triangle if she didn't want to," Letty tells me.

"She let me play the flute!" Berry says.

Berry hadn't liked playing the triangle because the group she was assigned to included a girl who had made fun of her last year after the girls cut their own bangs, so I'd mentioned it to Bram and he'd spoken with the teacher.

I turn out of the parking lot and into the school zone. "Windows down?" I ask.

"Yes, please!" they both chime.

I turn up the volume and we sing along to a radio-edited Sabrina Carpenter song as we head in the direction of home.

We turn down one of my favorite roads in Mount Astra, a double-wide street with a canopy of oak and linden leaves and extra-long yards with well-kept Queen Annes and Tudors and a Craftsman or two.

Berry points out the window. "Fern!"

And sure enough, just ahead of us on the sidewalk is Fern with her overstuffed backpack riddled with pins and permanent marker doodles.

"Fern!" the twins yell as I roll to a stop beside her.

She stops and turns. For a brief second, a wary cloud hovers above her, brows pinched together and eyes narrowed, but then her expression eases into something familiar when she realizes it's us. The same even, careful demeanor Bram carries is so present in Fern.

"Hey, Fern," I say in my friendliest but most noncommittal voice so as not to scare off the teen.[*] "Where's your car?"

She rolls her eyes and crosses her arms over her chest, assuming a position I am intimately familiar with. "Dad is waiting on a part to come in for my car and he said I can just walk home. But it's eight blocks. And not eight small blocks! Plus, I wore my new Doc Martens that I got when he took me back-to-school shopping because it was the student-government interest meeting today and I was going to see— Ugh, never mind."

---

[*] It's been observed that teenagers can smell the approaching lack of autonomy from up to three hundred meters away.

"Oh no," I say, horrified. "Breaking in Doc Martens is a gradual process. Not an *eight blocks in one day* kind of situation."

She rolls her eyes again. "Try explaining that to my dad."

I reach across the passenger seat and open the door. "Well, you're in luck. Get in! Your feet shall live to see another day. And I can show you a trick to break those in that involves putting them in the freezer."

"Seriously?" she asks as she slides into the front seat and buckles her seat belt.

I nod. "My brother's wife's best friend—wow, that was unnecessarily complicated—swears by this method."

"You're so much cooler than my dad," Fern says.

"Oh, I totally am," I tell her, and wish Bram could hear me say so. What kind of reaction might that get from him?

(Nope. No thoughts about Bram being super sexy when I'm in a car full of his offspring.)

For a minute, I think about bringing up Nolan and his wife, Bee, just to cement my coolness with the teenage demographic of one in my passenger seat. *My brother was in a super-famous boy band and now he's making movies on the Hope Channel!* There's a certain kind of thrill to it, because for so long no one around me cared about something as unintellectual and tacky as a boy band—Nolan's fame was actually kind of a liability, and my sister-in-law's career in sex work was a *super* liability—and so I haven't gotten to play the famous-sibling card in years.

On the other hand, there's no putting the former-heartthrob toothpaste back in the tube, so maybe it's better to stay quiet about it for now . . .

Fern pulls one knee up on her seat and begins furiously texting until we get to the house. The moment I turn off the ignition, she darts out of the car and up the stairs, letting herself in with her own key.

Meanwhile, the twins meander and rummage around the floorboard for things that had spilled out of their backpacks before they slowly make their way inside. While they run to the living room to check on Porcupine, I dig their folders out of their backpacks to leave out on the kitchen table for Bram. Then it's time for after-school snacks. I pile up some cheese and crackers, and after that, I get to work on my mom's chocolate chip banana muffin batter.

I am nowhere near as skilled at baking as my mom. But I remember finding such solace inside the little kitchen of our bungalow in our run-down neighborhood. Because if Mom was in the kitchen, she was having a good day.

It was just me and her pretty often, which meant a fair amount fell on my plate when her bipolar disorder was in a tough spot. But honestly, the real hardship was helping her navigate Medicaid and seeing the confused frown from the pharmacy tech when a new medication wasn't covered, or when an old medication suddenly wasn't covered, or when a rebate program had been discontinued and everyone forgot to tell us.

Nolan, my brother, took care of us as much as he could, but life changed in a big way when he joined INK.[*] And then again, when the band fell apart. Nolan is fine now—fantastic, even. When he's

---

[*] Yes, INK. As in the highly idolized early aughts boy band that met its tragic end at the hands of a greedy manager. For further reading, see *The Rise and Fall of INK* by Dominic Diamond and *Redemption Tour: How the Former Bad Boy of INK Rehabilitated His Career and Found Love Through the Miracle of Christmas Movies* by Nisha Sharma.

not wearing a top hat for the Hope Channel, he's got a great gig judging *Band Camp*, the reboot of the show where INK came together. He has Mom out with him in LA, and she loves the little cottage he has her set up in. She's constantly taking pictures of her herb garden and sending them to me. She even has one of those bird feeders with a camera that identifies the birds for you. She's happy. She's set. She wants for nothing.

But by the time my brother really got back on his feet, I was about to graduate high school. I didn't feel like I fell under the umbrella that his newfound financial stability afforded him. I wasn't a kid anymore. He did help me cover some expenses that my scholarships to Pepperdine didn't, and I don't think I'll ever stop feeling guilty about that.

When I graduated college and took the LSAT at Gentry's urging, I got into every law school I applied to but didn't receive a single scholarship. The tuition fees were astronomical. So I took out loans, because Gentry had made it very clear that his future wife needed a JD. It was the formula for creating a political power couple. I told myself that it wasn't just for Gentry. I really had been interested in going to law school. But left to my own devices, I probably would have chosen one with a cheaper price tag than USC.

Then Gentry told me he was positive his parents would foot the bill for my law degree after we were married. It was all part of the five-year plan. Graduate law school the same month Gentry wins his first primary. He wins against his opponent in November. He proposes at his victory party and we head to the state assembly as soon-to-be newlyweds. Goodbye, loans. Hello, perfect life.

And then three days before my first day of second year, I came home early from staying with my mom. Gentry was already at work, but there was a bra on the floor of the bathroom. One with a too small band and cups way too large to ever fit me.

He swore it was just the one time. That he was drunk. That he only did it because he missed me. He promised it would never happen again and I let myself believe him. Through the rest of law school. Until the minute Penelope Pike broke up with me on his behalf.

Sure, he might have been telling the truth about it only being the one time, but what did it matter in the end? Which was why I showed up here yesterday with an attitude the size of the Ninth Circuit Court of Appeals.

While the muffins are in the oven, I go over sight words with Letty and Berry, and I quickly discover that Berry is unexpectedly competitive. (The quiet ones always surprise you.)

In fact, I'm sure my sweet librarian friend, Junie, has some secrets of her own if I could just get a few drinks in her. Too bad I hadn't met *her* at the bar my first night in town instead of Bram. I've only hooked up with one other woman, but I do like them quiet and mousy. So if she weren't my sort-of friend, she'd be just my type. And that would have been way less complicated than whatever the fuck is happening with me and Bram.

No, whatever is *not* happening. Because yesterday was a onetime slipup. Really, it was just half a slipup. It's not like either of us came. In the moment, at least.

The scent of fresh-baked muffins lures Fern from her room, and the storm cloud hanging over her when I found her on the sidewalk has returned.

While the little ones take their snack plates and settle down for some predinner screen time, I pat the barstool at the island and pull up the plate of muffins.

With a truly impressive sigh, Fern joins me. There's nothing more cathartic than the heavy sigh of a teenage girl.

"Okay," I tell her. "Here's how this is gonna go. I feed you muffins. You feed me gossip. I am very hungry."

She rubs her hands over her eyes to reveal a pained expression.

And then I realize that—oh shit—I am the adult here, so I start my line of responsible-adult questioning. "Okay, wait. Are you in danger?"

She shakes her head.

"Does this involve anything illegal?"

She smirks. "You have no idea how boring I am."

"Boring can be good," I tell her. "And since there's nothing putting you in a compromising position that would require me to narc on you to your father, consider this discussion covered by attorney-client privilege."

"It's my ex," she blurts.

"I am genuinely triggered by those three words, but please continue."

A smile twitches on her lips before she takes a huge bite of muffin and talks through a mouthful, which is really the elite way to unload about an ex.

"We dated through eighth, ninth, and tenth grade," she says.

"Wow, that's like—"

"A long time, I know. Last year, at my family birthday dinner, my dad's friend Sloane, who is basically my aunt, told my ex—to his face!—that he was robbing me of my youth."

"Boss bitch move," I tell her. "I want an Auntie Sloane. Okay, so what's this little shitstain's name?"

"Simon. So he's been class president every year since seventh grade. And I've always run as secretary . . . which is—"

"A grunt work job."

"Exactly. But I like it. I like to keep track of the minutes and make sure we stay on task. I'm sort of anxious about details, so it's worked for me. Especially since Simon was more . . . the personality, ya know?"

I nod slowly. "He was charismatic, so I'm guessing you were constantly cleaning up his messes."

"Yes! And figuring out how to deliver on these impossible promises he would make."

"Did you see him at your student-government interest meeting today?"

"I did. Samira, who was elected last May to be the student body president this year, transferred to a boarding school in upstate New York unexpectedly. So now there's going to be a special election to fill her role and Simon decided that he wants to step down as eleventh-grade class president to run for student body president. And he's totally going to win and it makes me want to scoop my eyeballs out of my skull."

I tear a muffin in half and eat a small piece, like I'd learned to in the etiquette class I took last summer. (At Gentry's mother's suggestion.) "Well, we can't have any kind of eyeball scooping."

"He's already soft launching his campaign and taking credit for all kinds of stuff that I did over the last two years. Gender-neutral bathroom initiative in eighth grade? That was me. Organizing other students to go speak at school council meetings about lunch debt? Fighting against book bans? All me! He doesn't even care about half of that shit!" Her eyes cut to me. "Sorry."

I hike a thumb over my shoulder. "As long as you don't have the twins running around screaming *shit* over and over again, I don't care."

She laughs. "Trust me, they hear plenty of cursing from my uncle Leo* and uncle Joey."†

"Oh, I met Leo," I tell her as I recall the unnecessarily handsome and pompous piece of work who had followed Bram into my classroom. I resist the urge to say her uncle Leo strikes me as a fuckboy. Fuckman? Whatever. "Back to Simon. You have to run against him. It's the only way he'll learn."

Her jaw drops and then after a moment of shock, she's shaking her head. "No. No way. Maddie, I get that you've only known me for a couple weeks, but that's legitimately the last thing that I would *ever* do. Or would ever *want* to do!"

"But don't you get it, Fern? That's exactly why you *should* run. No one will see it coming."

"But what happens if I actually win? Unlikely, I know, but then I'd be stuck with a job I don't even want."

"It might not be the job you want, but it's one you're already doing from what I can tell, so why not at least take the official credit so you can add it to your college applications. And you know what, Fern? Simon sounds like a politician, and just because you're a good politician doesn't mean you're cut out for leadership. Sometimes the people who are the least interested in being in charge make the best leaders."

She thinks for a minute and bites down on her lower lip. "It *would* really, really piss him off."

"Just ignore me if this is too personal, but why did you two end it?"

Fern's shoulders sink. "He dumped me just after spring break

---

* Uncultured swine.
† A saint among men.

last year. He called it a break and said he needed to focus on himself."

"I hate when people give you those little sound-bite excuses. What does that even mean?" I don't know that it's wise to trauma-dump on Fern, but I wish I could explain to her just how much I truly do understand what she's going through. It is also possibly true that I want her to enact the kind of revenge on Simon that I wish I'd been savvy enough to do myself with Gentry.

"Right? Well, apparently, focusing on himself meant hooking up with the class VP and then boning his way through the statewide student government summit back in July."

"What a bastard," I whisper so the twins can't hear me.

Fern leans in and I can practically see the gossip endorphins hitting her system. "Our whole relationship was all about him to begin with. He was already completely focused on himself, because I can tell you that he certainly wasn't focused on me."

"Okay, listen. If I were a different person, I would tell you that you should keep your head down and dedicate yourself to things that will bring you joy. They go low, we go high, et cetera, et cetera. But sometimes when people are rats, you have to play dirty, and what better revenge than to take the thing this jackass wants most?" It is without a doubt the thing I would have done pre-Gentry, and a small part of me wants this just as much for me as I do for her. Maybe her victory over this shit bag will chip away at the last four years of my wasted youth.

She chews nervously on the skin around her thumb. I resist the urge to pull her hand away from her mouth, because that is exactly what Penelope would do. Actually, she would bat my hand away like I'd been a bad dog, but still.

Fern shakes her head and I think I've lost her, but then she shuts her eyes and sucks in a deep breath. "Okay. Okay, I'll do it."

I squeeze both her hands and squeal with excitement. "I'm going to plan the shit out of this campaign with you," I promise her. "Not only will Simon be sorry he ever let you go, but he will never forget the day he crossed Fern Loe for the last time."

She shivers. "Wow. You make me sound way sexier than I am."

I cringe a little. "Let's go for badass over sexy."

"Both things I've never been," she confirms.

The door to the tiny mudroom off the kitchen whines as Bram walks in. He makes every door he walks through look like it's the size of a doggy door.

It's the first time we've seen each other since yesterday and his nostrils flare for a moment, his gaze trailing from my neck down to the V of my blouse.

"Daddy!" Letty cries as she flings herself against his legs and Berry quickly follows.

"Hey, I left a little early today," he says, returning to the doting father I know him to be.

Fern pops up from her stool with a look of fierce determination. "I need a ride to the craft store," she announces. "I need posters for my campaign. I'm running for student body president."

"Okay," Bram says, and then looks down at the twins. "All crafty hands on deck. We've got a campaign to win. But no loose glitter, okay?"

"Sure! Whatever." Fern is already sprinting up the stairs, listing off everything she needs.

Bram glances back up at me, a pleased curiosity dancing at his lips. "You have something to do with this?"

I quirk my brow and lean back against the kitchen island. "You could say I'm a political visionary. And her ex-boyfriend sounds like a total shi—"

The twins preemptively giggle at me.

"A shih tzu," I finish. "A very high-maintenance dog."

"A real dog," Bram agrees. *Thank you*, he mouths, and then, *good girl.*

My cheeks instantly warm and I give him a short nod. I like being his good girl. I like it far too much.

CHAPTER EIGHT

Bram

The day after Fern decides to run for student body president, I find Leo Saint James in my office *yet again*. Last night, Maddie stayed well past her normal hours to help Fern come up with a plan of action for her campaign. Anytime I checked in on them, Fern waved me away and assured me they were *fine*.

Today, Leo is sitting in my chair, his expensive shoes propped on my desk and a glass of something amber cradled in one hand. His eyes are half lidded, predatory, even though he's staring at nothing more interesting than the soil monoliths another professor loaned me for my 600-level plant ecology class. He doesn't acknowledge my entrance other than taking a moody drink of whisky.

"Where did you even find that?" I ask. I don't keep any liquor in here, and the nearest bar is inside the Astra Hotel, at the edge of campus. And I know Leo didn't carry a glass of single malt all the way up the hill just to drink it in my office.

"A gentleman never tells his secrets," Leo says. He doesn't move from my chair or cease brooding at the soil monoliths. "And what does it matter? The world is full of thieves, and anything worth having must be stolen from the stealers."

"Happy Tuesday to you too," I reply, and set my satchel on the love seat. And then I pause, look over at Leo's Italian shoes, his dark expression. He looks like an AI-generated image of unprincipled wealth right now.

A thought occurs to me.

"Leo," I say carefully. "Do you know someone who can . . . find . . . things?"

Leo's eyes swing over to me. Interest flickers across his face, driving away whatever bad mood is plaguing him, and he sets his glass on the desk. "Ahem. Mr. *FernGully*. Aren't *you* someone who can find things?"

"Used to be." I sit on the arm of the love seat and regard him with a steady gaze.

A short, amused exhale once he realizes I'm not conceding anything more. Not that I have to—Leo already knows all my sins. "I'm not sure the statute of limitations cares too much about what verb tense you use, Bram, but fine. Yes, I know someone who can find things. What or *whomst* are we finding out about?"

I hesitate only a moment, although Leo still notices because of course he does. He's already smiling by the time I admit it.

"Madelyn Kowalczk's ex-boyfriend."

He kicks his feet in the air like a pinup girl before swinging them down to the floor and spinning my chair to face me fully, silver eyes sparkling like tinsel on a Christmas tree. "I knew it, old sport, *I knew it*! I knew it had something to do with the nanny!"

"Childcare provider," I correct.

"Say no more, I'll take care of everything," Leo says with a cheerful wave of his hand. "This contemptible worm will have no secrets from us by the time my friend is through."

"You have a friend?" comes a voice from the doorway to my office. Sloane Saint James, in wide-legged trousers and a gray vest with no shirt underneath, and with a vintage leather briefcase that looks like it was originally owned by someone who wore a lot of shoulder pads. She looks fabulous, but then again, Sloane always looks fabulous. (Even in messy buns and ripped Copperhead sweatshirts—even while chasing a tiny Fern back in the days when Sara and I used to beg, borrow, and steal any free babysitting we could get—Sloane has always exuded the kind of glamour you think is possible only in magazines.)

"Fuck you, Sloane," Leo responds fondly. "I've got lots of friends."

"Friends you don't pay a salary to? Or have sex with?" asks Sloane skeptically.

"My darling cousin, Bram is right here, and he's very shy about all the salaried sex we have. And may I just remark that you are looking very tastefully divorced this afternoon?"

Sloane comes around the love seat and sits on the other arm, setting her briefcase on the floor and then looking at Leo's whisky with undisguised envy. "I had a meeting off campus. I wanted to project a certain image."

"I'm sure the students were projecting several things by the end of the day, at least," Leo purrs, but he takes pity on Sloane and gets up to pass her the whisky, which she takes gratefully.

"How did your meeting go?" I ask when she lowers the glass and wipes her mouth.

"Dreadfully," she answers, and then takes another drink.

"Was the meeting at The Dry Bean?" Leo asks. "You should have had me come. I'm sufficiently terrifying when given the chance."

The Dry Bean? Sloane is a sexual health educator at Astra University, and while it's not unheard-of for her to do workshops or initiatives around Mount Astra at large, that usually means manning a tent during Pride or helping with the women's health van in a grocery store parking lot. Not a meeting at a run-down bar with a creative approach to health code compliance. I shift so I can look at Sloane. "You had a meeting at our bar? *Why?*"

Something strange happens. Instead of Sloane answering my very normal question, she and Leo glance at each other, and then look away.[*] She coughs. Leo gets to his feet.

"Don't worry about it," he says.

"Wait, so you know what this meeting was?"

"I may have heard some things," replies Leo evasively. "But we're getting off topic. The real topic is you and the nanny."

"Childcare provider."

"Having congress and not in a political science way," Leo goes on.

"*Leo.*"

"Congress with the nanny?" Sloane turns to me with wide silver eyes. "Bram!"

"No—the—" I blow out a breath and drag my hands over my face. "Look, the congress predates the childcare, okay? There is currently zero congress." Aside from Sunday, when I'd pinned her against my bookshelf and fondled the soft, wet cunt under her dress.

---

[*] The Saint James family telepathy is famous and is said to be the reason why Saint James Chocolate Co. is the billion-dollar candy monster it is now. It's also annoying as fuck.

But that hardly counts, right? It was a . . . a slip. A momentary lapse in control brought about by her bad manners and ridiculous accusations and the adorable jut of her jaw when she admitted she was jealous.

That she wanted me all to herself, even when I wasn't hers to have.

And Christ, did I know the feeling.

I come back to the moment to realize Leo and Sloane are arguing about my romantic history.

"I'm just saying, and with respect to you, Bram, that I don't think you ever dealt with the emotional fallout of having Fern," Sloane is saying, "and your grandparents cutting you off and how traumatic those early years were. You were learning how to be an adult and a husband and a father all at the same time, and then when the dust finally settled around money and your career, you had surprise twins. I just don't think you ever had a chance to learn what *you* want outside of scraping together the best life possible for the girls."

"My grandparents didn't cut me off," I explain patiently.* "They just said that if I was man enough to have a baby, then I was man enough to pay for it. So I paid for it." *It* being a shitty apartment and a car seat and a Pack 'n Play and cloth diapers and bags for breast milk and onesies and a little glowing seahorse that played lullabies and ocean noises. Sara scooped ice cream for people we'd gone to school with, for students our age completely unburdened by responsibility, for little kids like we were about to have, and I'd spent the summer working on a highway road crew until our first semester started at Astra, and

---

* They totally did.

then I transitioned to tutoring and after-hours janitorial work at the student bookstore. We'd finally snagged married student housing, used a combination of the campus's subsidized childcare and the goodwill of our friends to get through our studies, and somehow, eventually, clawed enough money together to make a down payment on a derelict house.

"And we were all okay," I add. "We made it through."

Leo snorts. "Yeah, I bet you were okay after your grandfather died and your grandmother decided to give you tons of regret money."

"People change," I say evenly.

My parents died in a car crash when I was a baby, so my grandparents were all I'd ever had growing up. They'd never said as much, but I knew they'd been extremely content turning their small plant nursery into a highly lucrative, multistate enterprise, and the presence of an unexpected infant in their lives seemed to have upset them as much as losing their daughter. I never doubted that they loved me, but their love had always been reserved. Conditional. Uninterested in the neediness of a child who was scared of the dark and bullied at school. They wanted me to be worth the work, I think, and when I had to confess Sara's pregnancy to them in the last year of high school, they realized I'd been a bad investment. No sense throwing good money after bad, after all.

But after Grandad died, Grandma had changed. She was older and lonelier and who wouldn't want to know a kid like Fern? Fern, who'd been the sweetest baby, who'd been raised underneath library tables and playing with lab goggles at our feet, chasing butterflies through fields while I collected samples, coloring on the floor of the student bookstore while I vacuumed. Fern, who learned to crochet before she learned to ride a bike, whose prized possession was an ancient Brother sewing machine that we found behind an old microwave at a thrift store.

So for the last few years of her life, Grandma had gotten to know Fern. She'd finally acted civil to Sara. She'd gotten to hold the twins when they were still tiny little burritos with red faces and lanugo on their delicate shoulders. She'd tried to apologize with money, and more money again, and when I'd explained that it wasn't necessary, that all was forgiven, she'd cried into my shoulder until my shirt was soaked.

My grandma *had* changed, she had tried to make amends and be better going forward. I can even believe that she'd tried her best when I was younger too. Her best still hadn't been good enough, but that's okay. I don't want to carry that kind of resentment—I just want to focus on making sure my kids never feel like my love is qualified by an invisible profit-and-loss sheet that only I can see.

Anyway, after my grandmother died, I sold the family nursery to the longtime manager, put the substantial inheritance into a trust for the girls, and laid the past to rest. It's done. We're all okay. We're all working to be good to each other in the creaky, cluttered house bought with spare change and sweat.

"I just think that you may have associated love with privation, that's all," Sloane finishes.

Leo waves her off. "That's not Bram's damage. The problem is that *he's too good*. No one ever taught him how to be selfish."

"Or," I say, "seeing as I'm the expert here, perhaps *you're both wrong*, and I'm simply focusing on my kids and my career. I don't have the time or energy for anything else."

I'm given identical silver-eyed stares of doubt.

"Really," I protest. "I'm not interested in"—I nod in Leo's direction—"whatever it is that you do with your love life."

"*Love* life?" Leo sounds offended.

"I'm perfectly happy with the way things are," I maintain. "And if there's anything I was missing, I wouldn't find it doing some kind of facile, drive-through intimacy."

"You're right," Leo says, earnestly. "I'd say you could only find it while actually driving. Or while parking. Or while having your parking spot stolen, perhaps?"

"Hmm. Why do you think she caught your interest when no one else has?" This Socratic musing is from Sloane.

"I have ideas," Leo volunteers, and starts counting on his fingers. "Spankings. Sweater sets. Parking revenge. Sounds made while spanking—"

"Ew," Fern says from the door. "Do I want to know?"

As one, we adults whip around to face the teen, terror in all of our faces.

"How much of that did you hear, sweetheart?" Sloane asks right as Leo splutters, "I was talking about an old woman who lives in a shoe!"

I push myself off the love seat and go to the door. It's warm out, the last of the truly hot days as September starts contemplating autumn, and Fern's cheeks are bright red. The fine dark hair framing her face is damp and clinging to her temples. "Did you walk all the way here from school?" The hike up the hill is no joke, even from the faculty parking lot.

"Maddie dropped me off near the student union before she took the littles to the park," says Fern. "She said that if I played my cards right, I could talk you into letting me use the laminator for some of my smaller flyers."

I smile at Fern. "Maddie was right. We'll laminate the heck out of your flyers."

"Flyers for what?" asks Sloane.

"I'm running for student body president." Fern looks terrified and proud . . . the same expression *I* wore when I cradled her little swaddled body for the first time.

"Baby's first campaign!" Leo says with delight. "How deep are your opponent's pockets, Fern? Actually, don't answer that, it doesn't matter, your uncle Leo's are deeper. Do you want a billboard? Let's get you a billboard."

Fern looks aghast. "Uncle Leo! We can't spend more than fifty dollars on our campaign!"

"And?" asks Leo.

"I mean, people might guess that I'm spending more than that if there's a billboard with my face on it."

Leo considers this. "And if I bought the billboard company?"

"I think they'll still measure the advertisement in value, even if it's technically free."

"Well, is there an auditing committee? Some kind of snitch line? Tell me what I'm up against, and I'll tell you how we get around it."

Fern looks to me for help, and I just shrug. "We should follow the rules, honey, but I can't lie, I'd love to watch you beat Simon."

Her shoulders slump at the mention of Simon—but it has the opposite effect on the Saint James cousins. They explode in noise and gestures—they both hated that kid—and Leo is already promising to buy off Midwest teen influencers to ruin Simon's life, while Sloane is planning out a series of elaborate shopping excursions to give Fern the perfect weaponized campaign wardrobe.

This continues as they follow us upstairs to where the laminator is, and then on our way home, Fern picks up the chatter where the cousins left off, talking about debate prep and what she should wear and if she should force Simon to engage on the policy items he stole or come up with even better ones on her own.

When we get home, Maddie has already served the twins tomato soup and grilled cheese for dinner and is reading them a Curious George book. After Fern wolfs down her own grilled cheese and pounds up the stairs to work on her plans for a debt-free lunchroom, I lean against the opening leading from the kitchen to the living room and watch Maddie listen seriously to Letty's suspicious questions about why the Man in the Yellow Hat doesn't take better care of Curious George, and then give equally serious answers. Berry is trying to burrow under Maddie's arm, and then against her thigh, and then behind her, between Maddie's back and the couch, and Maddie handles it with a matter-of-fact affection.

I . . . don't know how it makes me feel. Or rather, I *do* know how watching it makes me feel, but I don't know how I feel about the feeling. How I feel about the tight, possessive heat in my chest, about wanting to watch her with the twins instead of doing anything else—about how good she looks in my house.

It's primitive, the way I feel. I'm not a primitive person.

But later that night, as I'm braced against the shower wall with my forearm, my free hand working rhythmically below my navel, I am something worse than primitive, I've become something *dishonorable*. She makes me fucking filthy, into a man I barely recognize, someone so obsessed with her green eyes and her soft mouth and her tight pussy that he has to beat off in the shower just to hope for a chance at sleep later.

Why do you think she caught your interest when no one else has? Sloane asked today, and I don't know, I still don't have an answer, and even as I release thickly against the wall, I'm at a loss.

I press my forehead against the tile, water sluicing from above and dripping off my nose and lips, and tell myself to stop. Just fucking stop. She's too young. She's too on my payroll. She's too good at making me think and feel things that I don't need to think and feel.

And most important, she's just starting out here in Mount Astra. She's got a bright career ahead of her, and the last thing she needs right now is some sweater vest–wearing professor trying to swoop in and appoint himself her bossy, greedy, spanking-curious daddy.

CHAPTER NINE

Maddie

It was a Walmart parking lot night, which meant I woke up feeling busted. And looking like it too. When I pulled up to the rest stop I'd called home for the last few weeks, the exit was closed and full of workers re-striping the parking lot, so I had to return to my old Walmart stomping grounds.

It was the first truly chilly autumn night and I wake up freezing, thinking longingly of how cozy and warm Bram's house had been last night while I'd helped Fern prep for her debate, of how comfortable his couch was while a fire flickered in the grate and Fern and I scribbled on index cards.

And now I'm stiff and sore and shivering so hard that my jaw is clamped shut. I guess I've lost my winter fur after living in Southern California for seven years. A rough night doesn't need to make for a rough day, though.

Until it definitely does.

I stand dumbfounded in front of the sign at the student health resource center that says the locker rooms are closed until further notice while a plumbing issue is fixed. The student working the front desk informs me that he heard it was from the decades' worth of flushed tampons.*

"Way to victim blame," I tell him before stomping over to the student union, where I use the bathroom to freshen up as best as I can and get dressed.

It won't always be like this, I tell myself. *It won't always be like this.*

In fact, not only will it not always be like this, but these last few weeks are just a sliver of hardship compared to the reality plenty of people live with every day. I know that. I really do. One of the benefits to being Gentry's philanthropic arm was understanding what our constituents were up against. It made me want Gentry to do right by them, and it even made me wish a little bit that I could be the one to represent them, because even then, I didn't know that I could trust him to do the kind of job that people actually need.

And yet, I am a weak, weak woman, and the only thing that could possibly fix me right now is a pillow-top mattress and a hot shower. And coffee.

I can get a coffee! Coffee is a totally feasible thing that I can do. To the library!

As I walk across campus, I try to remind myself that I normally love this weather and that if I weren't currently camping in my car, I would be so thrilled for my first seasonally appropriate late September in years. Sweaters! I love sweaters! And Halloween. And pumpkins. And leaves. How could I forget leaves?

---

* False. The plumbing in the student health center is bad because that place is fucking haunted.

I might not be completely fresh, but I am wearing my favorite ivory wide-leg trousers and black-and-ivory-striped sweater paired with the camel coat my brother bought me for Christmas four years ago when I announced that I needed an Adult Coat that didn't make swooshing noises every time I moved.

Inside the library, Junie is in her element, assisting a student. She gesticulates wildly and her voice grows louder with every sentence. The student, a young girl in a Copperheads Volleyball hoodie, looks like she's getting far more from Junie than she ever asked for.

After filling up my reusable coffee cup, I top it off with a seasonally appropriate creamer, and the smell of pumpkin cheesecake is a balm to my weary soul.

The day is already better. Am I being optimistic? Is this personal growth?

Junie waves to me, and I motion over to her desk, where I plan on enjoying my coffee while I wait for her to be done so I can listen to her morning chatter. It's weirdly calming.

As I'm tightening the lid on my coffee, my red pointy-toed flat snags on a ripple in the ancient carpet that no one has fucking replaced ever because apparently no one cares about libraries. Or my favorite wide-leg ivory trousers.

I trip over my own feet, lose my grip on the coffee, and only narrowly miss falling face-first into the musty carpet, but my pants and sweater have not been so lucky and look like a Jackson Pollock–inspired failure.

"Fuck," I quietly grind out, and every head in the library whips around to witness my humiliation.

Suddenly, I'm not an adjunct lecturer with the godlike power to pass or fail my 184 students. I'm a clumsy girl who now has to walk around with coffee-stained clothes all day, because there is no possible way I can make it back over to my car and then all the way to Salih Hall in time for my morning class.

I love Junie, I really do, but she rushes over and immediately begins to pat me down with napkins and paper towels, making a fuss and only drawing more attention to me, like when you're young and your mom thinks she's helping but she's only deepening the mortification of whatever's just happened. My cheeks warm with embarrassment and my defenses are immediately up.

Without much thought, I push Junie's hands away and spit out "I'm fine" between my gritted teeth.

"Sorry, sorry, sorry," she says, apologizing over and over again, which only annoys me more. "Are you okay? You didn't burn yourself, did you?"

I need to walk outside before I lose my shit on this perfectly nice librarian (and my only friend in town, for that matter) for just trying to be helpful. "I'm good," I tell her. "I'm good, but I need to head over to my office early."

She steps back, the rumpled napkins clutched to her chest. "Oh. Okay."

I give her what I hope is a reassuring smile. I don't dare say another word. I've already acted like the world's biggest cunt. And while I definitely need to fix this, now is not the time.

My class today is later in the morning and only meets twice a week, so not only is the class bigger and rowdier, it's also an hour and a half instead of forty-five minutes, like my early morning three-day-a-week class.

When I stop at the adjunct office to check my mailbox, I find the door closed. Since it's a communal office, I don't even consider knocking. But I obviously should have because right there on my desk—well, the communal desk—are two adjuncts who I've only seen in passing with their tongues down each other's throats.

"What the fuck?" the man with a thick red beard says as he stumbles back, hands covering his crotch for very obvious reasons. "Have you heard of knocking?"

"Chill out, Martin," the other man with short twists in his hair says as he glances over his shoulder. "You must be the baby adjunct! I'm Anton. This is Martin. Sorry about this." He motions to the pile of papers they'd swiped out of the way. "The only other adjunct in the department has never actually used the office before."

"We honestly don't even know if she exists," Martin says in a softer tone once he realizes I'm not a foe even if I did ruin his boner.

"I'm Maddie," I tell them. "I was just coming to check my mailbox, but I can do that later. I don't want to ruin a good thing."

Anton laughs and then motions to my outfit with his chin. "Tough morning?"

I glance down to find that the stains are drying, which I think might be making them worse. "You've no idea."

"You could always cancel your class," Martin offers. "You get at least one bad-vibes-free pass[*] every semester. And no offense, but you're really giving bad vibes right now."

"None taken." I squeeze past the desk to my mailbox. "And I'd hate to use my free pass so early in the semester, so I think I'll just power through."

---

[*] An unofficial official rule that cannot be found in the faculty handbook but can be found in the hearts and souls of every professor at Astra University.

Fundamentals of Being a Good Girl

"Well, it was good to finally meet you," Anton says. "And, um, sorry you had to see—"

I hold a hand up. "Don't sweat it. I'll let you two get back to business, but maybe drape a sock on the doorknob next time."

Martin snorts as I close the door.

"She's funny," Anton says.

It's a coping mechanism, I nearly call back to him.

As I spin away from the door, I run directly into Dr. Salaza—I mean, Miranda.

"Maddie!" she says. "Are you okay?"

I motion down to my destroyed outfit. "Nothing a trip to the dry cleaner can't fix." And thank god it's free.

Her smile is tinged with slight pity. "I just wanted to say I really enjoyed your class I sat in the other day."

I force myself to stand up straight, because all I want to do is shrink back at the mention. The class was *fine*. Except that the tech in the room wasn't working and I had to lecture without the assistance of my slides, which are really pretty and a little bit funny. They give me something to hide behind when I'm feeling a little unsure of myself or like I have no business acting as an authority figure to a class full of people who are close enough in age to be my peers.

"Did you get a chance to send in that IT request for the lecture hall?"

"Yes," I tell her. "They say I should be all set now."

She nods to herself. "Good, good. Maddie, it's not my place at all, but I just wanted to check in and see how you're doing beyond teaching. We haven't really talked much about your personal life prior to Astra, but . . . I know what—or rather who—you left behind in California."

"Ah, I see."

"I wasn't looking to dig up your past or anything, but I remember you saying you'd worked on campaigns and did some charity work in your interview, so I was curious and . . . well."

I nod, a sigh blowing my hair back from my face. "I wasn't really the image that the Wade family was going for."

She rolls her eyes. "Would it make you feel any better if I told you that Gentry's father got so drunk at the correspondence dinner in DC one year that he pissed his pants and then blamed it on a waiter, saying a glass of water had been spilled on his crotch?"

A quiet laugh slips past my lips. "It actually does help quite a bit. Poor waiter."

"Yeah, people like the Wades are always looking for a fall guy . . . or girl. Either way, I'm sorry for whatever happened, but for what it's worth, you don't strike me as the type to be a politician's arm candy."

I give her a tired smile. "Yeah, the general consensus was that I didn't really have the looks to be anyone's arm candy."

She rolls her eyes and mutters something under her breath. "You're not hearing me, Maddie. You know, I read up on how you completely salvaged part of the Wade Foundation after the embezzlement scandal and managed to save face for the family. I can't help but wonder if you're less politician's wife material and more politician material."

I don't really know what to say. Thank you? Pretend that I've never even considered the idea? Because I have. Plenty.

But I've never had the money or connections Gentry has. And if people had a problem with a state assemblymember standing next to a fat woman, I can't imagine they'd be all that thrilled to vote for one.

I'm honored that Miranda would even think such a thing, however. Not because I don't think I could do the job, but because someone else sees it too. It's nice. It's validating. Even if it's never going to happen.

This particular section of Intro to Government is very heavy with Greek life students and athletes. Even though it's probably not fair to judge any of my students, it's very hard not to slip into old fat-kid trauma where I am in natural opposition with this exact demographic.

Being unshowered and covered in coffee stains is not helping the situation.

The class is already full, which means I have an audience as I walk to my podium. A group of carefully unmade up girls in very chic athleisure watch my every step as they whisper back and forth.

One thing I can say about my relationship with Gentry and all the media training we did is that I at least know how to act confident when I do not feel confident. So I hold my head high like coffee stains are the latest trend and I'm ahead of the curve.

"All right, class," I say, but my voice comes out frog-like. I clear my throat again, but it takes three tries to finally settle the class.

"Pig in shit," some douchebag says in two coughs.

I glance up, with one brow severely arched, and it's enough to quiet the class entirely.

"Right, we're starting off with a quiz today," I say, and elect two students from the front row to help me hand out the department-mandated quiz that's one of the uniform requirements across all Intro to Government classes.

"Professor," a guy at the back of the room calls, "you didn't even remind us."

"This quiz has been in the syllabus since day one and is one of your required grades. If you make anything below a ninety, you are allowed to make corrections for half credit."

There are a few groans, but the class quickly quiets except for a single phone playing videos.

It takes me a minute to find the culprits. A girl and a guy in the back center of the auditorium are doing a poor job of hiding their snickering as they watch something on the guy's screen.

"Please have some respect for your fellow classmates," I say to the class at large. "Silence your cell phones and sit quietly even if you decide not to take the quiz."

The girl pushes the guy's phone away as she hunches over her quiz.

Even though all I want to do is hide behind my podium so no one can focus on what a mess I am, I walk around the auditorium because it feels like the responsible thing to do.

The sounds start again, and it's even louder than it was the first time.

"Seriously?" I ask, turning back down the steps to the absolute man-child who needs his screen time.

I surprise myself and the whole row as I shimmy down the aisle to where the guy is sitting, still refusing to turn off his phone. The girl beside him purposefully angles her back to him and it takes everything in me not to say, *Clever girl*.

He's wearing sweatpants and a ratty T-shirt that says MY

Fundamentals of Being a Good Girl

GRANDDAUGHTER IS A PROUD ASTRA COPPERHEAD.[*] I refuse to smile at the irony of his shirt.

Students tuck up their legs and kick their bags out of the way to avoid them getting stomped on. I could really use Fern's Doc Martens right now. And I'm suddenly very nostalgic for a time when I wore stompy combat boots and ripped tights with short skirts and barked at boys who approached me and my friends at bars when we were sending clearly disinterested signals. A time before Gentry convinced me that in order to effect change in the system, you had to become the system.

I point toward the door so Grandma Boy understands what I mean when I say, "You're being asked to leave the room. You can make up the quiz later."

"Are you shitting me?" he says. "This isn't high school, you psycho. I'm paying to be here."

I take his paper that has nothing on it but his name and a dick and balls that look like a smiley face. It is so damn cathartic as I fold the quiz in half and say, "You don't have to make up the quiz later, then. I'll grade you on what you have."

It's only then that I realize he's filming me.

"You're live," he says with a smirk. "Everyone say hi to my cow of a professor who thinks she can just make me leave class like this isn't a free country. Freedom of assembly!"

"That's not how freedom of assembly works, you stale doughnut. Maybe you would know that if your brain wasn't made of trending sounds and memes."

The girl beside him snaps the phone out of his hand and rolls her eyes. "He's just being a dick, Professor Kowalczk."

---

[*] This is the perfect shirt. No notes.

He snatches his phone back from her and pushes past me on his way out of the classroom.

Fuck. I hate that he got a rise out of me.

Every single head is up and very much not looking at their quizzes.

"Ten more minutes," I tell the class as I make my way back down to the podium. "Then we're moving on to the lecture."

I want to go home. I want to go home. I want to go home.

But where the fuck is home?

CHAPTER TEN

Maddie

This is the day from hell.

Of course Dr. Wallace barged into my classroom just as I was finishing up. He took one look at me and asked if I'd like to borrow his stain stick, because I obviously needed it more than he did. I didn't even bother dismissing the class. Instead, I slammed my laptop shut, flipped on the lights, and then stormed out. And of course, Miranda was in the hall talking to another professor and I could feel her watching me as our conversation about not letting Dr. Wallace walk all over me rang in my ears.

Oh god, what if Grandma Boy complains about me taking his quiz and calling him a stale doughnut? I was within my rights to ask him to leave the room, but *stale doughnut* is definitely not in the classroom control toolbox, and if I lose this job—

No, I can't think about that right now. I'll think about it later, when I'm not exhausted and covered in coffee stains. Except now,

I stand in front of my street parking spot to find it unexpectedly empty. No car to be found.

Was it stolen? Why would someone steal my old Volvo? It guzzles gas like Nolan did store-brand SunnyD when we were kids.

But, oh fuck, if it was stolen, then . . . that car contains everything I own.

"Green Volvo?"

I turn around to see the meter officer talking to me. She wears sunglasses even though it's a cloudy day and her low ponytail is all business. The woman has never in her life broken a rule or allowed one to be broken in her presence. There is no talking my way out of this.

She hands me a slip of paper that is titled *Retrieving a Towed Vehicle*.

"Towed? Seriously? This is open street parking. It says right there. Every day from six a.m. to six p.m. and all day on the weekends."

She leads me closer to the sign and points to a much smaller stipulation at the bottom. STREET SWEEPING ON THE FIRST AND THIRD THURSDAY OF THE MONTH. TOWING STRICTLY ENFORCED.

"But—but—" She's not wrong. It's right there on the sign. This woman with her Founding Father's ponytail is absolutely correct.

I feel that fullness at the back of my eyes and tears begin to burn.

No. I am not crying today. I am not going to think about how it's going to cost me a small fortune to get my car back. I am not going to cry.

"The bus picks up at the end of the block," she tells me. "Goes all over town. And it's free for students and faculty."

Fundamentals of Being a Good Girl

"Great," I tell her, doing my best to regain my composure. "Thank you."

I am not going to cry.

It took me sitting through one and a half loops and studying the routes on my phone before I found the closest stop to Letty and Berry's school, but thankfully I wasn't late.

The girls are waiting near the car pickup line when Berry sees me waving from the patch of grass where the walking parents wait.

I wait for the crossing guard to let me cross the line of cars to retrieve them both and they excitedly take each of my hands.

Letty is brimming with energy at the change in routine and Berry is distracted by every weed disguised as a flower that we pass.

"I thought we could walk today," I tell them. "The leaves are starting to change, so maybe we can pick up some of our favorites for a special craft after your playdate with Aniq."

Once we cross the street into the neighborhood, Berry skips forward while Letty stops and picks a few dandelions.

"Berry's getting flowers for her boyfriend," Letty sings.

Berry marches over to Letty and throws the dandelions in her face.

"Letty," I warn. "No teasing. Berry, no throwing."

Letty's brows knit together and she thinks for a minute before begrudgingly apologizing. Berry mumbles something in return.

The girls' best friend, Aniq, lives only two blocks away and this playdate is a pretty regular occurrence, but the girls can get a little testy with each other over sharing a friend. They both simmer as we continue on and take my hands again after a few minutes of moodiness.

I can't blame them. This is not a good day.

"Did you spill your lunch?" Berry asks quietly.

"No," I tell her. Though maybe having something in my stomach before that disastrous class would have helped me not lose my temper. "I spilled a very delicious drink on myself."

Letty looks up to me, her little hand sweaty in mine. "Was there anything left?"

I shake my head. "Nope. It all landed on my clothes."

"I would have cried," Berry says.

"She would have," Letty confirms. "One time she dropped a meatball on the ground and Hester Prynne ate it before Dad could pick it up and Berry cried."

"It was the last meatball," Berry explains.

"Very understandable," I tell them as we stop in front of Aniq's house.

They're quick to run inside past Aniq's mom and I tell her to call me if there are any issues.

She promises that she will and then she closes the door and I'm left by myself.

Without a car, my only option is to go to Bram's until the girls are done.

BACK AT BRAM'S, I gulp down two glasses of ice water and eat three Oreos and a handful of baby carrots. Sometimes a girl just needs to hydrate and eat a snack.

The time on the microwave reads three fifteen, which means I have nearly two and a half hours before I have to pick up the girls. Bram isn't usually home until five thirty or six, and Fern has school newspaper tonight until seven.

I could be a good girl and tidy up the house and get started on dinner.

Or I could strip out of these coffee-drenched clothes and wash them while I treat myself to a hot shower.

With no chance of getting my car back tonight and no clue what I'll do after I get off work, I decide that the clean clothes and the shower take priority, especially when I think about the kind of shithole hotel I'll be able to afford for the night. Let's just say it'll be the sort of place where the shower curtain is just an Uber pickup line for mold and bacteria.

Bram's room is upstairs just across the hallway from the laundry room, so I quickly strip out of my clothes and start the machine.

I don't know why I thought Bram's room would be stuffed full of books and plants, but instead it's minimalist and tranquil. The dark green walls are bare and the only furniture is a wingback chair next to a fireplace and his king-sized bed with a fluffy white feather duvet. There are a few books stacked on the nightstand next to a framed photo of a much younger Fern holding the newborn twins, their sweet little faces red and scrunched up like they might be on the verge of crying the moment after the photo was snapped.

In his linen closet, I find stacks of fresh towels. Bless this man for having clean towels.[*] Gentry always had clean towels thanks to his cleaning service, but all my college hookups before that were

---

[*] Bram was born a fully grown adult.

deeply unhygienic. It's a wonder I didn't contract tetanus or impetigo. Or staph.

His shower is the shower of a grown-ass man and I didn't realize how badly I needed a shower that wasn't in a locker room and didn't require shower shoes and a travel toiletry bag.

As the room fills with steam, I open up his body wash and shampoo—and conditioner! Bram is a shampoo *and* conditioner man. No all-in-one for Professor Daddy. It's immediately clear that these are the source of his cedar and eucalyptus scent.

My nipples immediately pebble as the cedar bodywash suds between my breasts. If I weren't exhausted and if I weren't in my boss's shower, I might take better advantage of this moment, but the scalding hot water feels too good for me to do anything other than stand under the rainfall showerhead.

I take my time shampooing and conditioning my hair and when I've stayed in the shower so long that it's probably time for me to put my laundry in the dryer, I finally turn off the water and reach for my towel.

The towel is luxe and oversized and after squeezing the water out of my hair, I wrap it around my chest. The moment I step out of the bathroom, goose bumps tickle my skin and I am not looking forward to the wait for my clothes to dry.

Just as I'm about to open the bathroom door, it swings open and Bram's eyes are wide and frantic. His voice is clipped when he asks, "Where the hell are the twins?"

His pupils bloom the moment he realizes that I'm standing here, water rolling down my shoulders and nothing but a towel between us. But then it's gone and he's a parent of three again.

"Were you just in my shower?" he asks, like he doesn't have a fucking PhD. "Are the twins okay? Where are they?"

Fundamentals of Being a Good Girl

There's something about the tone of his voice. It's deep and stern, and startling. And I immediately feel like I'm in trouble. Like I've been irresponsible with the kids. Like I'm a horrible nanny and a terrible adjunct professor and a shitty adult. Because it's all true. All of those things are true, especially today.

So I cry. I finally cry.

CHAPTER ELEVEN

Bram

Maddie's face crumples so quickly that I barely track what happens—a dimple in her chin, a quiver of her lip, and then *tears*, streaming down her cheeks and racing down her neck to join the post-shower droplets still freckling her chest above the towel.

"Madelyn, are the twins okay?" I ask desperately, and when she nods, the wave of panic recedes.

"Playdate," she chokes out.

Fuck. *Right.* Having Maddie here for the last month meant that I was no longer on playdate management duty, and I'd forgotten.

I let out a breath—slowly, so Maddie won't notice. I didn't actually think the twins were in any danger, but the mammal-parent part of my brain immediately relaxes knowing where they are.

And then she starts crying even harder.

I might be a rare person in that tears rarely upset me. Crying is good for us, at least sometimes: it activates the parasympathetic nervous system, it calls forward endorphins and oxytocin, it signals a need for attachment and inter-individual response and can often succeed in strengthening social bonds. To that end, I've never tried to stop my children from crying—after I changed a diaper or bandaged a scraped knee or took away screen time, I always held or cuddled the little crier until the tears turned into sniffles and then into sighs, and never told them not to cry or to forget about it. What would be the point of that? Telling someone to stop crying is essentially telling them not to feel what they're feeling, and you might as well command the moon to wane or tell a prairie thunderstorm to settle down. Feelings are weather, and weather is . . . itself. The best thing you can do is take shelter together.

Except—

Except right now, I am not *not upset*. I am not serene and unruffled in the face of emotional weather. I see Maddie's shock dissolve into shame and hurt—and despair—

And I'm across the room somehow; she's in my arms somehow. I've pulled her tight into my chest, her head nestled well under my chin, her wet chest and arms and hair getting everything damp, and I want to fix it, I want to fix whatever it is, I want to tell her that I will make it better, and then I want to go and make it better.

Even if she's crying because of me. Because I was too stern or too stingy with my shower or because I scared her by walking in.

As that last possibility occurs to me, I loosen my hold and attempt to step back. Apart from her using my shower—which is objectively a little strange—she still has a right to privacy, and I have her crushed against my chest while she's still wet and basically naked. But when I try to pull away, she tightens her arms around my waist and buries her face in my chest, crying even harder. Full-blown sobs. Sobs like I would never have thought a sharp, perfectly made-up law school grad capable of.

And I don't . . . hate this moment right now.

I hate that she's upset, of course, I hate that I don't know what's happening and so I can't start helping. But I don't hate the feeling of her face pressed against my chest, of her fingers clutching at my shirt like I'm the only thing keeping her upright. Of her lingering jasmine scent mingled with the smell of my bodywash, my shampoo. In fact, smelling *me* on her makes me want to growl in pleasure. Makes me want to pet her, spoil her.

"Okay," I murmur. "Okay. Come here, yes, just like that. Good girl."

I've walked us over to the large wingback I have in front of the fireplace and I sit down, pulling her onto my lap. She goes willingly, pliantly, nestling right up against my chest again and continuing to cry through it all. If there was ever a time that I resented my high school growth spurt, having to duck through doorways, having to get blazers and jackets tailored for my shoulders, then I was a fool, because this moment, being able to hold Maddie— through whatever this is—is more than worth it. It's everything that could ever matter.

I stroke her wet hair. She's got her fingers twisted in my shirt, her knees pulled up as far as they'll go, and when I adjust the towel to keep her covered, she balls up all the tighter, like she wants to crawl inside my rib cage and hide there.

"It's okay," I soothe in a low voice. "I've got you. I'm not letting go."

The weather has been fussy—cool at night, a little too warm during the day—and so I still have the air-conditioning going to keep the edge off the heat. Which means that soon Maddie starts

Fundamentals of Being a Good Girl

shivering as she cries, chilled from being wet and in a now-damp towel. I reach for a blanket folded neatly beside the chair and pull it up over her, towel and all, smoothing it over her back and tucking it around her thighs.

And gradually, as she warms up, as I hold her securely against me and rub her back over the blanket, her ragged breathing starts to mend itself. Her tears slow. She doesn't stop gripping my shirt, however. She doesn't unbury her face.

It's not a good thing to do, it's not at all the right thing to do, but the itch to feel her skin under my palms is overwhelming, a craving that roars at full hunger nearly the instant I first recognize it: I slip my hand under the blanket to stroke her bare thigh.

From her knee to where the towel ends at the curve of her backside, and then back down again.

I can't see them, but I can feel the goose bumps rippling out from my fingertips, an opulence of them, everywhere I touch. And she's trembling again but not like she's cold.

She sucks in a breath as my fingertips trail higher, up to her hip, and then leave, like nothing happened, like I'm still on official childcare-provider-comforting business. But then I caress up to her hip again, treating myself to a scant second of pause, a flash of memory involving my hands and these same hips, and she lets out a shuddering exhale.

And then . . . shifts.

Instead of tucking herself into my chest now, she's sitting squarely on my lap, her head resting on my shoulder and her legs hanging over the arm of the chair. The hard-on that I hadn't realized was swelling is now roosted right under her warm, plush rear, trapped between us, and the pressure is . . . is almost enough, I think. I could come like this, with her sitting on me and nothing else.

She doesn't speak, doesn't tilt her head back to find my gaze. But her knees part. A little, and then enough that a hand could reach the warmth between her thighs.

"Madelyn," I say, and my voice is low and firm. "Are you spreading your legs?"

A short breath. And then a quick nod, her still-damp hair brushing against my jaw.

"Are you spreading your legs for me?"

Another nod, fast, urgent.

"Is it your pussy? Is it needy? Have you been neglecting it?"

Her head falls back a little as she whimpers out a *yes, Bram*.

"That's such a bad girl," I breathe as my hand moves between her legs. "If I can't trust you to take care of it"—my fingers reach silky curls—"then I'll have to do it myself."

The moment I part her cunt, she is all slippery lushness, like ripe fruit. I groan at the slick arousal, I groan again as I penetrate her with a finger and feel how hot she is inside. Blistering and tight and *fuck*, so perfect, fuck, fuck—

She's squirming now, her thighs as wide as she can get them, and both the blanket and the towel have slid down, showing me her tits, her bunched-up nipples, the flush creeping up her chest.

"Maddie," I say, "I am going to give you an orgasm now. Would you like that?"

"Yes, Bram" is her whined-out answer, and she's wriggling so much in my lap that I give her cunt a light slap. She whines again, her head falling back, her throat working.

"Hold still." It's half instruction, half threat, and it's only when she promises with a delirious sort of nod that I find her clit and begin.

I work the small bud carefully, with all of my attention. Like a doctor treating a patient, like a gardener tending to a rare plant. That night above The Dry Bean was frantic, panting, and angry, mostly dark and mostly clothed. But now, I take my time. I pay attention.

I *look*—watching the suntanned breadth of my hand wedged between soft, pale thighs, cataloging every glimpse I get of glossy pink Maddie. I commit to memory the feeling of her plump clit, her tight hole, the way her tits move with each quivering breath.

I study how she arches and gasps. I learn that she likes little breaks from her clit—short detours into her body, explorations up to her nipples and down to the pink eyelet below her pussy—and she hate-love-hates being strung along the edge, pawing uselessly at my forearm whenever I leave her teetering, her eyes flying wide to glare at me.

"Careful, Ms. Kowalczk," I warn, my chest lifting and falling with a deep breath. "A look like that is going to earn you another swat, and I don't care how wet that cunt is, it's not too wet to get spanked if I say so."

Maddie's wide, pouty mouth falls open. "Oh my god," she whispers. "Oh my god." She's trying to get her legs wider, trying to arch harder, and I can barely breathe, I'm so fucking ravenous for this, for Maddie, *my good girl*, splayed open and trying to fuck my hand, vacillating between bratty and pleading.

"Please, Bram," she's moaning, and I'm breathing harshly, heavily, my cock thumping with need underneath her writhing body, and I can't deny us both what we want next. This pussy, wet and clenching; my name on her lips; her eyes green and glazed and locked with mine.

I move back to her clitoris and stroke it with the strokes I now know she likes best—tight and hard—and it takes no time at all, mere seconds. She sucks in a breath, finding my face, something like panic all over hers, and then orgasms with a cry, her stomach and thighs quaking and her knees slamming closed and trapping my hand.

I don't stop, though, still rubbing and *rubbing* and watching her like I'm going to write a dissertation on Satisfied Maddie, and it's only an eternity later, when her body finally goes still and then loosens, that I stop. I don't pull my hand free right away, though; I savor all the soft, wet heat. I savor the sight of us, all of us, even though it's so fucking depraved that I feel like a bad, bad man, with the blanket half tumbled to the floor, her tearstained face, my slippery fingers.

My shirt is still buttoned. My shoes are still on.

"Bram," she whispers, and then she's twisting, rearranging, straddling me in the chair. The blanket and towel fall all the way down now; her hair has dried enough to make damp waves that trail down to her breasts and brush her nipples. She finds my belt, my zipper, and I don't help her; I silently watch as she spreads the placket of my trousers and pulls me out.

"Well?" I ask once she's got my dick into the cool air of the room. The skin of my organ is stretched so tight that it nearly shines. "What are you going to do with it, Ms. Kowalczk?"

A curl pulls at her pretty lips, and my heart flips over in my chest. She's almost smiling, and after seeing her cry that hard, an almost smile is a marvel.

"I think I need to make sure that you're not neglecting *your* needs, Professor Loe," she purrs, and then she moves so that her wet core is over my erection.

And sits on it.

I drop my head back against the chair as she starts rocking against me, my cock trapped between my stomach and her, all slick, soft pressure, and it's almost like being inside her, almost, *almost*.

She reaches down, like maybe she's thinking the same thing, and I catch her wrist.

"I haven't been bare inside someone for years," I grind out. "I won't be able to stop myself."

"What if I don't want you to?"

"Then you're a very bad girl. I thought you wanted to be good for me?"

"I do," she pants, her eyes wide and green and so beautiful in the afternoon sunlight. "More than anything, but I want your cock inside me too—"

It's too much. Her panting confession, her pretty eyes and pretty face and pretty tits. Her cunt sliding against me.

I grunt as jagged, angry bliss shreds through my stomach and tears its way up my cock, one hard jerk, and then full, thick spurts, coating her between the legs and staining my shirt.

"Fuck," she breathes, her eyes down between us, watching my erection swell and spill, swell and spill. "That's . . . fuck, Bram. That's so hot."

She pulls her wrist free of my grip and reaches down to catch some of my release on her fingertips. She licks it off, and my stomach clenches again, like my body needs to make sure that it drains every last drop around her.

The minute the orgasm lets me be, I fall back in the chair. Maddie and I are disheveled and sticky, and I can feel my heartbeat in my toes, behind my eyes, and I don't think I ever want to move—

but also, how the hell did I end up with my dick out and a naked adjunct perched on my lap?

Judging by the way Maddie's teeth are sinking into her lower lip, I'm guessing she has the same question.

I make a decision.

"We're both going to take a shower," I say. "Well, another one for you. And then I'm making you coffee, and you're going to drink it while you sit in my lap. Okay?"

She blinks, and in her eyes, I see the creeping shame and despair again, but there's a soft kind of relief in the shape of her mouth. "Yes, sir," she says, and I think the *sir* is a game attempt to tease me, to bring some levity to the moment, but all it does is make me push us out of the chair and into the shower together, where I get to my knees and lick her clit while water runs down my face and onto my cock.

I jerk myself so that we come together, so that I can know, at least once, what it's like to climax with Maddie's taste on my tongue.

CHAPTER TWELVE

Bram

If I've ever wondered what it would take to make my curvy brat docile, two back-to-back orgasms seem to do the trick. Because fifteen minutes later, we are back in the chair, both of us in old Astra University shirts and comfy sweatpants. Maddie is holding a cup of coffee with both hands while she's cuddled sweetly against my chest. I can see that she's still a little upset, but when I gently clear my throat to indicate I'm about to speak, she doesn't bolt, which feels like a good sign.

"I'm not upset you used my shower," I say, "and I'm sorry for being so brusque earlier. I should have remembered the playdate, and more importantly, I should have trusted that you had everything under control."

She seems surprised—taking a minute to sip the coffee and then frown down at her hands. "Thank you," she says slowly. "I wasn't expecting a— You don't need to apologize. You were worried about your kids, and I was doing something kind of—" Even from this angle, I can see her wince. "Invasive."

"You can use anything at the house," I assure her. "Although I wasn't expecting to find you wearing only a towel." The tips of my ears burn a little and I'm glad she's still looking down at her coffee right now. "But it wasn't . . . unpleasant."

She huffs a tired little laugh. "The only pleasant part of my day."

I think about her crumpling face, her tears and how they spilled down to fall on her chest. Those body-shaking sobs as she wept in my arms.

"Tell me about your day, Maddie."

She hesitates. "It was a little chaotic," she answers. "That's all."

I can practically feel her reaching for her armor, trying to cover up all the soft and vulnerable parts of her—and *no*, she's not allowed to do that, I'm not allowing it today. Right now, here in my lap with her body loose from the pleasure I gave it, her hair smelling like my shampoo and her hands cradled around my coffee mug, she's mine to take care of. Even if it's only for the next fifteen minutes.

I take care of what's mine.

"Maddie." My voice is firm. "Start with the shower and work your way backward."

She takes a deep breath. Blows it out.

And then she tells me about her day.

I'm frustrated for her when I hear about her car being towed; I'm irritated on her behalf when she tells me about the shitty students in her class. But when she gets to the part about the student health center being closed, I'm genuinely confused. "Why does the closure mean you couldn't take a shower this morning?"

Her thumb moves nervously on the coffee mug. "I don't have a shower where I live."

What?

"Where do you live?"

She ducks her head a little, so I can't see her face. "In my car," she says in a very small voice.

I inhale so sharply that my ribs hurt; something like rage and fear and a . . . a vast protectiveness fills me, swells me, unravels my neatly tied edges.

"You've been sleeping in your car?" I ask, and even I can hear how grim I sound, how dangerous.

Maddie shifts, like she's trying to scoot off my lap, and I seize her and drag her back. She's not going anywhere.

"Where have you been parking at night?" I demand. I'm shaking now, my hands, my thighs. My chest. I feel like an entire earthquake. "While you've been alone in the dark, unconscious and completely exposed?"

"I had the doors locked," Maddie protests, but the protest is thin, faint, like she knows it's not good enough. *Which it isn't.*

"Where, Maddie?" I demand.

"A Walmart parking lot," she admits. "And, um, this rest stop—"

I want to roar in pure animal outrage. I want to go to the rest stop right now and tear it down with my bare hands. I want to start pacing around her like a guard dog, snapping and rumbling warnings at anyone who dares to get too close.

She seems to sense this, because she's gone very still in my lap.

"And why are you sleeping in your car at a *rest stop*? Why, when you have two jobs, do you not have a place to stay?"

"Two *bullshit* jobs," she corrects, the words all the more corrosive for how accurate they are. "I make ninety-five hundred dollars a semester teaching—less than ten thousand dollars before taxes, and I'm not complaining about what you pay me, but I only work for you three hours a day and the agency takes their cut out of that too. And before I came here, I was a full-time student for the last *three years*, because my entire raison d'être after I met Gentry was to become the perfect politician's wife, and so I spent those years volunteering at the Wade Foundation and serving on stupid student boards and spending every spare second schmoozing with him at horrible, schmoozy events instead of clerking or doing paralegal work to earn cash. I lived with Gentry, I used student loans for tuition and clothes and my cell phone bill because he told me that his family would pay them off for me, and so when he had his campaign adviser dump me with no warning, I had nothing to call my own but my degree and my car. I had a little money squirreled away from the work-study programs I did, and that was enough to get me out here and feed me until my first paycheck. I couldn't afford to stay in California without asking for my brother's help, and now it turns out I can't afford to live in Kansas either. At least until next month, when I'll finally have enough for a security deposit, and even then, I have no fucking idea what I'm going to do in December when that first student loan bill comes due."

She's breathing hard now, fast, the coffee threatening to slosh over the sides of her mug as she trembles with emotion.

"But I'm doing *fine*. I don't need anyone's help, and I don't need anything to change, and I am not letting that cheating asshole turn me into a charity case when he's already taken so much from me. He's taken my goals and my pride and my favorite lipstick color and even my—stupid—hair because he needed me to look the part and that meant not looking like myself."

She's crying again. I carefully take the coffee mug from her and set it down on the floor.

"Your arms are so long," she complains tearfully. "You're too big."

"That's what Leo says. He's irritated he can't bully me anymore."

More sniffles. "He used to bully you?"

"Mercilessly. Then I had a growth spurt in eleventh grade and gave him a black eye, which for some reason he interpreted as an overture of friendship.[*] Now I can't get rid of him."

She's still crying but there's a half laugh among the sniffles now.

I find her chin and tilt her face so she has to look at me. "You live here. Starting today."

She stiffens. "What? No!"

"A live-in childcare provider would be easier anyway."

"Bram, no. Did you not hear the part about how I don't want help? About how I'm *fine*?"

I press on. "It'll make our schedules more convenient, and I have the extra room, actually two extra rooms, if you count the finished part of the attic."

"*Bram*. I can't live with you." I can feel a defensive pride roiling in her; she tries to move her head so she doesn't have to look up at me anymore. I don't let her.

"Why not?" I ask, searching her face. "I have the space, and we'll make boundaries around your time helping with the kids. And it's not forever, only until you have what you need to get into an apartment."

---

[*] When Leo decides you're his, you're his, no matter how little it makes sense.

"Just . . . no." Her full mouth is set in a stubborn sulk. "I don't need any help."

"You're sleeping in parking lots and at rest stops. It's getting cold at night, and today has proven that you're one obscure parking rule away from spending money you don't have on a hotel that will certainly have bedbugs. What was your plan for tonight? If you couldn't afford to get a hotel?"

Her eyes drop. Tears are caught on her long eyelashes—dark lashes, matching the near-black roots of her hair. "I was going to try to sleep in the adjunct office," she mumbles. "Or hide in the library."

"*Absolutely not.*"

"At least no one is forcing their pity on me there," she says, acid in her gaze as she looks back up to me, and I recognize it for what it is. A defense mechanism, a reflexive clawing at some dignity.

Another tear slides down to my fingers, and I want to kill somebody. (Somebody named Gentry.)

Also, I think I'd like to give Maddie a stern talking-to. Preferably while she's bent over a desk with her skirt above her hips. She is absolutely not allowed to put herself in danger, and she is not allowed to act like everything is fine when she's living in her car. She's not allowed to make everyone around her comfortable while she's hanging on by a thread.

She's worth more than that. She deserves more than that.

But I look at her, all tangled defiance and vulnerability and restlessness, and ask, *bluntly*, "Do you want Gentry to pity you?"

Shock blanches her expression. "Of course not! What the fuck, Bram."

I let go of her chin so I can cradle her face in my hands. "Then why are you letting him have this much power over your life? Over your future? You refuse to let him turn you into a charity case, but you'd rather he leave you homeless, desperate, and struggling to do your job?"

Heat reddens her cheeks, and her eyes are sparking with indignant fury.

Good. *Good.*

"Where do you see yourself at the end of this term? At the end of next term? Where will you be in five years if it takes you one year—or two or three—just to get your feet underneath you? What if you could get started on the rest of your life *right now*, and be building your future exactly the way you want it, and show the world exactly what you're fucking capable of? All for the scant price of sleeping in an unused room, in a place that's warm and safe and free of shopping carts? Don't live here because you're accepting my help, Maddie. Live here as a giant *fuck you* to Gentry and that campaign adviser and anyone else who made you feel like your time belonged to him. Live here so you can make everybody regret the fucking day they made Maddie Kowalczk feel small and alone."

Her eyes are burning into mine, bright green, alive, the same color as the inside of my greenhouse on a hot summer's day, and her lips are parted. She's breathing fast and swallowing hard and her nipples are poking against her borrowed T-shirt so prominently that I can see them even in my peripheral vision.

So my brat gets off on spite and revenge. Good to know.

"Okay," she whispers, nodding into my hands. "Okay."

"You'll live here?"

"Yes."

"You'll stop sleeping in cold parking lots?"

A nod. "Yes."

"You'll let me help you when you need it, so you can stop letting that asshole control your life?"

"Yes, Bram." And then, "You're swearing a lot right now. It's very sexy."

I give her a *be serious, Ms. Kowalczk* look.

She pouts.

"But I do think," I say, and this part I say a little reluctantly, "that this means we shouldn't . . . be . . . together. Again."

"Why? It's not against university policy and it's only a *little* bit against the agency's policy."

I drop my hands from her face and gently run them up and down her upper arms. She's soft and warm and I want to hold her until the stars come out. I want to haul her over to my bed, tie her to it, and drag out promise after whimpered promise that she'll be good for me, my good girl, after she's done being so very filthy and bad.

But this is more important.

"It's more than a little against the agency's policy, and anyway, I want you to feel safe here. I don't want you to feel like living here is contingent on sex. I don't want you to think that I expect payment in kind."

Her lips come together in a mulish shape. "I wouldn't think that."

"Still."

"Why are you helping me?" she asks. "You don't have any reason to."

"You could think of it as me supporting a colleague. Or maybe keeping my childcare options secure."

Her eyes flick over my face. "But that's not it, is it?"

Of course that's not it.

But I can't exactly say what it is, because it would terrify her and maybe terrify me too. The way I feel about Maddie—protective and tender and greedy and stern—it's not the kind of thing that would help either of us to admit. It wouldn't help her because she's just gone through an awful breakup, because she's *employed by me*, because she doesn't need Mid-Thirties Single Dad Baggage while she's making a fresh start.

And it wouldn't help me because . . . because I don't know the last time I've felt like this.

I don't know that I've *ever* felt like this.

Maddie slumps against my chest, and I take a moment to treasure it, what I assume will be the last time I have her in my arms.

"You're not going to answer me, are you?" she murmurs, but she sounds resigned to my reticence.

"I'm helping because I want to, Maddie. That will have to be good enough." *Because telling you the truth will send you running, and I need you here, warm and safe.*

"If only you could help me with those asshole students," she grumbles. "I know it's not the most important thing right now, but I'm just dreading going back in there and facing them."

"Actually," I say, sitting up a little. "I think I can help with that."

CHAPTER THIRTEEN

Maddie

Last night after Bram and I picked up the twins, we ordered Thai for dinner and told all three girls that I'd be staying here at the house under the guise that it would be easier to have a live-in nanny—or as Bram prefers: a *childcare provider*. I expected lots of questions, especially from Fern, but the twins squealed and flung themselves at me while Fern gave a nonchalant *cool* and took advantage of the moment to steal the last spring roll.

This is the first morning since arriving back in Kansas that I've had a bathroom all to myself without having to wait in line for it. It is the peak of luxury. Fern and the twins share the other upstairs bathroom, which connects their rooms, at the top of the stairs and I'm at the end of the hallway in the guest room.

After the kids went to bed, I tried to be a brave little toaster and sit on the couch with Bram while he watched some documentary about the history of national parks. But I fell asleep before the opening credits were even done. Bram woke me up and practically pulled me upstairs to the guest room. I let my fingers linger on his arm, hoping I might lure him into breaking his own rules, but either he was a gentleman or I was too tired to convince him otherwise.

I fell asleep in his T-shirt and under his roof, and for the first time in a very, very long while, I felt safe and looked after.

Today, I'm back in my ivory pants and striped sweater, now washed, and I smell like Bram from his body wash to his laundry detergent, and it's hard not to press my face into my own shirt and inhale deeply.

So yes, I am rested, but as I stand in front of the mirror, I can't stop noticing all the ways that the upkeep of my appearance has lapsed.

When Gentry and I became serious, his mother invited me to go to her salon with her before a big family wedding. I didn't realize that this was all just a ruse to ambush me with a makeover. But at the time, I felt spoiled and pampered. I walked into the salon with my dark brown, nearly black hair and came out with tasteful honey-blond layers that framed my face in a way that Penelope Pike later described as *aspirational yet approachable*. Then there was the eyebrow threading, the glowy spray tans, the biweekly nail appointments, the facials, and of course the personal trainer, who was actually wonderful despite being hired to help me achieve my "fitness goals"—or weight loss.

Now, my dark roots are coming in, my eyebrows are haphazardly plucked, my skin is pale, and my nails are bare. It occurs to me that Bram has definitely not seen me at my best.

And yet . . . and yet, he's made me feel sexier in a few weeks than Gentry did during the four years we were together.

When I go downstairs, Bram is waiting with a to-go cup of

coffee. "I got you something on my way back from dropping off the twins. I wasn't sure how you took your coffee, so I went with a latte."

"Thanks. I like a latte. The more froufrou the better."

"Froufrou . . . Next time, I'll have them add lavender," he says. "You look rested." His lips twitch like he has more to say, but instead he just motions for the door.

"Thank you," I tell him. "I haven't slept that well in a while."

He nods once, satisfied, a ghost of a smile on his lips as we walk out to his car.

"We can pick up your car after your lecture," he says as he reverses out of the driveway with his arm braced on my headrest as he twists to look over his shoulder.

"Um, I might need to call and see how much it is first, but they should let me get my stuff back, right?"

He stops the car and looks at me. "Madelyn, we are picking up your car today. That was not a question. I will pay the towing fee."

"You will not," I spit back at him.

He tilts his chin down, eyes a soft celadon green mixed with amber. "Consider it—I don't know—a vehicle allowance, but this is not up for debate. You need your car to do your job, and I need to know that you're not at the mercy of the well-meaning but underfunded Mount Astra transit system."

I don't like this. I don't like owing anyone anything, especially after being taken care of by Gentry and his family came at the cost of losing myself entirely. But Bram is right. I do need a car to do my job. "Okay," I finally say, my hands held up in surrender.

Today is my early section and since I drove in with Bram, I don't have time to stop and see Junie, which I need to do soon because I owe her an apology after I was so short with her yesterday.

Fundamentals of Being a Good Girl

When I get to class, students are still filing in. I connect my laptop and make sure my clicker is in working order. Just as the clock strikes seven thirty, I close the door only to feel it being tugged open from the other side. I let go and Bram is standing there.

"I thought I should come and observe," he says quietly.

My stomach curls into a fist and my pulse spikes. I know I asked him to help me, but I hadn't considered that he would actually watch me teach a class.

"You'll hardly notice me," he says.

I scoff. "Yes, because the six-foot-four Jolly Green Giant professor is so hard to miss."

He grins with his mouth closed and steps in past me, his torso brushing against my chest.

This is a starting point, I remind myself. I'm not scared of public speaking, but something about commanding a lecture hall full of students who are only three to six years off from me in age has had me feeling unsure that I have any business even doing this job.

"Okay, according to the syllabus, we're starting off with a quiz."

There's no reaction outside of a quiet *fuck*, which is already an improvement from yesterday's class, who took the same quiz.

Bram sits off to the side on the second row in the seat closest to the wall. Thankfully he's not in my direct line of sight.

While the class takes the quiz, I go over my notes for today's lecture, and as they finish, they bring their papers up one by one.

Jordan, the guy who had plenty of opinions about group projects the other week, takes the steps two at a time before jogging to the desk next to my podium. What I hadn't noticed before is that the kid has at least a foot on me. He's not as tall as Bram, but he's not far off.

I have to strain my neck to look up at him, and I suddenly feel very . . . small. Almost insignificant.

"Uh, yeah," he says loud enough for the whole class to hear. "I heard the other sections of Intro to Government had multiple-choice quizzes, but yours are short-answer questions. That's really not fair."

"Seriously?" someone asks.

"Jordan, the quiz format is at the discretion of the professor."

"You know that multiple choice is easier. I don't think it's very cool that we're all at such a disadvantage just because we're in your class. Doesn't seem very equitable if you ask me. Weren't we just talking about privilege in our last class and how it's about how everyone should have the same starting point? I don't think the short-answer format gives your class the same privileges as multiple choice does the other classes."

The way he frames his statement makes my skin prickle. He's using justice-oriented language for his own gain, and it's something I've seen and done enough times to recognize. In fact, if I weren't his teacher, I'd be impressed—even though he could use some polishing.

I can feel a roar building in my chest. A need to put him in his place, but then I remember how I was a total monster to my class yesterday. If students are talking about quiz formats, there's no way they aren't talking about my outburst yesterday. It's hard enough to be one of the youngest lecturers on campus. And I'd like to think that Bram might be impressed by my willingness to be the bigger person.

I peer up at him and try not to shrink back at our sheer height difference. "You know what, Jordan? You're right."

"Hell yes, I am," he says.

"I'm going to add a twenty-point curve to the quiz, and I'll take this into account for future quizzes."

He gives me a cool nod that makes me immediately regret my decision. It's the same feeling I'd get after making out with a guy only for him to turn around and act indifferent toward me or when male opposing counsel would whisper that I was getting emotional during a mock trial.

But I keep my mouth shut like a good girl.

The rest of the class goes by without any issue, until the door swings open at the exact minute class is ending.

Dr. Wallace walks right in and begins unpacking his satchel as I dismiss the class. "I've got a guest lecturer coming today for my constitutional law class," he says without even glancing up at me. "So if you could take any post-lecture discussions with your students to the hallway, that would be ideal."

"You're serious," I say.

"Quite." He leaves before I can say anything else and greets a man with bushy gray eyebrows and a thick head of hair that is definitely a toupee. A good toupee, but a toupee nonetheless. "Congressman Paulson."

Both men walk past me as though I'm invisible. Fucking boys' club.

I march out of the classroom with plans to take shelter in the adjunct office while I fume, but then a hand is wrapping around my wrist and pulling me into a smaller, empty classroom.

"You can't let Wallace treat you like that," Bram says before the door even closes all the way. His face is a little flushed, like maybe he had to stop himself from saying something to Wallace himself. "Especially in front of your class."

"You think I don't know that? Okay, sure," I say. "Let me put the most tenured professor in my department in his place in front of a class full of first-years." Miranda told me to handle the situation, but I can't imagine that's what she meant.

"And that lanky kid going on about fairness and quizzes. You should have shut that down."

I drop my bag on one of the desks and slide into the seat just out of view of the window in the door. "I was trying to be more agreeable. I really flew off on that other guy from my class yesterday and this seemed like a way to retain a little bit of goodwill. I'll change both classes over to multiple choice. It's not a big deal." I should have never asked Bram for help in the first place. I want to shove him and kiss him at the same time.

He leans on the teacher's desk at the front of the classroom with his trousered legs crossed and his arms folded over his broad chest, sleeves rolled up, looking like a whole-ass academic snack. This living together/working together thing is not going to work if I can't stop objectifying Bram.

"Madelyn." The way he says my name, like I'm being called to the principal's office, forces me to press my thighs together. "You picked short answer over multiple choice for a reason, didn't you?"

"Obviously," I say. "The other adjuncts do multiple choice, but it doesn't really lend itself to illustrating that a student grasps the material. It wasn't that long ago that I was a first-year, and shifting from high school to college is culture shock. The sooner they learn how to take the concepts and put them into their own words, the quicker they'll adjust and the more successful they'll be."

"Excellent reasoning," Bram says. "Good."

I wait for him to say *girl*, but he leaves it at that.

"It's not that easy," I tell him with a frown.

He saunters over to me, his whole body practically arching over mine once he reaches me. His focus is heavy, palpable. "It's not?" he asks mildly.

"You're likely the tallest person in every room, Bram. And you're a man. People—especially other men—automatically respect you. They look to you for what to do. How to act. You set the tone without even saying a damn thing. I'm not sure if you've noticed, but I'm five foot two, a woman, and plus-size. To a lot of those little dickheads, I might as well be invisible, so excuse me for trying to meet them in the middle before they paint me as a villain."

"It won't matter how they paint you if you let them trample all over you."

"Did you hear anything I just said? Fuck you."

"Make me," he says.

"What?"

"You're right. You're small. You're a woman. I'm the size of a clock tower and I'm a man. But you can't change who you are and how you look. And I *certainly* don't want you to."

My chest flutters. "You can't say things like that to me. You're playing dirty pool."

He raps a knuckle on my desk between each word. "Make. Me. Get. On. Your. Level, Madelyn. Make me feel small."

I feel flustered, and I hate that he's putting me on the spot, but then part of me—the part that feels like he's my own personal heat lamp—rises to the challenge.

With a backbone made of steel, I stand up and go toe to toe with him.

"Professor Kowalczk," he says. "I don't think it's fair to give your class short-answer quizzes when everyone else in the department is offering multiple choice." His body hulks over me, his back hunching to meet me, like he might press me into the ground with his gaze alone.

My neck snaps back. "Professor Loe," I tell him. "You will sit down when you speak to me."

"Answer me first," he drawls. I didn't even know Bram Loe *could* drawl.

"This is a question for after class. Please sit."

His firm lips curl into a smirk as he continues to loom.

I see what he's doing. I take a deep breath and fill my voice with certainty. Pretend I'm six foot four and that people have told me my time is valuable my entire life. "Take a seat, Professor Loe," I say, like it's a given, like it's an inalienable fact. I will tell him to take a seat and he will.

"Is that a demand?" he asks. "Or a suggestion?"

"It is a strongly worded suggestion."

The tension in his shoulders eases. "Yes, ma'am." And then he's sitting in the chair I just vacated.

Here, in this position, he is just below my eye level. "How did I do?" I ask shyly as my body drags itself closer to him until I'm standing with one of his thick, muscled thighs between my legs.

"You did well." His voice is a smooth velvet that has my center coiling with desire. "You were a very good girl."

A small whimper slips from my chest as he curls a hand around the back of my thigh just under my ass. I want to feel him. I want to know that he's feeling this and that he's as insatiably turned on as I am.

I lean down, my fingers skating along his inner thigh until I'm cupping the thick bulge contained by his navy-blue chinos. From the size and insistence of it, you'd think he was a soldier who'd been at war for months, not a man who'd gotten off twice last night.

"Who's playing dirty pool now?" he asks.

"It hasn't even been a day," I remind him, and immediately regret it.

"I guess we'll just have to start over," he says. "In just a little while."

He yanks me to him, and I use both hands to steady myself on his shoulders as he pushes my sweater up, his nose dragging along my stomach until he's nipping at the underside of my lace-covered breast.

"If we're going to break your rules, we oughta make it count."

"I can't fuck you in this empty classroom, Madelyn. That would be very, very bad."

"But how can I be good without being bad?" I ask.

He pushes my sweater up farther and presses his face in between my breasts, inhaling me like I am oxygen itself.

"Your good girl needs to be fucked, Professor," I murmur.

He grips my ass with both hands, and the muscle in his jaw twitches like the control he so artfully projects is mere seconds from cracking.

Then a door slams nearby, and we're immediately jumping apart.

He watches me with wide eyes full of regret. "We should go get your car."

My heart pounds in my chest and I am dripping with want, but the thought of someone walking in and catching the newest adjunct dry humping Professor Loe's thigh is enough for me to reluctantly agree.

"And Madelyn?"

"Yes?"

"You're right. Classroom dynamics will always be different for you. You're a woman and as you continue to remind me, I am a tree-shaped man. I want to help you in any way I can, but remember, there are women on this campus who eat men like Dr. Wallace for breakfast and then use the bones to clean their teeth."

"I do really like my department chair," I tell him.

"Dr. Salazar? She terrifies me."

"That's hot," I tell him.

He smirks. "Let me help you, but you should also seek out people like Dr. Salazar and find out what they're doing right."

"Okay." I nod. "I'll give it a try."

CHAPTER FOURTEEN

Bram

"And that's all until the guests get here," Ali finishes. We're in Nagel Auditoria, a Gothic building in the heart of Astra's campus, as we prepare for the upcoming seminar on pollinators. We're welcoming lepidopterists—or butterfly perverts, as Ali keeps forgetting not to call them—along with ornithologists,[*] chiropterologists,[†] melittologists,[‡] and other entomologists.[**] It's me and two assistant professors on the tenure grind who've been trying to keep up with Ali's tossed-out ideas all afternoon.

"And we're committed to online-only resources, Dr. Darwish?" one of the assistant professors asks. Dr. Diana Mensah, a Brit who came over as a grad student, and whom I adopted immediately as

---

[*] Bird perverts.
[†] Bat perverts.
[‡] Bee perverts.
[**] Insect perverts.

she was the only one in her cohort even remotely interested in a future as a bryologist.[*]

Her compatriot in suffering, a lanky man upsettingly named Maverick McGee, clears his throat. "I'm just thinking we might need more organization beyond throwing everyone's slides and handouts onto the cloud."

Ali pauses, then makes finger guns. "Let's do a seminar website, then. Thanks, guys!"

Diana and Maverick exchange a *dead inside* glance, which Ali misses as he's already striding up to the door, waving for me to follow him.

"You know, we'll probably have to build the website ourselves," I remark as we leave one of the lecture halls and emerge into the soaring stone lobby. "The web department won't turn it around in time."

Outside, the sun is fondly golden and the air is pleasant, despite the ever-present wind here on the hill Astra University is perched upon. The trees are waving and sighing, their full green leaves just starting to hint at the red and orange and yellow tumult to come.

"It'll keep the APs busy," says Ali. "Wouldn't want them to get bored this early in the year!"

I give him a wry look as we start toward Gerhart Hall.

"*Bram*, I promise I won't break the baby professors. I didn't break you, did I?"

"Isn't that how organizational abuse perpetuates itself, sir?"

"We should ask someone in Psych. But your concern about the website is duly noted," he adds, too quickly to take him at his word.

---

[*] Moss pervert.

"I'm happy to help with—"

He's already shaking his head. "Bram, stop. *Stop.* You have your hands full—great work on that proposal, by the way, you know how to titillate those National Science Foundation program officers—but you don't need to take on everything at Astra University that needs doing. Either the APs will get the website done, or we'll throw everything onto"—a heavy sigh, like it pains him to say—"Microsoft OneDrive. But you have got to get better about giving yourself away, because a university isn't like your greenhouse. You're never going to get back what you put into it. Maybe you'll get back what you put into teaching and mentoring, *to a point*, but never into the institution itself. A university will eat your health, your ideas, and your spare time, and it'll keep only half paying the bill until you're retired or you're dead."

"I'm . . . not sure what lesson I'm supposed to take away from that."

Ali stops in front of our building to squat down and extend his hand. Dr. Monty, who was lazing on his side on the grass near the entrance, gets up and starts rubbing his fluffy head against Ali's fingers.

"There's not a lesson," says my department chair. "I'm just telling you to do some shit for yourself for once. What does Bram Loe want when he's not being a professor or a dad? What do you do for yourself to unwind?"

I'm assailed by the memory of Maddie standing in front of me in a classroom yesterday. Sweater up, tits covered in lace. Heavily lidded green eyes and a bratty smile.

I push it away.

"Being a dad and teaching *are* the things I do for myself."

Ali gives Dr. Monty a final pat and then stands with the posture of someone about to casually throw down a decent hand of cards. "You know . . . Sara's worried."

I groan and start walking to the doors, away from this nonsense. The thing about bonding with the same professor as your spouse while you're both in undergrad is that time marches on for all of you and yet you still have this eternal, shared pseudo-parent in tweed.

"I'm serious," Ali continues, half jogging until he catches up. "She feels like she has Asher, and—well, glaciers, I guess—but you chose to *teach* science instead of *doing* science, and you're still alone after five years, and she's worried, is all. I'm worried. I'm not saying you have to download a dating app or take up ballroom dancing, but give yourself something, man. It doesn't have to accomplish anything other than bringing a smile to your face. It doesn't even have to make sense. In fact, it's even better if it doesn't make sense! Because then I'll know you're not being a scientist about it. Or worse, a *dad*."

He claps my shoulder and then pulls open the door to the building, entering as Dr. Monty headbutts my ankles and then darts inside to find a grad student's laptop to lie on.

I BEHAVE FOR a week. Seven days. Seven days of giving Maddie rueful smiles as I make sure not to touch her in the hallway as we pass, as I make sure I don't graze her in the kitchen as we clean up after dinner. Seven days of quietly pulling on my cock in the shower, trying not to think about what Ali said after the seminar meeting, trying not to justify and justify and justify what I want.

Give yourself something, man.

But I can't, I can't do it. It's not right.

Fundamentals of Being a Good Girl 151

That afternoon, I come home to three banged-up cars in my driveway and muffled yelling from Fern's room.

I set down my satchel on the sofa and peer up the stairs as Maddie emerges from the kitchen holding a bowl of denuded grape stems.

"So, there was a tie in the election," Maddie says without preamble. "And rather than doing a recount, the principal has asked Fern and Simon to co-govern as student body presidents."

Shit.

I can't imagine what Fern is feeling right now. It's hard enough to hammer things out with Sara sometimes and we're repeatedly told that we have the healthiest ex-relationship ever to have existed.

But Simon is a brain-rotted, cowardly piece of shit who deserves nothing but unskippable ads and diarrhea for the rest of his life for what he did to my daughter—and I can't do anything about the ads, but maybe I can work on the diarrhea if I use up a favor or two from Zoology—

Maddie catches my arm, and I realize that I've already started going up the stairs.

"I need to talk to Fern," I explain patiently. "Make sure she's okay. Let her know that I'm happy to go have a talk with Simon and give him a chance to do the right thing before I fill his car with potting soil. Or kill him."

Maddie isn't letting go. In fact, she's leading me to a kitchen chair and sitting me down, like I'm one of the stubborn students we practiced managing. "Bram," she says. Resolutely but with a sort of kindness too, like she understands the next part is going to be hard for me to hear but she doesn't have the patience to argue with me about it. "Fern is with her friends right now. *They* are making sure she's okay. *They* are hatching all sorts of plans that may or may not include ruining Simon's life. You can check in with her later, but right now, she's with exactly who she needs to be with."

A chorus of groans and shrieks comes from upstairs. It sounds . . . well, maybe not all the way happy, but energized. Comradely.

Maddie pats my cheek. Even with my sitting down, she's barely taller than me. "Fern needs to do this—at least partly—on her own. With her peers. She needs to figure it out without Dad rushing in to save the day. She needs to try to get through this, and maybe even to fail at getting through it, because otherwise she'll never learn how to pick herself back up again. It doesn't mean that you aren't going to talk to her tonight or give her lots of love in the coming weeks. It just means that Dad isn't the first person she needs to talk to, or even Mom. Not anymore."

I look down at my lap. At the hands that held a baby Fern, that held on to the handlebars of her bike while she learned to pedal fast enough to keep herself upright. "I hate that."

"She's seventeen. This is what seventeen is for. Learning how to get through hard stuff while the safety net is still underneath her. Practicing leaving the nest so that she can make her own one day."

"That's very wise," I admit. Grudgingly.

"Well, I remember being seventeen very well," Maddie says with a laugh. "It's a traumatizing age."

A knotty sort of guilt snags in my chest and throat as I think *Of course you remember it well . . . because it was only nine years ago.*

Fundamentals of Being a Good Girl

Because the difference in age between us is the same difference in age between you and my daughter.

I make myself stand up. "I should get some grading done before dinner," I say. "Thank you for this."

She steps back, her expression turning briefly uncertain and then resigned. "I'm a good advice machine. That one was on the house."

CHAPTER FIFTEEN

Bram

After dinner, bath, and twin bedtime, I check in on Fern, who's moved the anti-Simon conclave to some sort of group call on her phone, and get an impatient *I'll be fine, Dad* and a reluctant hug. I close her door, and more shrieking and giggling come through the wood as the conclave makes some biting observations about Simon's poor performance in Forensics this year.

I pause with a small smile to savor the giggles. I can't deny that I miss being able to scoop my baby up and hug away all her problems, but Maddie was right in the kitchen. I'm not the first person Fern needs to talk to anymore, and I don't think she would be cackling and scheming and ready to take on the Ex of It All without her friends.

It just doesn't feel fair that it's *so hard* to learn to be a parent in the first place, to give all of yourself, to be everything for this tiny, gassy, emotionally unregulated person, and then once you think you've got a handle on how to do it, you are abruptly required to *un*learn it all. To become the backstory so they can start their first act without you. To step back and let them make mistakes and hope they don't fuck up too badly.

The hallway is mostly dark, save for the light coming from underneath Fern's door and the light from around Maddie's partly closed door. I see her sitting on her bed with her laptop balanced on her knees, her face adorably scrunched at her screen.

Another round of shrieks from down the hall makes her face scrunch harder.

"Why don't you come grade with me in my office?" I suggest.

She twists, startled by my voice, and then squints at me. "Are you sure? I won't bother you?"

I know what she means, but for a moment, I want to tell her the truth. That she absolutely will bother me. In those sleep shorts that barely cover her ass, in the soft Copperheads T-shirt I lent her that she still hasn't given back. Her cute little feet in socks, her blond waves in a messy bun, wide mouth naked of lipstick.

She looks like a girlfriend right now, and I haven't had one of those since I was eighteen, and I suddenly want her so badly that my stomach cramps. Cramps with hunger pains for Maddie wearing my T-shirts, for messy buns, for the dark pressing outside the windows and us together inside.

"I'm used to grading with the twins narrating a Let's Play video for a game they're pretending to play and Fern counting her stitches out loud when she's knitting. Having a grown-up doing the same kind of work in my office will feel like noise-canceling headphones in comparison."

A jolt of Olivia Rodrigo comes from Fern's room, along with a polyphony of FaceTimed karaoke from her friends, and Maddie gives a decisive nod as she closes her laptop. "Office it is."

As Maddie goes downstairs, I check on the twins—both fast asleep on the floor with Hester Prynne between them. (They have beds, of course, but one of the joys of having *one* dog come stay with *two* girls is that the dog can't be in both beds at once. So Letty presented a solution to me: the twins would sleep in their sleeping bags on the floor so they could share Hester cuddles every night. I congratulated them on their problem-solving and helped them find old quilts and comforters to make an approximation of mattresses. I didn't tell them that Hester is a faithless creature who leaves the twins in the middle of the night to come snuffle my face and then curl up in a dog-croissant by my feet.)

Downstairs, I take the liberty of making Maddie some coffee (she's one of those people who can drink espresso like it's warm milk and then tuck herself right into bed after) and carry it into my office. I shut the door behind me—I doubt Fern will leave her room unless it's to forage for food, but I want Maddie to work without any other interruptions. And maybe . . . maybe I don't hate the idea of a little privacy.

For the sake of my own focus, of course.

Maddie has claimed the chair behind my desk—a chair that is indisputably *my* chair—and is perched there with her laptop open as I bring her the espresso with a little square of chocolate on the saucer.

"Oh," she says, looking at the espresso and then up at me. Her eyebrows have pulled up and created a kissable knot right above her nose. She looks stupefied. "This is for me?"

"You like late-night espresso, yes? Garishly en-sugared drinks in the morning, then grim brain fuel at night?"

"I do, I just—" Her exhale is a laugh. "Yes. Yes, I don't know why I'm surprised by what you notice anymore. And the little chocolate square . . . I feel like I'm in a hotel."

"A nice one, I hope," I say as I settle heavily into the armchair near the bookshelves. It's a good armchair, but unlike the one in my room or the one in the living room, it wasn't made with my proportions in mind. I always feel like I'm sitting in a dollhouse when I use it.

Maddie pretends not to watch me fold in my arms and knees, but she's biting her lower lip so she doesn't betray her smile.

So she stole my chair to get a rise out of me. *Interesting.*

"The nicest hotel I've ever stayed at," she confirms. "Even if I'm hoping for some more guest perks."

"Is that so?" I ask. A little gravely.

Maddie has this way of looking out from beneath her lowered lashes. It's a way that could be flirty, but it's more like she's about to take you apart bit by bit and she hopes you'll beg her not to when she does. It gets my dick so hard, and I breathe through my nose as I reach for my laptop and crack it open. I made it a week. I made it an entire week.

I can make it through the next hour or so of grading.

And I almost do, truly. Despite Maddie's bare legs and the way the cozy lamplight accents the upturned lift of her nose and the lush curve of her mouth—a mouth that's all plump, creased fullness in the middle of her lips and then sharp, sharp corners, ready to tip down into a devastating pout at a moment's notice. Despite the way her expression flickers as she's focusing on her work—her eyes *almost* narrowing in disapproval, her cheeks *almost* lifting in a smile, her jaw *almost* tightening in irritation, like her mind is moving too quickly and intricately for her face to keep up with.

Like every feeling, even the simple ones like disappointment or amusement, comes with an array of possibilities, scenarios, and outcomes, and she'll take a look at all of them before she gives you the pleasure of a reaction, thank you very much.

It's because I'm watching her so closely that I see it, the confusion in the high arches of her eyebrows, the suspicious uncertainty. It's one thing I've noticed Maddie never fails to express: her disbelief when she encounters something deeply, deeply stupid.

"What is it?" I ask. It's the first we've spoken since we started working, although my painful awareness of her every shift and sigh has meant I've barely been able to concentrate anyway. Alas.

She's sitting with one knee drawn up to her chest, the chair scooted close enough to the desk to keep her wedged there, and she brings her fingers up to pinch worriedly at her lower lip. "It's nothing," she says. "Just . . . nothing. I'll figure it out."

"I want to hear about the nothing." I close my laptop so that she has my full attention. Which she would anyway, but watching her play with the pink curve of her lip has me additionally riveted.

She doesn't speak right away, looking over at me with peevish stubbornness, which I return with a mild look of my own. She might be an unstoppable force, but I am an immovable object. My life's work is charting the generational growth of mosses—I am primed for an entirely different scale of time than someone who's spent the last three years playing politics.

As I suspect, I win, and she relents with a huff.

"Two of my students turned in bullshit for their Supreme Court assignments." She turns her laptop toward me, and I get out of my chair to look more closely, setting my own laptop on my desk so I can have both hands free to brace myself on the back of Maddie's chair as I lean over the top of her.

I can smell jasmine. Fuck.

"They're supposed to give me four paragraphs summarizing a seminal Supreme Court case of their choosing. And pretty much everyone did fine—or at least ChatGPT did fine—but these two..."

The first short essay is, in fact, very short. It's three sentences about Sandra Day O'Connor. And not even a case she ruled on, just her life.

The second assignment, when Maddie clicks over to it, is a PNG of disembodied testicles wearing a Ruth Bader Ginsburg–style collar. Both the collar and the testicles are drawn with an impressive amount of detail. Underneath the testicles, it just says *SCROTUS*.

"The lace work on the collar is..."

"I know," Maddie agrees. "I think it's hand-drawn too."

"Ah, throw them a bone and give them a point for it," I say, straightening up. "Maybe two, depending on how many points the assignment was worth."

Maddie's mouth twists to the side. I study her.

"What is it?"

She hesitates, like she knows what I'm going to say. "Well, it's just—if *two* people did this, maybe that means I wasn't clear about the assignment. Or the due date. Or something."

I brace a hand on the edge of the desk so I'm leaning forward. I want to see her face. "Madelyn," I say. "They didn't do the assignment. By any metric. You have to mark their work appropriately."

I watch as her teeth dig briefly into her lower lip, her sharp brain trying to find a way to justify this. "But—I don't know. They turned in something, you know? And maybe they had good reasons for not—"

"Stop doubting yourself," I advise. "You know these dinguses didn't do what you asked, and if they had real reasons why they couldn't do the assignment, then they would have come to you. They sent in this shit because they couldn't be bothered to try harder, and you can't reward that attitude. Plus, it's not fair to the students who at least gestured to the bare minimum."

She taps on the desk next to her keyboard with her fingers, lightly, indecisively. "My gut says that this is *find out* time. But my gut always assumes the worst—that everyone has an ulterior motive. Shouldn't I make an effort at assuming the best of human nature?"

"In a class that satisfies a gen ed requirement? Maddie."

A deep inhale that lifts her shoulders. And then a few taps and two clicks. The assignments are marked with one point each.

"Good," I murmur approvingly, and her next breath catches like a flag snapping in the wind.

Pleasure rolls through me, something not entirely good, not entirely healthy, and I force myself to straighten up and step back. I'm too close, I want to be closer, and . . .

Maddie turns and, with her eyes locked on mine, finds my hips with her hands. I freeze, every nerve ending flashing with contradictory signals. My body wants more and *a lot more*, but my brain knows I should stop this, pull away, make space, and before I can do anything, react in any measure except horny turmoil, Maddie leans closer and presses her open mouth to my dick. I can feel the shape of her lips through the thin fabric of my joggers; I can feel her *breath*. I was already half hard, but now having this brilliant, newly ruthless little thing with her hands on me, with her clever lips tracing over my shaft and head, I've got blood pumping to my groin so fast that syncope is a real concern.

She makes a satisfied purr as my cock kicks to life underneath her kisses, and that purr could be taxonomically categorized as carnivorous because it's eating me alive, Jesus fucking Christ, and her hands curl even harder around my hips, like she is a predatory animal in truth, and I've just been pounced on. I want to let her pounce. I want to let her sharpen her claws on me, nip at me, and then I want to have her curl up in my arms when she's done, exhausted but happy.

I want to set her loose on the world and then have her sit on my lap while she licks the blood from her metaphorical paws.

But—fuck. No. She's only got her mouth on me because she's sitting in *my* chair in *my* office. Because she lives here, because she's young and broke and watching my kids.

I stagger back, and Maddie's hands are still in the air, still holding invisible hips, and her expression should be one of confusion or shock or even rejection, but instead, she's beaming up at me, like she finds *me* adorable.

"Bram," she says.

"Madelyn." But it comes out too breathless to sound stern, and her cheeks are bunched into high, rosy apples right now. Her eyes are sparkling.

"I know you're going to have some reason why we shouldn't—"

"*Reasons*, plural—"

"—and I think we should just skip over that part and get to the part where we see how much of you can fit in my mouth."

Fuck my life, I can't—I need her to understand that I am actually going to pass out if she keeps saying things like this. No one has ever talked to me with such blunt, filthy honesty, and no one has ever acted like *not* having me fuck their face would ruin their night, and I'm uniquely ill-equipped to process any of it, because this part of Bram Loe has never been needed or required by anyone. Not even my ex-wife, who treated sex like she treated eating—necessary and occasionally done with gusto, but usually as only a pragmatic concession to biology.

And oh god, I don't even want to think it, but I can't help it, I am a *bad fucking person*, but having my nanny talk to me like this . . .

No, not my nanny! My *childcare provider*. What is happening to me???

I pinch the bridge of my nose. "Madelyn, we can't. It would be inappropriate."

"I like it when you use your exasperated professor voice on me," she says in a low hum. "Do it again."

Oh, I'll do it again. I'll do it again right now. I stride over to the glass board I have mounted to the wall, uncap a marker, and start writing. An impressive feat, given that my penis is currently starving my brain of blood.

I finish, cap my marker again, and then face the person responsible for my penile-focused blood flow. She's sitting primly in the chair, back straight, looking for all the world like a straight-A student. Looking like someone who knew even before she graduated college that she was going to be a politician's wife.

"Pay attention, Ms. Kowalczk, because there is going to be a test later. There are three exceedingly salient reasons why we should not have sex. Well, have sex again. Number one." I emphatically tap the board with the cap of the marker near the top item. "You live with me."

Maddie raises her hand and then speaks after I nod at her. "Professor Loe, if I may—isn't that an excellent reason to have sex?"

"It is not. I don't want your living here to feel like it's conditional. Zero impression of a quid pro quo. Now, number two," I say, before she can initiate a rebuttal of my point, "you work for me. It's against the agency's policy. It's also unethical, since I employ you, and would introduce complications for everyone if things go south."

She raises her hand again, her posture perfect, her eyes bright. This shouldn't be hot. *It's not hot.* I've never even considered any kind of classroom role-play because classrooms aren't sexy. They are made of linoleum and projectors that refuse to work at least once a month and they're haunted by all the unanswered emails in my inbox, wailing just under the threshold of sound.

But my dick is submitting a memo that it's a fan of this right now. Me at the board and Maddie with her hand raised. Me standing, her sitting. Me able to see the braless, perky tits move under her shirt as she tries to raise her hand higher.

"Yes, Ms. Kowalczk?"

"Counterargument: no one has to know that you're screwing your nanny." I make a face at her, and she rushes on. "Not the agency, not anyone who would think it's prima facie unethical. Plus, is it that unethical when you didn't know I'd be your nanny when we met on my birthday? Surely there's some nuance in there."

"I'm very glad you brought up your birthday," I say, and then I *tap-tap-tap* the glass next to item number three. "Because this is a very important one." I underline each of the six words I wrote there. "*You. Are. Too. Young. For. Me.*"

Maddie stands up and takes a few casual steps toward me. I don't back away—I don't want to give her the satisfaction—but I can't control the hot, primal quiver in my muscles as she steps close enough that she has to tilt her head back to peer up at me.

"Counterargument: I'm twenty-six."

"Counter-counterargument: I'm thirty-five."

"So you've got an upstairs ibuprofen bottle and a downstairs ibuprofen bottle, so what?"

"I'm not sold separately, Madelyn." I use the dry erase marker as a pointer and point at the ceiling. Upstairs, where my entire world is either sleeping next to a dog or doing FaceTime karaoke. "I'm a dad, a *pet frog–level* dad, and I'm an ex-husband, and I'm also in a deeply unhealthy relationship with my university. At twenty-six, you should be young and carefree and fucking equally young and carefree people who don't have goldfish crackers wedged between their couch cushions. Also, it's just . . . wrong. I'm nearly a decade older than you."

Maddie finds the dry erase marker in my hand. Steals it with a graze of her delicate fingers.

"I," she starts, uncapping the marker and writing on the board under my last reason, "just got out of the world's worst engagement, where my fiancé's aspirations dictated every phase of my future and every mundane aspect of my life, down to the brand of reusable water bottle I carried. The literal last thing I want is another scenario where my life is forced to fit around someone else's. I don't ever want that again, in fact. So I'm not asking you to go steady; I don't want to file taxes together. I just want you to fuck me until I scream."

On the board, in the pretty handwriting endemic to popular girls of every generation, Maddie has written *just sex, nothing else* and now she underlines the *nothing else* several times.

And then under my second reason, she writes: *No one has to know.*

And then under my first, she writes: *Living together means you can have my pussy for breakfast every morning.*

Time seems to slow and stretch, an infinity of shock, of erotic revelation, and I stare at the graceful handwriting, the precisely kerned letters of *pussy*, and everything is falling away, everything except that word, that image, the memory of her taste.

Everything except the idea of waking up, walking to her room, and treating myself to her sweet cunt before the day begins. Going to campus with my nanny still on my face.

I've taken hold of the marker, I'm pulling it away from her as I crowd her up against the glass board. The word *pussy* is right next to her ear.

"You're not paying very good attention to the lesson, Ms. Kowalczk." I clamp the marker horizontally between my teeth so I can use both hands on her waist to spin her around to face the board. I put her hands up on either side of it and then take the marker and write *it's a bad idea* underneath everything else and then circle it.

She turns her head so that I can see the side of her face—slightly snubbed nose, high cheeks, a mouth that looks even fuller in profile. "But what if it's a secret bad idea?" she whispers. "Our little secret? That you can't stop fucking your nanny? That you need to use her to keep your cock warm when the nights get cold?"

"Jesus Christ," I breathe, pressing my forehead to her silk hair. "You're killing me."

"You know what I think?" she murmurs. "I think for all your talk of behaving, of good manners, Bram Loe is actually very, very bad. And no one knows it but you. And now me."

I'm shaking my head no against her head. I'm a good guy

now, but there was a time when I wasn't. There was a time when I thought breaking the rules was a good thing, the right thing, if they were bullshit rules that shouldn't exist in the first place. There was a time when I did dangerous things, when I *liked* the danger, when danger felt as comfortable to me as repotting a plant or sketching while sitting in front of a mossy rock does now.

When I stopped, I stopped because I was tired, because living my actual life in the daylight started to make more sense than fighting for an abstract future in the dark, and there was a part of me that felt relief at being *good* again. I'd been a good kid, a good teen, and it was the detour into malfeasance and vigilantism that had been the aberration, and I was going back to the Real Bram, who'd always wanted to follow the rules to begin with. But sometimes . . . I wondered. Late at night, or on long drives, or in greenhouse reveries, I wondered if I could really think of myself as inherently good when I'd slipped *so easily* into being bad. And right now, I don't feel inherently good at all.

Right now, I want to have my nanny's pussy for breakfast every morning.

Fuck it. Why shouldn't I have this? It won't hurt anyone, it doesn't change anything, and don't I deserve this? Doesn't *she*? I have nothing that's only for myself, just like Ali pointed out, and Maddie's owed lots of non-focus-grouped depravity—as much as she wants—and so what if it's reckless and wrong? It'll be sex and nothing else, it'll be our secret bad idea, and maybe none of it matters, the reasons for doing it and the reasons for not doing it, because I was never going to be able to resist Madelyn Kowalczk anyway.

This has been inevitable since the moment she stole my parking spot.

CHAPTER SIXTEEN

Bram

I drag in a deep breath, a lungful of jasmine-scented academic, and then I slide a hand to the nape of her neck and pull her away from the wall. I guide her over to my desk.

"Professor," she says in a low voice. "What are you doing?"

"You were right," I reply, and I allow myself the satisfaction of cupping her between the legs. God, she's so hot there, hot and soft, a place made for me to play around in. She squirms back against me with a moan, searching for friction, which I don't give. Instead, I turn and carefully yet unyieldingly push her back onto my desk (after moving her laptop, of course, I'm not *that* reckless). She's lying along the length of it, some papers for who-gives-a-fuck-what underneath her, and her legs are dangling off the edge. "I want to be good, but I can't when I'm around a bratty little thing like you."

Her chest lifts with a surprised inhale; I'm already pushing her shirt up to reveal the softness of her stomach, her deep navel, her stiff nipples.

"You're a good student, Ms. Kowalczk, or you can be when you apply yourself. Tell me: What should I do about this? About this woman living in my house who gets wet for me? Who says I can have her cunt and no one has to know?"

"Oh god," she moans, hips shifting on the desk. "You should—you should do whatever you want with her."

"You think so?"

She nods on the desk, hard enough to send some papers sliding off the edge, and her hands go to her tits, to her stomach and then push down, like it's agony not to touch herself right now.

I stop her. "I don't think so, Madelyn. I think it's very bad of you to touch yourself when you know very well I'm first in line to play with your pussy."

"What—what are you going to do?"

I exchange the dry erase marker for a Sharpie and pull off the cap. "I'm going to mark all the parts of you that I have plans for. I won't mark anywhere that'll be in public view, but the marks will linger for a week or two. Is that okay?"

Another series of fast nods that sends a stray highlighter rolling to the ground.

"Stay still," I order, and I scan her from her unraveling bun all the way down to her cute, be-socked feet. A transect of horniness, a survey of obsession. I'd mark every part of her if I could.

I take a steadying breath and then lean over her, my brows coming together as I focus on my task. Her tits—yes, those need marking, certainly. I use the wet tip of my Sharpie to catalog the most urgent things I want to do. *Kiss, slap, squeeze, press together and fuck.* She shivers as I write metadata on the underside of both breasts, taking care to label each hard nipple. *Lick. Suck. Bite.*

I move down her stomach, *kiss kiss kiss*, and then write in the creases of her waist and the swells of her hips, *Grab, hold, stroke, bruise*. Each letter must tickle, because her ribs jerk ever so slightly, but she doesn't complain and I don't stop.

I pull her shorts off her hips, and then shake my head when I see the wet spot on her underwear. "You've been neglecting this again," I chide. "Do you need me to take care of it?"

"Yes." The word leaves her lips on an exhale, like she's been keeping it hidden in her lungs. "Yes, Dr. Loe. I need you to take care of it always."

"Hmm." I work her panties down and off her legs, and a pained, angry arousal stabs me in the groin when I get a good look at what I've uncovered.

Wet, pretty, with flat, silky curls and a swollen pink pearl at the top.

I peel off her socks, lift her feet up so that they're flat on the desk and her knees are pointed at the ceiling, and then I push her thighs apart and look my fill. My dick is hard enough to make an obscene tent in my joggers, my balls *ache*, heavy and full, and I won't deny myself this. Not when it's being so freely offered. Not when I've finally allowed myself to have it.

Finally, I squat down between her legs, take the marker, and start writing on the pale, velvety skin of her inner thigh. *Rub, kiss, suck, lick, fuck with my fingers, fuck with my tongue, fuck with my cock, ejaculate on, ejaculate inside of, have sit on my face.* I draw a neat arrow to her sex, and then to the cinched button below.

By the time I'm finished, she's shivering on the desk as if she's come down with a lethal fever. "Please," she whimpers. "Make me come. Fuck me and make me come."

I cap the marker and inspect my work like I'm about to submit it for peer review. My handwriting, while not as pretty as hers, is neat and matter-of-fact, made scrupulous by years of taking notes in classrooms and forests and prairie fields. She is an ordered index of hoped-for debauchery. She is as tidy as a lab report.

She looks fucking stunning wearing nothing but my handwriting and a rucked-up T-shirt.

"I'm going to fuck you with my cock now." My voice is rough, the need in it evident. "Does that sound good to you?"

"God, yes."

"Can you come on me like a good girl when I do?"

A vigorous nod.

"Let me just find a condom, I think I have one in my bag—"

"Professor—Bram—we don't have to." She's speaking quickly, and I think it's to prevent the protest already rising to my lips. "I've got an IUD, and I was tested after I broke up with Gentry, because of his history. I'm good to go, and you've already told me that you haven't been with anyone other than me since Sara."

I hesitate. After two surprise pregnancies, one *catastrophically* a surprise and one more of an *oh, what the hell, why not* kind of surprise, I don't take going without a condom lightly. For Maddie's future even more than my own, since my life is already woven into an I-only-own-plastic-cups nest to shelter young people. Her life is still completely hers and is still so, so fragile.

But also . . . I really want to. I really, really fucking want to. I want to so badly that my mouth is wet and my hands are shaking.

"Are you sure?" I confirm, meeting her eyes. "Completely sure?"

"Absolutely," she says, and then lifting her chin a little like the brat she is, she adds coyly, "But if you don't want to leave your come inside me when you're finished, then I guess I understand."

I growl, leaning over her and nipping at her lip. "You're trying to provoke me."

She makes a noise of agreement. "And I'd say it's working, wouldn't you?"

I press a full kiss to her mouth now. I explore her lips with the same exactitude with which I'd document what I found inside a quadrat frame, and then I invite myself inside her mouth and do the same. Stroking her tongue with mine, searching out every bit of her.

"What would you have written on my lips if you could have?" she whispers against my kiss.

I push the waist of my joggers down as I answer her. *"Kiss. Fuck. Push my fingers inside."* I move between her legs. *"Argue with. Listen to. Stare at while you tell me all the ways con law is taught incorrectly."*

"I'm glad that's one of your kinks because it will happen a lot regardless," she replies. She's smiling. She's on my desk in my old T-shirt and some Sharpie, papers everywhere, her work forgotten, and she's about to take me between the legs, and she's smiling like she's pulled one over on me.

Maybe she has. I can't say I mind at the moment.

I take my aching length in hand and press the head against her. She's slippery and hot enough to kill someone, and I trace the path from clit to hole several times before carefully fitting myself to her opening. Just an inch, just a barely inside inch, and my testicles have pulled close to my body, tight and hard. Sweat erupts near my hairline and on my chest.

I stop and pantingly brace one hand on the desk by her hip. I keep the other wrapped around the part of me that needs her so much.

She reaches up to touch my hair. "You okay?" she asks softly, her smile now one of concern.

I nuzzle back against her touch, still fighting for control. "The last person I was with—my ex-wife—couldn't do hormonal birth control because of her migraines. So it's been seventeen years since I've gone inside someone bare," I explain. "I need a minute."

"Seventeen years? So not even when Sara was pregnant with the twins?"

"She was on partial bed rest with the twins the whole pregnancy."

Maddie blinks. "What's *partial* bed rest?"

"It's when you can still do some sitting or standing, but only for short periods of time, and no sex, obviously. Because of the prostaglandins, and also the risk of contractions after orgasm." I pause. "This is weird to talk about while I'm touching your vagina, Madelyn."

She gives me a mischievous look. "But are you still going to blow your wad?"

With some elation, I realize she's right, that the climax has backed off a little. "You're an evil genius."

"You've already got my panties off, Professor, you don't have to sweet-talk me anymore."

I let out a short laugh as I flex my hips and push in again. Another inch, slicker and hotter than the first. Tight enough to make a lover see stars. Fuck.

I give her more, and more, and watch as my erection disappears inside, as I impale myself in slick Maddie right next to the stark, unequivocal words I wrote on her thighs. Possessiveness surges through me, delight at the juxtaposition of my words and her soft skin, at my greedy dick plundering amid all of it, and I'm turning into such a fucking satyr, but I don't even care, I *can't* care when I'm now all the way inside her, when she's making these soft, helpless noises and wrapping her legs around me and trying to pull me closer.

"You're so tight," I groan, pulling back and giving her a slow stroke. "God, you feel amazing."

"Make me come," she begs. "Please. *Please*."

"Can you be a good girl and come fast for me, Maddie? I'm afraid I won't last, darling, you feel too goddamn good."

She nods, wide-eyed and almost serious, like this is life-or-death, and it feels like it, it's got to be life-or-death, because why else would my heart be pounding like it's trying to escape my chest? Why else would I have goose bumps on my arms and no air in my lungs and tunnel vision only for her?

I tear my eyes away from her beautifully flushed face and look down to where I'm wedged into a slick heaven. I don't need to lick my thumb before I trace over her clit—there's so much slippery arousal between us that she's wet everywhere, and within a minute of working her with the focus of a scientist and scholar, I feel her grow even wetter. When I start thrusting, I can *hear* us, I can hear my dick moving in and out of her.

She likes small, firm motions on her clit and steady thrusts of my cock, and soon she's murmuring frantic, half-hummed words about that big part of me and how good it feels and how she wants to come on my tongue tomorrow, how she wants to ride my fingers after our morning classes. She wants me to pump her full and then she wants it to leak out of her all night. She wants me to leave handprints on her ass and then fuck her from behind; she wants to sit on my face and pull on my hair.

Every muscle in my body is taut, flexed hard against the relentless onslaught of raw desire coming from Maddie's lips, because it's hard enough to be inside her, stroking myself with her, skin to skin, but to hear the absolute filth she wants, the filth I now want to do to her . . .

It's a miracle that I make it until her back arches and she gasps my name. It's a miracle that I last through the rippling convulsions of her slick inner channel, which caress me, pulse against me, kinetic proof that I've given this girl what she needs.

And it's a miracle that when I do lose the fight and start spilling into her with a low, tearing growl, my hips moving fast and hard and my desk jerking across the floor, that I remember she wants to do this again. And again. And again.

That despite my vaunted decorum and ethics, despite all the reasons not to, we're going to have a secret bad idea starting right now.

I get to have pussy for breakfast tomorrow, and I come so hard that my stomach cramps and my vision blurs, and I let Maddie pull me down on top of her and stroke my hair as I stay buried inside and determinedly make plans for the most important meal of the day.

CHAPTER SEVENTEEN

Maddie

True to his word, Bram eats pussy for breakfast. Religiously. Like he's a growing boy.

After I told him about a favorite fantasy of mine, I wake up to find him between my legs; other mornings he greets me in the kitchen, while we prepare the girl's lunches before they wake up, and he bends me over the counter, devouring me from behind.

It's fucking filthy and I can't get enough of it.

Whether it's Bram's lessons or the release of tension every morning and on most nights, I show up to class relaxed and confident.

Even Junie, who graciously accepted my apology for snapping at her after my coffee incident, notices. "Don't take this the wrong way, but you look like you've been sleeping for ten hours every night for the last week and a half."

"New mattress," I explain, which isn't a total lie.

"That must be it," she agrees as I follow her through the stacks with my coffee cup in hand.

"And," my voice drops to a whisper, "I might have gotten a new vibrator." Because as much as I want to bond with Junie over world-class dick, riding my boss's face every morning like it's a roller coaster with no lines is still very much a secret.

Her cheeks pinken. "Oh!"

"Junie," I gently tease. "Does the word *vibrator* make you blush?"

"I am an adult woman," she quietly announces.

"That you are."

She nods once in affirmation.

"Junie Ellis, you do own a vibrator, right?"

She crouches down and studies the spine of an art history text on Louisiana Creole art before calling, "Just a minute!" With cheeks still just as flushed, she stands. "I better go help that student."

"I didn't hear anything."

She taps her ear as she flees the scene of the crime. "Librarian super-hearing."

As I walk over to my class, I resolve to corrupt Junie Ellis even if only a little bit.

Today my lecture is on the electoral college—a topic I have so many thoughts on that I don't even need notes. The last of my students trickle in just a minute before the start of class, and among them is an older woman I don't recognize in a loose pantsuit. She wears no makeup and her waves are pulled back with a . . . binder clip, I think? Frustratingly, the whole disheveled thing works for her—a privilege that only thin women are sometimes allowed to get away with. The look says *I'm busy and I eat nails for breakfast, but I put on this suit because I am playing the game. By the way, fuck you.*

Fundamentals of Being a Good Girl

Or maybe she's just another academic or administrator sitting in on my class. Something that is totally allowed, but it takes a good thirty seconds to convince myself to ignore her.

Besides, it's electoral college day and I have so, so many things to rant about.

I am unsurprised to learn that at least 40 percent of my class have no clue what the fuck the electoral college is. Another 40 percent are vaguely aware. The remaining 20 percent are either asleep *or* are the kind of kids who registered to vote on their eighteenth birthdays.

I don't know if it's my passion for how absolutely ludicrous this system of electing a president is or if this is the gradual result of my early morning class truly warming up to me, but most of my students are scandalized. And then—because it's the democratic way—they are disheartened by the unnecessary complexity of the electoral college.

One guy in the third row is anxiously running a hand through his hair as he verbally pieces it together. "So you're saying the whole country can choose one candidate, but if the math doesn't work out, the other person can still win?"

"But that's probably never even happened," says the person behind him.

"If only that were true," I say.

The class erupts then and I can feel their excitement in my toes. By the time class ends, the lecture hall feels like a beating heart, alive and engaged. I don't know if teaching is it for me or if it's just the first stop on the road of post–law school life, but I forgot how good it feels to have a group of people hanging on your every word.

Sure enough, Dr. Wallace is shooing me out of class, but I don't even care because my students are crowding around me, continuing the conversation, and I think I even catch a slight furrow in the great professor's brows that hint at jealousy. I smile at him prettily.

My students scatter as I make my way down the hall and I feel downright smug. I preen at the thought of telling Bram what a good girl I was today. Maybe I'll be rewarded—

"You're a hard woman to find."

I stop on the fourth step up to the department offices and turn around.

The woman in the suit leans against the banister at the bottom of the stairs.

My first response is fear. Who could possibly need to find me? I haven't violated any of Gentry's NDAs. I'm pretty sure the banks don't send out reminders in human form when your loans are about to come due. And Stale Doughnut Boy has retreated into sullen apathy (without any more gotcha livestreams).

After I realize I have no one to hide from, I stand a little taller with my shoulders pinned back.

"I'm not lost," I tell her as I double back down the stairs but remain standing on the bottom step so I can maintain an equal height with her.

She smiles then, and the way her lips widen is unsettling in a way that I am deeply intrigued by. "Maddie, I would like to speak with you. Perhaps we could grab a coffee if you're free?"

"Are you from a cult or something? I'm not interested unless you do the sort of polygamy where the women get to have multiple marriages." I start to walk back up the stairs when her next question stops me in my tracks.

"Have you ever thought about running for office?"

And then I laugh, because I have to. I have to laugh at the idea of something that would hurt too much to actually want.

She doesn't share my sense of humor, though. "Political office is funny to you?"

I pull my fingers together in front of my face and take a deep breath as an attempt to reset my demeanor.

"Ma'am—I'm sorry. I don't know your name—"

"Veronica Balentine. Now you know my name."

"Okay, well, I don't know you, Veronica, or why you think this is a good idea, but I've spent the last four years of my life in focus-group purgatory and I don't plan on making a second trip."

She digs her fists into her pockets and scuffs her heel against the carpet but says nothing, and I am way too satisfied with myself for having silenced Ms. Veronica Balentine.

"That life wasn't for you," she says once I've reached the landing halfway up the staircase. "You were just some boy's chess piece. Trying to fit into a mold that would eventually suffocate you." She drums her fingers against the banister, plotting her next move. "I'm going to go sit in that student union coffee shop for the next two hours. If I don't see or hear from you, I'll assume I have your answer."

I SAT IN the adjunct office for one hour and forty-seven minutes. Most of that time was spent staring at the blinking cursor in the Google search bar. With thirty minutes left on the clock, I'd typed *Veronica Balentine* and hit Enter.

There was approximately one photo in the image search of a much younger Veronica who seemed to give as few fucks as present-day Veronica. The search results were lacking, and if I had to guess that was on purpose. Veronica's name was only rarely mentioned in a handful of articles, where she was named as an adviser or consultant and once as a reliable source.

Penelope Pike and her firm were not under-the-radar people. They had a website, to start. But she and her firm also gave the occasional interview and were routinely reported on. But Veronica Balentine—whoever she might be—seemed to work in the shadows. And like her wolfish grin, that was enough to force me to stand up and walk my ass over to the student union.

As I sit down across from Veronica in the far corner of the Viper's Den,* she checks her phone. "I really expected to leave after two hours only to run into you on my way out of the building, but you're full of surprises, aren't you, Madelyn Claire Kowalczk?"

"I'm only here because your existence is basically scrubbed from the internet and I'm curious how anyone accomplishes that in the age of live-streaming your cat's birthday party and digging a tunnel under your house." I'm also curious to know how someone like Veronica even got my name to begin with, but I'm not showing all my cards at once.

"I like you," she tells me, and then leans forward, her elbow on the table and her chin cradled in her hand. "Speaking of live-streaming, that was quite the impression you made. What was it you referred to the student as? A *stale doughnut*?" She glances up and down the dark green silk blouse that I'd been told not to wear to a fundraising event because it read as a somber color. "You look much more put together today sans coffee stains. Though we will have to do something about those roots."

---

* Also the name of the basement in the family home Leo and Sloane lived in during their college years. The original Viper's Den may or may not be the original location of the first Best Night Ever.

Instinctively, I touch a hand to the crown of my head. I know I should at least try to cover the dark roots at home, but I've noticed that the new growth feels smoother. Healthier.

"I guess the perk of getting off social media earlier this year is that I don't have to witness myself go viral." I've never been one of those people who only saw the evils of social media, but after the breakup with Gentry, it was impossible to scroll through my feed without seeing someone we mutually knew or even tagged posts with Gentry himself. It should come as no surprise that I didn't retain custody of any of our friends. Calling them friends in the first place is probably a misnomer. Everyone in Gentry's circle existed to serve a purpose, and without Gentry, I had nothing to offer.

"I wouldn't go so far as to say you went viral. At least not outside the Astra University social media ecosystem. For what it's worth, I scoured that kid's online presence, and he really is a stale doughnut."

"I've always been a good judge of character." Except that wasn't true. How could it be when I'd let myself believe that Gentry was the person I should spend the rest of my life with?

"I had the video removed, by the way. Consider it a gift."

"Sounds more like a favor," I tell her. "And I really don't like being in the red."

She nods, and I can see that my response tickles her. "I'm looking for a fresh face to take over a House seat in four years."

"So this is just window-shopping?" I ask. "Checking out some far-fetched possibilities before the party settles on the same old white-bread wonder boy?"

"First off, I don't work for the party. Any party," she says with disgust.

I lean back in my seat, establishing some distance. I don't know that I ever do want to run for office, but getting mixed up with backroom, unsanctioned politics before whatever career I choose has even begun feels like a really sketchy start.

Veronica rolls her eyes, seeing right through me. "Don't get your ethically made period panties in a bunch. My work is legal. Technically. I am hired by donors to . . . acquaint myself with up-and-coming talent in the political arena. If a donor happens to like something I've found, then it's completely aboveboard for me to take the party chair out for coffee and talk shop. Drop a name or two."

"So your job is to find candidates that donors want to throw money at?"

She measures me for a moment as she chooses her next approach. "Maddie, don't pretend like you don't know how the sausage is made, or even that you find it distasteful. I've met plenty of idealistic prospects in this line of work. While I was highly impressed by the work you did with the Wade Foundation and even with the papers you wrote for your school's law review, you know that most victories require someone's hands to get dirty. Let's say I rub my hands in the dirt so that no one else has to."

"And what's in it for you? I'm guessing this whole *hardly put together* look of yours is by design too?"

"Blending in is underrated. And even though this meeting is about you and certainly not about me, I'll tell you that the only thing greater than being the king is being the kingmaker."

Her words send goose bumps up my arms, and I think that what she's saying should feel seedy. Immoral. But I appreciate her frankness. I might even find it a little bit sexy. "How did you even get my name?" I ask. "I am literally a footnote in Gentry's campaign, and I definitely haven't made any connections since I moved back to Kansas. Actually, never mind," I tell her. "It was nice meeting with you. You can send your little report on me up the chain. We both know that this first meeting is likely to be our last."

"The House campaign is in four years, Maddie, but next fall we have a state house seat and a couple of high-visibility municipal offices with wide-open fields. I think it would be a great chance for you to get your name out there before running for higher office. If everything pans out, the state campaign would kick off in January in the lead-up to the primaries. It wouldn't be much, but you'd be compensated out of the campaign funds. My donors own real estate. Some own law firms. We could get you a place and an employer to get you through until you would hopefully win your seat and take office. All of that is phase two."

"And what's phase one?"

"Donor support and party support. Then you launch your campaign."

"You don't strike me as the type of person to put all your eggs in one basket, Veronica."

She grinned that same wicked grin. "You know, you're almost too smart to be a politician. Just on the cusp, really. But yes, I've got a few horses in the race, though I'll admit that you're my current favorite."

"I'm your current favorite? Really? Some recently graduated law school student who hasn't even passed the bar and has no experience running for office?"

"A clean slate is a good slate." She pauses for a beat. "Miranda Salazar, by the way. Your department chair. That's how I got your name. She mentioned you at a dinner the other night. Miranda isn't easy to impress, so if she name-dropped you, I figured you'd be worth a look."

My chest flutters at the thought of someone like Miranda, who I am possibly starting to idolize, even thinking of me when I'm not in her presence. Let alone mentioning my name in conjunction with running for office. To stop myself from grinning like an absolute nimrod, I bite down on my tongue until I can taste the sharp, metallic tang of blood.

"And what if I'm interested?" I finally ask when I can almost trust myself to play it cool.

"Keep your head on straight. I see you're nannying right now on the side."

"Do I even want to know how you know that?"

She stands and tucks her phone in her pocket along with her car key. "Don't do anything stupid like fuck the dad."

I freeze, and she watches me for a moment, the crease above her nose pinched together. Then she laughs.

"I'll be in touch, Maddie. You really brought the heat with that lecture today, by the way."

"Veronica. Wait."

She turns back to me.

"I might be a realist, but I do have some very firmly held beliefs. Things I won't waver on. You should know that."

"Good," she says. "People get real boners for conviction."

"What about you?" I ask. "What are your convictions? I'm guessing your job isn't rooted in loyalty."

She laughs again. "I am convicted by money." She wiggles her fingers. "Dirty fingers come with a high price tag. Even if they're just a little bit dirty, dirt is dirt."

That afternoon, I pick up the twins and take them to their first gymnastics class. They'd begged Bram to sign them up after falling down a gymnastics rabbit hole on YouTube and we both had high hopes that it would serve to tire them out.

I sit on the bleachers and take a few videos to send to Bram while I replay my chat with Veronica Balentine. I know that I shouldn't—Veronica practically advertised her red flags, after all, and I know she seems to live in the same universe as Penelope Pike—but I like her.

Being with Gentry and working with Penelope felt like I was being handled with kid gloves. They were constantly searching for gentle ways to say very harsh things. Even though I didn't want to hear most of what was said to me, my stomach curdled at the way I was treated like I was fragile and that any word might be the one to break me.

But in my short time with Veronica, she spoke to me like an adult who could grasp the nuances of being both widely palatable and full of enough substance to actually stand for something.

When the twins and I get back home, there is a very nice red sports car in the driveway.

"Auntie Sloane!" Letty yells as they both barrel out of the back seat.

I follow them through the front door, and sitting there perched on the arm of the couch is a woman so stunning I have to stop myself from drooling over what a total mommy she is.

Fern is laying with her head resting against the woman's thigh like a pillow while the woman smooths her dark hair.

"You must be Maddie," the woman says as she gently lifts Fern's head and stands to greet me.

She wears tailored trousers that nip in at the waist and hug the wide curve of her hips and a sleeveless mock turtleneck with no bra, showing off her perfectly sloped shoulders and the subtle tease of nipples under the fabric. She looks like old money and sex—the kind you have to beg for.

"And I'm guessing you're Sloane."

She nods as she returns to the arm of the sofa and continues to play with Fern's hair. "I was just telling Fern here that it might be time for a makeover befitting a student body president."

The twins' feet pound overhead along with the sounds of Hester Prynne's nails scraping against the floor after them.

I empty the contents of my pockets onto the coffee table. My keys, my phone, and Veronica's card.

Sloane's cool gaze sweeps over the card as I sit down. "Have you heard of her?" I ask. "Veronica Balentine?"

All she gives me is a noncommittal *mmm*.

"A makeover?" I ask Fern. "I can't think of a better way to throw Simon off his game."

She nods, her gaze falling past my shoulders as she concentrates on some hypothetical version of herself. "I need something that says powerful but not intimidating. At least that's what Jules thinks."

"I like where Jules's head is at." I run my fingers through my hair, remembering what Veronica said about my atrocious roots. "Honestly, I've got to do something with my hair too."

Fern shoots up and bounces. "Oh my god, Maddie, you have to come with us. She can, right, Aunt Sloane?"

Sloane tilts her head toward me. "My hair guy doesn't take new clients, but luckily I only trade in favors, so I think we can get Maddie in right after you, Fern."

"Oh, that would be great." Except that if Sloane's hair guy is anything like I'm expecting, I definitely can't afford him. But I don't want to say no and reject her goodwill.

Besides, if I can't take care of my hair, what does that say about my ability to take care of constituents?

If constituents were even a thing I was going to have . . .

But I can't ignore how positively alive I feel at the prospect of this challenge. Right now, I am hungry in a way I haven't been for years. It's the kind of hunger that Gentry never left any room for. But without him or Penelope here to tell me I should shrink myself to fit the needs of his campaign, I let myself wonder: Someone's got to run. Why the hell shouldn't it be me?

CHAPTER EIGHTEEN

Bram

I'm humming as I carefully Jenga the month's Costco run into the back of my car. Applesauce, Pirate's Booty, enough bananas to make Sir Joseph Paxton wet his button-fly trousers, and then a box of Pocky sticks the size of a small shipping container for Fern.

I also picked up a box of plums for Maddie, because she steals them like a William Carlos Williams narrator, and also I enjoy watching her eat them very much. Just this morning, she took a bite out of a ripe, juicy plum at a stop sign as we were driving to campus together, and I stared at her mouth with such undisguised hunger that she unbuckled her seat belt, shifted to her knees, and . . .

Well. Thank God for the empty parking lot behind the basketball arena.

I can still feel the soft stretch of her lips around me.

I've progressed to whistling as I push the awkwardly wide cart into a corral, and I'm still whistling when I feel my phone pulse in

Fundamentals of Being a Good Girl

my pocket. I pull it out to see a text from Joey to the Andromeda Club group chat.

> **JOEY FUCKING KEMP:** Emergency Andromeda Club meeting. Bram's House. Now.

What???
NO.
I duck into my car and furiously try to tap out a response as the chat blows up.

> **ALESSANDRO:** I'M HERE IN MOUNT ASTRA I CAN FINALLY COME OMG

> **LEO:** We are aware how sticky Bram's house is, correct?

> **SLOANE:** I get off work in just a few minutes!

> **SARA:** If my signal is good enough, I want to call in to the meeting!

> **LEO:** . . . from the glacier?

> **ME:** Guys. Wait. We can't have an emergency meeting at my house.

> **JOEY FUCKING KEMP:** It has to be your house, Bram!!! Alessandro and Leo live in KC and no one wants to drive out to Lucien's weird compound.

I pause. This is true. Per the divorce arrangements, Lucien Méchant is giving Sloane four months of sole occupancy at his giant place outside KC, Persimmon Hill, but it's a drive from Mount Astra, and also it's really difficult to achieve casual human connection in a house with a dressage arena out back.

> **ME**: Let's meet at YOUR house, then.

> **JOEY FUCKING KEMP**: It can't be my house, dude! Riley is pissed at me and told me she couldn't look at my face tonight!

Oh, fuck me. Ugh. *Fine.*

> **ME**: In that case, emergency meeting at my house, but I have to get the twins to bed at eight. And no one is allowed to eat Fern's Pocky.

> **LEO**: Is Cole McKenney coming?

> **LEO**: That's right, he's not.

> **LEO**: Because he isn't real.

"And that's how we're related to the Medicis," Dr. Alessandro Ottaviano is saying as I stride in from the back door to find Maddie perched on an ottoman and staring raptly at him as he holds court in my armchair. He's wearing a three-piece suit, shoes from a brand I can't pronounce, and has his ankle propped on his opposite knee in a posture of erudite elegance.

He is also inexcusably handsome, with a long nose, thick brows, and smile lines bracketing a sculpted mouth that wouldn't look out of place on an ancient statue. He has russet-brown skin, tight curls that he's wearing a little longer these days, and glinting dark brown eyes that Maddie can't seem to stop staring at.

He throws her a quick wink after name-dropping the Medicis, and she beams back at him. I am abruptly grumpy.

"And of course, we're still the princes of Ottaviano—"

"Okay, okay, that's enough story time for now," I cut in before Maddie can absorb that Alessandro is (very, very *conditionally*) sort of royalty. "Maybe you should check on the twins—"

"Bram, is Sara's dog out? I need to run back to the car to grab the Perrier," says Sloane from behind me in the kitchen.

"Hester's upstairs watching a movie with the girls," Maddie volunteers, and Sloane nods and turns back to the door.

Alessandro eyes me from beneath his long lashes, as if wanting to study my reaction, and then leans toward Maddie with a lift of one of his adept surgeon's hands. I step forward to block her from seeing his handsomeness and undisputedly talented fingers, and then my front door flies open to reveal Leo holding a bottle of scotch, and—for no reason that I can immediately discern—a pumpkin.

"I see I'm tardy," he says. Then he sees Alessandro and stops. Looks down at his own pewter-blue two-piece and brown shoes. "You look better than me today. Fuck you."

"I always look better than you," Alessandro says, glancing down at his perfectly manicured nails.

"Bold words from a man who wears blue pajamas to work." Leo sniffs and then walks over to me and hands me the pumpkin. "Here's a pumpkin," he says, unnecessarily, and then moves past me into the kitchen with no further explanation.

Torn between setting the pumpkin somewhere pumpkins should go and making it so Alessandro can't impress Maddie anymore, I hover for a second or two, then decide to walk over to Maddie while holding the heavy orb.

Sloane opens the back door again with a nudge of her hip, carrying a cardboard flat of glass Perrier bottles that thunk and rattle on their way to the kitchen island.

"Where did you just *find* enough Perrier to supply an emergency Andromeda meeting?" I ask, instead of the real question, which is *Why didn't you bring a cardboard flat of Diet Coke instead?*[*]

Sloane freezes, like I've just asked her where she scores molly. "Uh," she says. "Um. Just a place."

"Just a place?"

"A place. A normal place. Like most people have. You know, normal."

Before I can follow up on this, the front door opens *again*. This time to reveal a tearful Joey, who is carrying nine pizza boxes.

"Hell is empty!" Alessandro says cheerfully.

"Joey, that is a lot of pizza," I observe.

He sniffles, tears running into his beard. "Why are you holding a pumpkin?"

"It's Leo's fault."

"You're supposed to bring your host flowers, Joey," Leo says,

---

[*] An important question when a full majority of those assembled work in education.

coming back from the kitchen with a glass of scotch. "Which you'd know if you weren't born amongst the proletariat."

"But you didn't bring me flowers," I say to Leo. "You brought me a pumpkin."

Leo takes a sip of his drink. "It's seasonal."

"It's a squash," Alessandro says.

Still holding nine pizzas, Joey says, "Pretty sure a pumpkin is a vegetable?"

"Botanically speaking, there's no such thing as a vegetable," I inform them for the ten millionth time since college.

Groans erupt all over the room.

"A pumpkin is a fruit—a *berry*," I say over their collective complaining. "And it's really a berry, unlike raspberries, for example, which are aggregate fruits. Aggregate fruits are easy to confuse with multiple fruits, by the way, but the difference—"

"Someone stop him before he gets to plant ovaries," says Leo.

The only other person in the room who had to remember the word *eukaryote* after graduation, Alessandro says, "Wait, I'm enjoying this. Do drupelets next."

"Will someone help me with the pizzas?" Joey asks in a disconsolate voice, and Maddie is the first to move, going over to take the stack of boxes.

"I'll bring some pizza up to the girls," she says as she passes me. "And I'll let Fern know there's some here when she comes home from the newspaper meeting."

"Thank you," I say, and then quieter: "I'll come up and check on the girls in thirty minutes. You'll be done working then."

I've learned that Maddie struggles with maintaining one particular boundary, and that's walking away from work (which I understand when work follows you around and asks you to read an

Elephant and Piggie book just ooone mooooore tiiiime) but it's cleanest and best for everyone if we keep Maddie's childcare hours carefully delineated from her non-childcare hours. I asked her to move in so that she wouldn't be shivering in a truck stop parking lot, not because I was trying to *Sarah, Plain and Tall* her.

Anyway, I've also learned it's easier if I simply *tell* her she's not allowed to work any longer, and so that's what I've started doing. If she needs someone to boss her into taking time for herself—someone to be the bad guy so she doesn't feel guilty doing things like eating, showering, sleeping, et cetera—then I'm happy to be the asshole. The asshole who makes sure she takes care of herself.

Plus, I would be lying if I said that it doesn't turn me on a little bit how squirmy she gets when I tell her what to do.

Like right now, when she ducks her head to hide her blush as she answers, "Yes, Bram." I want to press my lips to the blush, but I can't, because Joey Fucking Kemp has turned my living room into a nest of snakes and pizza. And they don't know about . . . well, they don't know about any of it. Us.

"Good girl," I murmur approvingly, and Maddie's cheeks flame even brighter.

She does dare a glance over to the others in the living room, where Alessandro is trying to steal Leo's scotch while Joey is looking on with tears running freely into his wet beard.

"Is he going to be okay?" she whispers, concerned.

How to explain? "Joey cries when the Chiefs lose a game. And when they win a game. He cries when his girls bring him art from school. Once he cried because he saw a very tall tree."

Maddie, whom I'm beginning to suspect only cries once annually, blinks at the giant bearded man wiping his face. "Oh."

"He'll be fine. We'll get some pizza in him and then we'll figure out what he and Riley fought about and then everything will be okay. You'll see."

"And so nothing will ever be okay again," wails Joey twenty minutes later.

We're circled in my living room, Sara on a phone propped against a bottle of Perrier, and Joey on my couch while Leo leans against the wall near my office, freshly en-scotched. Alessandro is still in my armchair, Sloane is next to Joey, and I'm sitting on the floor.

There's a moment of profound silence as we all process what Joey's just told us.

"Well," Sara finally says from the phone. "This is very triggering for me."

"And me," I add.

"Another Kemp baby," drawls Leo. "What does this make? Seven?"

"Four," Joey corrects glumly. "Four, and Riley says it's all my fault because I didn't use a condom the night she probably got pregnant. But the condoms were so far away!"

"Joey," Sloane begins in a delicate tone. "Does Riley want any support visiting a clinic or help getting mifepristone? Because I help students with reproductive health every day, and it would be no trouble."

"No, she wants four kids," Joey says, and sighs down at his last slice of pizza. "So we're doing it."

"She wants four kids?" Alessandro asks. "Then . . . why the pizza and the tears? Why is she angry with you?"

"Because she didn't want the fourth so close to the third." Joey's eyes fill as he picks up the slice. "She says it means we'll have two in diapers at the same time, and she's worried all the extra work of a new baby is going to fall on her, because I'll have to keep an eye on the big girls."

We ponder this. Joey is a good dad—if occasionally clueless—but four kids present some logistics issues even good parents can't easily parkour over.

"I mean, we did two kids in diapers at the same time, didn't we, Sara?" I ask my ex-wife, who is inside a motel room that looks like it's calibrated to the comforts of wind-grizzled fishermen. (Asher is behind her on the bed, wearing noise-canceling headphones and bopping while they do something with an Excel spreadsheet.) "How did we do it with the twins?"

Sara squints at nothing, trying to remember. "It's all a blur, honestly. And we were divorced by their first birthday, so maybe we're not the best people to take advice from."

That's true. "We did get very efficient at changing diapers, though," I say. "And we even did cloth diapers."

"Perhaps a factor in the divorce?" remarks Leo.

"My point is," I tell Joey, "maybe you can prove to Riley that you can find ways to make it easier on her?"

He stops chewing, swallows. "Like . . . like figuring out how to change diapers faster?" He looks hopeful for the first time since he got here.

"Sure," I say encouragingly. "That's a great start."

"When is she due?" Sloane asks.

"The middle of May."

We all exchange glances, including with Sara on the phone.

"Bro, it's October," Sara says. "She's, like, for-real pregnant."

"Well, she didn't know because she still hasn't gotten her period after Oksana, so it wasn't like she was late or anything. She was going in for some lower back pain today, and they wanted to do an X-ray, so they tested her first. And . . . surprise." The hopeful look has faded a little bit now. "Fuck, guys. This wasn't supposed to happen for another year or two."

Sloane rubs his shoulder and I decide it's time for beer.

"When do you need to be home?" I ask Joey before I select a craft beer to bring to him.

"I don't know. Never. By the time I came home from work, her sisters were there, and—" He shudders and we all shudder with him. Riley's sisters are formidable, and when they perceive injury done to one of their own, they form an impenetrable phalanx of judgmental looks and muttered remarks.

"Stay here tonight," I say, without thinking, and then remember the roommate that no one (but Sara) knows about. Shit. "Uh, or with Sloane. Or something. I'm grabbing something for us to drink!"

Very smooth.

I go into the kitchen and Sloane half follows me, peeling off to go into the dining room and rummage around my credenza for some gin. Leo and Alessandro have started offering less-than-helpful advice to Joey, interspersed with some actual advice from Sara, and so no one's paying Sloane and me much attention when she walks into the kitchen with a bottle of Tom's Town and says, apropos of nothing, "Have you ever heard of Veronica Balentine?"

My hands still over the bottle of beer I'm cracking open. "Yes," I say slowly. It's like asking if I've heard of nuclear reactors. Veronica Balentine can be used to power NICU incubators or blight entire landscapes. "She was the reason we took Topeka in the last election. But she also brokered that endowment to Geology from a *very evil* petroleum company."

"She's a sellsword," says Sloane as she gets a martini glass from a cabinet. "Her skills go to the highest bidder. I ran into her a lot via Lucien's, ah, circle."

Circle sounds so much better than *camarilla of rich monsters*.

"What about her?" I ask, and pop the cap off the beer. I attempt a joke to hide how much I don't like Veronica Balentine. "Does she want to endow Ecology next? We could probably find a way to do moss for capitalism."

Sloane's expression doesn't change.

"You're right, moss would actually be really hard to do for capitalism. Except, well, sphagnum is in its own category—"

"Veronica Balentine has been talking to Maddie," Sloane cuts in. "I think she might be tapping Maddie for office."

"Bram, where's your upstairs bathroom?" Alessandro asks from around the corner. "Leo is depriving me of the downstairs one."

"Up and to the right," I say absentmindedly. And then to Sloane, "Would you repeat that, please?"

Sloane uncorks the gin and pours some into her glass, then recorks the bottle before answering. "It's not certain—I mean, nothing in politics is real until you've filed, but it's looking like the party and the donors are in agreement: they want someone young. Maddie's got some name value from her work with the Wade Foundation, but she's still green and scandal-free. They want someone principled but maybe willing to get into the weeds a little. *Clean slate* is the current buzzword amongst those in the know." She takes a sip of straight gin and makes a face. "This needs something."

"A clean slate," I echo as Sloane starts opening up my cabinets and closing them again. "Like . . ."

"Like no affairs, no drugs, no secret money from Russia, no social media posts complaining about Disney's live-action remakes, no anything. Just a tabula rasa of a prestigious law degree, a pretty smile, and cleverness that Veronica will make sure is titrated out. You have to build up tolerance for an intelligent, strong-minded female politician, you know. Like how you can build up a tolerance for poison. Mithridatism, but for constituents."

I open a second bottle of beer. Thinking. Worrying. "Maddie hasn't said anything about this."

"She might not know how to bring it up." Sloane has found a cinnamon stick somewhere and sticks it in her gin. "How often do people immediately bring up future jobs to their current employers?"

I'm so much more to her than a current employer, but I can hardly say that, and I can hardly kick up a fuss about Maddie talking to Veronica Balentine when Sloane thinks my only contact with Maddie involves school pickup logistics and how to use an air fryer.

But then the worst possible thing happens.

Alessandro sticks his head around the opening to the kitchen and says, "Oh, Bra-a-*am*," in a singsong voice.

I look up at him, dreading whatever he's going to say next.

"Why is there a naked nanny in your upstairs bathroom?"

Of course this has to be when the living room conversation has organically fallen quiet. There's a brief pause, like the gap between a lightning strike and the clap of thunder, and then I hear the scrape of my couch, the glassy *thunk* of a drink being set down, a flurry of footsteps. Suddenly, I'm surrounded by Andromedas on all sides, all of them peering intently at me. They might as well be tasting the air, like actual snakes.

"Is Sara alone in the living room?" I ask, to delay the inevitable.

"She had to go," Leo says smoothly. "Now, about the naked nanny—"

"Is the nanny living here?" Joey asks.

"Childcare provider," I correct, pouring some firmness into my voice. The nanny talk is just for Maddie and me. "And she needed a place to stay, so I offered—"

"So she *is* living here?" Sloane asks. "Bram, what the fuck?"

I heave a deep breath. "Okay, yes. She's living here."

"Does Sara know?" is her loyal follow-up.

"Sara knows," I explain patiently. "I told her the day I offered my spare room to Maddie. She's living here until she can afford her own place because she spent the last four years dating an asshole. She's great with the kids, hilarious, smart, and it's just temporary. I have the room to spare."

They all stare at me with the same half-suspicious, half-amused expressions, and I regret everything in my life that means these people have known me for twenty years or more and can tell when I'm hiding something.

But that doesn't mean I can't keep trying to hide it. My breakfast of champions, my Sharpie notes, why the jasmine plant in my greenhouse gets me hard now, that should all be mine and mine alone.

"Anyway, back to Joey," I say quickly, grabbing a beer. "Let's have a toast to the fourth Kemp baby!"

CHAPTER NINETEEN

Maddie

The dark gray clouds are heavy and low above the fields of cornstalks. The rain cleared just long enough for the Mount Astra School District to go on as planned with their annual Fall Frenzy.

Mount Astra High School has two booths. Fern and Simon agreed that they would each take a booth and whoever raised the most money would decide what the funds from the event would be earmarked for. Fern wanted to dedicate money to making the menstrual products in the bathrooms free to use while Simon's plan was to fund a live band for prom instead of the usual DJ—who was just one of the teachers from the math department who called himself DJ Alge-bro. It's not that Simon's plan is bad. It's that Fern's is better. Which was why I highly encouraged her to use every advantage available to her.

The moment Leo heard there was competition to be had, he demanded that the Saint James Chocolate Co. sponsor Fern's booth.

So until just a moment ago, I've spent the last two hours helping Saint James employees and student volunteers give out free hot chocolate and s'mores truffles to everyone who purchases a ticket to the corn maze.

After I relinquish my apron to the next round of volunteers, I find a familiar scene just outside the tent.

"Where is that feckless little twat?" Sloane asks from where she stands with her arms crossed as she paces up and down the side of the Saint James Chocolate Co. sponsor tent. "Show your face, coward."

Bram stands at the mouth of the corn maze where Fern stationed him to take tickets. The orange volunteer T-shirt he wears over his green and black flannel is a size too small and stretches over his chest and biceps in a way that makes the other single parents notice and it's very difficult for me not to hiss at them in response. "I agree that Simon is a human stinkhorn mushroom, but maybe we could avoid calling Fern's copresident a twat. At least at a school function."[*]

"A stinkhorn would smell less like Target-brand body spray, at least," Sloane mutters.

"Or maybe he should avoid being a twat, has he ever considered that?" Leo asks lazily as he lounges on top of a picnic table between Sloane and Bram, his arms braced behind him and the core of an apple teetering next to his hip. He glances up and is immediately amused by my presence. "Ah, the nanny."

---

[*] Latin name for the stinkhorn family: Phallaceae. Originally called the *fungus virilis penis effigie* in the 1500s, and later called "the pricke mushroom" and "Hollanders workingtoole." (It looks like a penis.)

Fundamentals of Being a Good Girl

Bram's head snaps up and his pupils widen when he sees me. "Childcare provider," he corrects.

The smile I give Leo is nearly virginal, and Bram lets out a soft, involuntary hiss.

"Ah, the loiterer," I say to the chocolate magnate.

Leo scoffs, but I can see he's eager for a good verbal spar. "I am hardly a—"

"She's not wrong," Sloane chimes in as she taps a finger along the edge of her chin.

"You guys," Fern says, her face flushed as she rounds the corner.

Bram's attention immediately shifts. "What's wrong? Are you okay? Where are the twins?"

"Nothing. Yes. And with Jules and her family, because I had to run over here to tell you that Simon and I just raised the stakes of our bet. Whoever fundraises the least has to step down as co-president."

"Please say that was your idea," Leo says. "Does your ticket booth accept out of country wire transfers? We're going to bury this hormonal dipshit."

"Leo," Bram warns.

Fern snickers as Leo gives her a wink.

"No sketchy donations," Sloane says. "At least not yet. If Fern is going to win this thing, we need it to be above reproach."

Leo rolls his eyes and Fern skips off. "I have to go tell Jules!"

"Love you, sweetie!" Bram calls after her as he yanks the orange T-shirt over his head and tosses it right in Leo's face, which I'm sure is the first time his skin has ever come in contact with a polyester blend. "Cover for me."

"I'm not a volunteer," Leo clarifies. "I'm a sponsor."

"What's the difference?" Bram asks.

Sloane grins. "One has money and the other doesn't."

"Maddie and I are going to check on the kids," Bram tells the Saint James pair. "Be useful."

"Usefulness is so plebeian. You won't even let me buy my goddaughter the student government office she is rightfully owed," Leo calls as we press into the crowd and Bram's hand innocently hovers over the small of my back, his head shaking.

Behind us I can hear Leo and Sloane arguing over the fact that Joey is Fern's actual godfather. Leo calmly counters by saying that Joey is the royally appointed godfather and that Leo is the prime minister godfather elected by popular vote.

Terrell Farms is a historic working farm and former township just outside Mount Astra. It's the sort of place that exists for the sake of field trips and events just like this. And for the occasional wedding, if barn weddings are your thing. There are endless activities. Apple bobbing, face painting, cider stands, and hayrides.

"The twins should be pumpkin bowling with Jules and Fern," I tell Bram.

With his height, he only has to turn his head to confirm their location. But even with his memorable altitude, in this thronging sea of people, we are almost anonymous. It's too crowded for anyone to notice when his fingers wrap around my wrist and tug. "This way."

"What do you have in mind, Professor Loe?"

"We need to talk," he says

Well, that doesn't sound very sexy. Bram's been on edge for the last week, but I chalked it up to each of the three kids passing around a stomach bug. We haven't been alone together for days now, because if the currently sick kiddo wasn't with me, they were with Bram. He'd been on all-night dad duty with puke buckets and a rotation of kids curling up in his bed, except for Fern, who insisted on medicating with couch-and-documentary time.

His fingers slide against my palm until they're intertwined with mine. To an outsider, we might just look like two people together in a crowd trying to stay together, but this moment of us holding hands in public is not lost on me. An overwhelming part of me wants to let go and lose myself among the young families and rowdy teenagers, because even though I love the feeling of safety that comes with my hand tucked into Bram's, I am also fighting a sense of claustrophobia that tightens my throat.

But we're just fucking, I remind myself. He's pulling me along so that I don't get lost. He's not trying to publicly claim me or cage me into another long-term relationship where I am solely defined by my partner. We are simply holding hands. And having sex. A lot.

"You make it sound like I'm in trouble," I tell him in the hopes of distracting myself and getting a reaction from him.

"You very well might be," he says as we turn the corner around the side of the corn maze. But his tone isn't playful like it normally is.

In the distance behind the corn maze is a small white building that Bram seems to be walking toward. We're free of the crowd, and still, he holds my hand.

"What's going on?" A dozen different possibilities swirl in my head. Does the agency know I've broken their fraternization policy? What if Sara is pissed that I'm living in the house even though she seemed cool about it at first? Maybe one of the Andromeda Club members said something that made her change her mind?

"What do you want to do next, Madelyn?"

Next?

He asks it the same way your favorite teacher—the one whose attention you're always starved for—would, making it sound casual. Except it's not. It's one of those big, impossible questions.

"Well, getting an apartment is the priority."

"If none of that mattered," he says. "It does, obviously. But in the future. Teaching . . . is that what you want?"

A gust of wind whips around us, and Bram lets go of my hand only to pull me closer against his side.

My body sags against his. "I've missed this."

"It's been a very long week."

We approach the white building, which is labeled with a wooden sign that reads ORIGINAL TERRELL TOWNSHIP ONE-ROOM SCHOOLHOUSE IN USE FROM 1869–1963.

"Are you teaching me another lesson?" I ask as Bram opens the door for me.

"You didn't answer my question."

"Because I don't know if I have an answer." The door swings shut behind us. It's cold inside, but we're protected from the wind at least. There are about fifteen desks lined up in front of a teacher's desk with an old dusty chalkboard lining the far wall.

Bram weaves in and out of the rows, patiently silent because he knows that I'll talk. Eventually.

"I've been in survival mode for the last few months," I tell him. "I think I could love teaching one day. There are aspects I love about it now. But—"

"It's not enough."

"I don't know." There's a hint of frustration in my voice now. "I went from being Gentry's soon-to-be-wife with a whole future planned out for us to trying to figure out where to sleep at night.

I'd been with Gentry through every major decision-making moment of my life recently. The last year of undergrad. The end of law school. All of those moments when I would have decided what comes next were navigated with him in mind. Sometimes I wonder if I even know myself well enough to know what I want."

He leans against the desk, his legs spread out, and shakes his head with a grin.

"What?"

"Just the thought of you not knowing yourself . . . it's hard to imagine, is all. I've never met someone who seems so . . . so fully formed."

I'm drawn to him. Something magnetic in my veins pulls me to him and soon I'm standing between those tree trunk thighs. "I wish I could see myself how you see me."

He smooths my wind-tousled hair behind my ears and the way he looks down at me is so open and tender that I nearly backpedal away from him. "I do too, baby."

"I'm thinking about running for office. Um, there are a few different positions coming up for election," I say. It's the first time I've admitted it out loud. But besides being Bram's good girl, it's the only thing I can think about. Now that I've imagined it, my brain can't unknow the possibility. And maybe things are different in the Midwest than they are in California. Maybe people won't be so concerned about the fact that I have heavy hips and round cheeks.

"Good," Bram says, his hands resting on my waist. "You would be so well suited to that, Madelyn. You're fierce, engaging, and incisively intelligent—plus your poker face is the best I've ever seen. But Veronica Balentine isn't how you get there."

"How do you—"

"Sloane mentioned that she thought you might have spoken to her." One hand comes up to cup my cheek. "Do you know how hard it's been to stay away from you for the last few days?"

"Yes, in fact, I do. But don't distract me. Not yet. What do you think you know about Veronica Balentine?"

"I don't *think* I know anything. I do know that whatever she's promising you is not worth the price of admission."

"Oh, so you think that I can't handle myself around someone like Veronica? I've been playing chess with people worse than her for the last three years, Bram. At least Veronica is honest about what she is."

"And what's that?"

I can't help but bristle, especially because I admire Veronica in a way. And maybe I even recognize parts of myself in her—parts that haven't had much screen time but are there all the same. "Someone who's willing to get their hands dirty so other people can keep their hands clean. People like me. Besides, her only job is to get me into office. It would be up to me to stay there."

"I've been around long enough to know that everyone who works with Veronica thinks that the end justifies the means, but if you win with her, you will never stop owing her and the people who hired her. You don't want that."

"Funny how you think I'm so sure of myself but can't trust me to know what I want."

For a brief second, he appears wounded, but then his brow flattens into . . . not quite serenity, but something just as level.

"This isn't about me not trusting you, Madelyn. This is about me not trusting Veronica Balentine and the very deep pockets she works for."

I feel defensive and prickly, but also, this is the first time in three years that someone has thought of me first. Not the platform or the party or the constituents or the polls, but me.

And yet, I want this. I want to see where things could go with Veronica, because for so long I thought my best shot at navigating change was to be the smiling, charitable woman on Gentry's arm. There could have been power in that, yes, but being the actual candidate and not just the spouse could someday put me at the table where real decisions are made. And why shouldn't the chubby girl from a run-down neighborhood who had to navigate Medicaid on her mom's behalf get a crack at real power?

I've learned some things about Bram in the last few weeks. I've learned that he grew up without his parents, but that his grandparents took him in right away. That they owned a successful chain of plant nurseries, and the bills were always paid and there was always plenty left over. The first time he knew struggle was when he and Sara got pregnant, and even then, they could have had a safety net if they *really* needed it. A safety net I never felt like I had.

For as kind and fair that I know Bram to be, I also know that he hasn't had to confront the possibility of doing questionable things on the way to doing good things.

"I need you to trust me," I tell him. "I'm not looking to Veronica Balentine or anyone like her to be my moral compass. And hell, I'm not even her horse in the race yet. I might not know my way around a lecture hall as well as you do, but this is one arena I'm painstakingly acquainted with, Bram."

His throat bobs before he nods. "I can trust you. That is something I can do. But I won't stop or apologize for watching out for you. I want this for you. I want what you want, but it's important to do this the right way."

And that's where he and I disagree. Because when you're a big, tall white guy like Bram, the kind of guy everyone likes, then you always have the privilege of the right way. But I'm not up for that argument at the moment, especially when we are alone for the first time in almost a week. "None of this matters, because I am the last person on earth that anyone would elect for public office. The polls have made that very clear."

"No." His voice is unyielding as he pulls my chin up so that I have nowhere else to look but into his amber-flecked green eyes. "Fuck the polls, Maddie."

I start to laugh, but his grip on my chin tightens.

"I said, fuck the polls." He stands and his hand glides from my throat to the back of my neck.

My posture straightens like his hand is pulling on a string attached to my spine and he's freeing me of the ever-present decision of how to hold myself. With his hand still on my neck, he guides me around the teacher's desk to the chalkboard.

"It's time for your next lesson," he says.

My nipples tighten into hard points, and I push aside the thought that we should get back to the festival and I also push aside the very real worry that someone could walk right into this building as easily as we did.

With the hand that was on my neck, he takes the five-pronged vintage chalk holder and drags it across the board. "You're going to write me some lines, Madelyn."

I shake my head. "And what if I think that's a waste of time when I could be on my knees with your cock on my tongue?"

The weight of him at my back is gone, and before I can look to see where he's gone, there's a short swat against the curve of my ass, but it's not from his hand.

Fundamentals of Being a Good Girl

Then Bram is there again, his chest pressing against me, and the feel of his growing hardness nestles into my lower back.

From the corner of my eye, I can see the old wooden pointer stick in his hand.

My lips part, a moan slipping, and I arch back into him. I want him to feel as desperate as I do.

His lips dance across my ear as he asks, "Is this okay? The spanking, I mean."

"It's very okay," I assure him.

His hand is on my neck again and this time he's guiding me back to the desk. "Bend over, Madelyn."

Oh fuck, yes.

I'm quick to obey and he kneels behind me, sliding a hand up my thigh. The calluses on his hand press through the thin material of my tights as his touch comes to rest against my inner thigh just inches from where I am so, so starved for him.

He stands then and flips the back of my skirt up, tucking the bottom of it into the waistband before peeling my tights and panties down my hips. Bram moves torturously slow and every inch of revealed skin burns against the chilled air.

"You're going to be my good girl," Bram tells me as he yanks my wellies off one by one before pulling my tights the rest of the way down. "You're going to write your lines on the board, but first I'm going to have to punish you."

At that, my spine curves, pushing my ass in the air, presenting myself to Bram. I've never been spanked—at least not like this. Gentry gave me a swat or two in the heat of the moment, but never like this. Never as an event.

"You're going to give me five swats, pretty girl, and I need you to count them. We'll count this next one as your second." His hands grip my hips, with no attempt to shy away from the curves and folds there. "I need to know that you understand. Now, you tell me, what is going to happen?"

"I've been a bad girl," I say. The words feel filthy and my cheeks are ruddy with shame from how right it feels to be his bad girl—even more so than his good girl right now. "So you're going to give me four more swats and I'm going to count them out for you."

His mouth is on the cheek of my ass, teeth biting, leaving a mark, and a moan that borders on a scream dies just as it leaves my lips. "Bram," I whine, slick arousal pooling between my legs already.

"I know, baby," he whispers.

The rod comes down against my bare skin. Slightly harder this time, and I yelp as I rise to my toes. "Two," I say on a gasp.

The wood snaps against my skin again, and I squeeze my legs together in search of relief from the ache building there.

"Three."

Again, but incrementally harder.

"Four."

"You love being punished just as much as you like being rewarded. Isn't that right, Madelyn?"

My fingers dig into the edge of the desk as I nod.

"It makes the reward so much sweeter."

"Please touch me," I beg him.

"Soon," he promises. "Soon I'm going to fuck you so hard you won't be able to walk."

The rod lashes down against my skin again, and this time he doesn't hold back. The sting of it makes my eyes water, and I find myself thrusting against the desk, searching for friction of any kind. "Fuck," I whimper.

He chuckles as the rod clatters against the floor. "I think what you meant to say was five." His warm hand sweeps over my backside, gently rubbing along the tender lines left behind by my punishment.

"Now, darling, are you ready to write some lines on the board?"

"Are you fucking serious?" I ask. "What happened to fucking me so hard I can't walk?"

He chuckles darkly. "The fucking will be your reward. The swats were your punishment. And the lines are your lesson. Chalkboard. Now."

CHAPTER TWENTY

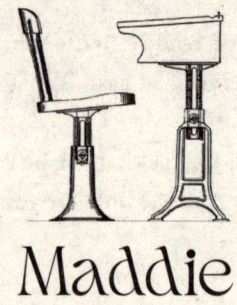

Maddie

I stand up straight, leaving the hem of my skirt tucked into my waistband. I am so starved for immediate gratification, but Bram Loe is a patient man, and he's always worth the wait.

His eyes darken as I meet him at the chalkboard and take the chalk from where it sits on the ledge.

I take his hand and press his fingers to my lips before taking two of them into my mouth, holding his gaze as I do. I refuse to be the only one suffering.

He holds his fingers there for a moment, pushing against my tongue, like he's testing me. I hollow my cheeks and suck, then he drags his fingers away only to dip his hand under the front of my skirt and presses those same two fingers past my slit. He cruelly avoids my swollen clitoris, but still thrusts deeper, his fingers finding no resistance as they sink into my wet cunt.

"There you are," he says. "You're dripping for me, Madelyn. Just absolutely drenched." He pulls his fingers out much too quickly and I gasp at the sudden vacancy.

A frustrated noise is all I can manage as he turns me to the board and takes my hand—the one holding the chalk—and begins to write the letter *F*.

"*Fuck*," he says as we spell the vulgar word out together. "*The. Polls.*"

There it is on the board, in some sort of mix of both of our handwriting.

"Repeat it back to me, Maddie."

My mouth is dry as the words gather in my throat. It's something I've thought plenty of times, but it's hard to get past the numbers. Even if I think the polls are bullshit, that doesn't stop them from mattering.

But polls aren't perfect, and I am more than a series of questions and answers on a scale of one to ten. I have to be more. That has to be true.

"*Fuck the polls*," I whisper.

He crouches down and gives me a sweet kiss just below my ear. "Now write it out. Do it for me, baby. Do it for you."

Dust falls from the chalk with each line as I write those three words. *Fuck the polls.*

"Good girl. Again."

I'm so enthralled by the words that I hardly feel his absence as I write the line again, and again.

But then his mouth—his goddamn mouth—is nibbling and kissing up the backs of my thighs.

I gasp, the chalk clattering onto the metal ledge below.

"Did I tell you to stop?"

"No," I say. "No, sir."

He lets out a guttural, feral moan, and I hear the sound of a zipper sliding behind me.

I begin to turn around, but his hands are on my ass, forcing my legs apart, and all I manage to see is him on his knees behind me, like I'm his final prayer. His last hope.

This fucking man.

For fear that he'll stop, I pick up the chalk and begin again.

His tongue traces along the lines left by the rod and then his tongue is between my legs, dangerously close to the pucker of my asshole as he laps at my pussy.

"Oh god," I manage to say as the chalk draws a jagged line that started as an attempt at a letter.

He sinks all the way to the floor now and wedges himself between me and the wall. Relentlessly strong hands pull me to his face so hard that I'm practically riding his mouth.

Finally—finally!—his tongue finds my clit and he swirls circles around the sensitive bud before sucking on it until the only things holding me up are the wall and his hands.

The chalk falls to the floor, my lines forgotten as I brace one hand against the board and the other in his hair.

I'm so close. I'm so close. The tension is building to the point that it hurts. It physically hurts not to come on this man's blessed tongue.

"N-no," I manage to sputter. "I want to come on your cock."

He shakes his head, his mouth still latched to my pussy.

"Oh my god, Bram. Fuck, fuck, fuck, I'm close."

He pulls back for just a moment, looking up at me, his face expression wild and his chin dripping. "You taste like honey. You're going to come for me now, okay? And then you can have my cock. But I need you to say it. I need to know you've learned your lesson."

My breath stutters in my chest as I manage to nod.

He slides two fingers into me without warning.

I can't stop my head from rolling back, but his other hand keeps me in place while his warm breath on my core is a constant tease.

"Say it."

"Fuck—"

His tongue swipes right over my clit, sending shocks down my thighs and into my toes.

I try again. "Fuck . . . the polls."

"Good girl," he mutters into my pussy before his tongue lets loose on my clit, his fingers thrusting in and out, making vulgar noises that should make me blush but only drive me closer to my finish.

His teeth drag against my clit, followed immediately by his soothing tongue, and that sends me over the edge. My orgasm is electric, sending volts of pleasure through me and I hardly register myself slithering down into his lap, his fingers still inside me, lazily thrusting as I'm hit with aftershocks of pleasure.

He cradles me for a few minutes and his lips trace patterns over my neck and cheeks and hair.

"You owe me your cock," I tell him when I can finally speak.

His pants are unzipped, but his erection is still clothed in his boxer briefs.

"Greedy, aren't we?"

I grind down on his crotch, and his hand on my hip tightens.

He quickly unbuttons his flannel shirt and tosses it out in front of us.

"On your knees, Ms. Kowalczk."

I quickly comply and let his shirt be the barrier between me and the hard floor.

He crowds behind me as he yanks my sweater up and pulls the cups of my bra down so that my breasts spill out. His fingers twist and tug on my nipples and he watches over my shoulder, hypnotized.

Gently, he pushes me forward so that I'm on all fours.

Because I love to watch, I glance back over my shoulder as he takes his dick in his hand, roughly fisting it three times before dipping it through my wet crease.

I purr as the tip of his penis nudges my clit.

He continues to toy with me, dragging his cock back and forth, like he's a predator playing with his food.

Stretching back, I press against him and he pushes just the tip inside me before pulling back out.

"Fuck you," I mutter.

"Yes, thank you," he says as he thrusts into me a little deeper this time.

He does it again, still not fully sheathing himself, and I've had enough.

This time as he starts to pull out, I ram my hips back and fuck myself onto him.

His fingers dig into my waist and the curve of my shoulder as I take him by surprise. "God, that's so fucking hot. I should punish you for that, but I love watching you use my cock and take what you need."

I rock back again, and this time he thrusts his hips to meet me and we both let out a chorus of groans.

Bram pushes me down so that my face is pressed into his flannel shirt and his cock slides even deeper.

"Touch yourself, Maddie."

I nod and slide a hand between my legs. My fingers find that overly stimulated spot and it doesn't feel as good as his tongue, but the burning stretch of his cock sliding in and out of me makes up for it.

Bram wastes no time picking up the pace and using my hips as an anchor as he drives himself into me.

My fingers move in tight circles and I clench around Bram's thick inches.

"I need you to fill me," I tell him. I've never felt as greedy for a man's come as I have with Bram, but there's something positively primal about how necessary it feels.

"Anything for my filthy little good girl."

He plunges into me four more times, pulling me upright and flush against his chest. One hand curves around my neck while the other replaces my hand on my clit, applying diligent pressure as he continues to buck into me from behind.

"Bram," I pant. "Bram. I'm—"

"Let go," he tells me. "Come for me."

As my mounting pleasure begins to unfurl, Bram bites down on the thin skin where my neck meets my shoulder.

"Fuck." It's the only warning he gives before his seed is spilling inside me. Warm and filling me full. So full that I can feel it dripping down his cock and between my thighs.

My head rests in the dip of his shoulder as we both shudder through our orgasms until he pulls me back into his lap and drapes the flannel shirt over us both.

Outside the gray sky is turning darker and soon the festival will make a turn for the spooky and be overrun with teenagers as the young ones go home with their parents.

"You're perfect," Bram says as he kisses along my hairline. "I need you to know that you're perfect."

For the first time in an incredibly long time, I feel like myself. I feel like the person Bram claims to see. And maybe I've been here all along, lying dormant and protected from the threat of Gentry and his family and Penelope Pike.

When we finally move to get dressed, Bram helps me into my tights, rolling them up my legs. We both make no move to clean his ejaculate from the inside of my legs. I want it—the evidence of us—there just as badly as he does.

We return to the festival, and I take the twins home to get ready for bed while Bram stays late with Fern and Leo and Sloane.

When they get home, Fern is buzzing. The numbers aren't final, but it looks like she has secured free menstrual products for every student bathroom at Mount Astra High School *and* is the reigning student body president. With the twins tucked in bed, the three of us celebrate Fern's victory with late-night pizza and the first *Scream* movie, despite Bram's protests.[*]

Fern falls asleep halfway through and Bram switches over to the nature series narrated by Barack Obama that he loves so much. I fall asleep splayed across his chest as he plays with my hair before loosely braiding it for me and walking me to bed.

The next day, Sloane takes Fern and me to her salon. When I sit down in the chair and see myself reflected back in the mirror, nearly an inch of dark roots coming in and the ends of my hair so

---

[*] Bram Loe is a notorious baby when it comes to scary movies, and while he has never admitted this as an adult, he has yet to sit through a single scary movie in its totality since he watched the three-part TV miniseries *Rose Red* in 2002.

obviously dead, I begin to swipe through the camera roll on my phone.

"What are we thinking for today?" the stylist asks as he snaps the cape around my neck.

"I think it's time to get back to my roots," I tell him. "And not as a metaphor."

CHAPTER TWENTY-ONE

Bram

"Time for the big reveal!" Sloane calls from the glassed-in walkway leading out to my greenhouse. I look up from where I've been helping the twins harvest basil for dinner to see Fern bouncing behind her honorary aunt, the apples of her cheeks a bright red and a big smile on her face. She comes in front of me and the twins and gives a little spin, making her newly shortened hair fly out around her face.

The twins clap and then a solemn Berry throws scraps of torn basil at her, like aromatic runway confetti.

"What do you think, Dad?" Fern asks me, and I open my mouth to speak, and then find that my throat hurts a little, and then take a minute.

"I think you look beautiful and so grown-up," I finally manage to say. With her hair cut away from her face, I can see her sparkling eyes, the almost-adult shape of her features, so much like her mother's. She has Sara's eyebrows and forehead and a little bit of my nose and she's my baby and also she's going to leave for college before I know it and—

"Aw, Dad, don't cry!" Fern pulls me into a hug. She smells like a salon only Sloane Saint James could afford. "It's just a haircut."

"I know, I know." My voice is gruff while I sniffle into her hair. "You look very pretty and I hope Simon shits his ileum[*] out when he sees you."

"Actually, maybe we don't want Simon to shit his ileum."

"Oh?"

"Yeah, so he wrote me this letter after I won our bet and I guess he started going to therapy after his parents separated over the summer and apparently he learned about this thing called weaponized incompetence and he apologized for using that to manipulate me into doing basically all of his work for him."

"That's a . . . good thing?" I venture.

"You need to be careful with the guys who overuse therapy vocabulary," Sloane warns.

"Oh, we're definitely not getting back together. Ever. But I did ask him if he would stay on as copresident. Plus, he's so good at doing the public-facing stuff like talking at pep rallies." She wrinkles her nose. "Maddie said I've got the upper hand now and I should call all the shots including making him do my bitch work."

"Your bitch work?" I ask.

She nods. "Yeah, all the stuff I don't want to do. And pep rallies are at the top of the bitch work list."

---

[*] Part of the small intestine. Dr. Alessandro says this would be very difficult to do.

"As long as you're happy, sweetie. Just let me know if I need to change my stance on him shitting out his ileum anytime soon. And thank you," I say over Fern's head to Sloane.

Sloane's expression turns a little devious. "You'll thank me even more in a minute. Girls, do you want to go upstairs with me while we put makeup on Fern and see what look suits her best?"

There's another cloud of bruised basil confetti, chants of *glitter gloss glitter gloss*, and then I'm alone in the greenhouse.

Well.

Not entirely alone.

Because coming through the walk is a brunette with a dark chin-length bob, bangs cut with an architect's precision, and lipstick so red it makes everything around her seem colorless. And the outfit she was wearing before—camel trousers and a button-down—have been replaced with a leather skirt that swings around her knees and a slouchy sweater that hints at a silk tank top underneath. It's still stylish, still TV-ready, but it's *Maddie* too, sharp and crisp and definitive.

And those bloodred lips . . .

So fucking bratty.

I'm staring at those lips with hooded eyes as she reaches me and stops.

"Well, Professor?" she asks in a smoky voice.

"Full marks, top of the class," I breathe, sliding my hand into her hair and leaning down. I don't want to mess up her lipstick, so I press my lips to the underside of her jaw. I savor the soft warmth there, and the subtle hint of jasmine underneath the scents of expensive salon.

"You look amazing." I speak the words against her neck, hoping I can speak them into her blood, into the air filling her lungs. "Gorgeous. Dangerous. Clever as a snake and bright as a star."

"Do I look like I could run for office?"

I pull back so I can take in the full effect of her again. Green eyes, red lips, the flawless hair that looks like it's been cut from the autumn shadows themselves.

"You look like the world belongs at your feet," I tell her, and I mean it.

She stares up at me. My hand is still in her hair and I drop it to her chest, feeling the warmth from her skin under her sweater. I want to figure out how to cold-wash and line-dry that sweater so that it stays soft for years. I want to feed her an orange from the small tree in the corner of the greenhouse. I want to sit her on this potting bench and push my fingers inside of her while she tells me every plan in her shrewd, feline mind.

"I don't think you should look at me like that," she whispers.

I can see my reflection in her blown pupils. "Like what?"

"Like you want to be the one to put the world at my feet."

For a moment, we don't move. And then she steps back, her bright red bottom lip tucked between her teeth for a single millisecond and then released again. I can see the pulse pounding in her throat.

"You don't want me to look at you like that?" I ask to clarify.

She hesitates. "I don't want *to want* you looking at me like that."

I flex the hand that had been pressed against her chest just a moment ago. It feels cold.

"When you look at me like you want to use those giant shoulders to ram people out of my way, I get this—" She gestures to her chest, fluttering her fingers. "That. Whatever that is, that's what

I feel. But then immediately on its heels, I feel . . ." She trails off. Her hand is flat against her stomach now, like there's a knot under her ribs and it's been tied too tightly and now something essential inside her is choked off. Bloodless.

And now I have a knot of my own. Because I've known what this is from the beginning—she wrote it out on my glass board, for fuck's sake—I knew what I agreed to.

Just sex, nothing else.

And it seemed like a good idea at the time. I have the kids and work, and I haven't dated since the divorce, and *well*, if I'm honest with myself, maybe I thought *nothing else* was all that life had left to give me. I'd had a pretty good marriage; I had good, adorable kids; I had tenure and moss grants. What more was I allowed to want?

But over the last few weeks, the idea of *more* has crept in, the way autumn creeps in, under the heat, under the soil, until one day you wake up and the air is keen and the trees are burning orange and gold. I woke up one day and wanted Maddie grading in my office as much as I wanted her bent over my desk, and I wanted her talking politics to me as much as I wanted her naked and wet in my lap. I wanted cuddling and complaining and helping at the Fall Frenzy and her meeting the Andromedas for real and for the things we shared to spore like moss and spread and spread until everything was covered in a soft, living blanket of *more*.

I don't say any of this, though. Because she doesn't want it, because it's not what we agreed to.

Because I abruptly feel foolish and . . . and old. Every bit a man infatuated with a younger woman.

And I don't need to say it, because Maddie guesses.

"Bram, I just got out of a relationship that defined me."

"I know."

"It ruined my life." Her eyes search mine. "I don't know if I can express to you how rare the thing between you and Sara is; if you can appreciate how unlike your divorce this breakup was for me. And I can't do it again. I can't."

I brush off the reflexive sting that she thinks anything between us—good or bad—would resemble her experience with that entitled jackoff. I carefully sequester the pain blooming in my chest. Instead, I simply say, "I know, Madelyn."

"And I can't have scandals if I want to start playing the game," she says, and now she's turning away a little, nervously sanding her fingertips over the wooden potting bench. "I can't be twelve years deep into a political career and have the press find out about that one time I fucked a dad while I was his nanny."

"Of course not."

She swivels her head to look at me and swallows hard. "Isn't the sex good enough? What we're doing? I don't want to change any of that. I just want things to be clear between us, that's all."

I haven't moved all this time, and I think it's because if I move, I will rip something vital, like an artery, or my lungs will tear open like paper, and I won't be able to inhale ever again. But if I stand still, if I stay right here, then I can say the right things. I can hold on to our agreement and give her what she needs. I can sound level and certain when I reaffirm that yes, the sex is good enough, that no, I don't want anything more.

But I take too long to answer, even standing still, and Maddie spins back toward me, something like panic in her face. "Bram? I don't want to stop. That's not what I'm saying at all. I want this. Please, don't think that I'm trying to end things."

"You just don't want me to look at you like I want to give you the world." I say it gently, a little teasingly, and it's the hardest thing I've ever done, acting as if this doesn't hurt right now. As if I'm capable of screwing her like nothing's changed, like of course I'm happy merely to fuck her while I scissor off my own feelings and prune away any unsanctioned desire for more.

Relief ripples through her, and she approaches me again, taking my hand, her entire expression one of *see, I knew you'd understand*. "It's so good, what we're doing, right?" she murmurs, pressing my hand to her cheek. "It's perfect. We both get off, and no one has to work for it. No one has to hurt for it."

No one but me.

But I accept it. I won't be petulant or covet what I'm not allowed to have. I give her the kindest smile I can. "It's very good, Maddie," I assure her, even as the pain in my chest radiates down to the soles of my feet and out to my fingertips. "It's so good."

She smiles back, beams even, those lush lips a shock of scarlet in my greenhouse, where even my roses don't get that red. "Plus," she teases, "you still have to teach me how to run a classroom."

I drop a kiss to her forehead and then step back, pull my hand away, under the pretense of cleaning up the dead basil parade the twins threw for Fern. In just a minute, I'll be fine, and by tomorrow, I'll have buried this somewhere deep, grown roots around it, trapped it somewhere where it can never see light again.

Just sex, nothing else.

"I have plenty more lessons in mind, Ms. Kowalczk," I say with a decent stab at flirting.

And then I stoop to sweep up the basil, damp and dark around the torn edges, and avoid the jasmine plant in the corner as I go to throw it all away.

CHAPTER TWENTY-TWO

Maddie

The door to the adjunct office is closed, so I talk loudly to one of the TAs about an ongoing filibuster happening in the Wisconsin state senate to make sure that if Anton and Martin are mid-coitus, they'll hear me coming.

But when I let myself in, the only person waiting for me is Bram in the much too small armchair in front of the shared adjunct desk.

He stands as I enter, and before I can even close the door, he asks, "How did it go?"

I shuck off my coat and hang it and my bag on the hook near the door and lie, because if I'm just not looking at him, I can lie. "Fine," I say. "He apologized."

"So you're saying you confronted Wallace about barging into your class earlier and earlier every day, and that it was fine, and that he apologized."

"That's exactly it," I tell him as I discard my slouchy cardigan as well and then smooth a hand over my bangs, a self-soothing habit I'd done since I was a child. I'd missed my bangs. I'd missed my dark hair. After three years of looking in the mirror and seeing a stranger, I finally feel a little more like myself.

With the signature bob I'd worn since middle school back, I'd found myself reaching for one of my favorite older T-shirts this morning. A black shirt so heavily faded that it was more of an acidic gray and in a tiny, dainty embroidered script across the chest it read I SUPPORT WOMEN'S WRONGS. I paired it with a burgundy-plaid pleated skirt and my beloved chunky loafers. When I came down the stairs this morning, Bram took one look at my shirt and let out a soft *mmmm* before saying, "Me too."

"Madelyn," Bram says now, in a voice that borders on scolding.

I turn to face him, my proud shoulders rounding into slopes. "It was a hard morning, okay?"

He steps toward me and takes my hand in his, his thumb running along the space between my thumb and pointer finger. "What happened?"

"Everything was fine. I visited Junie in the library and then just before class started, I got a text from Gentry asking me to please remove any photos of us from my social media because they're doing a scrub of the internet before early voting starts. I haven't even logged onto social media since I left California and there were all these awful messages from his friends saying how sorry they were to see us split and how everything happens for a reason."

His lips purse, nostrils flaring. "I'm sorry," he grinds out.

"It's stupid. It's not like I want any evidence of our relationship out there anyway. But it just . . . it made me feel like I'd done something wrong. Like I was the reason things ended. Or that I'm some kind of stain."

"Maddie—" he starts.

"I know that's not true, okay? But between that and the idea of facing off against Wallace today, it was just easier to let him walk in five minutes early and steamroll through the last bit of my lecture. I was mentally checked out anyway."

He steps toward me so that my nose is nearly brushing his chest and he keeps going until he's guiding me backward against the door. I inhale against his wool sweater and let myself become submerged in cedar and eucalyptus. A cool forest made of soft earth and muscled professor.

Beside my hip the lock on the door clicks, and Bram's fingers quickly move to the button and zipper of my skirt.

"Bram, this is a shared office," I remind him.

"I don't see anyone else here except for us," he tells me. "When's your department meeting?"

I glance up at the clock on the wall. "Twenty minutes."

"And will Wallace be there?"

He tugs my skirt down over my hips and it pools at my feet. He squats down and lifts my feet one by one before folding my skirt and placing it on top of the nearest bookshelf. Which he can easily reach, because of course he can.

"He'll be a little late," I say as his fingers skate up my waist and under my T-shirt. He rolls his thumbs over my nipples, the only barrier between us the thin deep-green mesh of my bra.

With careful steadiness, he lifts my arms and pulls the T-shirt over my head.

I check the knob on the door to make sure it really is locked. I may have caught Anton and Martin once before, but I'm not looking to repay the favor. Especially with my sometimes boss and sometimes colleague.

He bends down and his mouth closes over my nipple, his tongue dancing over the fabric as he sucks.

I throw my head back against the door. "Oh my god."

His mouth turns to my other breast, and why does the thought of him nipping and biting and sucking over the mesh of my bra make me so immediately horny?

We don't have much time. Only twenty minutes. But I'm not about to waste a second.

I make quick work of his pants and reach below the waistband of his boxer briefs to take his weeping cock in my hand.

Without any warning, I sink to my knees, his teeth snagging against my tit as he's abruptly forced to let go.

My hands move up his thighs, curving over the perfect roundness of his ass, and I pull his cock into my mouth in one rapid motion. He hits the back of my throat and I moan around him.

"Fuck." The word is more of a low noise than actual speech.

I look up at him through my lashes as I pull back and take him again. Just outside the door, there are footsteps and voices as the world beyond it continues none the wiser to this kind, gentle, and unrelenting man whose cock is pulsing in my throat.

I break eye contact for just a minute as I drag his thick, angry rod over my tongue, leaving a trail of spit and red lipstick.

"Are you fucking kidding me, Madelyn? I'm never going to forget the sight of your cherry-red lipstick streaked across my dick. Stand up. Stand up right the fuck now and bend over that table with your hands behind your back."

His fingers run through my smooth bob, and he tugs gently at

Fundamentals of Being a Good Girl

the roots as I stand to my feet. I love the feeling of him pulling my hair and using it to lead me along like I've been so bad that I can't be trusted to follow orders.

I bend over the desk, and neither of us bother to clear the stacks of papers as he presses my cheek into the ancient wood.

He yanks my ivory lace boy shorts down my thighs and leaves them hanging off a single ankle as he kicks the other leg open so that I'm completely spread for him on my own goddamn desk.

It's so vulgar. My panties caught around my ankle and I'm wearing nothing but my bra, lacy socks, and loafers.

"Fucking art," he says.

He presses his hips flush against my ass, the broad tip of his penis nudging at my warm, seeping slit. "Maddie, baby girl, do you know how powerful you are? How you demand that a room pay attention to you just by walking inside it?"

I shake my head and rock back against him. "Mmmm."

His hand reaches around my hips and finds my clit puffy and ready for his touch. My hips move in a circle, searching him out.

"Wallace is an irritable old dinosaur who can only wish to be a stepping-stone on the path of your life."

He holds my wrists with one hand at the small of my back as he plunges inside of me with one merciless thrust.

The scream that scratches against my throat is muffled as I bite down on my lips and I hold it there inside of me until it fizzles out into a whimper.

He is perfectly still, using me to warm his cock as he leans over and whispers in my ear, hands still fastened behind my back, "One day, you're going to look back on men like Wallace and Gentry and you will see how silly you were for ever letting them be anything more than the dirt beneath your heels. You'll be right where you've always dreamed of being, Maddie, and someone like me would be so lucky as to kneel behind you at your podium, eating your pretty cunt."

So tenderly, he presses his lips to my cheek and then pulls back so that he's gone from me except for just the tip.

He stands then, one hand digging into my hip, fingers punishing and bruising, while his other hand still circles my wrist in a way that's secure but not too tight.

His erection drives into me in short, rapid thrusts, moans turning into curses turning into prayers on his lips.

He lets go of one of my hands. "I want you to touch that sweet little bud, Madelyn. Rub your clit for me."

I do as he says. It's a compulsion. I can't stop. Someone could walk right in through that door and I wouldn't be able to stop. We're both so close to bliss. There are no words left. Just the rhythm of our bodies slapping together. The sound of him meeting my arousal.

"I'm—I'm—" The words die on my tongue as I'm flooded with sensual gratification that is all-consuming as it ripples through me, undulating.

Bram makes no effort to let up and only moves faster now that I've come all over his cock. His hips jerk as he paints my womb with his milky ejaculate.

He lays his head down against my shoulder, blanketing my body with his as he's electrified with the last few jolts of pleasure.

"I—" His breath tickles my neck. "I could fuck you every day."

And I feel the same way, of course, but the words are dangerously close to sentiments that ring *forever*.

After a moment of silent, panting breaths, he stands. But my body can't move. Not yet.

I stay bent over as I listen to the sound of clothing rustling and zipping. He doesn't have much dressing to do since he was nearly clothed as he fucked me. Yet another image that my perverted little mind gobbles up.

His broad hand smooths over my backside and he helps me up.

As I stand upright, his spend begins to leak out of me.

Wordlessly, he turns me around and pushes aside some papers for me to sit on the desk. With a studious expression on his face, he leans me back just a touch and crouches down before pushing his come back inside me.

A tiny gasp jumps from my chest and I bite down on my lower lip as I watch him.

"That's better," he whispers as he stands to retrieve my clothing and passes it to me.

I lean over to take my panties from where they still hang around one ankle, but Bram grips my wrist to stop me. He pulls the lacy fabric free and then balls it up before stuffing it in his pocket.

"Bram. Seriously? I need those back."

He shakes his head.

I pull the T-shirt over my head and then he reaches down to smooth out my hair for me.

"While I love the thought of my soaked panties in your pocket while you go about your day, taking office visits and lecturing, I really need those before going to my department meeting."

"You can have them back once you've completed your assignment."

His hand rests along my jawline as his thumb tilts my chin back before pushing past my lips.

I let my teeth graze the digit and then I suck for a moment. I don't think this is an argument I even want to win, so I finally nod.

"Now, go be my good girl and tell Dr. Wallace that he is no longer welcome to interrupt your class."

He pulls his thumb free and just like his cock, it's stained with my red lipstick.

"Yes, Professor."

CHAPTER TWENTY-THREE

Maddie

The department meeting is mostly a snoozefest except for when someone shows an animated video of the Oval Office recording of Lyndon B. Johnson ordering custom pants from the Haggar clothing company.[*] Dr. Wallace comes in among the laughter and is immediately cross. He huffs as he sits down and I wonder if he is angered by joy in general or just being left out of it.

At the end of the meeting, Miranda opens the floor for any comments or concerns.

It takes three other professors voicing their issues and then her calling twice more for any last topics of discussion before I finally manage to raise my hand.

---

[*] In said phone call, LBJ requested several extra inches from "where the zipper ends" and then back to his "bunghole." He also burped. A lot.

She offers me a warm smile and nods her head as the rest of the department faculty turn to me, several of whom I'm sure had mistaken me for a student up until now.

"Hi, yes, for those of you who don't know me, I'm the new adjunct, Madelyn Kowalczk. I just wanted some clarification on lecture hall etiquette. I'm so new to teaching, but I wanted to confirm whether or not it's appropriate for another professor to enter my classroom and attempt to prepare for their lecture when my class is still finishing?"

Salazar laughs and there are a few knowing smirks around the table. "I would say that goes beyond etiquette into just simply rude. So yes, please let's be mindful of our fellow professors and their time," she says to the group at large before she looks at me and her gaze briefly slides to Dr. Wallace, who is fuming. "Ms. Kowalczk, if this problem persists, please seek me out so that we can mediate the issue with the professor in question."

I nod sweetly and ignore the angry daggers that Dr. Wallace is staring in my direction.

Once we are dismissed, I gather my belongings and circle around the table to where Miranda is packing up the contents of her folio.

"Good job," she says. "Professional. Polite. But public. You made a statement without crossing a line." She gives me a neutral look. "It was more professional and polite than calling a student a stale doughnut, for example."

I wince.

"I've made a note about this in your evaluation file. You're young and you're new to this, but that's no excuse for being unprofessional in my department." Her voice is frank but level, and her gaze holds the kind of directness that is almost comforting.

Yes, this is a verbal reprimand, but I'm being given my feedback like an adult, like I can handle it.

I straighten my shoulders a little, pulling in a breath. "Yes, ma'am. I'm sorry, and it won't happen again."

She studies me a moment and then gives me a small smile. "I appreciate the apology, and also I've heard you've made strides in your classroom presence in the last few weeks."

"You have?"

"You certainly impressed Veronica. She's ready to stick a flag pin on you and drag you up and down the district."

Miranda leans back against the table, her arms crossed over her chest. Today she wears a leopard-print pencil skirt and yellow blouse with stiletto ankle boots. I've never been to New Jersey, but based on the PhD-research levels of reality TV I've consumed, I'd say she's representing her home state well.

"Miranda, I'm honored that you thought to mention me to her, but isn't it sort of counterproductive to give up one of your adjuncts when the department is so thinly staffed? Not to mention, how do you even know I'm fit to run?" Suddenly I remember that I am not wearing underwear. I am not wearing underwear and I'm having an important conversation with the chair of my department. Oh god.

No, I tell myself. *Maddie, mentally, you are wearing underwear. You are wearing underwear, goddamnit.*

She leans in, her neutral expression now conspiratorial. "First off, your contract as a lecturer is only through May, which is when the primary is. Perfect timing if you ask me. And academia will always be here, Maddie. Whether it's Astra or someplace else, if you decide that this is what you're meant to do, there will always be young, fresh-faced students for you to educate. And don't tell the career academics I said so, but sometimes you gotta get out there and have some real-life experience if you want to bring anything of value back to the classroom."

"And second?" She's not wrong about real-life experience, and I like teaching. I do. But I can't see it being the only thing I do for the rest of my life. I do, however, like the idea of it being something I sometimes return to. A place I can always revisit.

"And second, I don't know that you are fit to run. But there's no way to know until you do it. I can say that you're fiery as hell and if what you just did in this meeting showed me anything, it's that you're just the sort of person that could shake up the old guard without triggering a multi-person cardiac event. You know your way around politics, Maddie. That's obvious."

"I've heard that Veronica Balentine is a little bit . . ."

"Ruthless?" she asks. "I went to law school with Veronica. Well, technically, for a year. She dropped out once she realized what she wanted to do and that she didn't need to throw a ton of money at a piece of paper to make it happen. And yes, she is ruthless. But that doesn't mean she isn't good at what she does."

"Ruthlessness doesn't scare me."

"Good." She pushes off from the table and holds her portfolio to her chest. "Don't tell Veronica I said so—and if you do, I will lie—but she's not just good at her job. She's actually just plain old good too. Very, *very* deep down." She pats my shoulder as she steps past me toward the door.

Feeling relieved that Miranda trusted me to grow from doughnut-gate and a little smug that she saw political potential in me, I head back to the adjunct office for my coat before I head out for the day.

Dr. Wallace steps into stride with me and then in front of me, blocking my path. "Young lady," he says.

"You can go to Dr. Salazar with that, Dr. Wallace," I tell him, my tone never anything but polite.

He stammers for a moment, eyes wide and bulging. "Perhaps if you have a problem with me, you can address me directly and privately."

"Oh," I say, "I have, but I fear you have missed the point, *sir*, so please hear me when I explicitly say: You are not welcome to interrupt my class and undermine my authority. You may wait in the hallway until I am through. You will not speak over me, especially in front of a student, and you will not ever again in your life refer to me or anyone else as *young lady*. I'm sure that you woke up one day and realized the world had changed and that people who you had always thought beneath you were suddenly your peers and in some cases even your superiors. So here's a little advice for you: Evolve or go extinct. You decide."

The man vibrates with anger, but something behind his eyes changes. Guilt? Fear? Whatever it is, it's not my problem.

"Have a lovely day, Dr. Wallace," I practically sing as I spin on my heel. My body is charging with energy as I leave the old man speechless.

God, that felt so good. It felt so right!

My thighs press together as I remember Bram encouraging me and then pushing his come back inside me and sending me to stand up for myself with my panties stuffed in the pocket of his seemingly innocuous corduroy pants. Wow, we are a fucked-up little pair, and it really, really works for me.

After getting my coat, I march over to Gerhart Hall and straight into Bram's office, where a young man is trying to engage him in flat earth theories.

Bram looks directly over his head and right at me. "Corbin, email me those links and we can discuss after my next lecture."

The kid stands up and gathers his backpack as he looks me up and down and grumbles something about open office hours.

I slam the door shut behind him. "Is that kid really a flat earther?"

Bram shakes his head as he stands. "No, not seriously, at least. He just likes conspiracy theories. Last week, he tried to tell me birds aren't real."

"Do you know what is real?" I ask.

"What?"

"The way I told Dr. Wallace to fuck off."

Bram's plump lips split into a proud, beaming smile and the warm feeling he'd left in the pit of my stomach spreads to every inch of my body like sunshine after days of gray overcast.

He stands from behind his desk and takes my panties from his pocket. "I guess I owe you these."

I close my hand around his fist—well, as far as it will go, at least—and then stuff it right back into his pocket. "I rather like the idea of you keeping them."

The noise he makes is an approving rumble as he dips his head to kiss me, his arm curling around my waist until our bodies are pressed together. I try not to think too hard about how well we fit.

CHAPTER TWENTY-FOUR

Bram

"No, no, of course it's fine," I'm saying as I push my way out of the Eco meeting room where Ali Darwish and I have given everyone their final marching orders for the seminar this weekend. "The girls miss you, but we'll keep up the calls, and it will be okay, I promise."

Sara lets out a groan-whine thing that sounds like a ghost on a toilet. "I just—I *hate* being away from them for so long, and what if the twins forget who I am, and what if they make bad choices as teenagers, like playing organized sports, and it's all in a desperate bid to fill the void I left in their little hearts while they were six? What if they try to replace a parent's love with expensive shoes and travel tournaments and we have to learn what offsides is, because you know I can't do that, I'll never understand what offsides means!"

"First, Letty can't play team sports, she's too much of a tyrant for that. She's going to end up as a drum major or a stage manager, or maybe she'll get a job as a judgmental teen barista at one of those coffee shops that has only four things on the menu."

Sara makes a small, barely comforted noise.

"And right now Berry only wants to bring caterpillars inside and name them elaborate names from her made-up fantasy world, so I don't think sports are in the picture *quite* yet."

Even without the benefit of modern technology, I'd be able to hear Sara's sigh all the way from Alaska. "I hate this," she says in a small voice.

"It's a once-in-a-lifetime chance, having this grant extended another four weeks, and you know that I don't mean that figuratively. This glacier won't exist in another five years. This is important. Your work is important. And it's for Letty and Berry and Fern and the world they're going to live in too."[*]

"But also, are you going to be okay for another month? I won't be back until Thanksgiving!"

I reach the stairs going down to the floor my office is on, hearing the distant whoops and chants of students somewhere in the building. Loud-ass kids. "I've got help, Sara. Maddie has been fabulous, and she won't mind being kept on until Thanksgiving, I'm sure—"

Sara's voice is suddenly mischievous when she says, "Oh, I bet she won't."

I pause on the stairs. "What's that supposed to mean?"

"Nothing," she hums.

I narrow my eyes, even though Sara's not here and it's a poster

---

[*] Fun fact: Letty's and Berry's real names are Laurentide and Beringia, as they're named for Sara's favorite Last Glacial Maximum celebrities.

for a creek-bed cleanup getting the brunt of my suspicion instead. "The other Andromedas aren't gossiping behind my back, are they? This isn't like a back-channel text thread thing?"

"Does this mean there would be a valid reason for a back-channel text thread?"

I groan. "I'm saying goodbye, Sara. We'll tell the girls about your extension on your call tomorrow."

"For what it's worth, I really like Maddie!" Sara gets in before I end the call. I blow out a long breath, still glaring at the cleanup poster, and gather my thoughts. It's fine, it's fine, if Maddie and I were actually together, like *have to disclose it to HR* together, then I'd tell everyone. But since we're just fooling around, since it's our secret bad idea, it's not anyone else's business.

And . . . I don't think I can talk about it with anyone else. I don't think I can explain. Because then I'd have to explain that it's going nowhere, that it means nothing, and whenever I even *think* about how it's going nowhere, my chest hurts and my ulnar nerves thrum and the nape of my neck prickles with a prescient kind of fear. It's going to end at some point. It's going to end, and I'm going to be left segmented and starving, like a ringbarked tree.

Why would I want to share that with the class? Some things just aren't meant for show-and-tell.

Feeling steadier now, I finish descending the stairs and stride toward my office, the sound of whooping and chanting growing louder and louder as I do. Sounding more and more *adult* rather than *young adult* and sounding more and more like it's coming from my office.

And then I reach my office door and, with a deep sense of foreboding, open it to find Joey Fucking Kemp squatting on my floor with a pile of diapers, a creepy fake baby, and a stuffed ermine that has been passed around from building to building since I was in undergrad.* Leo and Alessandro hover above him with their phones out, recording the scene like they're camerapeople and this is *Sunday Night Football*.

The three of them turn to look at me like guilty children.

When I swing the door all the way open, I see Sloane standing on the love seat with a stopwatch in her hand.

"*Et tu?*" I ask, wounded.

She has the grace to look a little abashed, at least.

"Why," I ask as I drop my satchel onto the floor, "are we all in my office today?"

The men turn and look to Sloane, who somehow still exudes tasteful dignity while standing barefoot on my love seat. "Joey needs to practice changing diapers," she says reasonably. "So he can convince Riley that he'll help when the baby comes."

"Okay," I say, also reasonably, "and why are we doing that in my office again?"

"Well, we couldn't possibly do it in Sloane's office," Leo points out.

"It's at the bottom of the hill," adds Alessandro.

"The vibes are wrong," says Leo.

"She did let us borrow one of the babies from her student health building, though," says Alessandro. "It's even got a rubber fontanel and everything. But she only had the one, which is why we had to grab the ermine from the staff room."

---

* The stuffed ermine was stolen from the Rossi-Gill Museum of Natural History over a century ago as a prank and was passed around the Astra University frat houses for decades. By the time it resurfaced, the museum no longer wanted it, and it began its new life as a campus white elephant, being left in different buildings and occasionally thrown away only to mysteriously resurface later.

I rub my hand over my face. My house is never quiet. My classrooms are filled to the brim with hormones, anxiety, and unsubtle texting while I'm talking. Is it so much to ask that my office is a place of peace? On occasion? On the very rare occasion?

Alessandro and Leo pout at me.

"Sloane's office is closer to the big parking lot," I say, not because I think they'll listen to reason, but because I need to at least log the argument. "Again, at the bottom of the hill. You *don't have to walk up a hill* to get there."

Alessandro's eyes go wide. "But the big parking lot has students parking in it."

"The faculty parking lot is much better—and on the gentle side of the hill," Leo agrees.

"You're not faculty!"

Leo's mouth pulls into something deeper than a pout. Genuine hurt. "Don't use labels to box me out, Bram, I can't handle it today."

I turn to Sloane, who lifts a blazer-clad shoulder. "Joey's players have a football clinic on campus this afternoon, and since it's a block day and he only had a couple history classes to teach, he could leave school a little early and come do some diaper drills. So I grabbed the baby and some of the diapers we keep on hand to help the nontrad students and thought we'd give it a shot. It was Leo who suggested your office. And then Alessandro was already at Nagel for some speech he'd given the little premed zygotes, so—"

"Wait." I look around at the so-called friends assembled here. "So there *is* a group chat without me?"

The guilty faces grow guiltier.

"I've gotten my double-diaper turnaround time down to

twenty-three seconds," Joey volunteers in an unsubtle attempt to divert the conversation. "That's *with* wiping, Bram."[*]

I'm about to go back to the perfidious group chat when Leo's phone rings. He glances down at the screen and then says to me, "You're going to want me to take this," as he steps out of the office.

"Don't be sullen about the texts, Bram," Alessandro says cajolingly as he leans back against my desk and crosses his arms. (Another three-piece suit today. This one definitely Italian, and definitely tailored by someone who knew Alessandro's capacity for casually breaking hearts left and right, especially while on Italian suit–buying trips.) "We actually started it in undergrad when we thought you and Sara might need a bail network or whatever. And then we only brought Sara in last year when she thought it would be in poor taste to send her and Asher's boudoir photos to the main group chat."

"They were great pictures, though," says Joey.

"It's my fear that this secret chat is rife with speculation and hearsay, and—" I stop and really look at Sloane. There is white dust all over her blazer and trousers. Sloane is never covered in dust. Sloane has never even seen dust, to my knowledge.

Sloane follows my gaze, looking down at herself, and then her ivory cheeks go a deep pink.

"Darling," Alessandro starts, "have you misread the instructions on the cocaine again?"

"It's not . . . cocaine." She slaps viciously at her chest and then at her thighs.

---

[*] If you've tried to wipe a taxidermied weasel's ass, you'll appreciate the speed here.

Fundamentals of Being a Good Girl

"Not that we'd blame you, with the divorce and all," Alessandro says in a gracious voice.

"It's not cocaine!"

That's the moment Maddie steps into my office. She looks up at Sloane on the love seat, still slapping at herself, then down to the floor, where Joey is stacking diapers next to the stuffed ermine and the fake baby. And then to Alessandro and me.

"I didn't realize you had . . . this . . . going on, Dr. Loe," she says. "I'll come back another time."

"Stay," I say, an unstoppable instinct, really, to beg her to stay, but the naked honesty in my voice is hidden underneath Sloane's breathless, agitated "Don't go, I promise this is normal."

"Normal for us," mutters Alessandro.

Leo steps back into the office behind Maddie, and now, despite being a decent-sized office for Gerhart, the space is nearly shoulder to shoulder with unwelcome visitors, a weasel, and Maddie. I squeeze my way to my chair and sit, Maddie and Leo shuffle farther into the room, and Sloane is still on the love seat, slapping herself more gently now.

"Why do you have cocaine *all over you*?" Leo inquires, in tones of the delicately offended rich. "You don't have a lint roller for that?"

Sloane's face is red enough now to be medically concerning. "It's not cocaine," she growls. "It's *chalk*."

If she hopes this will shut down the discussion, she's sorely mistaken, because the entire room erupts.

"Chalk, like for sidewalks and children?"

"Is Student Health too poor for dry erase markers?"

"Did you travel back to the 1890s? Do you need a slate rag?"

"It's from a chalkboard," Sloane says through gritted teeth. "And I don't want to talk about it."

"Did the chalkboard give you the cocaine? Is that why?" asks Leo.

I'm just baffled. "Where on earth did you find a chalkboard on this campus?"

"I bet it was one of those folding ones you put out in front of cafés and shops," Maddie says, clearly trying to be supportive of Sloane. "Was it for a student health fair or something?"

"No, I was just cleaning it, and it was obviously the first time it's been cleaned in forty years."

Now Leo sounds truly offended. "Cleaning? You were cleaning?"

"Apparently with her tits," observes Alessandro.

"I don't understand," I cut in. "Did you buy this chalkboard? And it's vintage? And you didn't tell me about it first?"

Joey, this entire time, has been staring through everyone's legs to Sloane's open purse by the door, and then with a lunge that reminds us all of his college-ball glory days, he flings himself at her bag and then surges to his feet, a jangle of keys dangling from his hand. Seized between his fingers is the grubby leg of a baby doll—not from the realistic kind of doll that Student Health has, but from the kind of doll you find prehaunted at a thrift store.

We all go still, except for Maddie, who is scrunching her face.

"Why would you put a baby leg on a key chain?"

"So it doesn't get stolen," Joey says. And then with courtroom melodrama, he adds, "But this *has* been stolen."

"What?" Maddie laughs. "Sloane wouldn't . . ."

Sloane has gone from flushed to ashen, and we're all staring at her in various states of confused worry.

"She must have," Alessandro says slowly. "Because those are the keys to The Dry Bean's bathroom. In her purse. Sloane, why do you have the keys to The Dry Bean's bathroom in your purse?"

And that's when I notice that Leo is the only one not staring in confused worry. He's now leaning against the wall with his arms crossed, looking greatly amused.

Sloane clears her throat. Dusts daintily at her blazer. "I, ah, did not steal the keys to The Dry Bean's bathroom."

Joey is shaking his head. "Robbie never lets the baby leg leave the hook without his say-so. He would never allow a patron to just walk out of the bar with the baby leg!"

"Oh, but he would." This (smugly) from Leo.

Sloane clears her throat again. "So, here's the thing. About Robbie. And The Dry Bean. The bar has been . . . entered . . . into my possession . . . in a manner of speaking."

A beat. Then, "What?" from all of us, except for Leo.

Sloane laces her fingers together in front of her and, looking very prim for someone standing barefoot on a love seat, says, "I bought The Dry Bean. During the last Best Night Ever."

Joey's mouth falls open. Alessandro asks if she bought the business, the property, or both. And I look at Leo.

"You knew?"

"Yes, of course I knew," he says. "She needed the family lawyer to try to get out of it. But even though the agreement was written on a bar napkin and Sloane was impaired enough to sing in public, we couldn't actually fight the sale."

"Because Robbie vanished the next day," Sloane comes in. "I went back the next morning to tell him I was going to stop the funds transfer I'd made the night before . . . I found the bar empty and the keys on the counter with a note telling me when to expect the next shipment of olives. None of the employees had anything but a phone number for him—which turned out to be disconnected anyway—and none of his business neighbors knew where he lived. We tried hunting him down at the Lake of the Ozarks since we knew he had a boat there, but it turns out Robbie might not even be his real name. His deed was inked almost forty years ago, when it was possible to get by with shoddy identification, maybe, I don't know? But the upshot is that the transfer had already gone through, he closed his account the next day, I can't find him anywhere, and now I have the bar."

She takes a deep breath. "And I've been keeping it a secret because I was hoping I'd be able to get out of it, and also because it's all just so embarrassing. Like I didn't even have the good sense to take up with a younger man, postdivorce. I bought a sticky dive bar instead. Which is why I occasionally have spare pallets of Perrier and I'm covered in chalk dust." She glares at Leo. "Which you should have known!"

"Known that you would be cleaning a chalkboard related to your little property mistake?" Leo asks doubtfully. "I don't think so."

"You bought The Dry Bean," Joey says, a note of dawning awe in his voice. "Sloane, *you bought The Dry Bean*! Just like we always dreamed of when we were younger!"

Sloane dismounts the love seat and, with a huff and a hop, attempts to put on her high heels without sitting down. "You know, it's a lot harder than you think, suddenly being responsible for a bar, and it's bad enough to"—*hop*—"be dealing with ancient chalkboards"—*hop*—"and the glass recycling company"—*hop hop*—"and knowing that I'm throwing my energy into a giant dirty hole that no one will care about after I'm dead— *Alessandro, stop*."

Alessandro, who was making a delighted face, throws up his

long-fingered hands in innocence. "You were the one who said *dirty hole*, Sloane, I'm only a man."

Finally in her shoes, Sloane lifts her chin imperially and extends her hand, like a queen, to receive the dirty, key-jingling baby leg that Joey solemnly places there. Then she bends down and scoops up the baby from Student Health, grabs her purse, and opens the office door.

"None of you are getting discounts at the bar," she pronounces, and then leaves.

We stare at the open door as Joey's alarm goes off.

"Shit," he mumbles. "The players will be getting here soon. Can I leave the weasel in your office?"

"No."

"Thanks, man, you're the best," he says, and turns off his phone alarm. He leaves without taking the diapered stunt baby still on the floor.

Alessandro and Leo look down at the ermine and the pile of diapers next to it, and then Leo nudges the taxidermied rodent with a tip of his shiny shoe. "Well, Bram, I'd love to stay, but Alessandro and I are going back to Kansas City to eat in a restaurant that doesn't deliver pita wraps to dorm rooms."

"Why were you in Mount Astra anyway?" I ask a little plaintively.

"Work, business, numbers, I'm a very important man," Leo says. Then offers his elbow to Alessandro. "Mi'lord?"

Alessandro beams and tucks his hand inside. "Mi'lord."

They start to leave and Maddie does too.

"Ms. Kowalczk, wait," I say quickly. "I thought we could talk for a moment?"

"Okay," she says, smiling at me.

Alessandro discreetly takes his phone out of his pocket and sends a text while he and Leo leave the office. I hear Leo's phone chime, and from down the hall, Joey's phone chimes too. *My* phone doesn't.

Fake friends!

But the sting of their treachery fades the minute Maddie closes the door and I have her all to myself. I frequently have her all to myself, but it's never enough, it's never enough. I drink in the carmine lips, the dark, shining hair, all of her like she's water and I've just woken up at three in the morning completely parched.

"Sara needs to stay at the research site for another four weeks, and so I wanted to make sure it was okay with you before I brought it up with the agency."

Maddie bends down and scoops up the ermine, realizes there's no good way to hold a stuffed ermine, and then cradles it like a baby in her arms while she replies. "Meaning I would stay on to help with the twins for another four weeks? That's absolutely okay. I love working with them, and I'm still stockpiling the first few months of rent."

My stomach twists a little, as it does every time I remember that Maddie will leave, that she'll get her own place. That even if we carry on, it will be harder to see each other, and gradually we'll see each other less and less and less, until it's over and she's moved on and I'm in exactly the same place.

"Okay," I say, my voice a little weaker than I'd like. "And you know you're welcome to stay as long as you like, even if you're not helping with childcare. I have the spare room either way."

"I know, Bram," she says, green eyes soft. "But it'll have to happen eventually. And I think I'll have enough in my account for proof of funds by Thanksgiving, for sure."

My stomach twists again. I struggle against the feeling silently, determinedly. It does neither of us any good.

"So Sloane bought the bar," Maddie says, and I think it's partially to move us on from the semi-awkward silence we'd found ourselves in and partially because, holy shit, Sloane bought the bar.

I scrub a hand through my hair and lean back, still a little bewildered. "I can't think of a less likely person to own The Dry Bean."

Maddie's eyebrow lifts up behind her new bangs. "Why?"

"Why? Because Sloane is elegance embodied and The Dry Bean has a mural of a snake giving birth to a jar of pickled eggs in the bathroom."

"Maybe it's exactly the kind of new beginning she needs after her divorce?"

I think about my own divorce, about my greenhouse. But then I think about the box of wooden skewers next to The Dry Bean's toilet and make a face.* "I don't know. Would you want a grimy bar as your new beginning?"

Maddie nods, immediately, emphatically.

"Really?"

She gives the diapered ermine an idle pat, like it really is a baby. "Do you know who my brother is?" she asks.

I shake my head.

"Really?"

"Should I?"

"He's kind of famous," she explains, "but he uses a stage name, so maybe you wouldn't have guessed. It doesn't matter right now.

---

* These are there for a disgusting reason, and you will be changed as a person if you google why. See also: *poop knife*.

What does matter is that when I was growing up, he made a lot of money. A stupid amount of money. The kind that should have made everything okay forever, except his skeevy manager ran away with most of it, and by then Nolan had already blown his share. And my dad died and my mom had bipolar disorder and needed to be home, and money was so tight, Bram, like *Nolan paying for groceries one meal at a time* tight, and usually with scrounged-up change. And then Nolan made it big again. He's married and on TV and has a financial adviser, and he could afford to move Mom out to California and pay for the expenses at Pepperdine that weren't covered by my scholarships. And I met Gentry, and it felt like here was my Cinderella story, at last, thank God. But you know how that fairy tale ended."

She looks down at the ermine, her bob swinging forward to curtain her face. "All of it was outside my control. It was like life happened to me—money, lack of money, housing, lack of housing. I had no agency. No idea when things were changing. No way to change things myself." She blows out a breath, ruffling the precisely cut ends of her hair. "So yes. If you're saying that a new beginning would be a building with my name on the lease and a business that I owned, that I made the choices for . . ." She looks up at me through her lashes, a small, knowing smile on her red lips. "My answer would be *hell yes, please and thank you*. And not only would I have control of where things went, but I could actually make things *good* if I had my own place. I could make them the way they should be. So much of our lives is spent living in a world that's been made by other people, by their greed or apathy or well-meant intentions—doesn't the idea of making the world match what you *know* could be better make you excited? And if you had your own little world, like a

Fundamentals of Being a Good Girl

bar, then you could start right then, without delay, no waiting time required."

Her words dose me like caffeine, waking me up, jolting my pulse. I had felt like this too, once upon a time, like shaping the world for the better was not just a dream but a demand, and I'd answered the demand, me and Sara with some borrowed babysitting so we could go off to fight greed and plunder.

I think about that younger Bram sometimes, about what he was willing to risk to change the world. How I'd gotten so disillusioned with both the right way of doing things (research and protests and policies) and the wrong way (Sara and I clambering up construction equipment in the dark) that I'd ended up choosing the way most adults take by default . . . the slow way. The way of mostly meaning well and hoping that being a decent person in the same spot for twenty years would be enough.

My phone buzzes in my pocket and I pull it out as Maddie finds a place for the weasel on my windowsill.

> **LEO**: I didn't want to say anything while she was there, but my guy is writing his report on a certain Mr. Gentry Cooper Wade III now.

> **LEO**: God, who names their kid Gentry. It's so on the nose. It would be like naming me Distressingly Handsome.

> **LEO**: Looks like he's decided to run on the tried-and-failed "I can be just as narrow-minded as my opposition about things normal people haven't cared about for thirty years" platform.

> **LEO**: There's a video of him saying that America's literacy issues are tied to porn. LOL. As if typing out MILF isn't important spelling practice???

> **LEO**: Anyway, my guy is going to send the report sometime in the next couple of weeks or so.

> **LEO**: You can thank me by admitting that Cole McKenney isn't real.

I put my phone away and tap my fingers on my desk, feeling restless and energized and a little bit like that younger Bram again.

Maybe it wouldn't hurt to do the right thing the wrong way just one more time.

CHAPTER TWENTY-FIVE

Maddie

JUNIE: Happy Halloween!

MADDIE: It's the sluttiest day of the year! I saw you in your cat ears when I was walking over to Salih. So cute! I'm sorry I couldn't make it in time for coffee this morning. Got caught up with my boss.

JUNIE: You mean Professor Bram Loe, who was ranked as Mount Astra's third most eligible bachelor in last spring's quarterly release of the *Astra*?

MADDIE: Is that a real thing? I cannot wait to constantly refer to him as Bachelor #3. Do you know who took spots two and one?

JUNIE: I think—despite not even LIVING in Mount Astra—Leo Saint James bought his way to number one[*] and number two was John Stickney, the carpet king of Terrell County.[†] Anyway, big plans for Halloween?

MADDIE: Nah. Just taking the twins trick-or-treating and then prepping for my lectures next week. What about you?

JUNIE: Would it surprise you if I said I haven't dressed up for Halloween since I dressed as Joan of Arc in high school and then was relentlessly made fun of because, I guess, my costume didn't lend itself to enough lingerie?

MADDIE: Am I a bad friend if I say no?

JUNIE: 😂 No, no, you're not a bad friend. It was all very on-brand for me. Well, I might have woken up this morning and chosen violence when I bought two wristbands for the Terrifyingly Tipsy Bar Crawl along the Snake Pit near campus?

---

[*] This is shockingly false, though not for lack of trying on Leo's part. An exchange did occur between Leo and Dean Holmes, the journalist, if you can call ranking Mount Astra's most eligible bachelors journalism. The exchange, however, was more carnal than monetary.

[†] This title is controversial at best. John Stickney is the proprietor of the leading carpet installation company in the area, but only because his primary client is the university and by the time he finishes re-carpeting the entire campus, it's usually time to start over again. A truly respectable racket.

MADDIE: JUNIE. ELLIS. Are you getting drunk tonight?

JUNIE: Um. Not if I have to do it alone.

MADDIE: Say no more.

JUNIE: Would you be interested in a slightly scandalous couples costume?

MADDIE: Would I be interested in stumbling up and down a row of college bars with our barely covered asses on display on this chilly fall day with you? Yes. Yes, I would. It's time for you to reclaim Halloween, my friend.

IF I COULDN'T tell Berry and Letty apart before today, then Halloween would be the ultimate test of their individuality.

Letty is dressed as a miniature Chappell Roan with a huge red wig and blue eyeshadow that I watched her diligently apply as she stood on the counter of Bram's bathroom sink, because the only way to achieve her look was to have her nose pressed to the mirror. As someone who values a strong wing eyeliner, I cannot agree more.

And Berry—sweet Berry—is dressed as an ant. A fuzzy and startlingly accurate ant. Specifically, a sugar ant. Since he was out of commission at a seminar last weekend—something about butterfly perverts—Bram and I spent the last four nights working on her costume until the wee hours of the morning and finally, today at breakfast, she deemed it a success.

"Did kids always go trick-or-treating this early in the day?"

Joey asks as his wife—Riley—and Fern walk ahead of us and he pushes the stroller with his two toddlers, who are both dressed as little trees. Riley is dressed as Bob Ross, their oldest is dressed as a paintbrush, and Joey is a giant easel. The costume is incredibly unwieldy, and I think it might be some sort of punishment on Riley's part.

"When we were kids, we went trick-or-treating after dark and took our candy to be x-rayed for razor blades," says Bram, who is dressed exactly as he always is but with the insistence that today he is the Brawny paper towel man. Hester Prynne's leash dangles from his fingers as the dog walks unusually slowly as though the foam shark fin strapped to her back has somehow interfered with her legs.

I was unprepared, so the twins took to their dress-up wardrobe, and I am currently wearing a unicorn horn and have a red lightsaber tucked into the sash of my jumpsuit.

"What exactly are you supposed to be?" Joey asks. "There's a vision here. I'm just not seeing it."

I shrug. "A Force-sensitive unicorn?"

Beside me, Letty stomps her foot. "You are not a unicorn!"

Berry nods as she hands her bucket to Bram to carry. "She's right. You're a narwhal."

Bram grins, nearly laughing at an outraged Letty. "Clearly a narwhal."

Letty nods and then passes along her candy bucket to Bram as well, and the twins race off to Fern, who announced earlier this week that she is too old to dress up. I watched Bram nod and attempt a smile as his heart broke in real time when she told us. He was a little too pleased when she walked downstairs before we left this evening in a slouchy red sweatshirt with tiny little devil horns clipped into her hair.

When we both stared at her, she just rolled her eyes, a coy little smile curling along her lips, and said, "What?"

Bram's neighborhood is the kind of place you see in movies. The streets are shut down from nonresidential traffic and kids run freely up and down and across the neighborhood without having to pay too much mind to cars. Parents are at ease, and while I always loved Halloween growing up, it is nothing like the street I grew up on, where nearly every porch was dark. Mom always drove us to one of the richer neighborhoods or over to the Lieberman house, where we would join forces with Nolan's best friend's very large and very extended family as they prowled the streets of their HOA-controlled neighborhood.

As we turn the corner, Bram and Joey are intercepted by some other dads who they seem to know from high school, and I continue on, following behind the twins, who are now safely sandwiched directly in between me and then Riley and Fern.

I love watching them huddle together as they line up to approach a house. Both of them—even outspoken Letty—feeling clearly shy, but finding confidence in each other.

"What the fuck kind of AI-conceived Halloween costume is that?"

The voice on the other end of the scathingly good burn is Veronica Balentine in a historically accurate aubergine Edwardian gown with a matching feather hat and umbrella.

"Veronica? Are you— Do you even *have* a family? I thought you just pulled your body up to an electric car charger every night and then woke up the next morning fully charged and ready to take someone's money."

She laughs, like she is actually delighted by my admittedly rude question. "You will be surprised to know that you do not need a family to celebrate Halloween, but since you've asked, yes, I do." She says it in a hushed tone, like she is not actually comfortable with anyone knowing any sort of concrete information about her outside of her life as a hired political gun.

"Mommy! That house had the big candy bars!" A young boy slightly older than Berry and Letty storms Veronica at the knees. He's dressed as . . . a Victorian urchin turned thief, perhaps? I can't tell between his cable knit sweater and the too big watch on his wrist, so rather than guess at what he might be and dash his little Halloween dreams, I simply smile and wave as he becomes suddenly shy when he realizes that there is a stranger in his midst.

"Paxton, this is Mommy's friend Maddie," Veronica tells him in an uncharacteristically soothing voice.

My jaw drops for just a second before I recover. "Nice to meet you, Paxton."

"Come on, Pax," another woman says as she strolls up behind Veronica wearing an absolutely dashing Edwardian tuxedo with tails. She pushes a stroller with a very chill cat inside who seems in no way troubled by the red wig and red-and-black satin and lace dress she has been dressed up in.

The woman nods to me, her hair slicked back into a low bun, and guides the boy to the next house while Veronica turns back to me. She sighs. "Pax developed an obsession with both *Twister* and *Titanic* this summer but the cow costumes were on back order, so my wife, Holly, handmade that Rose costume for Giovani."

"The cat's name is Giovani?"

She doesn't even entertain my question. "And she had luck sourcing the rest of the costumes from a rental shop in Kansas City."

"*Titanic* is an interesting obsession for a kid Paxton's age."

"Well, he requested to see some of his namesake's films."

"You named your kid after Bill Paxton?"

Her expression is unflinching as I piece together that she is dressed as the Unsinkable Molly Brown and that her wife is dressed as Billy Zane. Amazing.

"Bill Paxton is an American treasure. He did for nineties movies what Churchill did for morale during the Blitz . . . and for whisky and soda as a breakfast-appropriate beverage."

"It's nice to see that you are an actual human," I tell her. "A family man, even."

Her eyes dart to her left and then her right before she takes me by the elbow and steers me across the street behind a tree.

"Ah, there she is," I say. "That's the clandestine Veronica Balentine I know and love."

She pops her umbrella open and uses it to shield us from any remaining view. "Speaking of family men. Please tell me that you were just coincidentally walking alongside Dr. Bram Loe just now and that you do not actually have any connection to that eco-saboteur."

"Bram?" I ask. "He teaches about moss at the university and has a pet frog named Porcupine."

Her eyes widen. "Fucking hell, Maddie. Are you screwing him?"

My cheeks immediately burn red, and I'm thankful for the heavily shaded street shielding the sun as it dips lower and lower. "What? No. He's my boss. Of course not."

"Your boss?" she nearly shouts, then drops to a whisper. "That man is who you are nannying for? Do you have any clue whose roof you're working under?"

"And living," I add. "Technically, I'm a live-in nanny." And a world-class good girl with a whole host of kinks I'm only just now discovering, thanks to said boss.

"Quit," she demands. "Now."

My head is shaking, and I'm telling her no before I can even consider what it might mean to tell Veronica Balentine no. "I just told him I'd stay on for a few more weeks. His ex-wife comes back at the end of next month and then I'm gone. It'll be like it never happened."

"Oh god," she says. "Stay even further away from Sara. Trust me when I say that their divorce was a national holiday in the natural gas industry."

"What the hell are you even talking about?"

"That man," she says, pointing through her umbrella to the general direction where I left Bram, "is responsible for some of the most costly corporate property damage, vandalism, and data leaks in the last twenty years, all because he wanted to save the fucking trees or something."

The thought of Bram—responsible, level-headed, even-tempered Bram—being a very bad, bad boy is making me way hornier than it should. And I doubt that was Veronica's intention.

"What does that have to do with me?" I ask.

"Have you ever heard of Fasse Global?"

"You mean the gas stations? As in Fast Fasse Fill-ups?"

"Yes." She leans in and through gritted teeth says, "As in the company I am currently working on behalf of, and the company that is very interested in a fresh, new candidate to support as they enter into the green tech and energy space after an absolutely devastating data leak twelve years ago that sunk stocks so low even James Cameron couldn't find them if he tried."

My heart flutters at the thought, and I think I know, but I still ask. Why is the thought of Bram breaking so many rules such a turn-on? "A data leak orchestrated by Bram?"

Fundamentals of Being a Good Girl

"Ultimately, no one could prove anything, but everyone knew it was him. There's bad blood there, Maddie, and getting caught in the middle would be political suicide. You're sure the nanny gig is worth that?"

Everything I've dared to dream for the last few weeks is suddenly blurry, like it's the goddamn Heart of the Ocean and it's just—*plopped*—into the frigid sea at the hands of some old lady who has no concept of how many mouths that priceless jewel could have fed. (I have *Titanic* Feelings™ if that's not clear.)

"It's just for a few more weeks," I assure her. "And if anyone even does find out, I haven't done anything wrong. I'm not out here chaining myself to trees." Though maybe I could be tempted if it involved Bram and limited clothing.

"No more social outings," she says firmly. "If there is so much as an eyewitness account of you two even brushing shoulders, Fasse Global will hear about this and not only will they axe you, but they will mark you as unelectable."

I scoff even though, yes, that sounds ominous and a little terrifying. "I know you're involved in some back-channel blurred-lines business, but I hardly think a company can just blackball me altogether."

"A, they can. And if you don't believe me, you're far more naive than I gave you credit for, and B, Fasse Global isn't the only company with a vendetta against Bram Loe. The man is a pariah as far as the big donors are concerned. So keep your head down and get the hell out of there the moment your contract is up. Do you understand?"

My arms cross over my chest, and I look her up and down with one brow raised. She has no idea how much more complicated the situation actually is. But that doesn't matter, because Bram and I are just sex. It's that simple. We've even discussed the fact because we are mature adults who communicate. Plus, Bram was disgusted to hear that I was talking with Veronica Balentine, so even if I ever wanted us to be anything more, I doubt he could stomach the political games I'm willing to play to get the job done. He is an amazing, incredible man and the kind of father who could be a blueprint for the ideal dad, but we're not a match. Not in the long term. And especially because I am in no way searching for the long term right now.

As much as it pains me to admit.

"Understood," I finally say. Because I do understand. Even if I disagree.

CHAPTER TWENTY-SIX

Maddie

Bram clears his throat as I wait for Junie and the Uber she is taking here that will then take us to the Snake Pit, which is Mount Astra's bar district and the area of town where Bram and I first . . . well, fucked. To say it's the home of much licentiousness is an understatement.

And tonight, dear, sweet Junie needs me to be her wingwoman and I am nothing if not a girl's girl, so when she bravely ventured into the nearest Spirit Halloween earlier tonight and sent me a picture of a very revealing costume of Daphne from *Scooby-Doo*, I told her I would happily be the slutty Velma to her Daphne.

"And you're sure you won't be cold?" Bram asks for the ninth time.

"I'm going to be fine," I promise him. "Junie will probably tap out after one drink and then we're crashing at her place and watching a scary movie, though I think her definition of a scary movie is on par with yours, because she floated *E.T.* as an option."

Bram shivers. "That thing's hands are grotesque. Just the thought of that pointy little finger touching me . . ." He shakes his head aggressively.

He glances at the clock on the microwave. The twins are in bed and Fern is doing a virtual movie marathon with a Canadian pen pal and has asked not to be bothered (and for no one else to stream anything while she's watching things). I do feel bad leaving him here alone, especially when I would like to see what he might do with me in this costume, but I also need a night away. After all that Veronica Balentine unloaded on me, I feel this weird, self-imposed distance from Bram. Even though I said all along that we were just sex, knowing that we can never be anything more if I ever want a shot at public office, especially in the State of Kansas, is . . . sobering. And I think I need a night of being decidedly unsober to deal with that truth.

The costume, though . . . it's a real tease and I know it. I didn't exactly have the cash to splurge on a plastic bag full of ill-fitting polyester, but I did have a red pleated skirt and an unfortunate clearance-rack orange turtleneck that I had purchased a year or two ago and have never worn, because the deal was too good to leave it behind. I also had a pair of cheap blue block glasses that felt very Velma-esque.

After trick-or-treating, I ran out to the local sex shop/stripper shoe store and picked up a pair of orange thigh-highs, which are definitely closer to knee-highs on my thick lower half, and have donned a pair of red patent leather heels that I was going to wear during an anniversary date to some celebrity-owned sushi restaurant that Gentry had planned to take me to, except we had to stop at a donor party first for his dad's reelection campaign and we got stuck in small talk purgatory.

Bram eyes the very heavy amount of exposed leg I'm sporting after rolling my skirt several times, like a walking dress code violation. His expression moves from concern to desire and back again.

I nearly give in for a little heavy petting, but then headlights flash across Bram's large picture window as the car pulls into the driveway.

He inhales through his nose and then says, "Be careful, okay? And just know that I am stopping myself from saying very toxic things about you leaving the house in this attire and other men daring to look at you and how I will snap their arms if they even think about touching you."

My chest is tight and warm at how overprotective he is, but my head is so, so foggy from how much I want to lean into that feeling as I nod. "Thank you for not saying those very toxic things, and yes, I will be careful. I'll be back in the morning."

I reach up and give him a quick kiss on the lips (no red lip stains this time, thanks to my liquid lipstick that is more stubborn than a gel manicure). "I know Halloween can be scary, so don't be embarrassed if you have to sleep with the lights on."

He kisses me back and then grumbles something about it being totally normal to be unsettled by movies that intend to scare you.

Outside, Junie—or someone shaped like her—is waiting for me in the back seat wearing a black cape with red antennae and eyes on the hood.

The moment I close the door, the driver reverses out. I hardly even notice the pulsing black lights that line the interior of his sedan as Junie flips back the hood of her costume and says, "Surprise!"

"Please tell me your slutty Daphne costume is under there," I say.

She shrinks as she slithers down the back seat. The word *no* comes out as a quiet peep. "I chickened out. I'm so sorry, Maddie. You look amazing, though!"

"I do," I admit. "But we were supposed to be a chubby, hot Daphne/Velma duo and now I'm just Velma with . . . with a vampire bug?"

"Mothman, actually," she says. "Who just so happens to be my favorite cryptid."

"I'm confused about what happened in between the time you texted me and we agreed on our great couples costume idea and . . . Mothman."

"Right," she says. "So I was going to grab the costume. Technically, it was displayed up high so I had to ask an employee to reach it for me, which is just a sales barrier and something they should really consider when doing product placement. Can you imagine how many shy consumers they're missing out on just because our worst fear is asking for something and being perceived . . . or even worse, being told no?"

I nod for her to continue as Bram's neighborhood slips away and there is an escalating number of drunk college students lining the sidewalks.

"So I was all ready to be a brave girl and ask the very intimidating teenage boy who worked there for help, but then this incredibly beautiful sorority girl who I helped last week with a research project about the scientific plausibility of *Jurassic Park* was there. I think she picked the topic as a joke, by the way, but it was fascinating. Truly. And she was actually very clever."

The car begins to slow as pedestrians clog the streets and we are getting closer and closer to the action.

"Anyway, the very pretty and also very smart girl had her huge boyfriend whose arms were as thick as an electric pole reach up and grab the costume for her and I just—I panicked. Because that was a hot girl costume, Maddie. And you—you are a very hot girl. But I'm—I'm the girl who dresses up as Joan of Arc or the girl who gets genetic testing done on her cats. I'm not a slutty Daphne."

I lean over and touch the spot just above her knee, which is covered in black fleece leggings. "That's not how that works, Junie. You must be the slutty Daphne you wish to see in the world."

She sighs in a forlorn sort of way and then nods. "Well, I looked for a Scooby costume or even Shaggy or Fred, but they were sold out, and then I saw this Mothman costume and—" She shakes her head and braces her hands on either side of her head. "It's Joan of Arc all over again. We should just go home. I'm so sorry, Maddie. We don't have to go back to my place if you're allergic to cats. I can just have the Uber take you back."

The car stops where the street is closed for the night, and I open my door, pulling Junie along with me. "Junie Ellis," I say. "We are going to have the night of our lives and it doesn't matter if you're slutty Daphne or Joan of Arc or a DNA-obsessed cat lady. Because we are grown-ass women and we can wear as little or as much clothing as we want on Halloween."

"Hell yeah," the driver says as he reaches out the window to fist-bump me. "I'd appreciate a five-star rating, ladies."

"Of course," Junie calls after him as she nods to herself and then at me. "Okay, okay."

"And you know what? Joan of Arc was a badass bitch. So let's go out and party for teenage Junie and for Joan of Arc and for the ability to DNA test your cats and for Mothman."

"Yeah!" she says, a fire lighting her eyes. "Who's to say Mothman isn't a total slut?"

"Woo!" some girl cheers as she walks past us, a very suspicious water bottle in her fist that is definitely full of something boozy and clear.

"Let's do Halloween up the butt!" Junie yells as a battle cry.

I laugh at how incredibly bad she is at being bawdy. "Wow, okay. Did not expect that. But yeah, let's sodomize the hell out of Halloween!"

10:42 P.M.

The Dry Bean is a sea of bodies, but Junie and I are diligent as we weave our way through the crowd to the bar. I search for Sloane, but if she's here, I'm too short to see her.

The bar crawl includes one drink and one shot from every bar in the Snake Pit, so we have some work to do.

I pull Junie along, refusing to let her get swallowed by the crowd. Her eyes are wide, but she's putting on a brave face.

When we finally make it to the bar, the bartender is quick to notice our wristbands and pulls two Jell-O shots from the windowed mini fridge on the counter behind him.

"Two Water Snakes for you, ladies!"

I pass Junie the small disposable cup full of blue gelatin and a gummy snake.

"Do we . . ." She eyes it thoughtfully. "Do we need a spoon?"

"Use your tongue!" I yell over the chaos.

She appears to be entirely daunted, so I take her hand and hold up my shot. "To slutty Mothman!"

"To slutty Mothman!" And then with absolute gusto, Junie tilts the cup back and tongues the glass like a thirteen-year-old attempting their first French kiss.

"Atta girl!"

The bartender hands us each a cup full of a glittery red drink that he calls the Skin of a Killer and tells us that we can take it outside as long as we don't leave the Snake Pit.

"That was disgusting!" Junie shouts in my ear. "I feel so cool!"

11:28 P.M.

"Oh my god, oh my god, I have to take your picture."

Junie's costume is a hit, but I was unprepared for the bloodcurdling scream that left a girl's mouth when she rushed Junie and hugged her just a moment ago.

The girl steps back and she's wearing the same cape as Junie except underneath is nothing but a red lacy lingerie set.

"I'm so jealous," the girl whines. "You look so warm."

"But you look so sexy," Junie tells the girl, her words slurred. "And I mean that in an empowering way!"

Everything feels fuzzy and light and this is the cutest thing I have ever fucking seen.

"A picture! You two need a picture!" I pat my skirt and then shove a hand up my shirt to feel around my bra, but my phone is definitely not in my bra or shoved into the little red boy-short underwear I opted for tonight. Shit. I left it at Bram's—but librarians are like Boy Scouts, right? Always prepared? "Junie, give me your phone!"

She does, and I creatively direct the greatest photo shoot of all time right there in the middle of Tombaugh Avenue.

"Okay, now make kissy faces!" And because I am nothing if not committed, I make a kissy face right along with them like the good stage mom I am.

12:19 A.M.

"Thanks for coming to the bathroom with me," I tell Junie. "I usually read on my phone when I pee, but I left it at home, so I really needed company."

She sits on the counter of the single restroom, her legs swinging, and doesn't even blink at the sight of me hovering over the suspiciously grimy toilet. "Boys pee standing next to each other every day. Why is it weird if I want to come into the bathroom with my friend and talk to her while she pees?"

"Exactly. They literally shake the pee off their dicks together and it's weird if you hang out while I take a little tinkle?"

"We need to reclaim the act of social peeing!" Junie says, her little fist curled and ready for rebellion. "Right after we finish reclaiming Halloween. When you close your eyes, do you see little dots? Do you think I'm having a stroke?"

I wipe and then do the stand/flush/hand wash dance. "I think you're just drunk, but if you still see the dots tomorrow, we can call Dr. Meredith Grey."

Someone pounds on the door, and we both jump.

"Wait your fucking turn!" Junie yells, and immediately slaps a hand over her mouth.

"That was so hot," I tell her. "We should stay in here for another few minutes and take some mirror selfies just to teach them a lesson."

Junie hands over her phone and hops down off the counter. I really shouldn't have left my phone at home, but here we are.

We pose a few times and I twirl around and stick my ass out a little so that it peeks out from under my skirt before snapping a mirror selfie over my shoulder.

"Now, *that's* a good one," I mutter, and immediately open Junie's text messages and type out Bram's phone number, which I memorized in case there were any emergencies with the girls. Because I! Am! So! Responsible!

After attaching the photo, I hit Send and pass it back to Junie.

When we leave the bathroom, some dumbass bro dressed as a cactus with giant balls snarls at us. "Fucking bitches."

I turn to the boy and step closer and closer to him until his back is pressed against the door. I sniff at the air, because I can smell his fear.

He quickly moves from annoyed to concerned as I square up to him.

And then I bare my teeth and growl before letting out a rumbling bark as I snap my teeth.

Behind me, Junie laughs and begins to bark as well.

A few other girls waiting in line join in, and before I know it, half of the women's lacrosse team all dressed as crayons are buying us shots.

"To slutty Velma!" Junie shouts, and the lacrosse team echoes.

1:31 A.M.

Junie and I sit on the curb outside a bar called The Library that she is very charmed by. We paraded around the place while Junie announced that she was indeed a librarian and we were treated to many shots. *Too* many shots.

"What if we die?" Junie asks. "What if our bodies are so full of alcohol that the little people inside of us who operate our bodies drown and die?"

My head lolls to the side as it rests on Junie's shoulder. It is cold.

Very, very cold. And I refuse to ever admit that to Bram. "The little people inside of us?"

"When I was a kid, I always imagined little versions of myself inside of me, clocking in for work, and pumping blood like a water pump and carrying food down into my intestines via—what's it called when a bunch of people work in a line to assemble something?"

"An assembly line?"

She kisses the top of my head. "How did I get so lucky to have such a pretty and smart friend?"

"*No*," I shout back at her, "you're the pretty and smart one. I am very stupid and a huge mess."

"Don't you dare talk shit about my friend like that or else—or else, I'm going to compliment you until your ears bleed."

A little burp slips out and I don't even try to cover my mouth. "I *am* a mess, though."

"Because you're totally doing Dr. Bram Loe, Mount Astra's third most eligible bachelor?" Junie asks.

"What the hell, Junie?" I sit up way, way too fast. "How did you know?"

"Well, you smile a lot in the mornings. You moved in with him." She leans over and whispers in my ear, "And sometimes you smell like . . . sex."

My eyes turn into saucers as I lean back and attempt to swat at her, but instead I swing at the air and lose my balance, somehow landing flat on my back.

Around me, people continue to walk, like this is totally normal and I guess at Halloween in the middle of the Snake Pit, it totally is.

I can't see many stars, but the lights and the flashes of shoes and bright, sparkly costumes feel a little bit like magic.

"Oh my fucking hell," Junie says in a voice that is suddenly very sober. "Maddie, we gotta go. Right now."

I moan and curl onto my side. "But I'm so comfy."

"Shoot, shoot, shit, shoot," she mutters. "Okay, I'll be *right* back, Maddie. Don't go anywhere, promise?"

"Oh, sure," I say. "Why not?"

"I'm going to be just around the corner of the building, keeping an eye on you." She groans, but it almost sounds like a shriek. "What the hell is he even doing here?"

I can't tell if the confusion is because I am genuinely confused or if I'm just that intoxicated. Who cares? My eyes slip closed and why have I never slept on the pavement before? It's so cozy!

I hear myself make those delightful little moans you make sometimes when you're so sleepy that the feeling of finally giving in to slumber is too good to resist.

"Madelyn," a smooth aristocratic voice croons. "Made-lyn, wake up, little bird."

When I open my eyes, a man with blond hair and an impeccable tuxedo is grinning down at me.

The man taps my nose three times. "Does Bram know that his little pet is drunkenly sleeping on the sidewalk in a garment that is more closely related to a belt than a skirt?"

"Mmmmm." All I can do is groan as he scoops an arm under my shoulders to sit me up. "Hey, I know you. You're Mount Astra's number one most eligible bachelor."

"I am indeed." Leo Saint James taps my nose again, which I find very annoying even though he seems to think he's sooooooooooo funny. "Six years and running. I have a title to maintain, you know, despite not actually living here. A mere technicality."

He sounds very snooty and I don't think I like his tone. "Well,"

I tell him, "I bet you're not fucking Mount Astra's third most eligible bachelor and letting him eat you for breakfast every morning because breakfast is the most important meal of the day."

Leo breaks out into a wide, brilliant, sparkling smile. "Oh. This is good. This is very good. Excuse me for a moment."

He takes out his phone and begins to type.

"What do you want?" I ask. I am losing my patience here. "I have dreams to sleep and snores to snore."

He pockets his phone, seeming all too delighted with himself. "Up we go."

"You look like someone made you in a factory for good-looking people."

"Thank you," he says, like it's a compliment he hears every day. He glances over his shoulder. "Correct me if I'm wrong, but was that person who was just sitting beside you a moment ago dressed as Mothman?"

"Slutty Mothman," I correct him. "Slutty *librarian* Mothman. Because Junie is a librarian, and if you're a librarian in real life, you're still one on Halloween."

He squints a little and then nods. "Yes, of course. Junie is slutty librarian Mothman. I think, if you'll excuse me—" And he straightens up, his eyes scanning the crowd like he's going to Richard Gere–style hunt down Mothman right this minute. Which is when I fall back over onto the sidewalk.

And then start giggling uncontrollably.

The single loudest sigh of all time leaves his body as he stares down at me. After a minute where he seems to have a long, internal argument with himself, he holds out his hands to pull me up.

"Standing up is overrated," I tell him. "I would like to sleep

Fundamentals of Being a Good Girl

here, please. File a permit with the city if you must. This is my home now."

Leo's eyebrow lifts. "And get killed by Daddy Bram and have my beautiful specimen of a body turned into potting soil? Not happening, little bird. I don't think you know what that man is capable of."

I pout and I whine, but begrudgingly I let him pull me up.

No matter how many times I blink, the world is still blurry, but I'm able to see that I'm at eye level with the fourth button down from the collar on Leo's pressed tuxedo shirt.

"What are *you* supposed to be?" I ask like it's an accusation.

"An indecently handsome person in a tuxedo."

I frown.

"Jay Gatsby," he says.

And then everything around me is moving.

No, no. That's not it.

Everything *inside* me is moving.

I begin to shake my head, like that might somehow stop the trajectory of the next ten seconds. "I'm going to—"

And then I puke. It's mostly blue and a little bit purple and thankfully chunk free. But I puke on Leo Saint James of the Saint James Chocolate Co., and I can say without a shadow of a doubt that this is the most expensive tuxedo I have ever puked on.

"I'm so sorry," I say, the words feeling like a cry. Suddenly, I just want to go home.

Leo takes a deep breath and sheds his jacket before cloaking it over my shoulders. "It's fine, Madelyn." He glances around like he's looking for someone, anyone, but after a moment, breathes a resigned sigh. "This was my Monday tuxedo, anyhow."

CHAPTER TWENTY-SEVEN

Bram

I was already pacing, phone in hand, warring with myself about whether secret hookups get to retrieve wayward brats or whether that's AITA material, when Leo calls.

"While I'd love to leave a very hot, very drunk Velma on your doorstep like a DoorDash order, I also remember very vividly that you are a gigantic motherfucker and I'd rather not test your godlike anger," he says when I pick up.

"What?"

"Madelyn is currently warbling 'Part of Your World' from *The Little Mermaid* while lying on a sidewalk outside an Irish pub," Leo explains. "She's pretending to have a mermaid tail. She also told me to do something absolutely disgusting with a knockoff Gucci belt we found abandoned in a potted plant."

I hear a trilling voice above the general clamor and shouting of the Snake Pit on Halloween, singing about bright young women sick of swimming.

"I'll be right there," I say, already going for my car keys.

"Spoken like a good Boss Daddy Bram," Leo approves, and then the call ends, leaving my screen open to the picture sent to my phone two hours earlier from an unknown number. Maddie in a strange bathroom, giving me a coy look over her shoulder, red lips pulled into a kiss, skirt flirted up just enough that I can see the juicy swell of her ass.

The thick-rimmed glasses and the thigh-highs she's wearing—obscene. Impudently filthy. I've already saved the picture to a hidden folder[*] on my phone.

With a growl, I text Fern to tell her that the house is hers for the next twenty minutes and then I go outside to my car.

TOMBAUGH AVENUE, THE main artery of the Snake Pit, is still in party mode when I get there, although only a few of the bars are still serving drinks, and the party has shifted from shots and well drinks to flasks and weed vapes. And it's not like the Snake Pit is Rome under Caligula or anything, but seeing all the reckless young people and the for-real grown-ups who definitely have no business partying like they're twenty-two is making me itchy under my skin. I need to find Maddie, see her, make sure she's safe, and then I want to ask her exactly what she thought was going to happen when she sent me that picture.

And then—*and then*—all sorts of raw, caveman reactions jostle inside me when the crowd parts, and I see the white glint of Leo's hair, and then Madelyn Kowalczk sleeping soundly at his feet. Flat on the cold, hard sidewalk in a delicious display of turtleneck and short skirt.

---

[*] Parents with children of any age know: your phone's pictures are not private.

I want to scoop her up, haul her home, and take her over my lap. And then hold her close, because Jesus Christ, seeing her passed out on the sidewalk while drunk, rowdy frat boys horse around just a few feet away . . .

I reach Leo, who, other than the drying vomit splattered on his tuxedo pants and dress shoes, looks like he just stepped away from a dinner with an ambassador. And then I drop down to a knee and gently rouse Maddie.

"Your nanny threw up on my shoes," says Leo, unnecessarily.

"Childcare provider. Where is Junie?" I ask Maddie, who's just opened her eyes behind her fake glasses. They are a shock of green in a world of cool shadows and golden streetlights.

Maddie manages to look scornfully defiant as I help her sit up—an impressive feat, truly, to still look like a czarina while reclining on a sidewalk—and I notice that her red lipstick is still immaculate when she replies, "She left me on the sidewalk because Gatsbys and Mothmen don't get along." She pronounces this statement with great import, like she's preambling a talk on bipartisanship and trade agreements.

Something dangerous rolls through me at the admission that she'd been left alone, a spill of red ink in clear water, and I bite back the words crowding behind my lips, piling on my tongue. I don't roar at the sky. I don't threaten to handcuff her to my bed so she can't go wander down dark, cold streets drunk and alone.

But, oh god, I want to.

"You were going to chase after Mothman," Maddie says to Leo, the suspicion as heavy in her words as alcohol. She's pointed a finger at him—or at where she seems to think he is, but it's currently pointed at a clump of frat boys who are dressed as different Dolly Partons. "That wasn't nice of you."

"I thought I'd say hello to Junie," Leo says, the neutral words layered with cool indifference. Maybe a graze of malice.

I meet his eyes, which are suddenly the dangerous silver of my high school bully. Of Junie's high school bully. There are a lot of years between that Leo and the Leo of now, but when it comes to Junie Ellis, I don't know that there will ever be enough.

"Okay," I say. "We're done here. Maddie, can you—no? Okay." I help Maddie to standing, my hands wrapped around her shoulders to keep her from toppling over. I grit my teeth when I feel how cold she is through the thin fabric of her turtleneck.

"Thank you for staying with Maddie until I got here," I tell Leo.

Leo lifts a shoulder, expression bored.

"And keep away from Junie Ellis," I add.

His beautiful mouth twists into something bitter, but he doesn't speak, only inclines his head in the way of someone acknowledging something has been said. And then he leaves, all wide shoulders and tailored wool and platinum hair, vanishing into the bustle and crush of the party.

"He even makes—*hic*—an exit like Gatsby—*hic*—" Maddie sways and I help her navigate the sidewalk until we get to the end of the block and past the pedestrian barricades. We get to my car and I help her inside, not waiting for her to try to buckle herself in before doing it myself, and then slide behind the wheel.

I take a deep breath before I start the car. I have never felt like this. *Ever.* I don't know what to do with all these wild instincts, which belong in a 1940s pulp fiction novel and *not* in a present-day, non-romantic, sex-based, 1099-implicated relationship.

We drive the seven blocks home in silence. I park and turn off the car, and then help her out of the passenger's side and up the porch steps. I stop her just inside the front door to kneel and remove her high heels. She has a small blot of pinkened skin on the side of her thigh with pinprick specks of blood trying to bead through. A scrape.

"Madelyn," I say calmly. "Have you seen what that sidewalk has done to you?"

Maddie blinks down at me and then narrows her viridian eyes. "You sound excessively judgmental right now," she says with disapproval in her tone. "That sidewalk was very good to me."

She hiccups, loses her balance, and then grabs onto my shoulders for support.

I finish pulling off her heels and set them to the side. And then I stand up, staring down at her, making a decision.

"To the shower," I say, and start guiding her to the stairs.

"*Ooh*, sexy," she says. "But wait, don't you want to screw me while I'm wearing these thigh-highs?"

I do want to screw her while she's wearing those thigh-highs. And that turtleneck, which clings deliciously to her pert tits and then the curves of her waist and belly. And that skirt, which starred so naughtily in that very improper selfie she sent me.

"You need a shower, Ms. Kowalczk, and then water, and then bed."

She looks back at me over her shoulder as we go up to my floor. Even soused, she manages an expression of such unutterable disdain that it nearly knocks me back.

Until I remember how cold her arms and feet had been when I'd touched her. Until I remember the scrape on her thigh.

"Up," I say sternly, and her disdain immediately melts into a pout.

"You're so *mean*," she mumbles as I herd her over the top of the steps and down the hallway, into the bathroom.

Fundamentals of Being a Good Girl

"I am going to undress you," I tell her as I close the door to my en suite. "I'm going to make sure you don't have any more damage from the sidewalk, which was very good to you. And then I'm going to wash you. Is that okay?"

"Is sex in there somewhere?" she asks, reaching for me.

I grab her wrists and give her a sharp look. "No. Behave."

It is a testament to my willpower that I'm able to peel off her thigh-highs without breaking my own rules, or that I'm able to pull her slutty panties down from under her skirt without bending her over and making her understand—*acutely*—how protective and possessive she makes me feel.

I somehow get her into the shower and propped against a tiled wall under the hot spray without doing anything untoward, and start soaping her soft, still-chilled skin as she stares unabashedly at the hard-on in my lounge pants. I've tucked my cock into the waistband, and the swollen head is just visible as it tries to peek out, and Maddie is watching it with the avaricious gaze of a Victorian opium eater.

"Why don't you get undressed and come in here with me?" she asks in a low, dick-jolting voice. "It would be better than getting your clothes all wet."

"You, my brat, are too drunk to have sex. And even if you weren't, I think I might want to spank you more than I want to do anything else. What were you thinking, putting yourself in danger like that? Completely drunk on a cold night in a town you still barely know? And that's not even touching on the Snake Pit of it all, with all the other drunk people. If Leo hadn't found you . . ."

"Oh, you're *big mad*." She sighs. "Can't you be *tiny mad* instead?"

I give her a forbidding look before I get the shampoo.

"It wasn't like we planned to be unsafe, it just happened, and I really needed a drink after Veronica Balentine told me we couldn't have sex anymore—don't worry, I'm not going to listen—"

"When did you see Veronica Balentine?" I ask, a fresh irritation nestling inside me. I hate the idea of her ensnaring Maddie into that circle jerk of donors, candidates, and power players. Of her perverting Maddie's hunger to get shit done into something wan and feeble and status-quo preserving. Or worse—ambitious and profitable.

"While we were trick-or-treating—she named her son after Bill Paxton, by the way—and then she told me that . . . that . . ." Maddie hiccups as I work the shampoo into her hair. "You used to be a criminal. For the environment or something."

I freeze. Only for a second and then I continue washing her hair, my thoughts alternately sprouting and dying, all of them failing to take root.

I should have known that this would come up. I should have known that I'd need to tell her about this, explain my past, make some attempt to justify it. But if there ever was a silver lining to *sex and nothing else*, then this had been it—that she didn't need to know. Not really. Why would she if she was going to leave and then we were going to be nothing?

"Yes," I finally say, and unhook the showerhead to rinse out the shampoo. "That's true."

Maddie turns to look at me once I finish rinsing her hair. "Really?" she asks with wide eyes. "That's so hot."

I snort, replace the showerhead, and move on to the conditioner. "Okay, little criminal. Close your eyes."

"But I don't understand why you stopped," she asks as I work the conditioner into her hair. "If you never got caught, why not keep going?"

I've never had to explain this before, which is strange to think about, but I suppose it makes sense in a way. Everyone else had been there—Sara and the other members of the Andromeda Club—and so there'd been no need to explain why it had started and why it had stopped. Everyone already knew.

"We were almost caught," I begin as I unhook the showerhead again. "Sara and I, together. They were building a pipeline through a wetlands area south of town—the wetlands are important to the Native American community here, and it's an incredibly biodiverse and ecologically fragile area—and we went to fuck up some construction equipment in the dark. We were careful, we always were, but someone must have seen us. The cops showed up, and we only got away by the skin of our teeth. And we realized that if we'd both been arrested, then we didn't know what would happen to our kid afterward. We could have been pinned with enough to mean jail for a long, long time, and we knew my grandparents wouldn't take Fern, and Sara's parents had too many health issues to raise a little one, and so we had to stop thinking like baby activists and start thinking like the guardians of a preschooler. In a way, even though we were already parents, it was the day we became adults."

I rinse Maddie's hair, savoring the wet silk of it through my fingers, savoring also the way her eyes roll back as I massage her scalp, her temples, the nape of her neck. Her eyes are closed and her mouth is open by the time I'm done. I give her a final rinse, replace the showerhead, and then turn off the shower, leaving her side briefly to find a towel, and then returning to bundle her inside it.

"Wait here," I tell her as she stands shivering a little on the mat, and then I go to her bathroom and return with her clear bag of toiletries.

And then carefully, with the slowness of someone who barely knows what they're doing, I use Maddie's makeup wipes to clean her face of slutty Velma makeup.

"So you stopped for Fern," Maddie says as I tilt her face up to make sure I've got everything.

"We stopped for Fern," I confirm. I find Maddie's moisturizer and squeeze some onto my fingers. I gently start applying it to her face. "But it was always stupid. We were white kids with a mostly middle-class upbringing, and so we thought playing Robin Hood was a game, an adventure. Coming to terms with our own recklessness and our own privilege was . . . disorienting." I set the moisturizer down and then pull Maddie into my bedroom and make her sit on the bed while I find clothes for her to sleep in. (Yes, she has her own pajamas, I know, but the primal pleasure of putting her in my clothes is too much to resist.)

I take an old T-shirt and sweatpants and help her pull everything on. "The hard part was that we did try to do things the right way, after," I tell her. "When it came to those wetlands, I mean. We threw ourselves into the research the university was doing, we went to all the town halls, all the planning meetings, we went to protests and wrote to politicians and spoke to newspapers. No vandalism, no data leaking, no sabotage. Just all the things you're supposed to do with community and science and asking your political leaders to help. And it didn't matter. It didn't work. They built the pipeline anyway."

"I'm sorry," Maddie says softly.

I smile at her, brushing some wet hair away from her jaw. "It's okay. For a while, I let big defeats keep me from smaller wins, but the smaller wins are worth it too."

Maddie's mouth pulls into a *watch me* smirk. "But you know what's even more worth it? *Big* wins."

I laugh. "That's my brat."

Dressed in my old, baggy clothes, Maddie goes back into my bathroom to brush her teeth, and I follow. It's confusing to brush your teeth with someone who only wants sex—it's an act that's bound up in the feeling of playing house, of cozy routines and small intimacies—and I fight off a wave of pained yearning as we do it.

"To bed," I tell her when we're done, pulling off my own shirt and lounge pants as I crawl into bed with her.

She acts up again, trying to kiss my neck, her hands cupping my cock, but I know she can't be sober yet, so I flip her around so her back is to my chest and pull her in tight, wrapping my arms around her and cinching her close.

She yawns. "I feel like I'm being swaddled."

"Just until you can be trusted."

"You're such a daddy," she murmurs.

I almost point out that I am literally a daddy, but I know what she means. "I like taking care of what belongs to me," I say simply.

"Do I belong to you?"

Her words hang in the air, curious, dangerous, still undeniably drunk. She wouldn't ask this sober.

She wouldn't admit to wanting to know the answer sober.

I just hope that she's too drunk to remember the way I hold her closer and quietly admit, "I want you to, Madelyn. So fucking much."

CHAPTER TWENTY-EIGHT

Maddie

It feels a little risky and a little wrong—okay, a lot wrong—but I wake up in the morning in Bram's bed and burrow into his chest. I should run upstairs before the girls wake up. I definitely shouldn't enjoy the fact that his sweet, unconcerned face with his lips just slightly parted is the first thing I see when I open my eyes.

I fell asleep with him holding me tightly to him and it was soothing enough that I fully understood the magic of Temple Grandin's hug machine. I fell asleep wishing that I could feel this safe and looked after every night.

Last night, as I brushed my teeth, I watched Bram from the corner of my admittedly fuzzy vision. The panic I expected to feel while standing alongside someone who I was also sleeping with as we brushed our teeth never materialized.

That's probably due to the fact that I haven't been that drunk since my last year as an undergrad, during Model UN, when we used the bathtub in our room to make trash can punch. Luckily, the alcohol likely killed any bacteria lurking in the bathtub of that particular Holiday Inn Express.

Along Bram's forehead are the beginning of very faint worry lines, and I can't stop myself from tracing each crease.

Bram's eyes open slowly, blinking until I come into focus. "There you are," he says.

"I'm sorry about last night. I was definitely a drunk brat," I tell him. Most everything after Junie panicking and running is a little blurry, but I'm sure I did or said things to embarrass myself. I'm certain I puked on Leo. So I don't know in entirety what I'm apologizing for, but I do know I was a handful.

"I like when you're a brat," he says through a yawn. "And you are a very adorable drunk, but I was worried for your safety. I know I'm too overprotective. I just . . ." His gaze wanders down to where my palm is pressed against his bare chest and he covers my hand with his, like my touch alone is enough to regulate his beating heart.

We kiss. It's slow and soft. We're quiet. I sling my leg over his hip so that he can slip inside me as we lie on our sides.

When we come, I bite down on his shoulder to stop myself from making a sound.

I allow myself to stay like that with him for a few more moments before I sit up and scoot off the edge of the bed.

He stretches his arm out across the span of mattress between us. "You could stay," he says. "You could just sleep in here at night. We go to bed after the kids and wake up before them."

I turn my head to the side to catch a glimpse of him. "Bram . . ." I can't give him what he's asking for. I can't give myself what he's asking for. Because I feel something happening. As much as I want to ignore it, I have this sense of unraveling, and if I give in to a simple request like sharing a bed, my heart won't be able to unlearn the feeling of waking up next to Bram Loe. Even if him and his stability and his perfectly structured and full life is the last thing I need right now.

"It wouldn't have to mean anything," he says, but his voice is flimsy and unconvincing. "But I like being around you, Maddie. There's nothing wrong with that. People who just have sex can enjoy each other's company."

"I like being around you too. But I think it's better if we don't. I don't want to confuse the girls." *Or either of us*, I nearly add.

"Right," he says, his tone returning to logic. "Of course."

JUNIE CALLS THAT afternoon in near tears and fumbles over her words. She apologizes to an excessive extent and explains that she and Leo have a history of sorts. She's vague, but says she lurked in the shadows like a real-ass Mothman to keep an eye on me until Leo left, but he never did leave and then Bram showed up and . . . well, since Junie knew I was safe, she called a car and went home to her genetically analyzed cats.

I plan on digging deeper to find out what the hell it is about Leo that is severe enough for her to literally hide from him, but those are buttons to push a different time, when she is far less tearful.

The next week is good. I've found my sea legs in the classroom and among my department. Word very quietly spreads that I pushed back against Wallace, and other professors from my department give me encouraging nods and knowing smiles. I'm even invited out to lunch with a group of tenured professors (who are much younger than Wallace) one afternoon and they fold me into their conversation and banter like I've been there all along.

I know that teaching isn't my endgame, but it feels good to be more certain of myself and to know that I can do this. I can do this and I can enjoy it too.

I'm capable. I am entirely capable.

"At least I don't have to worry about adding a stylist into your campaign budget. At least not while you run for local or state offices." Veronica Balentine hovers beside me, eating olives out of her martini and then swirling her glass before throwing back the remainder of her drink in one shot.

I sip from my lime club soda. After last weekend, it's going to be a few more weeks at least before I can stomach an adult beverage. "Thank you, but you are welcome to divert that budget to keratin hair treatments and a shopping allowance."

Veronica texted me on Thursday and told me to meet her at the Astra Hotel on Friday night, where the Democratic party was hosting a dinner honoring U.S. Representative Gretchen Bailey and the bill she successfully introduced and passed during the last congressional session, Caden's Law, which limits an insurance company's ability to deny coverage to children seeking somewhat experimental treatment for life-threatening illnesses.

It also just so happens that Representative Bailey is the state party leader and the woman who they are currently seeking a replacement for when she retires in four years, so when I was told to dress like I was the most charismatic person in the room who you would also trust with your grandmother's notebook full of passwords, I knew exactly what to wear: the forest-green skirt suit I wore to the Pepperdine alumni luncheon last fall, where Gentry was invited to accept a philanthropic award on behalf of his family when all they actually did was donate a heap of money after one of his cousins got caught masturbating in a computer lab.

Veronica navigates me around the room, making introductions, and when I realize that I'm the only potential candidate on her arm, I turn to her in a moment between new faces.

"Don't you have other ponies to parade?" I ask.

"Not at the moment," she says.

"Am I to take that to mean that I'm the last one standing?"

"There are always—and I can't stress this highly enough, Maddie—*always* other options in the wings, but yes, at the moment, you are my primary focus."

I take a sip of my drink to hide my smile.

"Don't look so pleased with yourself," she tells me. "You still have plenty of chances to fuck this—" She strides forward and discards her drink on a tray of canapés. "Representative Bailey!"

I follow close behind as she and the congresswoman take hands and give each other fake little cheek kisses. Apparently, Veronica Balentine can schmooze, which is incredibly unsettling.

"Representative," she says, "I'd like to introduce you to Madelyn Kowalczk. This little firecracker is young, but I think it's safe to say that she's got quite the future ahead of her."

Congresswoman Gretchen Bailey is the kind of woman who sets you at ease. She doesn't look like she's had work done, which means the work she has had is incredibly well-done. She is calm and serious but smiles and laughs just enough to remind you that she is not a law-passing robot.

"Representative," I say, "congratulations on the bill, and I have to say I truly enjoyed watching you put Matthew Flowers in his place during the judiciary hearings you presided over while his pharmaceutical company's privacy terms were being investigated."

"Ah, yes," she says, "I believe he called me a—"

"Prehistoric battle-axe," I finish for her. "I can only hope that one day a slippery pharmaceutical exec accuses me of being the same." I lean in like we're just girls sharing secrets and give her a wink. "It'll mean I've done my job well."

And at that Representative Bailey lets out a genuine, barking laugh. "Oh," she says through a giggle, "this one is as cheeky as you said she'd be."

I allow myself a moment to preen before the congresswoman loops her arm through mine.

"You know," she tells me, "I just pretend that the term *battle-axe* refers to Kansas's own Carrie Nation."[*]

Representative Bailey regales me with historical facts as she begins to introduce me to her inner circle. Our heads huddle together as she gives me the CliffsNotes on every guest, and for the first time in my semiprofessional life (if you can even call being Gentry's arm candy that), I feel like I've been invited into the back room and that I am not just aware of the secrets, but I'm in on them.

All around the room, people begin to watch me and speculate, because it turns out that I might be someone worth watching. I might just be the party's next shiny, new star and a formidable one at that.

Every once in a while, I search for Veronica in the crowd, but she's slipped into the shadows like a mother who knows that the most important lessons a child will master are meant to be gained on their own.

---

[*] A suffragette and prohibitionist who was known to walk into bars with a literal axe and destroy fixtures and bottles of liquor. She sold miniature souvenir hatchets to raise funds and refused to wear a corset. Icon.

I am delighted by the thought that the people I am meeting tonight might be future chess pieces to accomplish the sort of change I've always dreamed of. Big changes that would rewrite the future of health care and resources for financially insecure families and protections for women and the queer community. Things that would have made a monumental difference for little Maddie.

But there's also this quiet curiosity in the corner of my mind as I watch Veronica slip through the room, whispering in ears and shaking hands. She's a puppet master, and while that might sound sinister to most, I'd be lying if I said I wasn't fascinated by the very necessary—if at times morally gray—work that she does.

At the end of the night, I wait for my car at the valet stand as I chat up a young state senator who talks to me like I'm his peer. It's a small moment that most people might be unfazed by, but I wish I could document it and send it to Gentry. *Look at me now. You thought you'd used me. That I'd served my purpose and needed to be discarded because there was nothing of value that I had left to give. But Gentry Cooper Wade* the Third, *you were wrong about me and one day that will hurt. It will hurt so goddamn bad.*

When I make it back home, the house is dark. All three girls are spending the weekend with their grandmother, and Bram is already in bed.

The floorboards creak as I take the first step to my room, but then I pause.

Tonight was perfect. So perfect that for a moment, I think I could just have it all. I could have the job and the power—the kind of power that women are called dirty for even wanting. I could have a family. I could have a man like Bram who is far too good for me. A man who feels things like right and wrong in his bones. A man who I thought would be horrified if he knew just how willing I am to do a little bad for the sake of good. But then he told me about the man he used to be, once upon a time.

My heels echo across the hardwood floor as I walk to his room.

Bram is lying in bed, glasses on, his shirt neatly folded in his armchair, and one leg propped up. He holds a thick, heavy book from the spine with just one hand, his chin resting on his chest.

"Hi," I whisper as I kick off my heels and shed my suit jacket so that I'm only wearing my pencil skirt, stockings, and silk camisole.

He places his book flat against his abdomen and pulls back the covers.

Without letting myself think too much about what exactly this means, I climb in next to him, curling on my side in the narrow space between his body and the edge of the bed.

I lay my head across his chest and I feel far too comfortable. Far too at home under this roof. In this bed. Alongside this man. In his fully formed life.

CHAPTER TWENTY-NINE

Bram

For the second time, I wake up with Madelyn Kowalczk watching me, a little line between her brows and her eyes flicking over my face like she's trying to commit me to memory. It makes me feel like a king, because she's *here*, she wants to be here, this lovely, sharp thing who could be anywhere.

Having her in my life is like having a finicky, fickle plant in my care—a maidenhair fern or a string of pearls or a red-lipped Habenaria—and knowing that sometimes you can do everything right, have all the right calibrations of water, sun, soil pH, and watch the plant wither anyway. Still have the plant not choose you. And right now I feel like the plant has chosen me. Like I'm staring at vibrant petals, shining leaves, an overflowing pot, and it's alchemy, it is lead into gold, the singular gardening victory of my life.

Somehow I got it right, and I'm waking up to Maddie looking at me like I'm a fight she's going to win.

Fundamentals of Being a Good Girl

I reach up and trace her mouth with a curled knuckle. Her lips are soft and pink, free of lipstick, and I can see every crease in the middle where they're almost too full. The sharp, sharp corners, like they were drawn by an artist concerned more with drama than anatomy.

I think of the way she looked last night coming into the bedroom: silk blouse, *watch me* heels, victory all over her face like a lioness with blood on her muzzle. I'd gotten hard so fast it hurt.

"You're terrifying," I murmur to her, and pull her close. She's still in her silk camisole, but her skirt, stockings, and panties are discarded on the floor, leaving her naked below the silk. Her legs part in an unspoken invitation, and I trail a hand down to where she is warm and still damp from what I gave her after she slid into my bed.

She sighs happily, as if I've said the swooniest thing a non-boyfriend can say. "Thank you."

"You looked like a goddess last night," I say as I start stroking her. She sighs again and stretches in my arms, moving to her back and opening her legs even more. "Not the flowery sea-foam kind, but the helmet-and-spear kind. Like you'd just razed a city to the ground and had the survivors erect a temple to you there."

"Mmm, I like that," she breathes. She's properly wet now, and I indulge myself by playing with her, circling the opening of her, sliding deep inside and crooking my fingers. The house is empty for another day and night yet; we have nowhere to be, and I want to take my time in the late autumn sunlight. Maybe this will end, and maybe it will end soon, but I have right now, and I won't waste a second of it.

I draw out her orgasm, sucking on her hard nipples through the silk, murmuring to her about how ruthless she is, how beautiful, about how I want her to have everything and how it's hers to take. And when I finally give in to her arches and whimpers and I caress her clit like we're on the clock, she climaxes with my name as a sigh on her lips. *Bram.*

I want to crawl on top of her and trap her with my arms and legs and make her say my name over and over again, just like that, *Bram Bram Bram*, like I'm the plant in the greenhouse that needs talking to in order to thrive.

I resist the urge, somehow. Mostly because I want to feed her. I kiss her forehead instead, ghosting my mouth over the shapely line of her brow, the delicate skin of her temple.

"Breakfast?"

IT'S LATE FOR breakfast, but I don't let that stop me from spoiling my brat with the works: French toast, cut fruit, bacon so crispy it's nearly burnt. She sits on the counter in these little shorts that drive me to distraction and an old Astra sweatshirt that she's brazenly stolen from me as she tells me about the event last night.

". . . and after we talked, I think there's a real opening for the state's department of education to make green-tech academies a statewide resource. Wind is our largest single source of electricity, and the jobs are there *now*, and so we can focus on trade certifications and prepping future engineers and innovators—oh, thank you"—I've just handed her a hot latte, doctored up with whipped cream and cinnamon on top—"and Veronica says there's a real chance we can get some of the other side to join us as long as we focus on *jobs* and not the *dying planet* of it all."

I pull open the dishwasher while she crosses her legs and sips the latte I made her. "Do you think the *dying planet* part is really a flexible part of the narrative, though? The more it gets erased, the easier it is to subvert."

"Does it matter if we say *sustainable domestic initiatives* instead of *mitigating climate change* if it gets us to the same place?"

I think about this as I start putting away the clean dishes. "It honeycombs the core message," I say after a moment. "It allows special interests to quietly lobby for subtle changes that weaken legislation. It hazes over the clarity and necessity behind *why* a change is initiated, which means legislators and civil servants, and in this case, school boards and superintendents, aren't all pulling in the same direction, even if they think they are."

"Or it allows something to get done instead of nothing," Maddie posits, humming a little as she sips her latte. She gets whipped cream on her nose and I step over to shamelessly lick it off, which makes her laugh.

"Do you think," she asks as I go back to the dishwasher to finish unloading, "that, on a legislative level, it's sometimes okay to do the right things for the wrong reasons? Or at least the less-right reasons?"

"Less right. Like . . ."

"Like how public libraries are meant to make an educated voting populace, which is kind of soulless and abstract when you think about it, that education is only for civic duty and not for individual enrichment or opportunity—but then libraries also act as free warming and cooling centers and safe places for kids after school or for unhoused people. Or like how we went into space to keep up militarily with the Soviets, but ever since, it's been wildly important for all kinds of science things, maybe even more than for the military things. Maybe the words we use to get important stuff done are all just—" She waves a hand. "Marketing."

"My experience with marketing is that it gets very tempting to change the product to suit the pitch, rather than the other way around."

"Or we don't do that, we say *jobs* a lot in the legislation, and then have a toast after when we've managed to make the world a better place without having a bunch of pointless fights with the oil shills. Also, you look so hot doing that. I could watch this all day."

I look up from the pan I've started scrubbing, not feeling particularly sexy in my old T-shirt with a dish towel slung over my shoulder. But Maddie is watching me with predatory eyes.

"Sara trained you well," she says with a nod to herself before she lifts her latte to her mouth.

I laugh. "And she bemoans every day that no one is putting me to good use."

"You two really do have a good thing." She sounds admiring—and jealous. Not of any potential unresolved feelings between Sara and me, I think, but jealous that we ended things as friends.

"There were painful parts," I tell Maddie as I finish with the pan and move on to the breakfast dishes. "I don't want you to think that it was all easy. But it wasn't a catastrophe. Have you ever heard people say that you shouldn't marry someone you wouldn't also want to get divorced from?"

Her eyebrows pinch together. "Uh. No. I have not heard that."

"It sounds stupid, I know—because why would you marry someone if you were already considering divorce? But the idea is that you wouldn't want to marry someone who you couldn't trust to—on the worst day of their life, on the very, very worst day—still treat you with respect and kindness. Sara and I did that, accidentally. We were too young to do it on purpose, but somehow it happened anyway."

Fundamentals of Being a Good Girl

I start putting the rinsed dishes in the dishwasher, feeling some tenderness for those babies who got married in a panic, trying to figure out how to have a baby with no money and only partially ripened frontal lobes. For those adults five years ago trying to figure out how to make a fresh start without fucking the other person over. "I remember when we first dragged it into the open, the feeling that the marriage was fading for the other. And we decided that we wanted our ending to feel like autumn. Like fall. Not a struggle or a fight, not a death, but something organic and necessary. And there was grief and friction too, but we held strong to our autumn plan because we believed in a new spring and summer for ourselves, and for each other. It worked."

I close the dishwasher, start a cycle, and then wash my hands. When I turn to face Maddie, she's looking at the latte cradled in her hands. Her eyelashes are so long they nearly rest against her cheeks as she does. "Everything about being with Gentry felt like a struggle. Like I had to struggle with myself to be the kind of girl who *he* didn't have to struggle with, if that makes sense. A smart but quiet blonde who was content to stand in the background and prove his good taste."

She shakes her head and looks up at me, a rueful smile on her face. With her dark, dark hair, dramatic brows, and wicked mouth, she is the furthest thing from the girl she just described. "Sometimes I think . . . I think that it doesn't matter as much as it should? The years I wasted on Gentry, my childhood worrying about Medicaid and bills and groceries—if I were writing a memoir before I launched a campaign, all that low-key trauma would be my spider bite story, the explanation for why I'm the way that I am. But maybe I would have always been like this?"

"Like what?" I ask.

"Sharp," she replies. "Hungry. Too fucking stubborn. I see a problem like a dare, and I look for problems that aren't even problems yet. I want to win, but I want to win in a way that no one has ever thought of before. I want to make the impossible real, and then I want to keep going. I want to be harder and meaner than every hard, mean thing in this world, and cleverer too, and I'd rather be called bold than brave, and I'd rather be trying and fucking up than doing nothing at all. I don't want to settle for what they tell me to settle for; I want to make the world better and I won't accept less than more and I won't accept it slower than right now."

Her lips part as she inhales and then looks away.

"Not very good girl of me," she finishes, with a self-deprecating laugh.

I set the dish towel on the counter and walk toward her, planting my hands on either side of her knees.

"That's okay." I lean in, touch my forehead to hers but don't give her the kiss she starts seeking. "I only want you to be a good girl *for me.*"

Her exhale brushes against my lips. "Oh?"

"I think," I murmur, dipping my lips to her jaw and then her neck, "that you should be as ferocious as you want to be. As cunning as you want to be. And that's how you'll be my good girl. By being the sharp, hungry Maddie you need to be everywhere else."

"*Oh*," she says, not a question this time, because I'm kissing her neck and she's shivering and shivering.

"You want to practice?" I ask against her neck, and then pull back a little to watch her face. "You want to be Sharp Maddie right now?"

"How?"

Fundamentals of Being a Good Girl

I straighten up and take her latte from her hand, set it on the counter of the kitchen island. "Tell me what to do."

"Now?"

"Yes."

"Here in the kitchen?"

"Yes."

I stand in front of her, my T-shirt dotted with dishwater, the sunlight pouring in and showing everything. Every gray hair of mine, every fine line around my eyes. Every place where her near-black hair reveals the subtlest hint of light brown, a barely there freckle across her nose, the shallow cleft in her chin. This isn't a game played in the dark or a moment stolen with our tweed or lipsticked armor in place. This is stripped of all pretense, all gloss, the honesty of it undeniable. I see it in her seeking eyes, in the hesitation parting her lips.

But then that sharp, hungry Maddie comes through. Her eyes drop from my face to my shoulders to my hips and the thick length already starting to stir there. Her tongue comes out and dabs at her lower lip.

"Tell me," I say again. "Make me."

A flush is blooming on her neck. She exhales.

"Take off your shirt."

CHAPTER THIRTY

Bram

I obey Maddie and take off my shirt, reaching behind my head and pulling it off from the neck. I fold it and put it on the counter. The way her gaze goes ardent and keen at the sight of my bare torso has heat crawling up my thighs.

"I love the hair on your stomach and chest," she says on a sigh. "Fuck, it's hot. Take off your pants too."

I should feel self-conscious undressing in the middle of my kitchen in broad daylight, but there's only eagerness to do what Maddie wants, to gratify her, and when she makes a happy noise at the sight of my dick and my (just as hairy as my chest) thighs, pleasure surges in my belly. I love giving her what she wants.

It takes her a moment to speak, but not like she's having second thoughts. More like a general surveying the field, choosing where to outflank the enemy.

"Stand just there." She picks up her latte, leans back on one hand, and uses the mug to indicate a spot by the entrance to the dining room with the air of someone gesturing to movers where to put a couch.

I obey, of course.

It's a good spot for someone to stand naked; from here, I can see into the living room and parlor and into my office, I can *feel* the open space of my house around me, the distance to the walls, the brush of air currents from the house's little system of easterlies and westerlies, the unfiltered sinfulness of standing naked in full daylight in an open space. But it's also shielded by various angles from view; despite the many tall windows in the house, there's no danger of neighbors or passersby seeing anything other than Maddie slouched on the kitchen island, one leg now dangling idly over the edge as she sips from her mug. If they happened to notice the sultry curve of her mouth, or that her eyes are glintingly fixed on one spot, well. They would never be able to see why.

I stand with my feet apart and my hands at my sides, ready for her to make me do whatever she wants. Which I have a guess about, but coarse satisfaction still floods me when she says in a clear imperative, "Jerk off for me."

My cock is hot to the touch when I take it in my hand, hot and swollen enough that the first brush of my fingers has pleasure rippling through my stomach. Maddie watches with undisguised gratification as I take a moment to collect myself, cupping my balls, running a hand up to my chest.

Well, it *was* a moment to collect myself, but now I'm preening a little bit, showing off. Spreading my hand wide as I move it back down over my chest and stomach, letting her take in the hair she says she likes so much, the tight lines of muscle moving under my skin. I cup my balls and widen my thighs. When I start stroking myself, I don't use the quick, efficient *you have five minutes in the shower so make them count* motions, but the long, grazing *make it last* kind. I make sure she can see the muscles in my arm and shoulder bunch and tense; I want her to see the flex and release of the tendons in my forearms and wrists and hands. I want her to see the three veins meandering thickly up my dick, like vines, scandent and seeking, and I want her to see the clear glisten of desire pooling at my slit.

She's trying to play it cool still, her latte in hand, her dangling foot, but the mug is frozen halfway to her mouth and I can see the jut of her nipples even through her sweatshirt.

Ahhh, *fuck*, I like this.

I like this a lot.

Is this how she feels coloring her lips bright red? Putting on a skirt that she knows will have me hauling her into a corner at the first opportunity? I'm not an exhibitionist; I don't have any internal craving to be watched or perceived. And yet showing off *for her*, making her throat move and her cheeks pink just by existing . . .

That's potent.

And it's exhilarating to realize in my mid-thirties that I'm actually sexy to someone. Sara and I got together when I was short and awkward and stammering, my teeth everywhere, my body a mix of knobby bones and soft places.[*] And so nothing changed for me romantically or sexually after the muscles and the hair came, or after my features caught up with my teeth and nose. Sara loved the clumsy youngster and the big, quiet man just the same, and so I guess I never reconsidered my own attractiveness. Attempting to

---

[*] *Ugly duckling* is a kind way to describe a young Bram Loe. *Bully's dream* is more accurate. Just ask a tenth-grade Leo Saint James.

date after the divorce, even this attachment with Maddie—well, I know what I can do for people. Make them feel good. Make them feel cared for. And I like doing those things, honestly.

But it does feel nice to have Maddie look at me like I should be on the cover of a magazine. Like she's memorizing the sight of me to rub her clit to later.

"Go faster," she says. The mug has been abandoned and she's scooted to the edge of the counter. Her chest is moving up and down under the sweatshirt. "I want to see how you do it when you're getting yourself off alone."

"Can I come?" It seems important to ask her this, to know exactly what she wants.

Her eyes are so, so dark with pupil now, despite the light filling up the house. "No," she says, her voice shaking a little, with lust and maybe with the power of it too, the ability to deny me something we both know I want. "Not yet."

"Then I won't," I say, although I'm already in the danger zone, already feeling that pull deep in my groin. The shimmering mirage of relief just a few hard pumps away. I take a breath and try to steady myself as I wrap my hand securely around my cock and start working the thick organ with the kind of strokes I like in private—steady, short, rough. You could set a metronome to how I fuck my fist, and Maddie seems to have set her heartbeat to it, judging by the fast heave of her chest and the unconscious squirm of her hips.

I'm there so fast, my balls cinching up and my thighs trembling, and I feel the first dangerous swell of my penis, the tight, angry knot at the base of my spine, and I yank my hand away with an agonized noise, my ribs jerking with futile, uneven breaths.

Her breathing is just as uneven, her lower lip wet from licking, her right hand up and kneading her breast, as if it's aching and needs relief.

"Good," she says, her voice a little hoarse. "That's so good, Bram."

I grunt, my entire body clenched against the release, a string of shining pre-come dripping from my tip.

She watches me strain for a moment, clearly enjoying my struggles, and then comes to some kind of decision, because her lips curve wickedly.

"Again," she declares, "but this time—"

She wriggles out of her shorts, which have nothing underneath. She's wearing only the sweatshirt now, and then it's all plump, creamy thighs and that ass and those hips and the adorable smile of her belly just above her bare pussy.

"This time I'm going to come while I watch you," she says, perching on the edge of the counter and spreading her legs wide. The sunlight means that I can see immediately how worked up she's become watching me jerk off, and when she runs two fingers up the center of herself, they come away wet. "But you still can't come."

"Maddie." It comes out as a growl. A warning.

"You said I could tell you what to do," she purrs as she licks her own arousal off her fingertips.

Fuck. Me.

My cock gives a painful jerk in the air, without me touching it. Another string of pre-come drops to the floor.

She touches herself again, this time focusing on the needy bundle of nerves at the top of her sex, relaxing back on one hand again and looking for all the world like someone having a casual self-care session. Like someone treating themselves to a nice morning with some porn. It's so goddamn hot, and without meaning to, I grab myself again, stroking as I watch her fuck herself. Delicate fingers, her nails varnished the same killer red as her lipstick, fucking against all sweet, wet pink.

"I did this thinking of you after that first day when you showed up on my doorstep." The words come out jagged and harsh. "That night. I got in the shower and I thought of fucking your mouth until you had pink lipstick all over your chin. I thought of bending you over my desk and spanking you until you were begging and squirming, and then making you take me as deep as I could go. Making you come on me while my handprints were still glowing on your backside."

She sucks in a breath, her fingers moving faster. "I fucked myself that night too," she admits, her hips moving now to meet the pleasure. "In the library bathroom. I had to bite the side of my hand to keep quiet. I thought about you calling me a brat. I imagined you finding me on campus and making me take your cock before class." Her gaze is on that same cock now, like she's jealous of me for touching it and also like she's . . . proud of it. Like it belongs to her, a treasured possession that she can demand at any time, and oh god, it's true, it belongs to her as much as the rest of my body and my mind. As much as my heart.

"Tell me the worst thing you thought about," she demands breathlessly. "The filthiest thing. The thing you would never even imagine if you were in your right mind."

"Maddie, don't," I groan, jerking myself harder despite my protests. "Don't make me say it."

"But I'm in charge right now, and I want to know," she says, brat and queen all at once. "You're always so good, so careful, but now I know that you've been bad before too. That there's a streak of it in you. That you want to be bad with me." The last part comes in a low voice—the words broken as her hips move even faster into her touch.

And I shouldn't, it's awful, it's nothing like the person I want to be, nothing I would ever even think with anyone other than Maddie, but—

"I thought about you being the nanny," I grind out, ashamed and aroused and maybe a little angry, even, to be forced to admit this. "*My* nanny. The pretty nanny walking around my house in her flirty little skirts, flaunting herself at me, knowing full well that I already knew how good her pussy was. I thought about having her whenever I wanted—available, wet, forbidden, but still mine mine mine."

"Me too," Maddie whispers, eyes fluttering. "Oh god, I thought about it so much. So fucking wrong, but I imagined you using me whenever you needed relief—*fuck*—"

We're merciless with ourselves, and the *noises* right now, the wet noises, the chafing, slapping noises, the whole scene is beyond indecent. With our shared nanny fantasy hanging in the air, it's just plain wrong. And yet, I'm there, and I'm so fucking depraved because the orgasm clawing its way up my groin is fueled by our filthy words . . .

"Don't come," Maddie gasps right before she cries out my name. Her entire body shudders, rolls, fucks, as she keeps rubbing herself through the cataclysm shaking its way through her. It's wet on the counter underneath her, on her thighs, and I'm about to die because I can see the quiver and pulse of her climaxing cunt.

I make a noise I don't even recognize from myself—something like a roar and a whimper together, one breaking apart into the other—and force my hand away from myself, having to curl my bare toes into the floor and brace every muscle in my body against

Fundamentals of Being a Good Girl

the pleasure threatening to tear its way up my cock. It surges angrily in the air, redder than the rest of my body, so swollen that the skin is satin and gleaming, the veins huge and furious and beating with my rabid heart.

But it holds. With several shredded breaths and more fluid leaking out of the tip, my orgasm holds itself at bay.

Maddie is still quivering, still riding it out, the flush on her cheeks and throat matched by her flushed cunt as she comes to the end of her trembling contractions. She takes a slow breath and lifts her hand from between her legs. Wet, wet, wet.

"Come here," she whispers, and I'm helpless but to comply, coming to the counter and then accepting her fingers when she pushes them into my mouth. I groan at the taste—sweet, light, all Maddie—and then let out a guttural, animal sound when she hops off the counter and grabs hold of my thoroughly edged flesh.

"Follow me," she says, like I have a choice with those red-tipped fingers wrapped around my dick. Like I'd ever do anything different. And then all five foot two of her leads all six foot four of me by my tender, throbbing cock up the stairs and to my bedroom, where Hester Prynne vacates the bed with a huff and stalks off to find somewhere else to leave an imprint of fur.

"Lie down" is my next order, and I do it, not bothering to pull down the covers, my mind fixed only on relief. I'll do anything she says to get it. I'll have her sit on my face. I'll rub myself against the soles of her feet. Literally anything so long as she'll let me come.

She doesn't make me wait. She crawls over me, swings a leg over my hips, and then mounts me like I'm a service she's paid for.

I clench my jaw as she impales herself, the squeeze of her channel so unfairly tight, all of her like silk, like a slippery glove I barely fit into, and when she sits up straight and starts using me with her hands braced on my chest, I find clenching my jaw isn't enough. My hands are fisting in the blankets, my breathing is coming in gusts from my nose like a bull's, and after she whips off her sweatshirt to reveal her pert, bouncing tits, I have to close my eyes for a few seconds because I can't handle it. I can't handle it.

"Bram," she says, her voice husky, private. "Bram, look at me."

I look at her. I keep my eyes on her face, on those jewel-green eyes with those long lashes, on her upturned nose and wide mouth.

"I know," she says. She says it like a benediction and a confession also. "I know."

She's riding me and I'm dying and she is looking at me with every version of herself—the brat, the lioness, the good girl—all of it is in her eyes and her face, all of herself, and I know that I could spend a thousand years with each version of her and still not get enough, and still need more, and maybe she sees *that* on my face, because she says, in a strange, bewildered kind of voice, "It's never felt like this."

And then she jerks forward, her hot cunt clamping down on my length like divine vengeance, an act of God, and I grab her waist, brace my heels, and start fucking up into her with every minute's worth of denied frustration, with every day's and week's worth of longing and need. I fuck her like I'll die if I don't; I fuck her like I've never even heard the word *good*.

I fuck her like I love her.

And then with her still orgasming around me, the climax catches fire, burning me from within, searing up my cock and exploding as I start unloading pulse after pulse deep into her pussy, every jet of semen coming with a rush of pleasure so intense that static fuzzes around her, that my fingers are going numb and tingling.

It's never felt like this.

It's never felt like this.

My ears are fucking ringing.

Her green eyes are the only thing in the world.

I'm spilling into her body, each surge coming with a hard thrust from underneath, my orgasm leaking out around us as I stab up into the tight kiss of her cunt over and over and her hands scrabble at my chest as her head falls forward and she shudders and shudders until we—finally—both go slack.

I'm still seeing sparks.

Maddie collapses onto my chest, warm and quiescent, and I stroke her back with fingers that have yet to fully regain circulation.

"Good boy." She sighs happily, and a rush of satisfaction floods through me. No wonder she likes being called a good girl. It feels fucking great.

I keep stroking along her spine, enjoying her little shivers since I'm still deep in her body. "What you said earlier," I start. But I'm not sure how to finish.

"Mmm?" She nuzzles my chest and snuggles in closer.

"When you said that it's never felt like this . . . it's the same for me. Which is strange to say with having been married before, but that was different, and this is different, and I want—I want . . ."

I don't know what to say next without terrifying her. Without running roughshod over all the rules we agreed to.

I finally settle on: "I want this, Madelyn. I want all of this."

"I know." It's a murmur against my chest, dozy, sweet. Like she's agreeing with me.

"You're growing all over me. Like wisteria. Like—" I smile even though she can't see it. "Like jasmine."

And it's a bad idea to murmur the rest, but I don't stop myself,

I won't, because she is right, she is right. It's never felt like this. "I want to keep you, Madelyn. Let me keep you. Let me water you and feed you and move you into the sun. Let me . . ."

I don't quite have the courage to finish the last sentence, though.

Let me love you.

Let me love you.

But maybe I don't need to. Maddie props herself up to look at me, her hair tousled to hell and back, her cheeks still flushed. Her pupils are big and there's a softness to her face that I rarely see. "You'd be a good gardener of me, Bram," she says. Her voice is full of something, and I can't quite name it, but it feels fragile and hopeful, and it makes my heart beat twice as fast underneath her.

I love her. I love her, and this, whatever this is, is the only thing I've ever had just for myself, and she is the only person I've ever let have all of me—my attention and my friendship and my care and my carnality. My darknesses and worries and certainties and the joys closest to my heart, and I want everything of hers in return, and I'll nurture it, all of it, the thorns, the carnivorous parts, the clever, seeking roots. The sweet, silky petals that bloom only under the right touch.

And yes, I'd be a good gardener of her, but she's already the best gardener of me, the only one I ever want.

"It's just as well," she says, closing her eyes, "because I suck at gardening. I can't keep a plant alive to save my life."

"Everyone can keep something alive," I tell her, a fond amusement curling around all the other emotions blooming in my chest. "Even a preschooler can keep an aloe plant happy."

Maddie opens one eye to glare at me. "Tell that to my graveyard of dead aloe vera plants, Bram. I killed an air plant last year. They said I was supposed to mist it. But how much mist? And how often? Oh, one mist too many? Dead. You know what? It's gaslighting, that's what those plants are. Succulents too, they can fuck right off."

I laugh, shaking her where she's lying on top of me, which makes her laugh in return.

"I'll make a plant mommy out of you yet," I say, and lift my head to kiss her. She kisses me back, that soft hope staying in her face and making a summer inside my chest.

"You make everything out of me," she says. "And you make me want things I shouldn't want."

"Who says you shouldn't want them?"

She moves to kiss me, her dark hair falling around my face, her eyes going from green to black as her hair screens our faces from the sunlight. "I don't think I know anymore," she whispers, and presses her mouth to mine.

CHAPTER THIRTY-ONE

Maddie

Bram was made for playing house. We stay in bed for a while, and I show him funny memes and videos on my phone. A few of them he doesn't fully understand, and I have a good time laying into him being such an old man.

Then we take a shower, and I reward him for being such a good boy earlier with his cock in my mouth as the warm spray of the shower cascades down my back.

And then Bram decides that I am going to own a plant and that this time is going to somehow be different because I've never gone plant shopping with Dr. Plant Daddy Bram Loe. With the girls still at their grandmother's, it's just the two of us as he leads me out to the oversized shed at the end of the driveway.

He unlocks the old rolling door to reveal an old but organized collection of every lawn and gardening tool a person could ever want, including bags of soil and a rusty old baby-blue truck that is definitely older than me.

"My first car," Bram explains. "It was my grandfather's, and he and my grandmother saw no point in me driving a vehicle that couldn't potentially haul dirt or ferry around larger plants and small trees. So I held on to it, because by the time Sara and I could afford a new car, it wasn't really worth anything. This thing guzzles gas like a freshman pre-gaming for their visit to the Snake Pit, but I only use it to go back and forth to the nursery or to pick up supplies for the greenhouse. And okay, I have also moved many couches in my day."

"Bram Loe, environmental crusader, owns a shitty-ass old truck that basically leaks fuel."

"It does *not* leak fuel," he informs me as he walks me around the truck and helps me up into the cab.

The truck bounces along down the road as we drive to Taking Stalk, the nursery formerly owned by Bram's family. It's different to see Bram in a vehicle that he actually fits inside as opposed to his very eco-friendly compact SUV.

"You know, I'm not sure this plant field trip warranted a ride in your dilapidated truck."

"First off," Bram says, "this beaut is not dilapidated. And second, if you're going to keep this plant alive, you need the full plant-buying experience, and for me, that includes a ride in the truck."

"Okay, well, thank you for this immersive experience."

"Nothing but the best for Madelyn Kowalczk."

Bram rolls the windows down as we drive across town. The last few days were pretty windy, so only the most stubborn of leaves are still hanging on to their branches. As he turns the wheel with one hand, Bram reaches over the middle seat where my hand is resting and laces our fingers together.

We're out in broad daylight, driving around, and now Bram is holding my hand and I think at this moment that Bram and I feel more like a couple than Gentry and I ever did.

I know that in the moment when bodies are molded together, panting in unison, it's easy to say things. Things you don't mean. Things you wish you could.

But earlier today with Bram, something was different. It wasn't just that I was in charge or that we had the house to ourselves. Those things heightened the experience, of course. But it felt so . . . domestic. Him making breakfast. Having the luxury of that spiraling out into raw, unfiltered desire. Then at the end, in those final moments with me on top as he let me use his body like it was my own, we were two hearts in one rib cage.

Somewhere inside me, a wall fell down, and I started to imagine not just tomorrow morning with Bram but every morning with Bram. Picking up the girls when he and Sara were busy. Coming home to find his friends loitering. Falling asleep on his chest while he watched the same documentary for the eighth time. Listening to him talk about campus politics. Him listening to me talk about actual politics.

It all felt suddenly possible to love Bram Loe.

"This is the original location," Bram explains as he parks the truck, pulling me from the rose-colored fantasy occupying my thoughts. "By the time I was born, my grandparents already had three other locations, but this was the one where they had the company office. It's the one where Sara and I worked together in high school."

Bram comes around to open my door, and as I begin to slither out because there's no foothold, he grips my waist and guides me to my feet. "Thank you," I murmur.

He places a kiss on the crown of my head and takes my hand.

His hand envelops mine, and I love the feeling of it too much to pull away. This is more than daytime sex in multiple locations in his house or holding hands in the truck. This is us in public. In a too-small college town where there are no unfamiliar faces.

"They didn't always have the whole shopping center," Bram explains. "But as businesses moved out, they snapped up the other storefronts until they'd taken over the whole place and eventually bought the property outright."

The shopping center is low and wide in true mid-century modern fashion and the sign is angular with teal starbursts. The letterboard beneath the sign reads GO BIG OR GOURD HOME.

When we walk in, the kid behind the counter waves to Bram, who at first grabs a basket but then opts for one of the small shopping carts instead. "Just in case," he explains.

I appoint myself the official shopping cart pusher, and rather than walk alongside me, Bram hovers behind me with his hands on my shoulders and the rise and fall of his chest brushing against my back.

"So," he says. "It sounds like an air plant was not the best option for you. And I can understand your frustration. A lot of tending plants is intuitive, which isn't always user-friendly for the casual plant owner."

"I'm going to kill this thing," I tell him. "I'm going to kill it, and you're going to be so disappointed in me."

He bends down and tsks in my ear. "Baby, you could kill an entire greenhouse and I wouldn't be disappointed in you."

My breath hitches at the completely standard pet name that couples everywhere use. I let my head drop against his chest for a moment. "Okay, Bram, lead the way."

We weave up and down each aisle, and in and out of the open air part of the property in the back.

The only time I waver for a few moments is when I see a display of small pots. One of them is the exact shade of red lipstick I wear, with small hand-painted gold constellations.

"Plant first," Bram whispers.

I watch as he examines a table of snake plants and mutters to himself about the pros and cons of owning one. At one point, he finds a hose and waters a section of mums and asters only to arrange some of the succulents based on how the sun has shifted now that our days are shorter.

I watch him work and I can almost see that teenage boy who hadn't fully grown into his build yet but was just at home in this quiet place where not a single plant asked for anything, and yet it was Bram's job to know exactly what they needed.

I wander a little as he continues to situate the succulents until I stop in front of a table of purple cacti.

"Santa Rita," he says from behind me. "It's a prickly pear that turns purple in the fall—or when it's in distress. They bloom in the spring. They're pretty self-sufficient in the wild."

"Like me," I say under my breath.

He presses his lips to my temple and I can feel his smile there. "Yes," he says. "But they can truly thrive with a light amount of care. And they're perfect for beginners."

My fingers brush along the metal table as I inspect each plant, letting myself see the small variations among them.

"Do any speak to you?" he asks.

I hum as I point to one in the direct center of the table. "That one."

Bram reaches past me and plucks the plant off the table. It has a single paddle with deep purple coloration. It is perhaps the size of

Fundamentals of Being a Good Girl

my hand and is scattered with smaller spikes and then there are a few very sharp clusters that look sturdier.

"The small hairlike ones are called glochids," he explains. "And these others—the ones that look like they can really do some damage—are spines. You would think the big guys would be harder to handle, but it's the glochids that surprise you. They shed easily and get under the skin with little effort."

"Like me," I say again.

This time he laughs. "Exactly like you."

Bram pushes the cart and grabs an extra bag of soil, which I imagine he just likes to have in abundance based on the tower of bags in his shed.

I loop my arm through his, and his chest falls in a sigh as I rest my arm on his biceps.

He doubles back for a snake plant and picks up some poinsettias for Sara's mother before we loop back around to the pots and he tells me to pick out the one I like best. Of course I reach for the red one with the gold stars while Bram gets me a small watering can and mister.

I attempt to buy my own plant and pot, but Bram is adamant that this is a gift. "You will not rob me of the honor of buying Madelyn Kowalczk the first plant she will keep alive."

And I let him, because it feels like the kind of thing your boyfriend does for you and just for today, I'd like to think that Bram Loe being my boyfriend is a very real possibility.

Bram loads up the truck while I take the cart back inside.

For a moment, I am distracted by the small selection of gifts just by the cash register. One of them is a small vintage hotel-style key chain that reads PLANT DADDY.

I take one to the counter and the teen running the register smirks as I hand her my card.

As I step out of the store into the small breezeway where I left the cart, someone tugs on my elbow and turns me to face them.

Uh-oh.

Veronica Balentine is mad. Very, very mad.

CHAPTER THIRTY-TWO

Maddie

Veronica Balentine is so mad that her lips barely open as her words grit through her teeth. "Please tell me I did not just watch my leading candidate buy Bram Loe a PLANT DADDY key chain after she canoodled all over this establishment with him."

"Ah," I say, in an attempt to lighten the mood. "I much preferred you in your role as the Unsinkable Molly Brown."

Beside us the automatic doors keep opening and closing, unable to decide if we are going in, out, or staying put.

"This has gone beyond playing with fire." She shakes her head, features hard and unforgiving. Nothing about her feels almost warm like it did on Halloween night. "You're done," she says, and turns for the door.

This time it's me who is yanking her elbow, forcing her to turn back. "No," I tell her. "You can't do that."

She pulls away from me but still stands there in the open door. "You received strict instructions, and you were unable to follow them. Not only were those instructions—oh, I don't know, actually important, but what does this say about your ability to cooperate in the future?"

"I'm not your fucking puppet, Veronica."

"Oh, trust me," she says, "you've made that very clear, and it's actually what I like about you. But there is a game to be played, and either you're willing to play or you're not. If Bram Loe and his years of baggage are worth throwing away everything at your fingertips, then that's for you to decide. You're a big girl, Maddie."

I cross my arms over my chest in an attempt to appear confidently defiant, but squared up against Veronica, I look defensive, like I have something to apologize for.

And the truth is that I do. Veronica is right. She never lied to me about the rules of the game. I let myself get to this point knowing full well that Bram and I would never be able to be anything more than—

"Physical," I blurt. It's a lie the moment I say it, but the truth I do know is that the only person who can guarantee my future is me. Even if I do love Bram Loe and I tell Veronica to move on to the next most eligible candidate, Bram and I could simply just not . . . work. It's cruel, but it's true. It's a gamble I can't afford. At this moment in my life, I am not in the position to say no to someone like Veronica and the people she works for. I wish I had the luxury of exploring what things could be with Bram, but after four years of belonging to someone to the extent that it was the first thing and most important thing to know about me, I can't spend another moment making a decision that is not entirely for my own future.

"It's just physical, Veronica. I'm—I was stupid and I let things get out of hand. I never should have gone out in public with him.

But I'm done working for him in less than two weeks, and then we have no reason to even be in each other's proximity. You can rest easy—Bram Loe and I will basically be strangers by December."

She shifts from foot to foot for a moment and then rubs her eyes with the heels of her palms.

"I don't give second chances," she says, her gaze trained on some point beyond me, like she's thinking of every version of this going south. She snaps back to me and points a finger, nearly poking me in the chest. "Do not make me regret showing you mercy. End it with the moss doctor. If you don't, I will personally see to it that you are unelectable, and I don't just mean in certain natural gas or big donor circles. I mean everywhere. There's plenty of skeletons to choose from. Your brother marrying a sex worker. Lying on your mother's medical forms several times. The video of you yelling during your lecture that I scrubbed from the internet. I could ruin you for the most mundane reasons, and I promise I would enjoy it. I don't break promises, Maddie."

"Neither do I," I tell her. My heart hardens into a fist, and I want to hate her, but I see too much of myself in her narrowed eyes. I know that her sharp edges were all born out of necessity. "It's over, Veronica. I promise."

She gives me a single nod before disappearing into the parking lot, where I spy her son and her wife loading up a very shiny and very expensive SUV with pumpkins and gourds of all sizes.

I look down at the key chain that I'd been rubbing between my fingers for our entire conversation and I tuck it into the pocket of my jeans.

This is fine, I tell myself. *This was never permanent. This was always about feeling good in the moment. Neither of us promised the other the future.*

I walk outside through the electric door that's been wide open for a few minutes now and as I turn the corner, Bram is standing there with his arms crossed over his chest. The same chest covered in coarse hair that I'd run my fingers through just hours ago.

"Strangers by December," he echoes, his voice low and rumbling.

"Bram—" I start.

But he's already turning around and heading toward the truck. "We should get back."

The car ride is agonizingly silent.

I want him to be mad at me. I want him to scream.

But Bram is focused on the road ahead. His mouth is pressed into an unmoving line, and it's not until we are parked at the back of the driveway next to the shed when he unbuckles his seat belt and turns to me.

"I can understand," he says, his words slow and steady, "if what you told Veronica Balentine about us being physical was just words. I can understand if you didn't actually mean it but needed something in the moment to say to her. I know what my reputation means to the donors she works with, and I understand the position it puts you in. We can set this aside and move on."

I am desperate to tell him that I didn't mean it. That what I said to Veronica meant nothing. He wants to hear it, and in so many ways, so do I. But I can't continue to hurt Bram like this. I can't make him believe in something that we can't have. "And then what?" I ask quietly. "And then I've lied to her and she either ruins me, or we have to exist in the shadows for how long, Bram? That's not fair to you. Or the girls. Or me."

The rise and fall of his chest has become more rapid. "Is it just physical, Madelyn? Answer me that, at least."

Fundamentals of Being a Good Girl

"I know what you want me to say, Bram. I do. And there's a version of me who wants that too, okay? A version of me who wants to be yours to keep. But that's just the problem. That would be only one version of me. One version among many."

"And I'm pretty sure I love every version of you," he says, and it's the kind of thing that you would die to hear spoken to you, but his words are dripping in sorrow.

"You can't love me, Bram. You can't love something you don't know, and I don't even know myself."

"Learning yourself isn't something you have to do alone." His voice turns stern when he adds, "And don't you dare tell me I can't love you, because I do and I have and I will. If you're changing and growing, I want to be there to witness it. Can't you see that? I don't want to stifle you. I want to be the one who creates the perfect conditions for you to flourish. I want to be there to watch you germinate as much as I want to be there to watch you bloom. Those aren't different versions of you. Those are stages, Maddie, and each one of them requires specific circumstances and conditions. But above all, it is you at the heart. You are Maddie in every form."

My eyes are burning with tears. I hadn't cried in years until that day when Bram caught me getting out of his shower, and now the threat is there all over again.

I count to ten and swallow back the sting in my throat. I can't cry, because if I cry, he will comfort me, and if he wraps his arms around me, I will never allow him to let go.

"I can't give you what you want. You need someone to be there for you too. You need someone who can give *you* the environment that you need to grow. You can't just be the gardener. You can't just give and give until you have nothing left, Bram. And selfishly, I cannot join your life at a time when mine is so uncertain. Because the world you've created—this beautiful fucking life of yours—is too big for me to not simply be consumed by it. I will never know what could be if I'm absorbed by the life you've spent years nurturing. It's a life, by the way, that you should spend with someone who deserves you and can give you what you deserve in return."

He grips the steering wheel, his knuckles turning white. "You never answered my question. Was it just physical? Is that what we were to you?"

The difference between Bram and me has been and always will be that I understand just how crucial it is for someone to be the bad guy. I understand that sometimes the road of truth is paved with lies.

It takes sitting on my hands to stop myself from reaching over and touching him.

I want to be greedy. I want to live in this bubble for just a while longer, but I know that the longer this goes on, the more it will hurt for the both of us.

And so, once again, I decide to do the hard thing. The thing no one wants to do. I break Bram Loe's heart with one single word.

"Yes."

CHAPTER THIRTY-THREE

Bram

I nod, as rust creeps up my throat and fills my mouth with the bitter taste of metal and heartbreak.

How foolish I am. How very old and besotted and ridiculous and selfish, selfish.

And how greedy, I add to the list. *To want more when your life is already overflowing with plenty.*

It's a bad person who wants more than enough. Isn't it? Who looks at their perfect kids, at the job of their dreams, at nosy, messy, loyal friends who've stuck with them for years and years, and thinks *but I want more*?

Not everyone has a day in their life that they can point to and say that was the day they chose to be a good person, but I do. Sara and I emerged from our hiding places in that field, covered in burrs and mud and scrapes, and we decided. *I* decided. I chose rules and logic and consent and equanimity. And this version of Bram right now, trying not to cry inside the cab of a truck that might as well be an oil spill, his ribs cracking open like dry, termite-eaten wood over someone who has been more than clear from the beginning . . .

This is everything I've chosen not to be.

I've chosen to be a good man. And I need to act like it.

"If you'll go inside with the cactus, I'll put everything else away?" I say, careful to frame it as a suggestion and not as an order.

Which doesn't matter. Maddie shifts to look at me. I don't look over, keeping my eyes on my hands instead.

"If we're going to fight, then let's fight," she says. Her voice is steady, pointed. Fighting is where she feels the safest; to her, conflict is clarity, and clarity is relief. Funny to think that ten weeks ago, she was a complete stranger to me, and now I know this indelible thing about her.

"I'm not trying to choose the field of battle, Madelyn. I just want us to be warm."

I can feel her hesitation, the way she takes temperature after temperature of the moment, wondering if this is a trap, if there's some angle that she can't see. Even though it hurts physically to do it, I make myself look at her. I give myself over to her searching green gaze.

"I meant what I told you months ago," I say quietly. "I've got nothing to hide. If you want to ask me something, I'll tell you the truth."

"You did have something to hide, Bram," she says, a sad kind of impatience in her voice. "Not that it makes much of a difference in the end. It was still never going to be . . . more."

Her eyes rake over me one last time—making sure that I mean it when I say I'm not trying to strategize my way into winning, whatever that looks like here. And then she unbuckles her seat belt.

I get out of the truck, walk around the front, and open the door for her. I don't think she'll want me to hold her by the waist like I did earlier, but I do offer my hand, which she takes with a polite nod, and help her down. And then she retrieves the cactus from the floorboard and goes into the house.

In the fading daylight, I move the potting soil into the shed and the poinsettias into the greenhouse so I can keep them happy until I give them to Sara's mom. I turn the truck back on and roll it into the shed, turning it off again and getting out. The creak and slam of the rust-eaten door is as familiar to me as my hometown; it's the sound of high school, of my first job, of those early days with Fern driving all the way to Topeka and back to get her to fall asleep.

I wonder if my grandparents ever did that with me in this same truck. I wonder if my parents did before they died. I'll never know, and by the time I was old enough to think of a question like that, I was old enough to know not to ask it. My grandparents didn't like to talk about my parents, and they weren't the sort to tell you stories about yourself when you were little. They didn't allow night-lights, they didn't read you books at bedtime, and hugs were brought out like the good dishes—on special occasions, and then handled so gingerly that the experience wasn't all that enjoyable anyway.

The first person to hug me like hugs were things meant for sharing was Joey Fucking Kemp. In sixth grade, I spiked a crucial volleyball serve in gym class, winning the match, and he ran up and threw his arms around me like it was something people did all the time. Like it was nothing.

Maybe my parents would have hugged me like that if they'd still been alive.

I stare at the truck, allowing myself just a moment to ache for what I didn't have then and for what I don't have now. A moment of crawling loneliness so deep that it frosts over my bones.

And then I go inside to finish being broken up with.

MADDIE IS STANDING in the middle of the kitchen holding her cactus, just a few feet away from where she told me to masturbate in a shaft of golden sunlight this morning. When she turns to face me, her lips are open and her eyes are blank, like she doesn't know how she's gotten there. Like she's lost.

But then her eyes sharpen and her shoulders go back. Her chin lifts. She's holding the cactus the way someone would hold a sacred artifact to ward off evil.

"We said sex and nothing else," she starts before I can say anything at all.

"I know," I say.

"This always had an expiration date."

"Yes."

"So this is it. The expiration date." She says it not like a question but also not like a proscription, almost like the echo of a thought. Confirming to herself that something is true.

I take a breath. And then I take another. Draw the air past my aching throat into my lungs, into my alveoli, feel my body trade oxygen for carbon dioxide. Something scalding races down to my jaw. I exhale as I wipe my face.

I'm not ashamed of crying, but I don't want to make this harder on her when she's done everything right and I'm the one asking for more.

"Excuse me," I murmur, and quickly walk to the downstairs bathroom with my head down, taking a moment inside to seal up the breach inside myself. I deadhead and prune. I pull all the sap out of my branches and go dormant.

The tears stop. There's still a swelling at the base of my throat, but I can talk through it.

When I go back out to the kitchen, passing a dozing Hester Prynne stretched out over the vent and enjoying the heat, Maddie has set the cactus on the counter and is pacing, her head dipped in thought. It snaps up at my approach.

"I have less than two weeks left on my contract," she says, getting right to the point. Which in a way, I can appreciate. It is what's immediately necessary—figuring out the money and the logistics. The heartbreak can hollow me out in its own time.

"I'll call the—" I start, but Maddie cuts in.

"No, I'd like to continue. I mean, if it's all right for you. I think it's best for the twins to have some consistency since they're so young." She pauses and then adds, with some reluctance, "And I still need to work as much as I can right now."

I don't know how I feel about this. I want as much of her as I can have, and the twins and Fern love her. And yet just looking at her hurts right now.

But I summon up my equanimity, my belief that we should do what's categorically best for ourselves and the girls. "As you'd like," I agree.

"Is that . . . okay with you? Me staying on with the girls for the last two weeks?"

"Yes." *No. Maybe. Don't leave me. Don't look at me with those cat-green eyes, I can't take it.* "It's what's best for the kids, I agree. And you're welcome to stay here as long as you need, Maddie. I mean that. I'll do everything you need to feel comfortable here."

Quickly, so fucking quickly, she blurts, "No. No, I-I can't. I can't stay here."

My capacity for being hurt by a person I've known for less than three months is astounding. "Okay," I say softly. "We'll figure it out."

Hester Prynne clicks over to Maddie from her spot near the vent and noses Maddie's hand for attention. Maddie gets down to a knee to pet Hester with both hands. I wonder if she does that so she doesn't have to look at me.

"I can see if Junie will have me for a bit, or Sloane," she says, her eyes on Hester's panting face. Then she glances up with a weak smile. "Or maybe Joey and Riley will need some preemptive childcare and take me in on a barter system."

I give her a weak smile back. "Maybe."

She stands up and steps a little closer. Not much, but enough that I can see the infinitesimal quiver of her chin. "Bram . . . I want you to know that even though this was a physical relationship and even though it's ending, it was still important to me. You are still important. And the time we shared, and getting to hang out with the girls, and all the advice you gave me—it mattered. I wouldn't have wanted to spend these last two and a half months any other way."

A cynical part of me feels like she's already playing the role of politician, throwing a bone to a demographic that's about to be sidelined. *We value your voice; we won't actually change our existing plans for you, but you should feel appreciated all the same. Because we said so.*

But I do think she means it.

"You are important to me too," I say. And then I add, because I know it's the only time I'll say these three words to her and I want that, selfishly, at least once, "I love you."

A broken exhale, like she's fallen from a height. "I never asked you to."

I nod, because I know.

"And I never wanted this to hurt."

I know that too. I step closer and allow myself one last liberty: I take her hand in mine and give it a careful but lingering squeeze. "It's okay," I tell her, meeting her eyes. "It's going to be okay."

"It would have hurt worse if I dragged it out, right?" She bites her lip, her brows lifted in a kind of plea. Begging me to absolve her. "If we carried on until I felt too trapped or until Veronica caught us again. It's got to be better to make a clean break of things, you know?"

"That's right." My voice is soothing; I squeeze her hand one last time and let go. "Tomorrow, we'll light up the phone tree and find a new place for you."

I leave her in the kitchen with another weak smile and then go to my room. Hester Prynne, the canine Judas, doesn't follow and stays with her most recent admirer instead. Which is fine, I know what to do. I did it for years coming home with schoolyard bruises. I did it before then as a little kid scared of the dark and knowing that if I asked for comfort, I'd be told to be stronger, braver.

I go into the empty corner of my room and slide down to the floor, wedging myself as far back as I can so it feels like the walls are holding me. And then I wrap my arms around myself in a hug and pull my knees up to my chest. And just like I did when I was a lonely little boy, I pretend that in a minute someone will come in to turn on the light.

CHAPTER THIRTY-FOUR

Bram

Two days later, and Joey and I are carrying plastic totes of clothes up the narrow stairs leading to an apartment above The Dry Bean, and Sloane is on the phone with a plumber, trying to get Robbie's DIY shower up and running before Maddie stays her first night.

"So when Robbie said he was renovating up here, he didn't mean renovating in the commonly understood sense, did he?" Joey observes, setting a tote down on the kitchen table and gazing around at the shag carpet and faux wood paneling. The carpet is a shade of orange that I last saw on a couch in my grandparents' farmhouse before I hosted the estate sale.

"It's clean at least," Sloane says, coming around the corner. "I had the same team that does Persimmon Hill come out and give it a once-over."*

---

* Persimmon Hill is the name of the property belonging to Sloane's

"Well, it looks like they got most of the nicotine residue off the walls," Joey says cheerfully, and then squints upward at the jaundiced tiles of the suspended ceiling. "Maybe not everywhere, though."

"It's too bad." Sloane does a slow, sighing spin. "This building is a hundred and thirty years old. Hardwoods, brick, tinplate, all sorts of lovely things just hiding behind layers of bad decisions, and all it needs is time and money. And those are precisely the two things I can't give it right now."

As Joey agrees with her, I go downstairs to get the last of the totes. I've just looked at the latest polling numbers in California and it appears like Gentry is all but guaranteed to win his district, and stomping up and down the stairs is the only release of aggression I have time for right now. After that, Joey volunteers to run to the store to get a few basics for the kitchen. Sloane and I watch him lumber down the stairs, meowing the tune of Billie Eilish's "What Was I Made For?" and then we look at each other, realizing at the same time that Joey Fucking Kemp probably thinks kitchen basics are Cinnamon Toast Crunch and Gatorade Zero.

"I'll go with him," Sloane says.

"I think that's a good idea."

She gets her purse from a questionable recliner Robbie left behind. "I'm really glad I had this unit open," she remarks. "There's supposed to be a tenant moving into the second apartment in January, but this one is still unleased, and there's no reason for it to stay empty."

---

ex-husband. The Méchant family informally calls the compound of tennis courts, cascading swimming pools, and guesthouses "The Farm," on account of the farmhouse that was knocked down in order to build it.

"It was nice of you to cut her a deal on everything," I reply. "Thank you, Sloane. Truly. She needed this."

Sloane looks at me sidelong, gray eyes curious. "It was a little unexpected," she says delicately, private school manners on display. "We all assumed she was content to stay with you for the time being."

I muster a smile. I've been doing a lot of that the last two days. "She was ready for her own space."

"Were you ready for her to have her own space?" Sloane asks, and she says it teasingly, but I know what she's really asking.

"That obvious, huh?"

She bumps her shoulder against my arm. (Sloane is taller than Maddie, but it's a rare person who can reach my shoulder with theirs.) "Just a little obvious. The secret group chat was really pulling for you two, you know. Seeing you smiling and relaxed and happy—it was nice. You needed it."

"I didn't think it would hurt this much," I admit. "And it's stupid. I met Maddie in August. How can I be brokenhearted in November?"

"Oh, Bram," Sloane says with a sigh, leaning her head against my shoulder. "You don't give your heart away very often, but when you do, you do it completely. It's not a bad thing."

"I've done it twice and wound up alone twice, so there might be a flaw in the design," I say.

Sloane pulls away, and when I look down, I see her flexing the hand that used to have Lucien's ring on it. "There are worse things than being alone," she murmurs, and then subtly shakes her head, as if banishing bad memories. "I'll be back with Joey, and hopefully things like bread and milk and not tubs of protein powder."

I wave her off and then go down to get the final thing I'd

brought for Maddie's new apartment: the cactus, in the pot she chose. I pick a windowsill that'll get some southern exposure and tuck an index card with handwritten instructions next to the pot. Instructions for how to water it and check the soil for good drainage. When to move it outside to the little fire escape in spring. When she can expect fruit and how to tell when it's ripe.

In the 1700s, the prickly pear was imported to Australia so dye could be produced from the cochineal insects who liked the plant. But it thrived far too well in Australia's interior and grew into dense, impenetrable forests, sometimes up to twenty feet tall. It drove farmers off their farms; it grew so quickly that it crushed houses.

I think of this now, looking at Maddie's prickly pear. Like the plant, she is remarkably self-sufficient. Like the plant, she is covered candidly, honestly, in her needles and prickles and barbs.

Like the plant in Australia's soil, she has taken hold in my heart. A twenty-foot-tall forest of Maddie, stabbing and sweet, a crush of clever beauty that I can't regret even now.

"Okay, okay, pillows *can* count, but I still think it would be more fun if the game were The Floor Is Pyroclastic Flow," Asher tells the twins, who tilt their curly heads at Asher and consider this.

"That doesn't make sense," Letty declares. "If there's no lava, then we *can* be on the floor and there's no game."

"I think it doesn't make sense because a pyroclastic flow wouldn't only be on the floor," says Sara as she navigates the couch cushions tossed around Riley and Joey's living room. "It would be more like The Floor Is Hot and the Air Is Hot and I'm Breathing Rocks While I Burn Alive."

"Cool," Berry whispers solemnly.

Sara hands me a beer where I'm sitting against the wall, having died a few moments ago from touching the lava floor, and then she goes to give Asher a quick kiss before returning to the family room.

"Oksana is licking the doorknob," Letty informs the room. Asher and I look over to see that, yes, indeed, Joey and Riley's youngest has decided she's done waiting for Thanksgiving dinner and she will start with a doorknob appetizer.

"I've got her," I announce, and get to my feet. With the beer in one hand, I scoop up the baby with the other and tickle her while she's tucked under my arm. I carry her like a football into the family room, where Fern is patiently playing Barbies with the other two Kemp daughters, Dorothy and Kristi.[*] I whoosh Oksana down to the floor like a landing airplane as Sloane and Alessandro sit at the table between the kitchen and the family room and argue about the dwindling public appeal of the symphony while they sip cocktails.

Leo is slouched in a chair in the corner of the room, all lidded eyes and long limbs, a glass of scotch dangling from his fingers and his mouth set in a dangerous line. So, typical Leo.

"I can't believe you had an entire situationship while I was gone," Sara complains from the Barbie zone, where she's settled next to our oldest and the Kemp girls. "You met someone, fell in love, *and* broke up, all while I was on a fucking glacier."

Fern glances at the two of us and then back down to the Barbies, trying not to look like she's eavesdropping. Maddie and I had

---

[*] Before Riley Kemp was the coxswain of the Astra University rowing team, she was a competitive figure skater who suffered a knee injury at seventeen. She gets to name the Kemp babies by mutual agreement. (Joey gets to name the goldfish.)

been too close for a perceptive young person like Fern not to get suspicious when Maddie abruptly moved out; after I'd explained everything to Sara, we agreed that it would be healthier in the long run to give Fern a brief (and very redacted) primer on the circumstances. I told her that Maddie and I had dated for a short time but mutually decided to part ways, that it had happened warmly and honestly, that we still liked each other very much. I could tell the curiosity was burning inside of her, though.

"I acknowledge that it was a faster timeline than everyone is used to from me," I say, trying to sound fun and jokey and not at all heartbroken. Like the steady, kind dad I'm supposed to be. "But nearly the same ingredients. We're even at the peaceful co-parenting stage now."

And that part is true. Maddie and I have the same routine we did before, with school pickups and some dinner help, and we don't avoid each other, we don't avoid speaking. We smile faintly in passing. We eat at the same table, clean up together, commit the occasional *extra fifteen minutes of screen time* sin together. The twins barely notice anything has changed, except for Maddie not being there in the mornings and around bedtime for the last two weeks.

It's all very gentle and respectful and respectable. An autumn, organic and necessary, a much-needed winter coming to freeze the lingering lust and love between us. At least in theory.

I only wish I felt like spring would come again.

"Sloane said it was our youthful, um, shenanigans that did the two of you in," Sara says, the euphemism for Fern's benefit. (We're waiting until she's older to tell her about our crime era.) "I am sorry about that, Bram."

"It was a lot of things," I reassure her. "Not just that Fasse Global still has a picture of me tacked to their wall."

"Food is almost ready!" Riley announces from the kitchen, as her mother and sisters swarm the china cabinet to stack dishes on the counter buffet-style. Sara and Fern get up and help Dorothy and Kristi put the Barbies away, and Joey and Sara's dad come in from the back patio with the fried turkey in a disposable aluminum roasting pan, trailed by a very interested Hester Prynne.

It's just me and Leo in the family room now, and when I get to my feet, Leo says, in the first words he's spoken all afternoon, "Did you get the email I sent last night? About our friend Mr. Footlicker95?"

"I did," I say. Neutrally.

"Which Bram read it?" Leo asks, lifting the scotch to his mouth but not drinking. "Good Guy Bram or Fuck Shit Up Bram?"

I take a swig of my beer, eyebrow lifted.

Leo laughs suddenly, a laugh that is rich and chilling and beckons a person closer even as it promises certain peril.

"What are you going to do about it?" he asks.

"About Gentry Cooper Wade the Third?" A real smile pulls at my mouth. The only thing better than ruining that piece of shit before the election would be to ruin him badly enough after the election that he'll need to step down before he's even been sworn in. "Got anyone else you'd like to bury this weekend?"

Leo looks like I've just proposed, and beams. "Always."

CHAPTER THIRTY-FIVE

Maddie

"I think I killed the tofurkey," my sister-in-law, Bee, announces from the kitchen while Mom hovers over her simmering homemade cranberry sauce like a witch closely monitoring her brew.

"I don't know how to tell you this, babe, but it was never alive," my brother says as he runs in from the backyard where he's been frying a real turkey with Bee's moms, who are visiting from Texas.

Bee lets out a fretful whimper, and from where I'm setting the table I can see the tears brimming.

Nolan drops the utensils and serving platter in his arms and rushes over to coo at Bee, who is in her third trimester. Apparently, a few months ago, her pregnant body decided that she could no longer stand to eat meat, citing the texture. Bee, who loves a Thanksgiving spread, was determined to make the best tofurkey of all time.

As I lay my last utensil, I make my way into the kitchen and hover behind Mom to get a whiff of all the various sides she has waiting in the wings.

"The sides are the best part of Thanksgiving," I assure Bee. "One year when we were kids, the only thing I ate was Mom's rolls with homemade cranberry sauce and little molded pieces of butter in the shape of corn, and you know what? Best Thanksgiving ever."

Bee takes a deep breath as Mom turns and gives me a soft kiss on the cheek. LA has been good to my mother. She's thriving in her little studio apartment behind Bee and Nolan's house, and when I flew in on Monday, she walked me through her garden, pointing out all the different things she would be using for Thanksgiving dinner. It made me think of Bram, and that made me cry. It only took a split second for Mom to get over the shock of seeing me cry before she was pulling me into her arms and rocking me against her chest.

"You're r-right," Bee says as she absentmindedly strokes her belly and Nolan cradles her hips.

It's sort of gross to see your brother be so physically affectionate, but goddamn is he happy. It's actually a little painful to watch at the moment.

Bram and his snakes rallied together and got me moved into one of Sloane's apartments above The Dry Bean. In fact, I can see my cozy patch of sidewalk where a very amused Leo and a stern Bram found me on Halloween night.

Bram insisted on getting the place ready for me while I stayed with the girls. When Junie and I drove over later that night with the rest of my belongings and a hot pizza, I found the kitchen stocked with the essentials and my cactus on the windowsill with handwritten instructions from Bram.

I cried. It was the first time since I'd ended things with him, and those tears broke some sort of seal, because over the course of the last two weeks I have cried more than I have in my entire life. It didn't help that I'd also just learned that Gentry won his election within thirty minutes of the polls closing. It was a blatant confirmation that everything people like Penelope Pike and Veronica Balentine preached was true. The focus groups mattered. The donors mattered. Getting into office required the right package, and there wasn't much room to veer from the plan. So maybe ending things with Bram really was the only choice I had if I wanted to keep hope alive for a future of my own.

I wanted Bram to hate me. I wanted it so badly. In fact, I was angry at him for not hating me. How could he not see how much easier this would all be if he could just hate me?

Junie stayed with me for a while that first night. She turned a movie on and didn't mind or push too hard when I spent most of the evening just staring at that prickly pear cactus.

At first, Bram's gentle demeanor felt like a game to be won. Who could out-polite the other? But after a day or two, I remembered the way he'd described his divorce from Sara and how, for him, the end of a relationship required just as much care as the relationship itself.

It was healthy and good, and when I got over the urge of wishing he would just scream at me, it began to hurt. Truly hurt. The immediate moments and days after the breakup were full of me appearing overly confident in my decision in an attempt to convince myself that I'd done the right thing. And then came the hollow sadness as I began to realize that the choice I made wasn't just about ending something I'd sworn was only physical. It was about choosing between two very different lives. The life I thought I should want and the one that took me completely by surprise.

I don't know how long it will take me to decide if I've made the right decision, but what I do know is that after living so long in the service of someone else's ambition, I have chosen a future that belongs to me. At the very least, I can say that.

Nolan heads back outside to monitor the turkey with his mothers-in-law while Mom takes over the job of salvaging the tofurkey and I help Bee on drinks.

She pauses for a minute and sets the water pitcher down while she presses a hand to her stomach.

"Everything okay?" I ask. I am totally good with kids, but I don't know the first thing about being pregnant, so as far as I know Bee could turn to me and say she's going into labor.

She nods once and then lets out a long burp followed by a happy sigh. "Sorry, my whole life is basically a Russian roulette of bodily functions right now." She frowns. "I almost peed my pants last week."

"That sounds terrifying," I tell her.

"It is . . . humbling, and I say that as someone who actually got stuck while filming a stuck porn."

That makes me laugh for the first time in weeks. Bee is a semi-retired sex worker turned bona fide Hollywood actress and is way too good for my brother, but at least he knows it.

"The dark hair is a good look, by the way." She nudges me with her elbow. "Your mom actually cried when you sent her a selfie from the salon. You just look like you."

Mom tried to hide her worry when I began to change into this predetermined person whose purpose was to complement Gentry, but the blond hair really bothered her. She tried to disguise her concern and tell me that it was a nice change or that it was good to be adventurous, but I felt angry with her for not seeing that this was what I'd wanted.

Of course, my mother knows better than anyone else that I have to make my own mistakes. Even if that mistake cheats on you after encouraging you to turn into a person you hardly know, only to dispose of you for never quite fulfilling their vision of the ideal partner.

The rest of Thanksgiving Day is a rotating door of familiar faces from the life Bee and Nolan have built here. There's a FaceTime call from his best friend, Kallum, his wife, Winnie, and their ever-growing brood, who are back in Kansas City visiting family.

Bee's best friend, Sunny, swings through with her husband and Nolan's former bandmate, Isaac (who also holds the honor of being my first crush—along with that of many other girls, except I had to suffer the pain of him witnessing me hit puberty). They only stay for a moment on their way to spend a month visiting every Christmas market they can manage in search of the perfect hot nuts and with a scheme to hit as many photo booths as they can. Their oddly specific plan feels like an inside joke that none of us are privy to. The monthlong journey will culminate in their meeting up with Isaac's old bodyguard, Krysta, and her wife, Addison, while the four of them hole up for the holidays in Edinburgh. They are very adamant that I one day visit their favorite hotel there, The Balmoral, and say hello to their favorite whisky ambassador, Fraser. I nod along and jot his name down in my phone. I smile and pretend like there will ever be a time when I might want to go on a grand adventure like that with someone I love.

Around dessert, we are treated to a parade of Bee's former colleagues from her adult-film career. There's Luca, the costume designer, and his animator husband, Angel. They tell us about their (really, Luca's) plans to host a New Year's party while in LA that would make Martha Stewart jealous. And then there's Steph and her husband, Teddy, the sometimes porn producer and *the* current name in the Christmas movie biz. I remember meeting him as an older teenager and him always slipping me hard candy and five-dollar bills like I was still young enough to believe in Santa Claus. He and his wife leave early because they have to get home to the two absolutely unstable German shepherds they have recently adopted before they both escape their crates and eat the couch for the second time.

By the time the house is quiet and free of visitors, Bee's moms are yawning from the two-hour time difference and excuse themselves to bed for an early night.

In a totally out of character move, Mom leaves the kitchen full of dirty dishes for tomorrow. "All I want is for the four of us to sit down with some hot cider and turn on the fireplace," she says.

"Mom, it's seventy-four degrees out," I tell her as my body melts into the velvet sofa that is flush with beautiful throw pillows as well as slightly disturbing embroidered ones with a focus on eyeballs that speak to Bee and Nolan's offbeat style.

"Don't tell Greta Thunberg," Bee says as she flops down across from me and adjusts the air-conditioning app on her phone to an obscenely low number that would definitely piss off Greta.

Nolan flicks on the fireplace and Mom bustles in with a tray carrying four steaming mugs.

Sitting here in this dark room, surrounded by the three closest people in my life, I'm able to inhale deeply for the first time in weeks.

CHAPTER THIRTY-SIX

Maddie

Growing up, no matter how hard things were, Mom always went to great efforts to create holiday magic for us. It warms me to my core to know that, with the help of Bee and Nolan, the picturesque ideal Mom had always strived to create in our old, little house (that had the worst insulation but somehow never felt cold) is possible. The reality of the holidays finally has met the version in her head.

Life is tumultuous and uncertain and full of an aching pain right now, but I can at least say that I am no longer worried for the well-being of my mother. I know that she is taken care of now. It's not as though we never had the desire to before, but money. Fucking money. It always came down to money. And I'm filled with a fiery anger all over again—the same anger that had me falling for Gentry and the future we could build. The anger that had me eagerly saying yes to Veronica Balentine and the power she could help me garner. The power to make a dent in our broken—no, nonexistent—mental health services.

Mom sits down next to me, and Nolan passes over a cozy blanket for us to share. I take a sip of my cider before setting it down and laying my head in Mom's lap.

She makes a pleased noise as her soft, dish soap–scented fingers brush through my hair.

A single tear slides over the bridge of my nose and into the line of my hair.

"Why are you crying and what have you done with my sister?" Nolan asks.

Bee smacks him *hard* on the arm and he chokes on his cider.

"What?" he asks. "The only time I can remember Maddie crying when we were kids was when INK broke up because she was using a quote from Kallum as an INK endorsement when she ran for class secretary in fifth grade."

"It was a weak campaign," I tell them. "You know it's bad when your platform is that you're INK approved."

Mom smooths my hair back and my bangs away from my forehead. "Is it Gentry?" Her voice drips with an indignation I did not think her capable of. "I can't believe anyone voted for that buffoon."

"No, actually," I tell them. "I mean, yes. It starts with Gentry."

"You know what," Bee says, her finger jabbing angrily in the air. "You're broken up, so I can just say it now. I hate that motherfucker and I always have."

Above me, Mom nods as Nolan says, "Hell yeah, baby."

"And I shouldn't even be surprised by his horrific sex worker registry stunt," Bee adds.

I'd read more about it over the last few days now that my news feeds were more Southern California–focused again.

Fundamentals of Being a Good Girl

It was always part of Gentry's plan to run on family-first policy and to straddle the line of liberal and conservative, and if it was for the sake of pushing through legislation that truly mattered, I understood why he would do that, even if my younger self would have been horrified. But I really hadn't seen that family-first olive branch coming in the form of a California sex worker registry so that you could see on a map if any sex workers lived in your neighborhood. The map was supposedly anonymous but did give specific addresses, just like the sex offender registry.

It was the kind of policy that would (hopefully) never pass, especially in a state built on the entertainment industry, but I've thought that before about absolutely inane bills that were then used to amass attention and dominate news cycles.

And it worked, because in the last week of his campaign, when thousands of base supporters had already voted early, Gentry began to float this new idea of his and immediately piqued the interest of zealous extremists who wanted to rid the earth of anything that they deemed sexually deviant even if it meant burning it all to the ground just to build it back up.

The furrow in Bee's brow is riddled with genuine concern. The registry would greatly impact many people she knows and possibly even Bee herself. Even if I don't know how much truth there is to it, I feel compelled to comfort her. "The good news is he's only a junior lawmaker," I assure her. "He's only doing all this to make some noise. Very few people would actually vote for this."

"I hope so," she says as Nolan pulls her under his arm and kisses the top of her head.

And I do too. The word *registry* in conjunction with anything outside of babies and weddings is almost always a bad idea.

"Okay," Mom begins, "so we are in agreement that Gentry is an awful mother . . . effer."

"Mom!" Nolan and I both say at the same time, his voice full of alarm and mine full of delight.

She shrugs. "I've said the actual word before."

"What else are you keeping from us?" I ask.

Bee snorts. "Maybe you should ask her about her contractor boyfriend."

I shoot up now to face her, and Nolan is on the edge of his seat.

"What the ever-loving fuck, Mom?"

Mom rolls her eyes as she pulls me back into her lap. "Oh, hush, you two. It was one dinner date."

"And three coffee dates," Bee adds.

"And four brunches," Mom continues.

My brother's nostrils flare. "I'm going to beat the shit out of this guy with his own tool belt."

Mom giggles. "Donald doesn't wear a tool belt on most days. He's the contractor, dear. And you're the one who hired him to rebuild the steps and pergola in the backyard. And he's a very kind gentleman."

"He didn't even kiss her until the third date," Bee says, trying to prove Mom's point.

"And how exactly do you know all of this?" Nolan asks.

"I'm observant, okay? And it was more entertaining than my book club book when I had to back out of filming for that new Hope After Dark movie last month because I was already showing too much."

"So you and Donald are a thing?" I ask, feeling a little hopeful for our mom.

"We are taking it slow," she confirms. "But perhaps we are . . .

Fundamentals of Being a Good Girl

the beginning of a thing." With a huff, she turns her attention back toward me. "Enough about me. Maddie, talk to us, baby."

Nolan nods. "Yeah, we've hardly heard from you since you left for the gig in Mount Astra."

I groan and bury my face in the blanket Mom and I share, but she silently squeezes my shoulder, and I know it's finally time to tell them everything. Not just about Bram.

My first confession comes in the form of my nonexistent law school scholarship and how it was an informal guarantee that Gentry and his family would pay for my student loans once we were married.

Nolan leans forward, like he has a lot to say, and I'm sure he does—mainly that he would have rather paid for law school than have me in debt to a bank or the Wade family. But Bee pulls back on his shoulder and encourages me to continue.

I walk them through how desperate I was to leave Southern California and then getting the childcare job with Bram to help offset expenses.

"Where in Mount Astra are you staying?" Nolan asks.

"Well, I was staying with Bram and his girls."

"So you were a live-in nanny?" Mom asks.

I frown as I think of how Bram would gently, but quickly, correct her by saying *childcare provider*.

"Sort of . . . um, so Bram . . . he offered me his spare room when . . . he . . ." I take a deep breath. I'm either telling them the truth or I'm not. I'm fine now. I have an apartment, so any of their worry would be retroactive. "He realized I was living in my car."

"Maddie!" Nolan and Bee shout just as Mom weighs in with an outraged "What the fuck?"

I sit up again now. "Okay, that didn't go very well. Though, Mom, I am impressed by your usage of a four-letter word."

The three of them sound off with more questions and general outrage.

I explain. I don't expect them to understand. But I explain. I explain that I thought I had to do this on my own and that Bram proved me wrong. Nolan grits his teeth, and I tell him that I love him and that he doesn't owe me generosity. He grumbles about paying off my student loans whether I want him to or not. I tell them about the girls, and I can feel my whole face light up as I go on about Fern and how she conquered her boy troubles and how Letty and Berry are like salt and pepper and how one complements the other. I tell them a little about Junie and our morning coffee dates. I tell them about Veronica Balentine, and they all seem cautiously optimistic at what the future might hold.

And then comes Bram. With tears on the verge of spilling, I tell them about Bram and his greenhouse and his eco–bad boy past and I tell them about how I was having a hard time in the classroom at first and how Bram helped me find my footing.

I leave out the best parts, of course, even though I'm tempted to tell my brother a little too much to make up for the time I caught him and Bee in his childhood bedroom a few months after they got together.[*]

"This Bram guy sounds like he likes you a little too much," Nolan says, his chest puffed out in big brother mode. "You think

---

[*] Maddie is still haunted by the way his favorite childhood stuffy, an off-brand Care Bear with a tennis racket embroidered to its belly, was used as a wedge pillow to achieve a position she'd only ever seen in a very pornographic anime that was playing at a bar once in college.

I need to send Kallum down the road to have a word with him while he's in KC?"

"Trust me," I tell Nolan, "if anyone needs a talking-to, it's me."

"Oh, Maddie," Bee says. "What happened?"

I shake my head. "He fell for me. I fell back. Maybe even harder. I don't know. And then I broke it off, because he is basically enemy number one to everyone who might consider donating to my campaign. Veronica gave me an ultimatum and I'm a heartless power-hungry bitch, so I dumped him."

Mom grunts at my self-burn. "You are not, Madelyn."

"You say that like it's a bad thing," Bee says as she reaches her foot over to lovingly poke me. Nolan might be a total doofus in the eyes of his sister, but he chose well when he chose Bee.

The three of them let me tell them even more about Bram and his group of friends and Hester Prynne and Porcupine the frog and the way I absolutely reinvented the school pickup line. Bee is on the verge of violence as I regale them with the story of Professor Wallace and how I stood up to him with Bram's encouragement. (The PG version.)

"So does this Bram guy have anything to do with the cactus you were forlornly holding when I picked you up at LAX?" Nolan asks.

My lip trembles. "He gave me that stupid cactus, and we're not even together anymore and now I'm just responsible for it! I have to keep it alive somehow and I don't want to give him the satisfaction of me killing it without him." (Even though that is the exact opposite of how Bram would react.) "So I brought it on the plane so I could keep an eye on it and so that it wouldn't die of neglect."

"It sounds like you're really projecting a lot onto this cactus, little sis."

"I just think it's rude that he would leave me with something to be responsible for when I can hardly keep a roof over my own head. It's like he's trying to prove how incapable I am without him."

"Babe," Bee says with a soft smile. "It's hard to say for sure without meeting this plant daddy myself—"

"Can we call him literally anything else?" Nolan asks.

"What?" She shrugs, and I love that she organically found her way to Bram's nickname without me even saying so. "He's a plant person and a father. Plant. Daddy."

Mom chuckles. "He sounds lovely. What were you saying, Bee?"

"Before I was so rudely interrupted by the father of my unborn child, I was saying that"—Bee looks down at me—"with love, I think you're completely delusional, Maddie."

I roll over onto my back like I'm in a therapist's office and the pillow is my mother's lap. "I know," I concede. "But it's just easier to hurt when there's something to be angry about, you know? The pain has a place to go."

"You're so much like your father," Mom says softly.

I hardly knew him. Nolan remembers more than I do, but my father is more foreign than a mythical creature to me. The sadness in my mom's voice, though . . . For the first time I feel like I truly comprehend the way her voice sinks and then floats anytime she mentions him. Sad to have lost him but happy for what they had.

Bram is alive. Thank God. And we were so short-lived, but our relationship feels more impactful in a matter of months than mine with Gentry did in four years. For as angry as I want to be, for as much as I want Bram to fight me, I can't find it in me to regret a thing. Like Mom, I'm sad it's gone but happy it existed at all.

The conversation shifts to Bee and Nolan, and they swear us to secrecy as they list out potential baby names. We watch our first Christmas movie of the season, the Hope Channel's attempt at a lower-budget ode to *Die Hard*. I slip in and out of sleep, as does Mom. Nolan offers to walk her out back to her studio, and she holds a hand out for me to come with so we can cuddle up like we did when I was a child and Nolan was away on tour and it was just the two of us and the act of sleeping in separate beds seemed like a useless boundary to maintain when all we truly had was each other.

I feel like myself. Telling them everything, even if they don't have all the answers, feels like fresh air. And it feels so, so good to be Maddie again instead of the Gentry-shaped fiancée I had folded myself into. The girl who spent each holiday with her family, trying to make them see how lucky she was to have such a handsome and smart guy from a wealthy, established family interested in her.

Being fat for much of my life always meant trimming myself back until all that was left was the version Gentry wanted to see. Especially because he was this traditionally attractive guy, and if I let myself become anything other than what he needed, his light might stop shining on me. It was already hard enough to get anyone to take me seriously, but with Gentry by my side, I was so certain we could be this power couple and that the world would see what he saw in me. Worth.

But I and my desires would always come second, so maybe I owed a thank-you to Penelope Pike for breaking up with me. I definitely wouldn't have found Bram, and even if he and I are over, now I can say that I know what can be. Thanks to myself, of course, but thanks also to him and his encouragement of every good girl, bad girl, sharp, hungry girl part of me.

CHAPTER THIRTY-SEVEN

Maddie

On Sunday morning, I try to give my mom the cactus. I tell her how happy it will be in her mild California climate, and how, unlike me, she will actually keep it alive.

She gently pushes it back into my hands as Nolan loads my suitcase into the trunk of the car.

Then she gives me a crushing hug that pushes the air from my lungs. "I love you, my sweet, fiery jalapeño of a girl." She steps back and tucks a strand of hair behind my ear as her other hand runs over my bob, like she's memorizing this image of me and replacing the blond stranger that she's had to live with for the last few years.

We say our goodbyes and Bee wonders if maybe we should make a last-minute change of plans and do Christmas in Kansas so Nolan and Mom can see some old friends and help me settle into my new place.

The airport is holiday chaos, and as I go through security, I feel

Fundamentals of Being a Good Girl

like an overprotective mother as I try to shield my cactus from any rough handling, but I and the prickly little thing make it through.

Because the LAX drop-off math is a constant mystery and you can only be there way too early or five minutes before your flight, I am at my gate three hours before it is time to board.

I perform the required act of confirming that, yes, my gate does indeed exist, and then I'm off in search of overpriced food that doesn't taste like cardboard.

After settling on a dumpling place with my ideal ordering process—free of humans and from the safety of my own phone—I settle in at the bar to read a few bookmarked articles on my phone with my cactus currently taking up residence on the counter.

Two dumplings in, I hear the stoic voice of a reporter coming from the giant screen above say, ". . . Gentry Cooper Wade the Third, the California assemblyman elect of a notoriously upper-middle-class suburban district that is a stronghold not just for one party but for the Wade political dynasty in general. Political pundits have been eagerly awaiting the debut of the youngest of the Wade prodigies, and it seems that he isn't waiting for his swearing in for his first political scandal. And viewers, I have to be honest when I say, it might just be his last."

My heart skips a beat as I allow myself to look up. Whoa. This is national news. What the hell could Gentry have done to get himself in the national spotlight?

"For those who did not follow the race, Wade announced a rather controversial policy proposal just a week before Election Day and made a name for himself as he rallied support for his California Sex Worker Registry plan. Well, we here at CTB have confirmed with a reliable source that the youngest Wade's interest in pornographic material is perhaps more personal in nature."

The reporter, her hair a short brown crop, her eyes twinkling with glee, continues on as I sit there with a half-eaten dumpling hovering in front of my agape mouth.

"Footlicker95, also known as Gentry Cooper Wade the Third, was identified in what is being called a guerrilla data leak similar in nature to the Fasse Global leak investigated by this reporter ten years ago."

My dumpling and chopsticks clatter to my plate then. My chest is alight with a burning excitement and something akin to hope. But above all, I feel like a predator satisfied.

Bram. Holy fuck. He's still got it.

I am way too turned on right now to be sitting in an airport eating dumplings. Oh god, and I am still so, so sad. Sad and horny. What a combination.

I don't care that Gentry watched porn. A handful of times we even watched it together—though it was rather vanilla and definitely free of foot fetishes. But I do care that he was so dead set on vilifying sex workers and also framing porn as a dirty little secret.

I push my lust and curiosity aside as I force myself to metabolize the rest of the report.

"The leak appears to be targeted, as no other identities outside of a few financial heavy hitters and a US House representative from Kansas have been named. The leak also includes services rendered, featuring receipts for video chats and escort services paid for by Wade. We can also confirm that Wade, over the time frame the data leak covers, was in a serious relationship with his longtime girlfriend, Madelyn Kowalczk. While Kowalczk had only just begun to venture into the limelight, what many didn't know was that she is the younger sister of Nolan Shaw and sister-in-law to Bee Hobbes. This reporter can't help but wonder if Gentry was a fan of Bianca Von Honey, Bee Hobbes's adult film alter ego. When asked for a statement, Gentry's office did not respond."

Gentry never did like Bee, and I wonder now if his breakup with me was preemptive in anticipation of this new front-running policy of his. Among many other things.

"I told him that registry would kill his campaign, but did he believe me? Of course not."

I glance over and right there just two seats down is Penelope Pike with two glasses of half-drunk wine (one red and one white) sitting in front of her, along with a bowl of edamame carcasses.

"Penelope Pike," I say. "I hope you're not planning on flying a plane after double-fisting two glasses of wine, are you? Not after all the lectures you gave me about not giving a shit if I ever actually drove drunk, but only caring if I got caught."

To her credit, Penelope laughs, and it's the first time I've witnessed such a thing. If it weren't for the two glasses of wine, I might not notice anything amiss. Her dark blond hair is pulled back into a chignon and her suit jacket is carefully draped over the back of her chair to avoid creasing.

"I am sorry about this debacle," I sweetly lie through my teeth.

She waves her hand like she's clearing the air of a bad smell. "Oh, I did my job. I got the dolt elected. His grandfather always said the Wade genes became more and more diluted with every birth. It only makes sense that little baby Wade would be the dullest of them all. He didn't even have the soundness of mind to use a fake billing address, if you can believe it."

"Wow. So I'm guessing the cheating wasn't a onetime thing, then?"

She frowns. "That depends on how you look at it. Some political wives don't count physical interactions with sex workers as cheating. For their own sanity, of course."

Oh god, that makes me cringe. "Well, I'm still sorry you have to clean this up."

She takes a swig of the white and chases it with the red. "Oh, there's nothing to clean up. The elder Wade is about to release a statement condemning Gentry's behavior. The family will urge him to step down or face retaliation. If he has any bit of sense, he will, and the best Gentry can hope for is ten years on the charity circuit in the lead-up to a comeback campaign one day."

"That is very satisfying."

She nods. "I do like being right, so yes, in a way it is."

"Where are you off to?" I ask.

"Taking a little vacation back to the Midwest to visit family in Iowa. I need a fucking break from the coast. Just stuff me full of potatoes and feed me some salads that are free of vegetables and full of mayonnaise."

"Amen to that," I say, and hold a dumpling up to *cheers*.

She returns the sentiment with her glass of red. "Maddie, I don't often apologize, but I don't take pride in how we let you go."

She says it like I was laid off from a job, and I guess I sort of was.

"I hear Veronica Balentine is absolutely smitten with you. She's got a good head on her shoulders."

"Good to know."

She throws back the rest of her red and starts digging through her overstuffed Hermès bag before coming up with her wallet. "I don't know how you do it," she tells me. "Kids like Gentry are made for this. The personality is practically bred out of them, but being a normy and then putting yourself out there for the public to pick apart and consume after someone like me has already ruthlessly done so . . . it takes thick skin, Maddie. You're made of some strong stuff."

My lips twitch into a smile. "It's the Midwest in me."

She guzzles the rest of her white. "I couldn't take it. It's why I dish it out instead. I don't want to be the person in charge. Just the one who pulls their strings." She shivers greedily at the thought. "Yo-ho, a pirate's life for me."

Yep, Penelope Pike is shit-faced. But more surprisingly, I think I might like the woman just a little bit.

She stands and holds her hands out for a moment and checks her balance. "Yup," she says proudly. "Good to go."

"Have a safe flight," I tell her, "and if you do fly the plane drunk, just don't get caught."

She thinks about that for a minute. "That really is shit advice, isn't it?" She tugs on her blazer and throws an extra twenty on the counter after I already noticed her tipping 30 percent on the app as she closed out her tab. Good tippers can't be entirely monstrous, right?

She points at me, her finger focused more at the artwork of a panda on the wall behind me. "And if you ever want to throw your name out in California, I think we would make an absolutely gruesome twosome."

To my shock and slight horror, she throws her arms around my shoulders and kisses each of my cheeks before whispering, "The world could use a few less Gentrys and a few more Maddies, if you ask me."

She pulls back, noticing my cactus for the first time. "What's with the plant?"

I open my mouth to answer, but then with a slightly sloppy shrug she adds, "Never mind. I don't actually care. See you around, Maddie!"

As she expertly (and impressively) weaves through the crowd, I watch her go with an unexpected smile on my face.

I sit there for the next two hours and help myself to a celebratory, overpriced cocktail as I watch the breaking-news ticker scroll across the page. Two other reporters in new time slots give the same report on Gentry along with a rundown of all his family's prior scandals and their own hot takes. Unfortunately for the Wade family, it's a slow news day.

I want to feel warm and fuzzy and satisfied, but the only person I want to talk to about all of this is in Mount Astra, Kansas, probably chasing down a frog, a dog, and three girls as he gets them ready to go back to school after the holiday.

Penelope's words stir in my chest. *More Maddies. Less Gentrys.*

But I'm only one person. One woman who feels more like a girl on most days, who is so often guided by calculated anger. Who is too cunning and unlikable. And too fat. With a severe haircut and poisonous red lips that aren't approachable or accessible.

But I am one person who has the ability to find others like me. Not only that, but I have the ability to make those women electable and I think—I truly think—I can accomplish that without forcing them to give up so much of themselves. Maybe it's not about losing yourself. Maybe it's a matter of curating yourself and saving the softer, private parts of yourself for the pieces of your life that aren't up for public consumption. Maybe it's about having a hard shell so that you can protect your soft interior.

I don't think I want to fight the battle of one person. I want to build an army so that it can fight a war. And there's only one man who I want waiting for me every night when I return from the front lines.

Fundamentals of Being a Good Girl

The echoing voice of overhead speakers crackles as a gate change for my flight to Kansas City is announced.

Quickly, I pay my bill and gather my bags, all while wedging my cell phone into the crook of my shoulder and my prickly pear cactus in one arm.

The line rings four times before I get an answer. I'm practically running to my new gate now as I realize it's on the other side of the terminal.

"Madelyn," Veronica Balentine says into my ear. "Are you heavy breathing into the phone right now? Please tell me you've not accidentally called me while in the act."

"No," I pant. "Running to my gate at LAX." I cannot and will not miss this flight. I know what I want and I want it right now.

"That should be an Olympic sport. Now, that would get me invested in—"

"I don't want the job," I blurt.

"Pardon?" she asks. "You don't want to run for office with a war chest at your back. Is that the job you are speaking of? This better not be for something silly like love."

"It's not," I tell her. "Well, it is. And also, I love Bram Loe. So I'm fucked anyway and you do not want me as your candidate. Trust me. But it's more about me and figuring out who the fuck I am and what the fuck I want, and Veronica, I *do not* want that job."

"I presume you've received another job offer?"

I skitter to a stop at what I think is the line for my flight. "No, not exactly. But I know what job I *do* want," I tell her.

"Oh? And what job might that be?"

I hand my ticket to the gate agent and step with purpose onto the jet bridge. One step closer to home. One step closer to him.

"Your job," I tell her. "I want your job."

CHAPTER THIRTY-EIGHT

Bram

It's the last week before finals, and it hits the department like an asteroid. I find Dr. Mensah swaying on her feet in front of the vending machine, blinking hopelessly at a can of Diet Coke stuck in the chute, and Ali is in my office more than a Saint James cousin, anxious about this funding deadline or that professor taking family leave in the spring, and there is an unending parade of TAs with questions, problem cases, and mean emails from parents that they have no idea how to respond to. And that doesn't even touch the students themselves, some of whom are overly scrupulous about their grades and some of whom feel entitled to extra credit or eleventh-hour make-up labs to earn points they didn't seem to give a shit about earlier in the semester.

With Sara thankfully back, though, it means I can pass the parenting baton (and Hester Prynne can go back to a life free of menacing frogs) and I can work as late as I need. It means that when I leave Gerhart in the breath-puffing dark of December, the lights are out everywhere in Salih except in the stairwells, and I don't have to wonder if Maddie's looking out her window at a sleep-deprived dad in a peacoat and congratulating herself on making the right choice.

I don't have to wonder if she saw the news about her ex-fiancé... if she's figured out it was me. And that's fine, because I didn't do it hoping that it would send her running back into my arms. I didn't even do it because I hate hypocrisy—even though I do hate hypocrisy—or because I'd hoped something about the scandal would show Maddie that she deserved so much more than what that self-righteous clot of a man and men like him could give her.

No, I did it because he hurt her and he needed to burn for it. It was that simple. There is plenty in this world that I can't fix, but this... this I could do. This I *wanted* to do.

And if I am alone at night, if I miss her snorts and sighs while she grades next to me, if I miss the way she looks in my old college shirts and the way she looks slipping off her heels after a bloodless victory, well, then I have no one to blame but myself. I went and fell for her. I chose to plant my heart in the earth at her feet. I can't be upset when she tears it up at the roots.

It's what you do with a weed, after all.

Friday comes, and with it, a feeling like an inhale. Not quite relief, not yet, but the certainty that for better or for worse, everything will be over soon.

I'm checking over my test materials one more time before I close my laptop—just for Bio 1, Plant Ecology will have presentations instead—when I hear a knock on the door. I look up to see

Sloane in a red wool coat, her platinum hair gleaming with caught diamonds. It must be misting outside, but when I look out the window, it's too dark to tell.

"You have to follow me," announces Sloane, in the kind of voice you use after someone in the room taps a champagne glass with a fork.

"Uh," I say. "Follow you where? Because if Sara or Joey put you up to this, tell them I can relax at home alone with the frog, and I don't need to be cajoled out to someplace noisy and hostile to contemplative thought."

Sloane gives a look that says *I'm too well-bred and gracious to say what I'm really thinking.* "This has nothing to do with Sara or Joey—or Leo or Alessandro, for that matter. And it barely has anything to do with me. Now, get up, get up! Put those long legs to use!"

With a sigh, I push away from my desk, pack up my satchel, and stand up to get my coat.

"How was your week?" I ask as we leave the office and I flick off the light before closing the door. "I haven't seen you much since..."

"Since my new tenant broke your heart?"

"Yes, that," I say wryly.

"It's fine, I guess." Gerhart is mostly empty as Sloane leads me downstairs and out the front door. Dr. Monty, the primordial campus cat, trundles roundly across our path and then across the sidewalk-faceted lawn to the library.[*]

---

[*] There is a forbidden cat door installed on the less-picturesque back side of the library, where the dumpsters are. Junie also sets out forbidden cat food next to a forbidden cat bed. The secret arrangement remains undiscovered, since the cat door leads into a storage room so creepy even the spiders don't go there.

"Are you sure?" I ask. "I know you're supposed to move out of Persimmon Hill soon."

Sloane's delicate exhale is nearly lost in the bitter wind dancing between the limestone buildings. "The condo I'm supposed to buy, the one on the river, won't be ready in time. Some construction delay or another. So I'll either need to move into a hotel or hope some poor student drops out of school midyear and frees up an apartment. I don't relish either option, honestly, but Lucien is . . . firm . . . about my leaving Persimmon Hill in a timely manner. Which is his right."

"He barely lived there when you were married," I grumble, irritated on her behalf. Lucien was gone, always, it seemed, for work or for work-adjacent things, for barely disguised affairs that never seemed to dent his obsession with Sloane for as often as they occurred. Sloane was left to keep up appearances and semi-parent his teenage son, who had zero respect for his young stepmother and spent his last two years of high school making her life hell. "It's only to be a dick that he wants you out now."

"He's angry I wanted out," Sloane says with a sad sort of smile. "That's not how it's supposed to work, you see. I was supposed to stay the same tender, malleable ingenue who married him. I wasn't supposed to hate his affairs or have my own career or decide no amount of money or glamour was worth staying for. Here we are."

I pause. We've come to Parker Hall, the oldest building on campus, symmetrical, stone, and forbidding. Also half dark—it's after five and the bursar's office and counseling offices inside are shutting down for the weekend. It's a gorgeous building, possibly the heart of the university, but I step foot in here maybe once a semester.

I turn to Sloane. "Why?"

Sloane takes my arm and pulls me up the shallow stone steps to the door. "Because you have a class tonight."

"*I* have a class tonight?" I'm completely baffled. And tired. And wishing I was at home nursing a beer and sketching something in my greenhouse, shading in the night shadows and capturing the feeling of growth in the dark.

"That's what I just said. You don't listen so well."

She's hustling me through the central atrium with its historic, coffered ceilings and down the hall, which is mostly dark.

"Just through there," she says. "Last one on the left, with the lights on."

"Wait—"

But she's just pressing her chilled lips to my cheek and then walking away, her red coat the only bloom of color in the building.

I turn and look at the door she'd indicated—a massive wooden one with an old-fashioned transom window above it. Golden light glows from inside.

Utterly confused, I go to the classroom and open the door. And then freeze.

The classroom is one of the few classrooms left on campus that *looks* like a stereotypical college classroom—rows of wooden desks attached to seats, maps hanging from walls, a long wooden desk for the professor with a bust of Walt Whitman on it. The chalkboards have been upgraded to dry erase boards, and the usual chandelier of technology hangs from the ceiling, but otherwise, this classroom is much the same as it was a hundred years ago.

And at the front, trailing a dark red fingernail over the edge of the desk, is Madelyn Kowalczk, wearing a black skirt with a slit up the thigh, a black, long-sleeved shirt with buttons marching up to her neck (not that it matters, the shirt is see-through, showing the flimsy camisole she's wearing underneath), and a pair of dark green heels that should be illegal based on the ankle straps alone. Her hair, still dark and flawlessly cut. Her lips a brighter red than Sloane's coat.

CHAPTER THIRTY-NINE

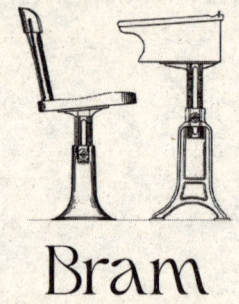

Bram

"Take a seat, Mr. Loe," she says, looking over at me.

Longing rips through me, followed by empty, cramping pain. I haven't seen her in two weeks, and my memory has played me false, because she's more beautiful than I remembered, more arresting. Just her eyes on mine is enough to make me want to drop to my knees. And beg. Beg beg beg.

But there is some animal sense of self-preservation buried in me yet, and I don't move. It hurt enough to muster all that polite grace when we had to share the twins' afternoon and evening routine—I don't know that I can endure being told again that I'm an impediment to her future, that I'm a decent fuck and nothing else. It's so much easier to be dormant, frozen, the structure of myself and nothing more, than be here and present and looking at her.

Then Maddie taps her finger on the desk, angling her chin so that she's looking at me with a cool sort of impatience. "Don't keep us waiting."

Fundamentals of Being a Good Girl

I—I don't know what to make of this, but there's something about the way she regards me, with the authority I taught her to wield, in clothes nothing like her focus-grouped florals, that has me obeying like I am indeed a sheepish first-year late to class. I close and lock the door behind me and then walk between the desks.

"Good boy," she says, and I feel the tips of my ears heat as I pause in the middle of the classroom to take a seat. "No, no, not there. At the front. So you can show me that you're eager to learn. Excellent."

I carefully remove my coat and scarf and drape them over a chair. And then I take a seat at the front, my frame barely fitting in the desk-chair combo, and fold my hands together on the desk. They're shaking a little. She's so close. She's so close and I don't know if I can handle whatever this is, but right now, she's looking at me like she'll follow me if I leave. Like she's already got a taste for my blood.

"I know you're used to seeing me teach political science, but today, I'm teaching anatomy," she says crisply, walking over to the dry erase board and uncapping a marker.

"Maddie—"

She looks over her shoulder at me, the long lashes and upturned nose and carmine lips in profile. She doesn't speak, but the curve of her eyebrow says it all.

"Professor Kowalczk," I correct myself. "We don't have to—I don't want to—" I stop, because I don't actually know what I want to say next. I don't want to autopsy our relationship on a cold Friday night; I don't want to have my unwanted love dragged out in the open like Exhibit A.

I also want to spend the next thirty-seven hours committing the dimples above her exposed knee to memory.

"I think we do have to," Maddie says, turning back to the board. "And I thank you for not interrupting me again, Mr. Loe."

Her voice is smooth and emotionless and immovable—she's an extension of the building itself now, made of limestone for how affected she is by my interjection. If I weren't so nervous, I'd feel a little bubble of teacherly delight at that. If nothing else, she has *this* now, this strength in commanding a room.

"So," she says, drawing a little circle with a smaller circle inside it. "Our anatomy class starts with this." Two stick figures are drawn above the circle, one with a dress and the other comically larger.

I shift in the tiny chair, the wood creaking ominously under my ass, trying to reach for the calm everyone says I'm famous for. I'm nearly frantic with the terror that this lesson is going to leave me in the corner of a room again, trying to coax the comfort of a hug out of the walls themselves.

Maddie ignores the creaking. "First, we have me. The half-orphaned girl who spent her adolescence watching money disappear out of her brother's hands like it was leprechaun gold. The girl who thought the biggest way she could change the world was by marrying one of the changers. And then was kicked out of her own life and had to build a new one with no notice, with no idea who she wanted to be or how.

"Next," she says, tapping the marker next to the giant stick figure, "we have you. The divorced professor who loves his babies and moss. The good guy with a secret bad guy past. The orphan who never felt at home." She turns to face me. "I talked to my landlord about you this week. Do you know what she told me?"

I shake my head. I have no idea what Sloane would have said about me to Maddie.

"She told me that your grandparents sucked. Really bad. She told me that when she first met you, you still slept with a nightlight on, even though you were the biggest guy she'd ever met. She told me that sometimes you'd cry when people hugged you."

I look away, at the windows, my throat hurting and my jaw tight. I'm not upset that Sloane told Maddie these things—it's knowledge in the public domain—but it's still not easy to have it all reflected back to me. It wasn't easy as a kid and as a teen, when it was bullies like Leo doing the reflecting, and it isn't now, when I've finally had enough therapy and internal security to be able to do things like sleep in the dark, like exchange a hug without the oxytocin taking me out at the knees. I'm not that Bram anymore, and it's embarrassing to know I used to be.

"Bram," says Maddie softly. "I'm sorry."

I don't turn my head, but I move my eyes to where she stands at the board.

"When you grow up without a lot of money, it's easy to think that anyone who had it better than you must have been universally blessed, that they must have had everything. I assumed because you grew up comfortably that you must have grown up happily, and I'm sorry for that, because it led me to unfair conclusions about you."

"Don't," I start, and then pause to swallow, because my voice sounds like how I feel. "Don't be sorry. Please. My childhood wasn't that bad, and also it wasn't your fault."

"No, but this is my fault: I misunderstood you. Everything about the way you live your life. I thought you didn't know what it meant to *want*, to have to scrape and scrap and claw out just the tiniest piece of happiness; I thought you grew up with happiness in the air and soil and so it was a part of your DNA. I didn't see what I should have, which is that you were only able to make a house full of plants and daughters, full of cuddles and mess, a home because you did have to fight for it. Because you had to choose it. And you were trying to choose it with me."

There's the faintest flicker of movement in her throat, just under the ruched collar of her sheer blouse, but before I can observe it again, she's turned back to the board.

"Next part of the lesson," she says, drawing two little bean shapes. "What fuels us. I want to change the world." She labels one of the little beans and then moves to the next one. "What fuels you, Mr. Loe?"

The answer is immediate. "The kids. My job. Watching you change the world."

A slight tremor in her hand as she labels the second bean. Then she draws a couple ovals with squiggles inside. I'm starting to see what's happening, I think.

"Now to what we actually need," she says quietly. So quietly that I barely hear her. "Because I thought that I wanted complete autonomy, unfiltered progress. I thought I wanted to be exactly where Gentry is now. I thought if I could stomp my way to the center of everything and just *fix* it, then I'd have anything I'd ever wanted. But I ran into Penelope Pike at LAX, and together we watched the news cycle about Gentry's peccadilloes, and it made me realize that I don't need to be Gentry. I need to be the person who makes sure there are better options than Gentry, and that there are better options not just in one district but several. And I need . . ."

A pause. She looks down and to the side, so I just make out her profile beyond her near-onyx curtain of hair. Her eyes are almost closed and her jaw is taut with some kind of misery.

I want to get up and leave before she can say whatever she's about to say next. I want to stand up and take the marker out of her hand and scrawl *I love you* all over the board.

"You," she says after a deep inhale. "I need you."

My heart beats once, hard enough to shake my ribs, and then collapses into a frantic arrhythmia.

"But," she says raggedly, "there's this." A big oval smashing against everything else she's drawn. No squiggles, but she tilts her hand sideways and starts writing without stopping. *What if I'm wrong what if I'm making the same mistake what if I'm weak for falling in love right after a breakup what if this ruins my future what will people say what if I love you more than you love me—*

I push out of my desk chair, my skin made of sparks, my heart both doing too much of its job and not enough, and I walk to the board. She doesn't move, one arm still lifted to her badly sketched vacuole, her shoulders moving with every breath.

Even in her heels, she's so much shorter than me, and it's too easy to take the marker from her. I start drawing something like a ribbon folded unevenly on itself, with little circles around it. She stays frozen, but frozen in a way where I think she feels—as I do—the vanquishing gravity of the single inch between us. The way that every movement of my hand, every deep breath, shrinks the space between us to almost nothing.

I finish drawing. The Golgi apparatus. The processing and shipping department of the cell. "What if you're wrong?" I ask her.

"What?" she whispers, sounding dazed. I wish I could see her face.

"What you wrote in the vacuole—I'm asking you to answer the question because that's what a classroom is for. Answering questions. So what happens if you're wrong about needing me?"

"Then I—" A breath. "I'll be okay. It'll hurt a lot, but I'll be okay."

"And if you're making the same mistake that you made with Gentry?"

"I can't be," she murmurs. "Because I'm not the same person who made that mistake. I might make different ones, but not that one ever again."

"And what if it ruins your future?"

Her voice is stronger now, threaded with relief. "No one else gets to define ruin for me. Not anymore."

"Professor Kowalczk, turn around and tell me who loves whom more."

She takes a second. A long second, and I know that I've done something unfathomably stupid, that I'm laying my soul bare for her again, but I want this—this anatomy of us, this diagram of our broken edges, of our rupture, to mean what I think it means. I want to hope. I want to look into her eyes and feel something vital take root between us.

She does turn, and when she looks up at me, there's a shine in her viridian eyes. "I don't know."

I cup her jaw, gently, and she trembles. "You don't?" I ask tenderly.

"It can't be you," she says thickly. "Because I love you so much that even my ribosomes hurt with it."[*]

The confession makes me close my eyes. I'm floating, a spore, a samara off a maple tree, spinning and spinning.[†]

---

[*] The cell machinery that makes proteins or something like that. Science is Bram's love language and Maddie did her homework.

[†] No one else in Mount Astra calls those twirly seed things samaras. They are helicopters.

"You love me."

"I love you," she repeats in a whisper. "I love you and it scares the hell out of me."

She turns again and takes the marker. I open my eyes to see her draw a cell wall around everything—nucleus, chloroplasts, vacuole, Golgi apparatus, and mitochondria.* She writes next to it.

I fucked up. I'm sorry. I love you.

I find her fingers around the marker, wrap my fingers around both, and then write my response.

I love you. There's nothing to forgive.

"I lied," she whispers. "About things only being physical between us. It was so much more, and I knew it, but I lied anyway. And I thought your past meant we could have no future, but watching Gentry's secrets unravel on national television . . ." A shaky laugh. "Bram, your past is everything I need for my future. I need a partner in crime and I need someone to pull me back when I want to go too far. I need someone who's charted a path along the edges of morality, and I need someone who found their way back again. I need someone to give me five different layers of advice, who will be as merciless on my behalf as I am for the things I care about, who will make sure I never stand alone, no matter where I find myself."

I drop my lips to her head. Her hair is the glossiest silk. Jasmine is everywhere.

"Forgive me for lying," she breathes. "Forgive me for clutching a dream I didn't even want in the end. Forgive me for being so

---

* Mitochondria is the powerhouse of the cell.[1]

  [1] Bram would like you to know that mitochondria *are* the powerhouse of the cell, since *mitochondria* is the plural form.

preoccupied with what a just-broken-up woman is supposed to do that I couldn't even see what I *wanted* to do."

A dream I didn't even want in the end. "You no longer want to run for office?"

A small shake of her head, like she's being careful of my lips on her hair. "There's a way to do so much more, behind the scenes. *That's* where I'm meant to be. That's what I'm going to do."

"Whatever you want," I murmur, and I mean it. Whatever she wants, whatever she needs. I'll be behind her, beside her, underneath her when she needs to sit on my lap and hear about how perfect she is.

"Forgive me," I add now, guiding the marker down to the tray and then finding her waist with my hands. "Forgive me for breaking our rules. Forgive me for pushing for more when you'd made your lines in the sand clear. Forgive me my greediness, that I want so much of you, to keep you and care for you, to be the soil and water and sun. That I love you past all logic even though logic demands I should let you go now, that you should get a chance to build your life without a lonely dad weighing you down."

She twists so she can glare up at me. "To be clear, logic can go to hell."

"It'll have to," I murmur, nuzzling her hair again. "I'm too selfish."

"And if it doesn't work, well, then we all know you're the world champion at breaking up. And it will be okay."

It will be okay. *We'll* be okay. And that's how I know this thing between us can't be all bad, because in every version of the future, even the ones where we don't end up together, we will both be okay. Sad, maybe. Lonely for a while, perhaps. But respected and cared for and okay.

Her waist is so warm under my hands, so soft through the

expensive material of her clothes. "Is class dismissed, Professor Kowalczk?"

She arches a little so that her breasts push out and her curvy bottom grazes my lap. I let out a wounded hiss at the contact, my trapped and swelling cock trying to surge closer to her.

"Not even a little," she says, satisfaction dripping from the words.

"Does that mean you have more anatomy to teach me?"

In response, she guides my hands up to the perky handfuls beneath her blouse, and then grinds back against me as I squeeze them. I'm fully hard now, and with the door locked, I don't waste any time. I slide a hand under her skirt and find her completely naked.

"Such a bad girl," I grunt, checking to see if she's wet—she is— and then I start unbuckling.

"Oh god, oh god." She's shuddering and yanking up her skirt and trying to arch her back even more, and the minute the head of my cock slips against her opening, she starts begging, pleading, words falling from her lips like a closing argument—*you have to, you must, feel how much I need it, if you don't, I'll die, I'll die.*

The words break into a moan as I push inside, nerve endings on nerve endings, soft around hard, hot against hot. I make a noise too, engulfed by silk, by the slick squeeze of her inner walls, buried in a snug, velvet cunt from root to crown. I'm about to grab her hips to fuck away every last moment we weren't together when I catch sight of her high heel out of the corner of my vision.

"These bratty little heels," I growl, and then use her hips to push her to the desk. She stumbles, catches herself on her hands, and then with a saucy look back at me, bends at the waist, knowing that it's only a skirt that separates me from what I want.

I yank it up impatiently, guide one knee so it's resting on the desk and her cunt is right there for the taking, and then I fit myself right back into her body like I never left.

"Be a good girl and make yourself come," I tell her, thrusting into her with deep, demanding strokes. I keep one hand on her hip and then slide the other to her foot, trace my fingers along the ankle strap. I want to rub my cock on it. I want to come all over it. I want to fuck her in these heels every night.

"Not a problem," she breathily replies, her hand wedged just where she needs it and her fingers hard at work. "This is—*fuck*, this is so hot—"

She's telling me. I've got Stern Teacher Maddie bent over a desk in a classroom, her ankle-strapped heel in one hand, her moans filling the air as she masturbates and I use her pretty pussy for myself and—

She comes with a keening wail, and I go rigid, letting the rippling clenches of her core take me all the way home, extracting the pleasure out of my body like a debt to be paid, and then I fold over her with a groan as I release pulse after pulse of my orgasm inside her. So much of it, a lonely man's worth, and she's giggling underneath me by the time I finish.

"Been a while, Mr. Loe? I can already feel it running down my thighs."

"Stop—*ah*—stop laughing, it hurts," I grumble, wincing as she giggles again and it squeezes my sensitive organ.

"I'm sorry, I'm sorry. I promise I'll start taking anatomy very seriously."

"You already did. I'm actually impressed." I carefully work my way free and then wince a second time after I see what a slick mess she is. "Stay here."

I go to get my scarf while she sighs happily over the desk.

"I'm glad you appreciated it. And I didn't even get to the endoplasmic reticulum."

I use the scarf to clean her up, and then I help her rearrange her clothes after I make sure she can stand without swaying.

"You know—" I start, and she does get a little serious then, her lips pressing together as she nods.

"I know. We need to talk more. Figure out what happens next. Take an inventory of where we stand."

I run my hand down the row of still-buttoned buttons on her blouse. "Actually, I was about to say that the kids are all with Sara, and I have the house completely to myself this weekend."

Maddie's lips part . . . and then curve into a catlike smile. "In that case, Mr. Loe, I have so much more anatomy to teach you."

CHAPTER FORTY

Maddie

My and Bram's love is slow and then sudden like the changing seasons.

After my classroom lesson in December in the midst of finals, I spent the weekend at Bram's and I never left.

After a week of leaving bits and pieces of my belongings in his room and in his bathroom, he asked me how I felt about laying down roots. Here. In this house. And not in the guest room up on the second floor with the girls, but here with Bram in his bed. He asked me early in the morning as the day spilled from the horizon, and I whispered a yes into his ear before he could finish the sentence.

Before I even got home from celebratory end-of-semester drinks with Junie that day, Bram and Joey had cleaned out my apartment and Bram had paid Sloane for the next three months of rent. (A fact I only later found out, thanks to Leo's loose lips, and a fact that became an argument that Bram refused to have.)

Fundamentals of Being a Good Girl

Today, Sara was on back-to-school duty, so it was an incredibly quiet return to real life after the holidays as Bram and I had lazy, sleepy morning sex before he showered and headed over to campus.

I, on the other hand, put on my best sweatshirt[*] and spend the day prepping for my first day at my new second job, which isn't until next week. I'll be adjuncting through May, though I only have classes two days a week, and then I'll also be working for Veronica Balentine. I won't actually be doing her job—at least, not at first—but watching her do her job and learning from her as her shadow will be the next best thing.

The house is quiet without Hester Prynne, and Bram is slowly giving in to my cat adoption campaign. After Bram gets home, we're going to visit a middle-aged brother and sister duo whose bios read that they are only motivated by shredded cheese.

Most of the morning is spent building a dossier on potential candidates for the next election cycle that I'll be presenting to Veronica, who called me on Christmas Day.

"I don't think I can ever forgive you for your bad taste in men," she said in lieu of hello. "Though to be fair, most taste in men is bad taste in men, but over the last few weeks, I was dismayed to find that I missed the Madelyn Kowalczk interruptions in my life."

I smiled as I stepped into the mudroom at the back of the house, while Bram, Sara, Asher, the girls, Hester Prynne, my mom, Bee, and Nolan all snoozed in and out of a Hope Channel movie called *The Last Letter*, written by Bee's friend Sunny Palmer.

"Oh, Veronica," I said in a whisper as I closed the door behind

---

[*] All the best sweatshirts belong to Bram, including this one.

me. "If you're trying to woo me back into a campaign, I'm sorry to say I'm not your girl."

"I know, I know," she said. "Though I've been thinking about it and I think with the right donors, maybe we could actually capitalize on the good professor's bad boy past if—"

"No. No, thank you," I told her. "Now, I'm assuming you're not calling to wish me a Merry Christmas."

She huffed. "No, I'm calling because my wife says she won't talk to me until next year unless I just pull the trigger and offer you a job. Next year is only a week away, I know, but the woman is the only person I enjoy talking to, so that would present a problem."

My jaw dropped as I paced back and forth, tiptoeing over discarded shoes and jackets.

She took my stunned silence to mean something else entirely. "All right, I can see this is going to take some negotiations."

My heart immediately skipped a beat at the scent of blood in the air.

Ultimately, we agreed that I would spend a few months shadowing Veronica before I would be allowed to take on my own clients. I told her that I wouldn't work with just anyone, and she coolly replied that as long as my moral compass didn't put her in the red, that was fine.

Which is why I am currently running all over the house with my laptop open and balancing it in one hand as I hunt for my charger. Bram's theory is that if I just leave it in the same place every day, I'll be able to find it, but that doesn't account for my changing mood and the fact that some days I want to work in the greenhouse or in bed or in the window bench of his—

Bram's office! Yes, of course.

Fundamentals of Being a Good Girl

Quickly, I slide down the hall in my fuzzy socks, the red battery angrily blinking at me in the corner of the screen.

I swing the office door open and right there sitting on Bram's desk with a small note attached is my charger.

Right where you left it. Funny how that works. —B

I stick out my tongue, knowing that I'll always choose to be his brat when it comes to this silly little charger that always seems to be missing.

Just as I plug the laptop in, the screen goes black, so I plop down into Bram's chair as I wait for it to charge enough so that it will power back up.

While I wait, I use Bram's desktop to browse the county courthouse page and brush up on the campaign filing rules and deadlines.

The cursor hovers over a menu option that reads *How Do I . . .* There are several options. Pay a traffic fine, receive an exemption from jury duty, receive housing assistance. And then at the very bottom of the list is *file for a marriage license*.

I nearly exit out of the page before it can even load. But then I remember my mom whispering in my ear about what a good man Bram is as he and Nolan lay on the ground the day after Christmas, fake snoring and pretending to be asleep as the twins attempted to wake them while Fern downloaded Bee on her crush on a girl named Adelaide.

I let myself look over the page and I can't get over how easy it is to just go to the courthouse with the person you love and make things quietly official. How you can go to the historic two-story building in the heart of Mount Astra and walk in as two and out as one.

For just a moment, I let myself imagine a short little white dress and a nonsensical veil because why the hell not. And red lipstick. Always red lipstick.

It's just the two of us in my imagination. Our lives are full of people we love and treasure, but I like the idea of this moment taking place discreetly in a building where lives change in big and small ways every day. That our union is a contract, a promise, and not at all a performance.

I leave the browser open on purpose right there next to Bram's inbox, because almost everything I do is for a reason.

Sitting in the windowsill is my prickly pear because Bram said that the lighting in his office was ideal at this time of year and that this office is ours now, and he likes that it shows evidence of me. The soil appears to be a little dry, so I take out the mister and shower her with a little bit of water.

It feels silly to hope, but every time I check on the spiky little thing in her shiny red pot, I get a little giddy as I catalog every minute change and development. It all feels very subtle, but Bram has promised me that one day this spring, we will wake up to find that she is flowering all at once. And because we will have witnessed her every day until that moment, Bram and I will know that even though her blooms will appear to be sudden, the truth is that they have been finding their light little by little every day for months.

I leave the cactus in the window and go back to the desk to retrieve my laptop and charger, taking one last look at the open web page on Bram's browser, and I know that for anyone else who might see it, the silent and completely informal proposal might feel abrupt, but for Bram and me, there's never been any sort of casual space between meeting as strangers and a deep, life-altering connection. So this—the idea of us committing ourselves to each other in a legal and binding way—was a seed planted early on before either of us even knew what we might become, which was in no way sudden and yet, like spring, abruptly lush and alive all at once.

EPILOGUE

Best Day Ever

As told by Joey F***ing Kemp (Bram's Version)

One Month Later (Seriously)

"I can't believe these devious little scabs," Leo says, taking the courthouse steps two at a time, his coat fluttering cinematically around his heels. "During the day! A weekday! Some of us have jobs!"

"You never seem to work at yours," Sloane points out. The accusation comes with the signature breathlessness of trying to speak outside during a prairie freeze.

"Seriously, though, I had to get a sub at the last minute," complains Joey. Not that he minds missing this afternoon, secretly. His students are doing the Second Industrial Revolution right now and he hates having to spell *laissez-faire* in front of an audience.

"First they didn't invite us," Alessandro complains. "And now I'm on call in an hour, which means that Bram and Maddie need to be quick about it all."

"Isn't *quick about it all* the heart and soul of a courthouse wedding? Of their very relationship?" Leo asks, yanking the courthouse door open. "I can't believe we're here. I can't believe someone we know is getting married at a courthouse *like French people do*."

Sloane's phone rings and she crosses her arms over her chest the moment she hears the voice on the other side. "Yes, I am participating in the charity date auction this year. No, I will not be attending as Lucien's plus one despite what his RSVP card might say."[*] With a roll of her eyes, she ends the call and rejoins the group.

"Did you ask if they'll have the deviled eggs again?" Joey whispers into her ear.[†]

Sara is standing just inside the doors with Asher and all three kids.

"We're going to be flower girls," Letty announces to the Andromeda Club before anyone else has a chance to speak, and in concurrence, Berry holds up a basket filled with what looks like an assortment of petals, leaves, and snipped herbs from Bram's

---

[*] Sloane has participated in the Saint James Foundation charity date auction at the annual gala every year since she turned eighteen, and every year Lucien Méchant has bid on and won a date with Sloane. This is the first time she will be attending as a free agent in sixteen years.

[†] Joey looks forward to the gala every year so that he can reunite with his one true love, the deviled eggs sprinkled with orange roe and edible gold flecks. He has informed Riley that he would never dream of asking her for a hall pass unless he met the person with the recipe for those eggs. Riley approves and maintains that her hall pass is and always will be Tessa Virtue and Scott Moir. At the same time.

greenhouse. Joey sees a few plastic-wrapped logs of string cheese peeking out from under the mess of random flora and gives Berry an approving nod. Game recognizes game.

Meanwhile, Sara is staring at them with dark-eyed horror while Asher is quietly cracking up behind her.

"Bram is going to be so *pissed*," Asher chokes out between laughs. "Oh my god."

Sara lifts her hands. "How did you even—it's supposed to be a *secret* ceremony, a private thing, family only—"

"First, how dare you imply the Andromeda Club isn't family," Leo prosecutes, "and second, if it was supposed to be secret, then why did he have it written down on his desk planner where anyone who'd let themselves into his office and sat at his desk could see it?"

"Why were you looking at his desk planner?"

Leo gives her a look that says *please, we have real things to discuss*. "You may as well tell us where to go now. We're not missing noble Dr. Loe dirty up all his laudable ethics because someone finally wore red lipstick in front of him. Shall we?"

Sara glances at her fiancé—who is still laughing too hard to help—and sighs. "Fine. *Fuck*. Fine. This way."

As a herd, they tromp their way through the marble-floored courthouse until they come to a room with a closed door. They crowd inside—Leo bickering with Sara, Fern trying to remind the twins not to throw their petals until everyone is back outside—and find Bram and Maddie handing clipboards to a court employee as a very, very short judge waits behind the podium.

Bram and Maddie turn as a unit, and Bram's ears go bright red above his suit.

He stands up and strides down the courtroom to the other Andromedas, meeting Leo in the middle of the aisle.

"No," Bram says. "Under no circumstances. This is supposed to be *private*."

"I'm private," whines Leo.

"Nope."

"And Sara gets to be here," Leo says with a pout. "And Asher. And Fern. Fern's supposed to be in school, Bram. Just like your twins. Are you saying that you care more about destroying the intellectual flowering of young minds than you care about your friends? Your very oldest friends?" He gestures back at the Andromeda Club, all of whom immediately strike poses of wounded, wide-eyed fellowship. Joey tries to beam memories of roller-skating parties and square cafeteria pizza slices directly into Bram's brain.

Maddie has come up beside Bram and laces her arm through his. She's wearing a short, sheer white dress of pleated tulle with a slip underneath and a thick black velvet ribbon that ties at the back in a dramatic bow and cascades into a train against legs clad in sheer black tights with seams up the back. In her short black wedding veil, dotted with pearls, and crimson smile, standing beside Bram with his tweedy suit and well-loved brogues, they couldn't look more different.

"I like that they're here," she tells Bram, still smiling at the Andromedas. "It means they love you."

"Their love is like a mint plant!" Bram hisses, and anyone who knows Bram knows that is *not* a compliment.

They all try harder to have big, sad eyes at him, especially Leo, and Leo's big eyes could make the pope himself consider *sola scriptura* for a hot minute.* They're going to win. They know it.

Bram's narrowed gaze takes them in, and then finally, with a huge sigh, he says, "*Fine.*"

"We're here because we love you!" says Leo, and the others chime in to agree, except for Joey, who's already started to cry. He always cries at weddings.

He's silenced his phone, but it buzzes in his pocket as Bram and Maddie make their way to the front, where the tiny, wrinkled judge awaits them. Joey discreetly pulls it out and sees a text that makes his blood run cold.

> **RILEY:** They said I'm measuring too big at my checkup, and so they took me back for an unplanned ultrasound

> **RILEY:** It's twins

Twins???

Oh fuck, oh fuck, he is so cooked, what the fuck. He doesn't think Bram even has a second stuffed weasel to practice on. Oh no. Oh god.

Before the podium, Maddie and Bram are listening to the judge, staring at each other with undisguised excitement and love, and then they start repeating their vows, pledging care and fidelity and respect, deciding to start a lifetime of devotion right now.

---

* For anyone who wasn't paying attention during Joey Fucking Kemp's European history lessons, *sola scriptura* is the Protestant doctrine that the scriptures should be the sole authority for the faithful. This contrasts with the Catholic doctrine of *sola pointy-hat-a*, where the pope and his friends also have a say.

Everyone cheers and whistles when they kiss—except for the twins, who make *blech* faces—and even though Joey is in a fog of panic, he whistles the loudest.

And then they spill outside, the twins throw handfuls of hellebore petals and oregano, and Bram and Maddie kiss another time, just for the hell of it. Bram is grinning at all of them now, clearly having remembered that they were his very best friends in the whole world, and in the frigid air, with his red-lipped bride under his arm on the courthouse steps, he says, "It's too bad Cole McKenney isn't here."

Next to him, Leo screams.

And somehow it's decided that the twins will go with Fern and everyone else will go to The Dry Bean for wedding shots, except for Joey, who is going home to Riley to process the twin thing together.

"Best Day Ever?" he asks Bram before he goes to find his car in the blue-skied cold.

Bram smiles at him, a wide, handsome smile, and he pulls Maddie even closer to dip her in front of the courthouse.

"Best Day Ever."*

---

* Brought to you by the Best Night Ever.

ACKNOWLEDGMENTS

The experience of writing this book has been a giddy thrill, and we want to thank everyone who enabled us over the last year (and didn't once tell us that we packed too many tropes into one book or that we didn't need to make yet another small town filled with troublemakers—or that of course we shouldn't *put footnotes in a romance novel* because why would anyone do that*).

As always, love to our ever-supportive cinnamon roll John Cusick, who's managed to be a schedule shepherd, a cheerleader, a calmer-downer, and an intrepid inbox warrior while we've juggled all the flaming bowling pins. And super-duper love to our editor, May Chen, who good-naturedly joined us in Mount Astra, Kansas, found all the ways we could make Bram and Maddie's story even punchier, and loves Leo just as much as we do.

Thank you to the team at HarperCollins who turned our puddle of words and footnotes into a whole entire book! Alessandra Roche, for being the Librarian of All Answers; DJ DeSmyter, Kelsey Manning, and Julie Paulauski for spreading the word of

---

* But who doesn't want their romances to feel like a Tolkien appendix??? We're this close to inventing our own language.

our good girl all over campus; Diahann Sturge-Campbell for the beautiful interior of this book; Hope Breeman, Andrew DiCecco, Brittani DiMare, and Hope Ellis for turning our professor-ly fever dream into a real book. Also we can't thank Natalia Sanabria and Kerry Rubenstein enough for making us the absolute bestest cover. Even Maddie would approve, and trust us, she's full of opinions.

We'd also like to thank Dr. Laci Gerhart and Dr. Ann Rossi-Gill for talking to us about science, ecology, who can date whom on campus, service loads for faculty, and soil monoliths! And our gratitude also goes to Vermont State University, who awarded their campus cat Max a degree in *litterature*, and from whom we stole that joke. Big thanks to the reader in St. Louis who let us memorialize the name Gentry by giving it to the book's arch-dirtbag, and our forever fondness to the city of Lawrence, Kansas,* for being the inspiration for Mount Astra.

Thank you to Ashley Lindemann, Flavia Vazquez, Serena McDonald, and Candi Kane for nudging us always toward writing—and away from Canva, Mailerlite, inboxes, etc. We literally couldn't do this without you.

We owe so much to our collective brain trust: Tessa Gratton, Adib Khorram, Ashley Lindemann, Nana Malone, Natalie C. Parker, Erica Russikoff, and Flavia Vazquez. And huge love to all of the people in our lives who gave us hugs, advice, or serotonin-laced TikToks while we were writing this: Aubrey Bondurant, Megan Bannen, Kenya Goree Bell, Jo Brenner, Becca Mysoor, Kennedy Ryan, Jean Siska, Nisha Sharma, Nikki Sloane, QB Tyler, Rebekah

---

* LFK!

Weatherspoon, Julia Whelan, and Julian Winters, along with Ashley Brown, Marianne Devin, Kate Fasse, Juliet Johnson, Ariel Larson, Ashley Meredith, Morgan Moore, and Carley Morton.

Our families! Bob and Gail, Liz and Bob, Emma, Roger, Vivienne and Aurelia, Ed Bisceglia, Dana, Doug, Sandra, and Kathie and Milt. And the people closest to home: Ian, Josh, Noah, and Teagan. Thank you for having lichen-like patience with us while we somehow survived writing a squillion words this year. We promise to stop having the sleep habits of college students any day now.

Finally, we want to thank every educator, from the teachers working with tiny tots all the way up to the professors sparking critical thinking and curiosity in higher ed.* To all the researchers, adjuncts, librarians, and especially to all the support staff who make all the lunch-y, spreadsheet-y, insurance-y, clean floor-y work of education possible. You're better than good, you're the best.

---

* Julie would like to shout out Professor Jocks, Dr. Payne, and Dr. Salih, and Sierra would like to thank a former nun named Ms. Wurtz for attempting to teach her math and Mrs. Greiner for introducing her to *Hamlet*.